SCOOBY-DOO
ALL WRAPPED UP!

Written by:
Chris Duffy
Terrance Griep, Jr.
Michael Kraiger
Michael Kupperman
Matt Wayne

Colored by:
Noelle Giddings
Lee Loughridge
Patricia Mulvihill
Rick Taylor

Illustrated by:
Bill Alger
Mike DeCarlo
Manny Galan
Tim Harkins
Andrew Pepoy
Bob Smith
Joe Staton

Lettered by:
John Costanza
Phil Felix
Tim Harkins
Ken Lopez

VP-Executive Editor
Brazwyn Taggart
Dana Kurtin
Editors-original series
Mike Brisbois
Chuck Kim
Assistant

...s

...Editors-original series

...tt Nybakken
...Editor-collected edition

Robbin Brosterman
Senior Art Director

Paul Levitz
President & Publisher

Georg Brewer
VP-Design & Retail Product
Development

Richard Bruning
Senior VP-Creative Director

Patrick Caldon
Senior VP-Finance & Operations

Chris Caramalis
VP-Finance

Terri Cunningham
VP-Managing Editor

Alison Gill
VP-Manufacturing

Rich Johnson
VP-Book Trade Sales

Hank Kanalz
VP-General Manager, WildStorm

Lillian Laserson
Senior VP & General Counsel

Jim Lee
Editorial Director-WildStorm

David McKillips
VP-Advertising & Custom Publishing

John Nee
VP-Business Development

Gregory Noveck
Senior VP-Creative Affairs

Cheryl Rubin
Senior VP-Brand Management

Bob Wayne
VP-Sales & Marketing

DC Comics, 1700 Broadway, New York, NY 10019
A Warner Bros. Entertainment Company.
Printed in Canada. First Printing.
ISBN: 1-4012-0513-5
Cover illustration by Joe Staton.
Publication design by John J. Hill.

 WB SHIELD ™ & © Warner Bros. Entertainment Inc.
(s05)

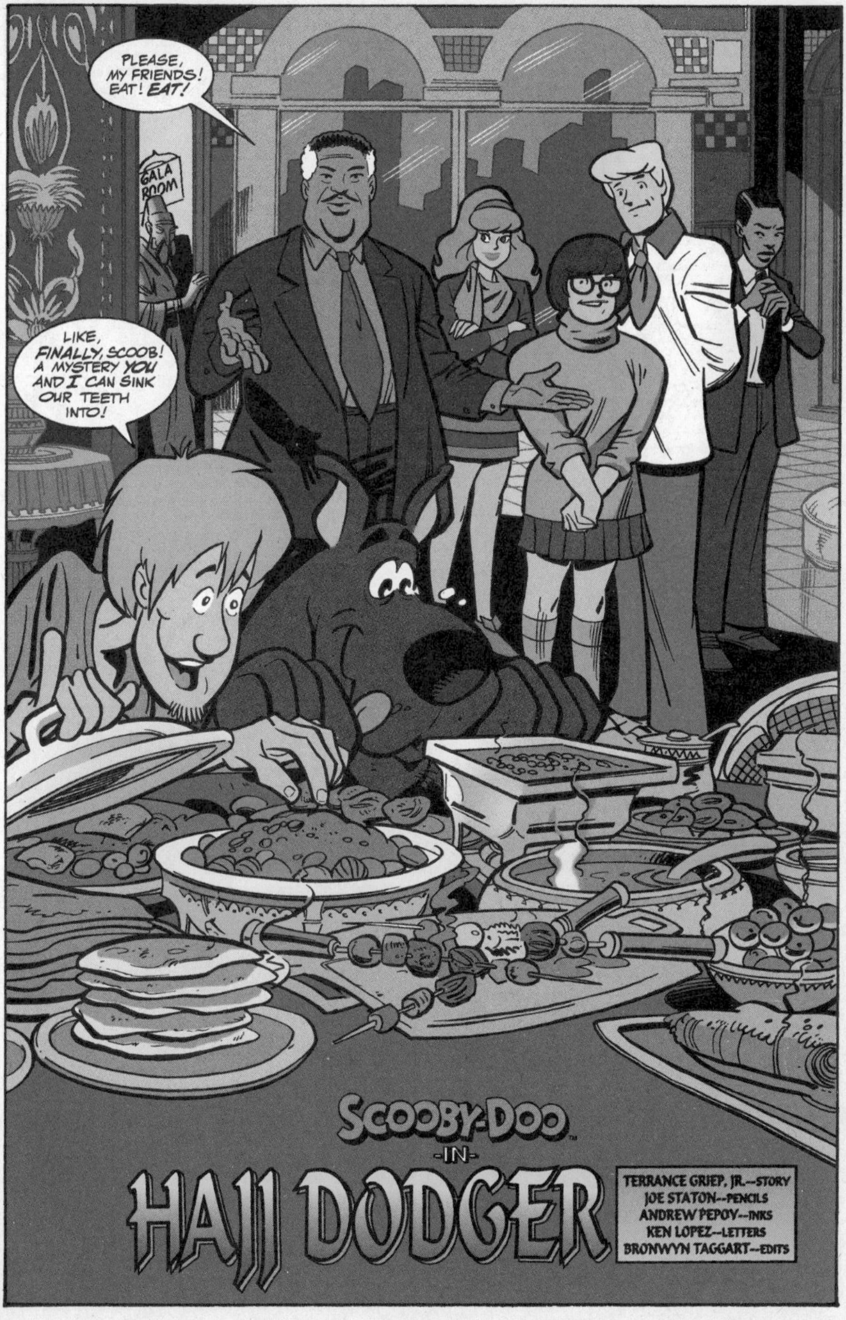
PLEASE, MY FRIENDS! EAT! EAT!
GALA ROOM
LIKE, FINALLY, SCOOB! A MYSTERY YOU AND I CAN SINK OUR TEETH INTO!
SCOOBY-DOO -IN- HAJJ DODGER
TERRANCE GRIEP, JR.--STORY
JOE STATON--PENCILS
ANDREW PEPOY--INKS
KEN LOPEZ--LETTERS
BRONWYN TAGGART--EDITS

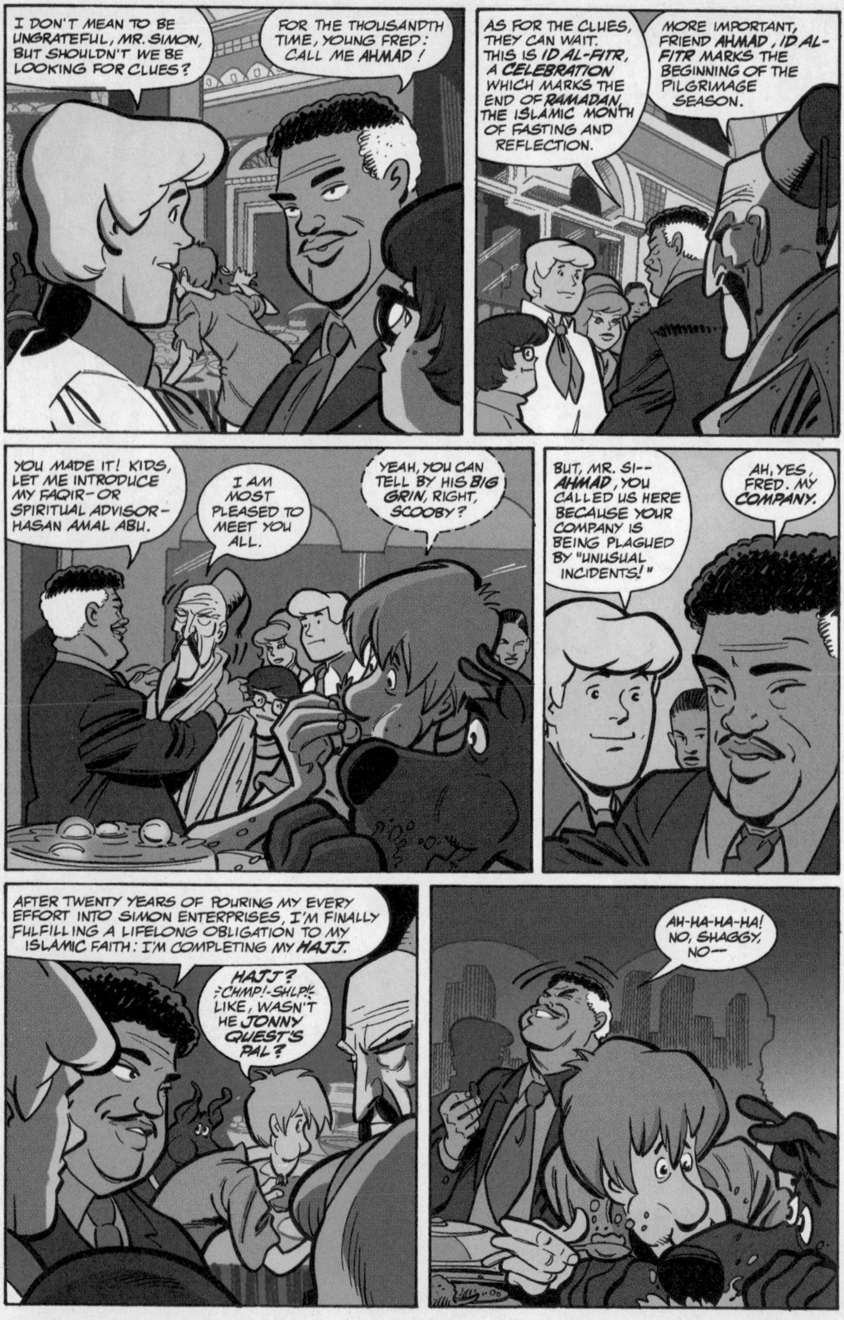
I DON'T MEAN TO BE UNGRATEFUL, MR. SIMON, BUT SHOULDN'T WE BE LOOKING FOR CLUES?
FOR THE THOUSANDTH TIME, YOUNG FRED: CALL ME AHMAD!
AS FOR THE CLUES, THEY CAN WAIT. THIS IS ID AL-FITR, A CELEBRATION WHICH MARKS THE END OF RAMADAN, THE ISLAMIC MONTH OF FASTING AND REFLECTION.
MORE IMPORTANT, FRIEND AHMAD, ID AL-FITR MARKS THE BEGINNING OF THE PILGRIMAGE SEASON.
YOU MADE IT! KIDS, LET ME INTRODUCE MY FAQIR-OR SPIRITUAL ADVISOR-HASAN AMAL ABU.
I AM MOST PLEASED TO MEET YOU ALL.
YEAH, YOU CAN TELL BY HIS BIG GRIN, RIGHT, SCOOBY?
BUT, MR. SI-- AHMAD, YOU CALLED US HERE BECAUSE YOUR COMPANY IS BEING PLAGUED BY "UNUSUAL INCIDENTS!"
AH, YES, FRED. MY COMPANY.
AFTER TWENTY YEARS OF POURING MY EVERY EFFORT INTO SIMON ENTERPRISES, I'M FINALLY FULFILLING A LIFELONG OBLIGATION TO MY ISLAMIC FAITH: I'M COMPLETING MY HAJJ.
HAJJ? CHMP!-SHLP! LIKE, WASN'T HE JONNY QUEST'S PAL?
AH-HA-HA-HA! NO, SHAGGY, NO--

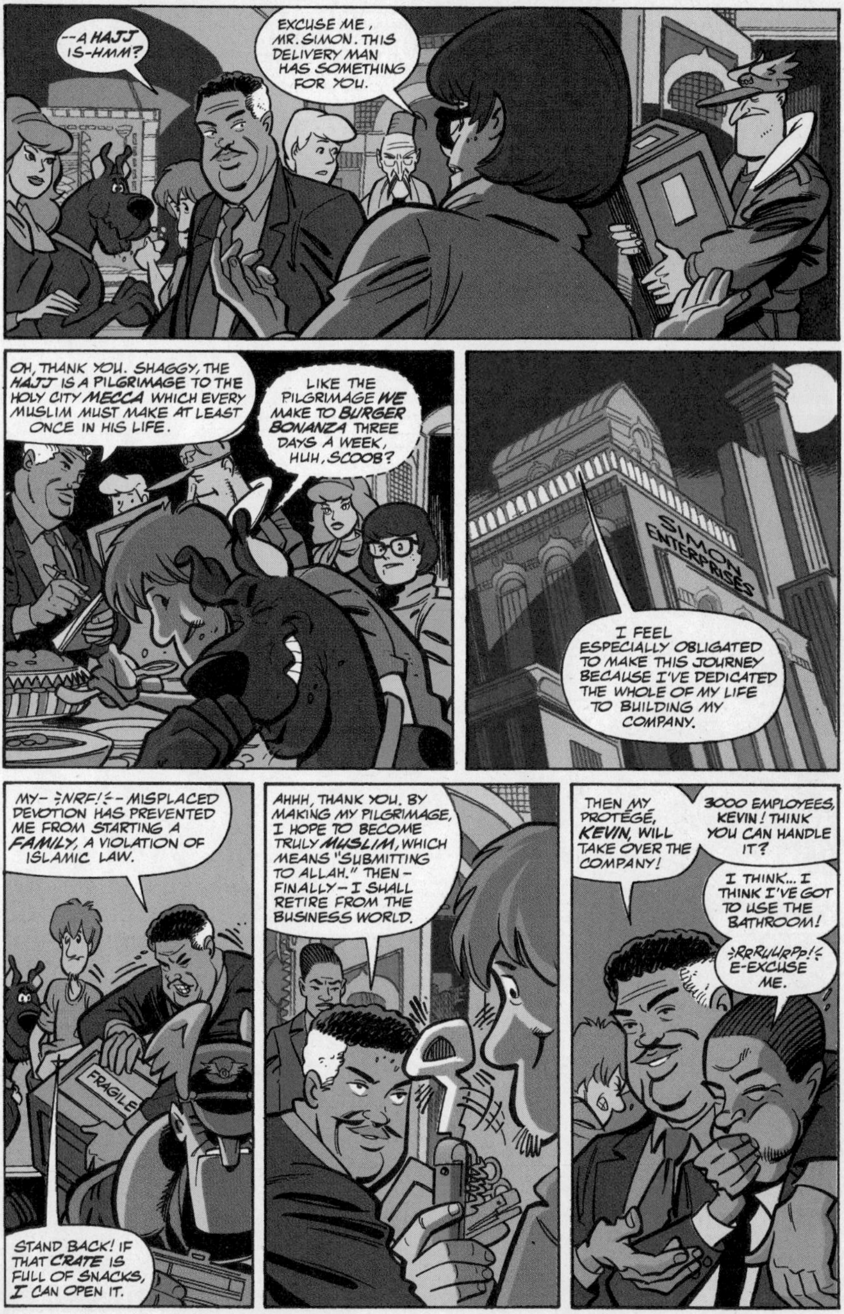
--A *HAJJ* IS-HMM?
EXCUSE ME, MR. SIMON. THIS DELIVERY MAN HAS SOMETHING FOR YOU.
OH, THANK YOU. SHAGGY, THE *HAJJ* IS A PILGRIMAGE TO THE HOLY CITY *MECCA* WHICH EVERY MUSLIM MUST MAKE AT LEAST ONCE IN HIS LIFE.
LIKE THE PILGRIMAGE *WE* MAKE TO *BURGER BONANZA* THREE DAYS A WEEK, HUH, *SCOOB*?
SIMON ENTERPRISES
I FEEL ESPECIALLY OBLIGATED TO MAKE THIS JOURNEY BECAUSE I'VE DEDICATED THE WHOLE OF MY LIFE TO BUILDING MY COMPANY.
MY- *NRF!* - MISPLACED DEVOTION HAS PREVENTED ME FROM *STARTING* A *FAMILY*, A VIOLATION OF ISLAMIC LAW.
FRAGILE
STAND BACK! IF THAT *CRATE* IS FULL OF SNACKS, *I* CAN OPEN IT.
AHHH, THANK YOU. BY MAKING MY PILGRIMAGE, I HOPE TO BECOME TRULY *MUSLIM*, WHICH MEANS "SUBMITTING TO ALLAH." THEN - FINALLY - I SHALL RETIRE FROM THE BUSINESS WORLD.
THEN *MY* PROTÉGÉ, *KEVIN*, WILL TAKE OVER THE COMPANY!
3000 EMPLOYEES, *KEVIN*! THINK YOU CAN HANDLE IT?
I THINK... I THINK I'VE GOT TO USE THE BATHROOM!
RRRULURPP! E-EXCUSE ME.

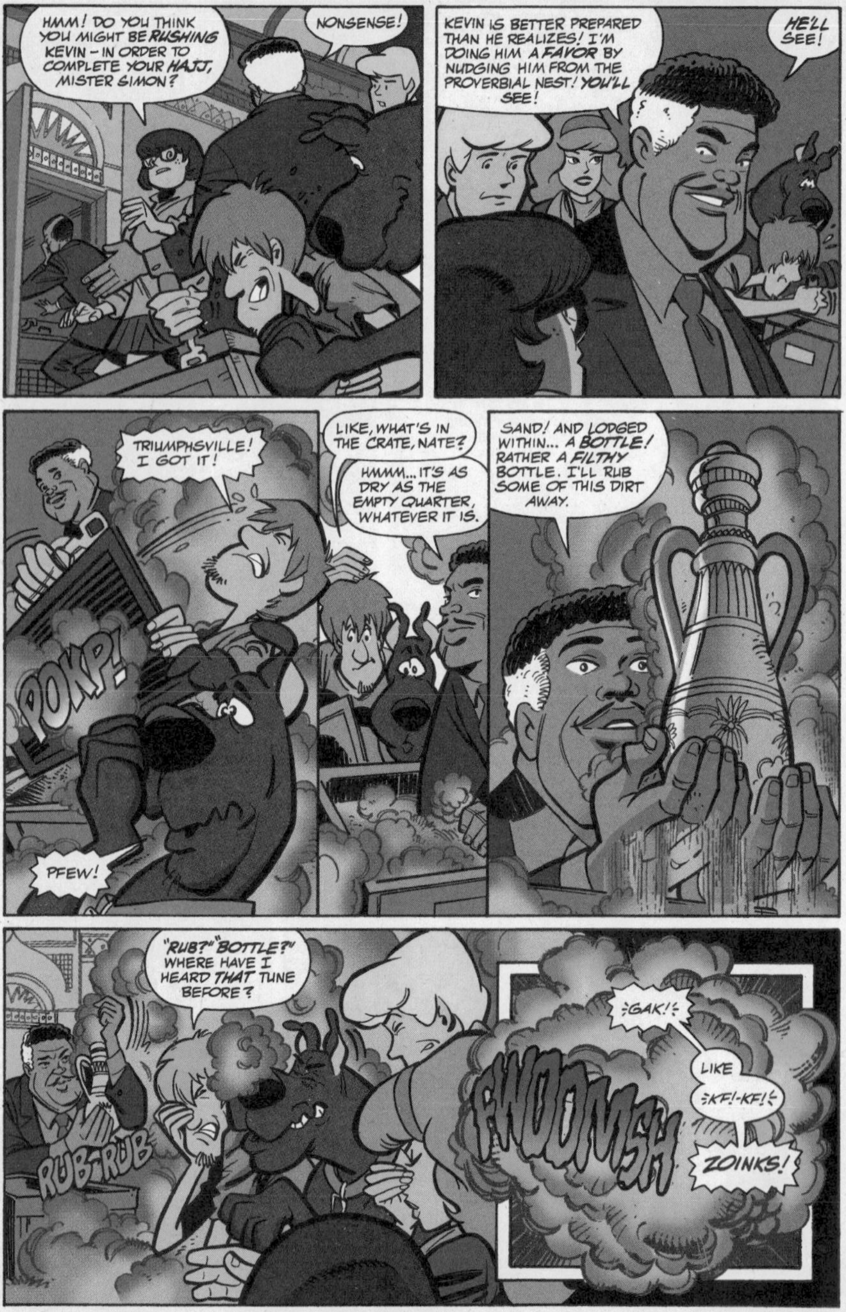
HMM! DO YOU THINK YOU MIGHT BE RUSHING KEVIN – IN ORDER TO COMPLETE YOUR HAJJ, MISTER SIMON?
NONSENSE!
KEVIN IS BETTER PREPARED THAN HE REALIZES! I'M DOING HIM A FAVOR BY NUDGING HIM FROM THE PROVERBIAL NEST! YOU'LL SEE!
HE'LL SEE!
TRIUMPHSVILLE! I GOT IT!
POKP!
PFEW!
LIKE, WHAT'S IN THE CRATE, NATE?
HMMM... IT'S AS DRY AS THE EMPTY QUARTER, WHATEVER IT IS.
SAND! AND LODGED WITHIN... A BOTTLE! RATHER A FILTHY BOTTLE. I'LL RUB SOME OF THIS DIRT AWAY.
"RUB?" "BOTTLE?" WHERE HAVE I HEARD THAT TUNE BEFORE?
RUB-RUB
FWOOMSH
GAK!
LIKE
KF!-KF!
ZOINKS!

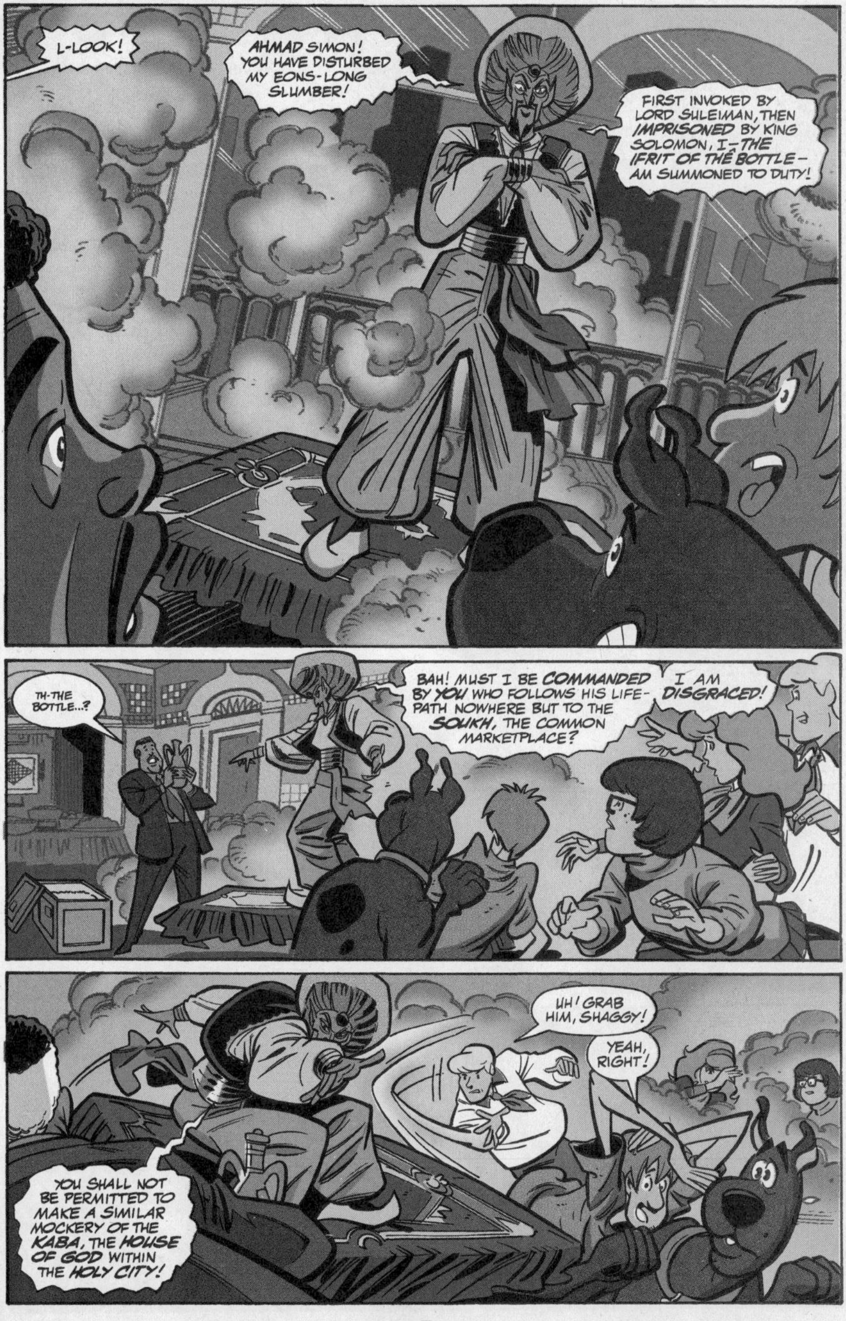
L-LOOK!
AHMAD SIMON! YOU HAVE DISTURBED MY EONS-LONG SLUMBER!
FIRST INVOKED BY LORD SULEIMAN, THEN IMPRISONED BY KING SOLOMON, I--THE IFRIT OF THE BOTTLE--AM SUMMONED TO DUTY!
TH-THE BOTTLE...?
BAH! MUST I BE COMMANDED BY YOU WHO FOLLOWS HIS LIFE-PATH NOWHERE BUT TO THE SOUKH, THE COMMON MARKETPLACE?
I AM DISGRACED!
YOU SHALL NOT BE PERMITTED TO MAKE A SIMILAR MOCKERY OF THE KABA, THE HOUSE OF GOD WITHIN THE HOLY CITY!
UH! GRAB HIM, SHAGGY!
YEAH, RIGHT!

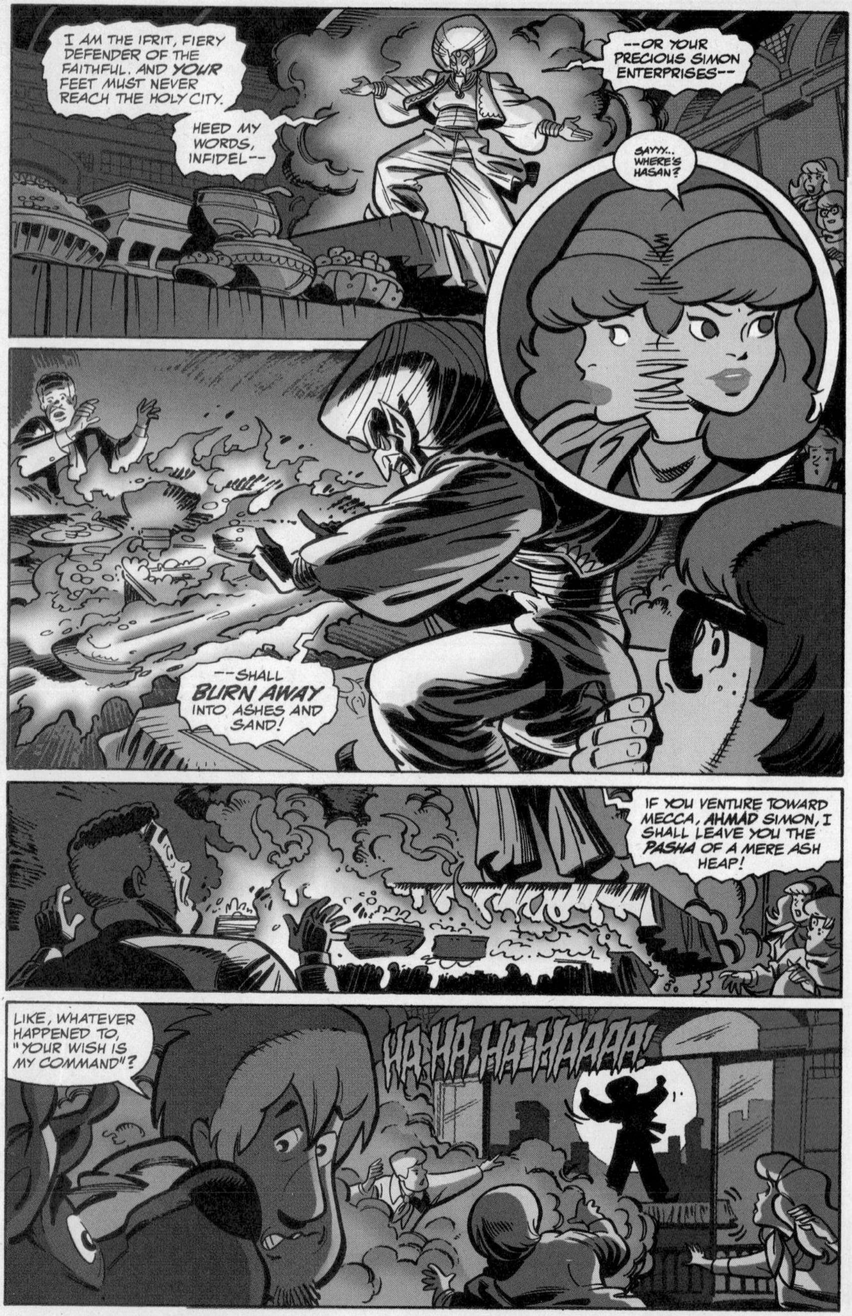

I AM THE IFRIT, FIERY DEFENDER OF THE FAITHFUL. AND YOUR FEET MUST NEVER REACH THE HOLY CITY.
HEED MY WORDS, INFIDEL--
--OR YOUR PRECIOUS SIMON ENTERPRISES--
SAYYY... WHERE'S HASAN?
--SHALL BURN AWAY INTO ASHES AND SAND!
IF YOU VENTURE TOWARD MECCA, AHMAD SIMON, I SHALL LEAVE YOU THE PASHA OF A MERE ASH HEAP!
LIKE, WHATEVER HAPPENED TO, "YOUR WISH IS MY COMMAND"?
HA HA HA HAAAA!

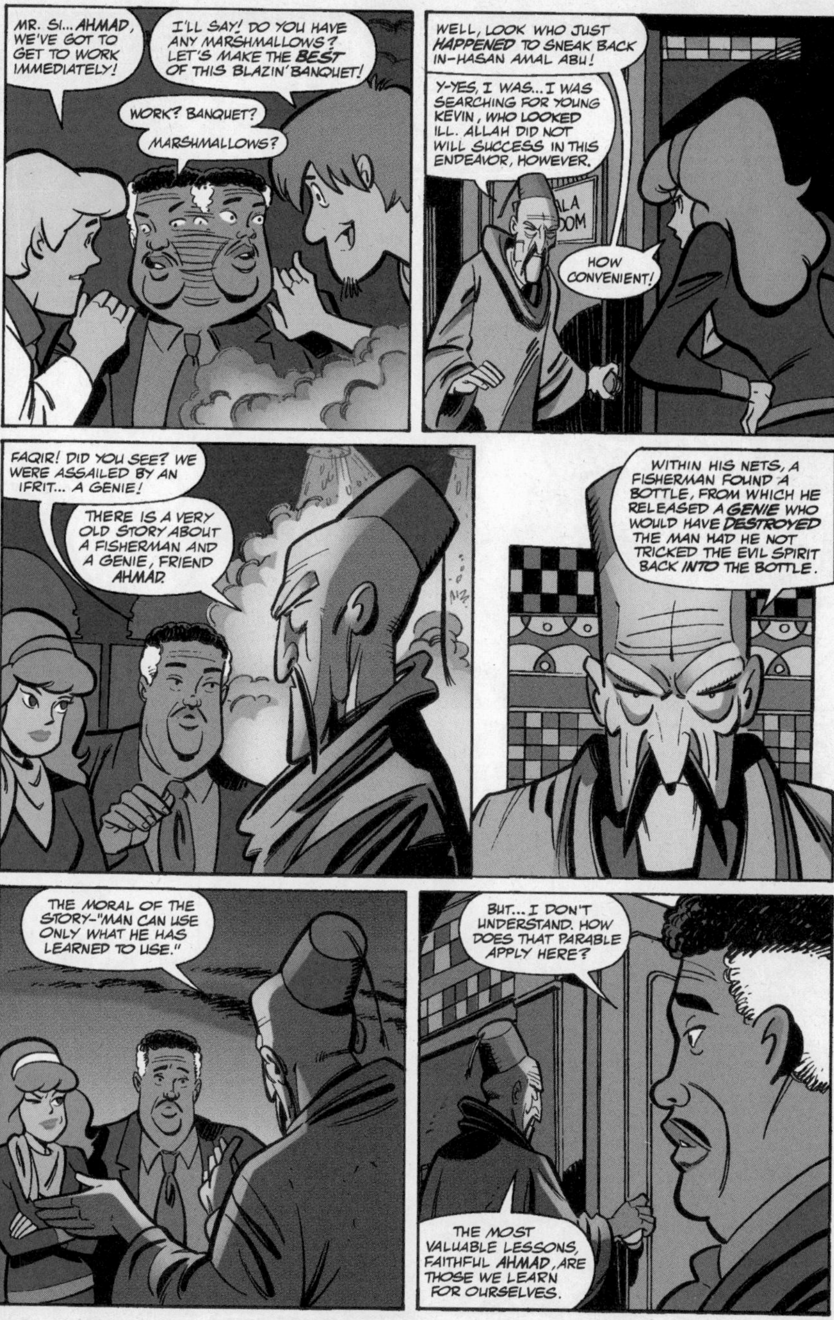
MR. SI...AHMAD, WE'VE GOT TO GET TO WORK IMMEDIATELY!
I'LL SAY! DO YOU HAVE ANY MARSHMALLOWS? LET'S MAKE THE BEST OF THIS BLAZIN' BANQUET!
WORK? BANQUET?
MARSHMALLOWS?
WELL, LOOK WHO JUST HAPPENED TO SNEAK BACK IN-HASAN AMAL ABU!
Y-YES, I WAS...I WAS SEARCHING FOR YOUNG KEVIN, WHO LOOKED ILL. ALLAH DID NOT WILL SUCCESS IN THIS ENDEAVOR, HOWEVER.
HOW CONVENIENT!
FAQIR! DID YOU SEE? WE WERE ASSAILED BY AN IFRIT... A GENIE!
THERE IS A VERY OLD STORY ABOUT A FISHERMAN AND A GENIE, FRIEND AHMAD.
WITHIN HIS NETS, A FISHERMAN FOUND A BOTTLE, FROM WHICH HE RELEASED A GENIE WHO WOULD HAVE DESTROYED THE MAN HAD HE NOT TRICKED THE EVIL SPIRIT BACK INTO THE BOTTLE.
THE MORAL OF THE STORY-"MAN CAN USE ONLY WHAT HE HAS LEARNED TO USE."
BUT... I DON'T UNDERSTAND. HOW DOES THAT PARABLE APPLY HERE?
THE MOST VALUABLE LESSONS, FAITHFUL AHMAD, ARE THOSE WE LEARN FOR OURSELVES.

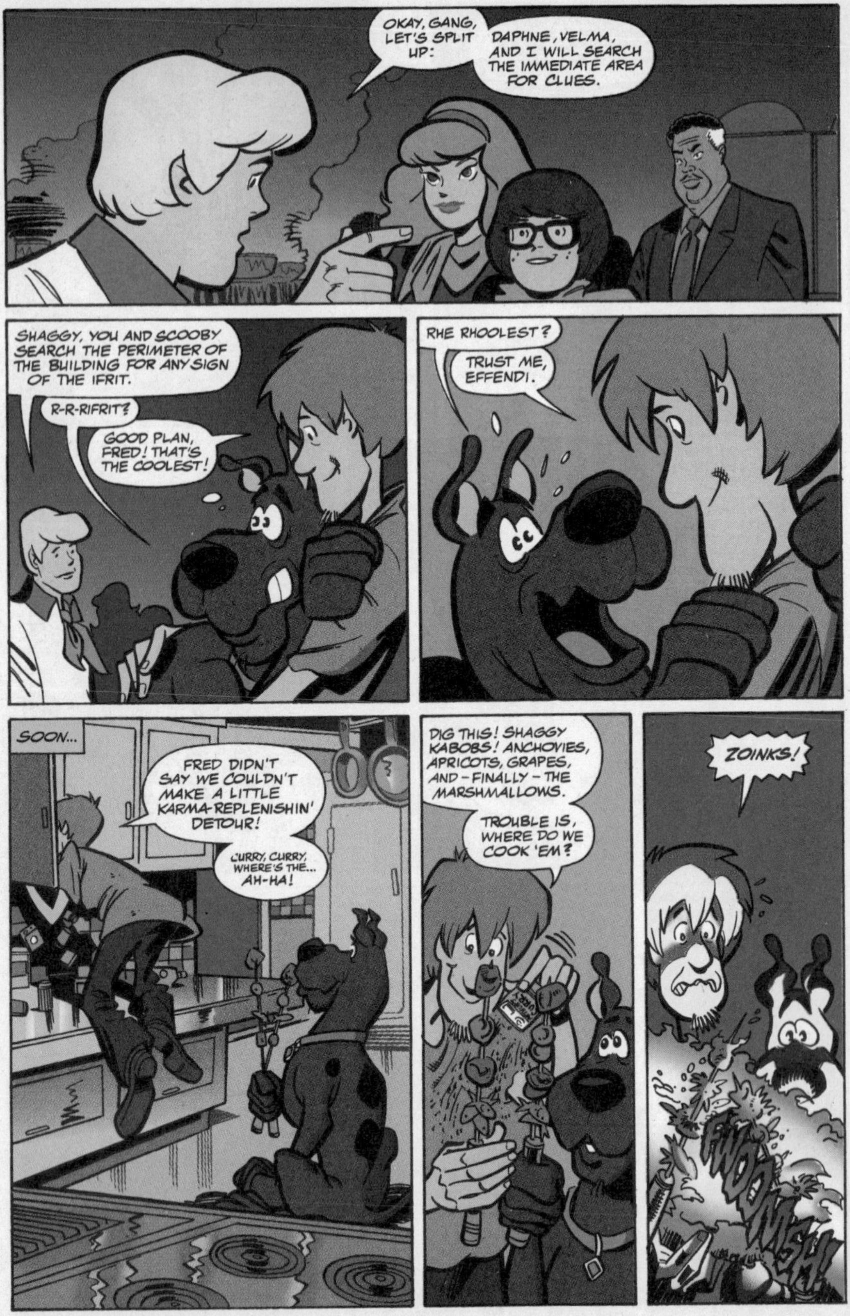
OKAY, GANG, LET'S SPLIT UP:
DAPHNE, VELMA, AND I WILL SEARCH THE IMMEDIATE AREA FOR CLUES.
SHAGGY, YOU AND SCOOBY SEARCH THE PERIMETER OF THE BUILDING FOR ANY SIGN OF THE IFRIT.
R-R-RIFRIT?
GOOD PLAN, FRED! THAT'S THE COOLEST!
RHE RHOOLEST?
TRUST ME, EFFENDI.
SOON...
FRED DIDN'T SAY WE COULDN'T MAKE A LITTLE KARMA-REPLENISHIN' DETOUR!
CURRY, CURRY, WHERE'S THE... AH-HA!
DIG THIS! SHAGGY KABOBS! ANCHOVIES, APRICOTS, GRAPES, AND - FINALLY - THE MARSHMALLOWS.
TROUBLE IS, WHERE DO WE COOK 'EM?
ZOINKS!
FWOOMSH!

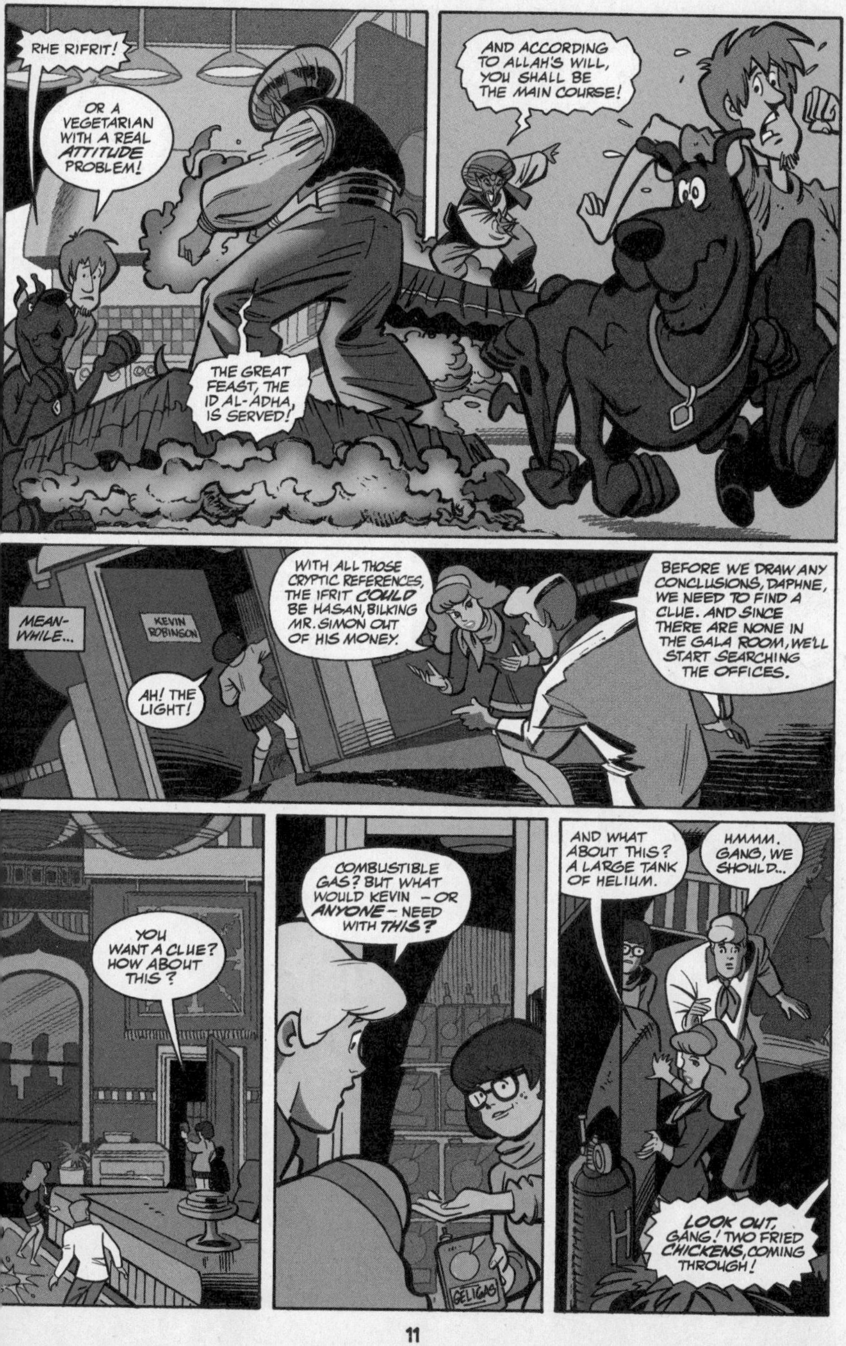
RHE RIFRIT!
OR A VEGETARIAN WITH A REAL ATTITUDE PROBLEM!
THE GREAT FEAST, THE ID AL-ADHA, IS SERVED!
AND ACCORDING TO ALLAH'S WILL, YOU SHALL BE THE MAIN COURSE!
MEAN-WHILE...
KEVIN ROBINSON
AH! THE LIGHT!
WITH ALL THOSE CRYPTIC REFERENCES, THE IFRIT COULD BE HASAN, BILKING MR. SIMON OUT OF HIS MONEY.
BEFORE WE DRAW ANY CONCLUSIONS, DAPHNE, WE NEED TO FIND A CLUE. AND SINCE THERE ARE NONE IN THE GALA ROOM, WE'LL START SEARCHING THE OFFICES.
YOU WANT A CLUE? HOW ABOUT THIS?
COMBUSTIBLE GAS? BUT WHAT WOULD KEVIN —OR ANYONE— NEED WITH THIS?
GELIGAS
AND WHAT ABOUT THIS? A LARGE TANK OF HELIUM.
HMMM. GANG, WE SHOULD...
LOOK OUT, GANG! TWO FRIED CHICKENS, COMING THROUGH!
H

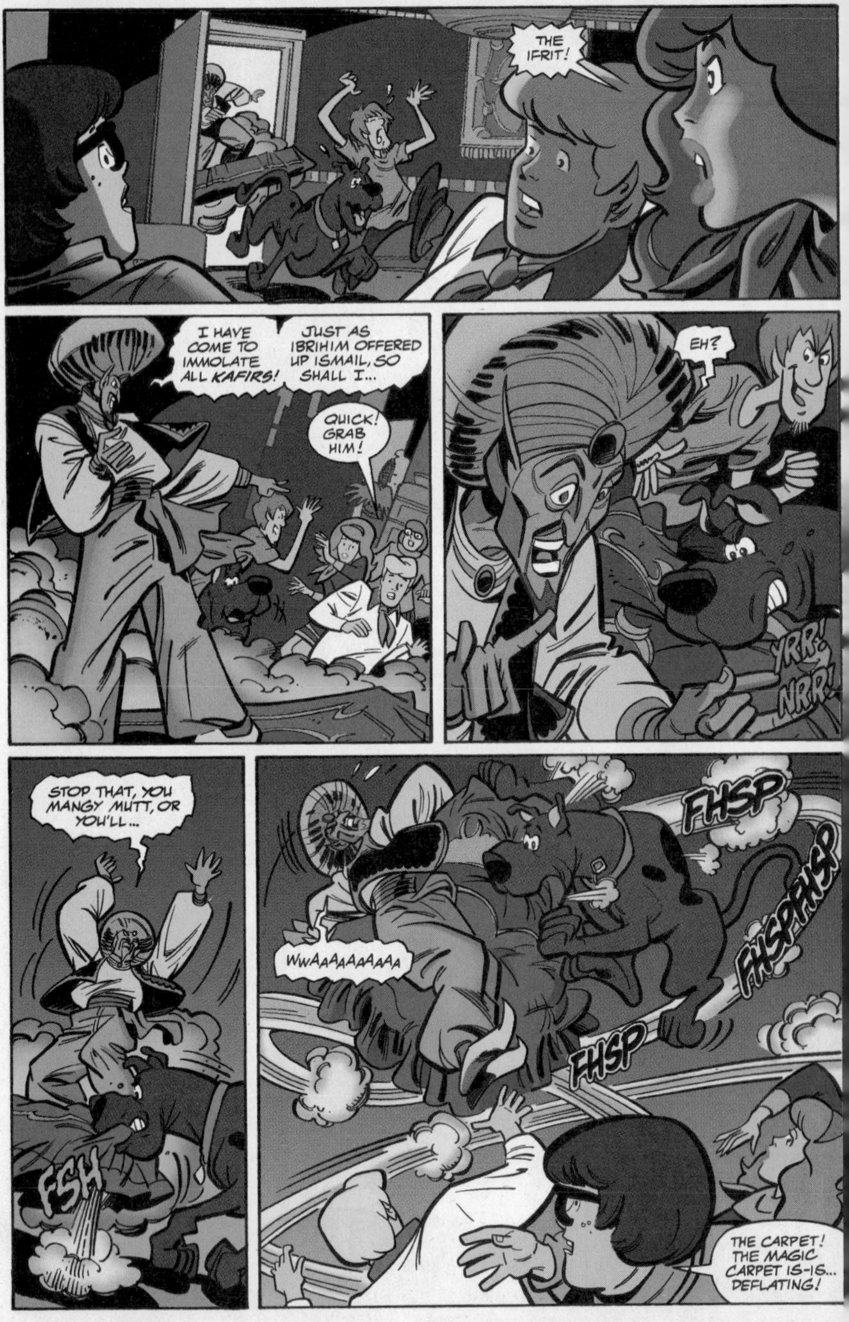
THE IFRIT!
I HAVE COME TO IMMOLATE ALL KAFIRS!
JUST AS IBRIHIM OFFERED UP ISMAIL, SO SHALL I...
QUICK! GRAB HIM!
EH?
YRR! NRR!
STOP THAT, YOU MANGY MUTT, OR YOU'LL...
FSH
FHSP
WwAAAAAAAAA
FHSPFHSP
FHSP
THE CARPET! THE MAGIC CARPET IS-IS... DEFLATING!

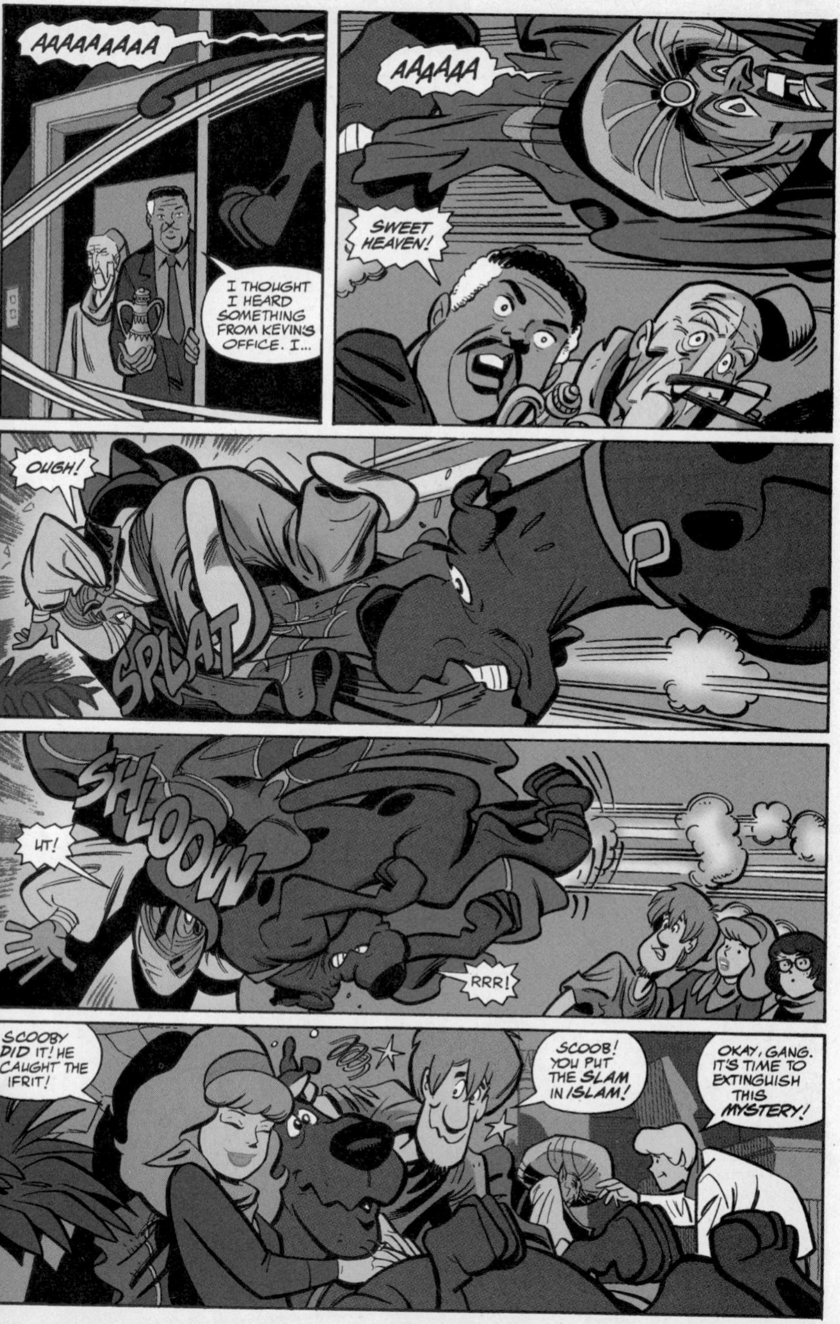
AAAAAAAAA
I THOUGHT I HEARD SOMETHING FROM KEVIN'S OFFICE. I...
AAAAAA
SWEET HEAVEN!
OUGH!
SPLAT
SHLOOW
UT!
RRR!
SCOOBY DID IT! HE CAUGHT THE IFRIT!
SCOOB! YOU PUT THE SLAM IN ISLAM!
OKAY, GANG. IT'S TIME TO EXTINGUISH THIS MYSTERY!

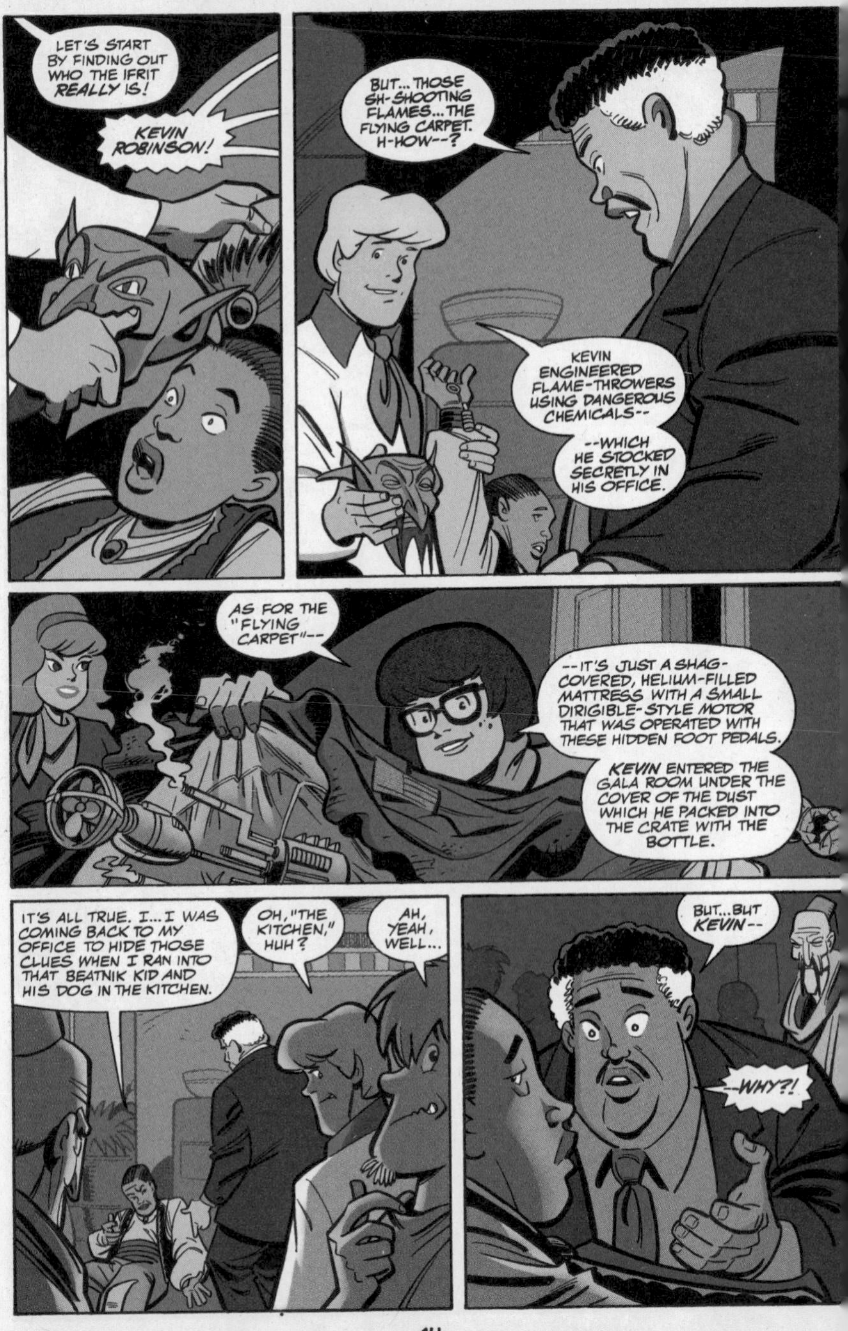
LET'S START BY FINDING OUT WHO THE IFRIT REALLY IS!
KEVIN ROBINSON!
BUT... THOSE SH-SHOOTING FLAMES... THE FLYING CARPET. H-HOW--?
KEVIN ENGINEERED FLAME-THROWERS USING DANGEROUS CHEMICALS--
--WHICH HE STOCKED SECRETLY IN HIS OFFICE.
AS FOR THE "FLYING CARPET"--
--IT'S JUST A SHAG-COVERED, HELIUM-FILLED MATTRESS WITH A SMALL DIRIGIBLE-STYLE MOTOR THAT WAS OPERATED WITH THESE HIDDEN FOOT PEDALS.
KEVIN ENTERED THE GALA ROOM UNDER THE COVER OF THE DUST WHICH HE PACKED INTO THE CRATE WITH THE BOTTLE.
IT'S ALL TRUE. I... I WAS COMING BACK TO MY OFFICE TO HIDE THOSE CLUES WHEN I RAN INTO THAT BEATNIK KID AND HIS DOG IN THE KITCHEN.
OH, "THE KITCHEN," HUH?
AH, YEAH, WELL...
BUT... BUT KEVIN--
--WHY?!

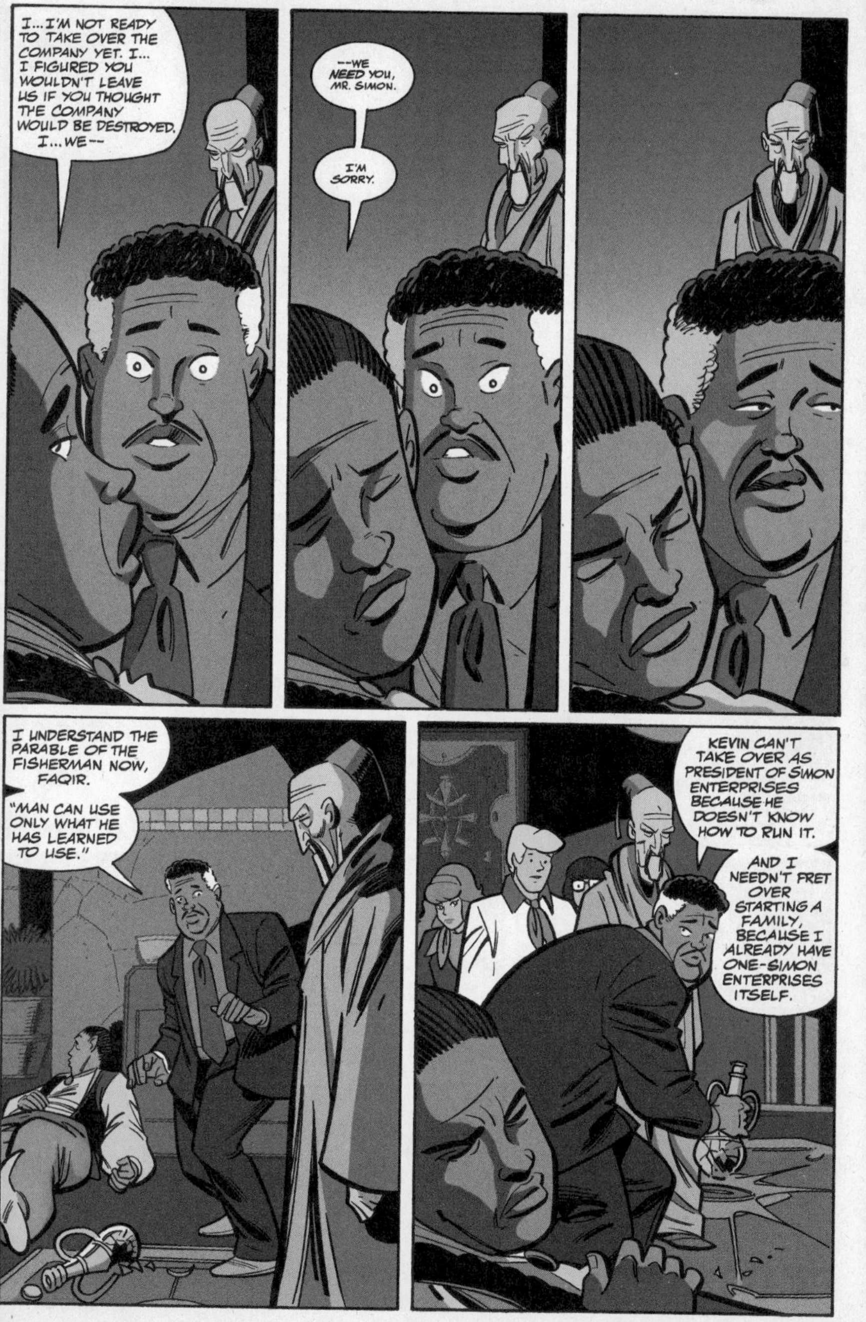
I...I'M NOT READY TO TAKE OVER THE COMPANY YET. I... I FIGURED YOU WOULDN'T LEAVE US IF YOU THOUGHT THE COMPANY WOULD BE DESTROYED. I...WE--
--WE NEED YOU, MR. SIMON.
I'M SORRY.
I UNDERSTAND THE PARABLE OF THE FISHERMAN NOW, FAQIR.
"MAN CAN USE ONLY WHAT HE HAS LEARNED TO USE."
KEVIN CAN'T TAKE OVER AS PRESIDENT OF SIMON ENTERPRISES BECAUSE HE DOESN'T KNOW HOW TO RUN IT.
AND I NEEDN'T FRET OVER STARTING A FAMILY, BECAUSE I ALREADY HAVE ONE-SIMON ENTERPRISES ITSELF.

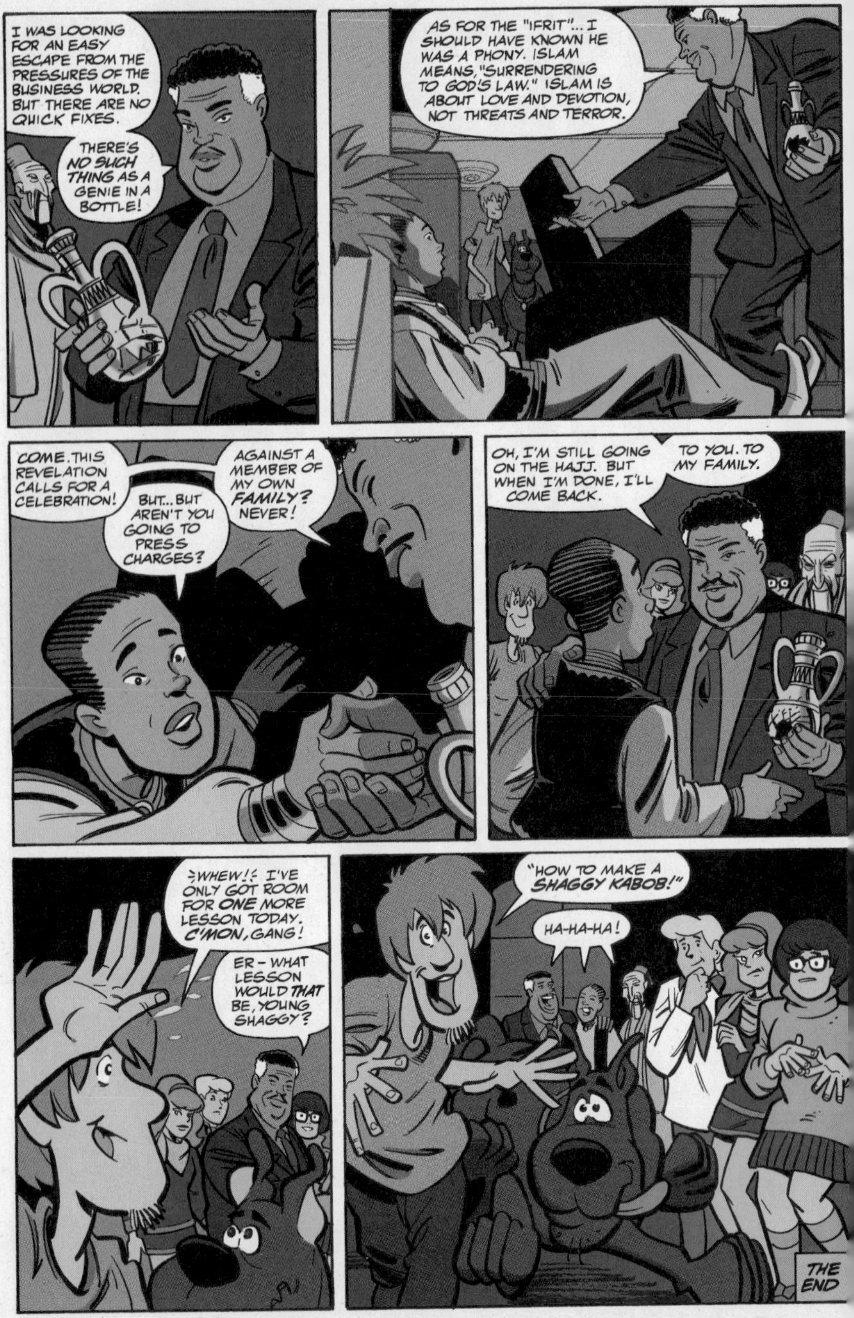
I WAS LOOKING FOR AN EASY ESCAPE FROM THE PRESSURES OF THE BUSINESS WORLD. BUT THERE ARE NO QUICK FIXES.
THERE'S NO SUCH THING AS A GENIE IN A BOTTLE!
AS FOR THE "IFRIT"... I SHOULD HAVE KNOWN HE WAS A PHONY. ISLAM MEANS, "SURRENDERING TO GOD'S LAW." ISLAM IS ABOUT LOVE AND DEVOTION, NOT THREATS AND TERROR.
COME. THIS REVELATION CALLS FOR A CELEBRATION!
BUT... BUT AREN'T YOU GOING TO PRESS CHARGES?
AGAINST A MEMBER OF MY OWN FAMILY? NEVER!
OH, I'M STILL GOING ON THE HAJJ. BUT WHEN I'M DONE, I'LL COME BACK.
TO YOU. TO MY FAMILY.
WHEW! I'VE ONLY GOT ROOM FOR ONE MORE LESSON TODAY. C'MON, GANG!
ER– WHAT LESSON WOULD THAT BE, YOUNG SHAGGY?
"HOW TO MAKE A SHAGGY KABOB!"
HA-HA-HA!
THE END

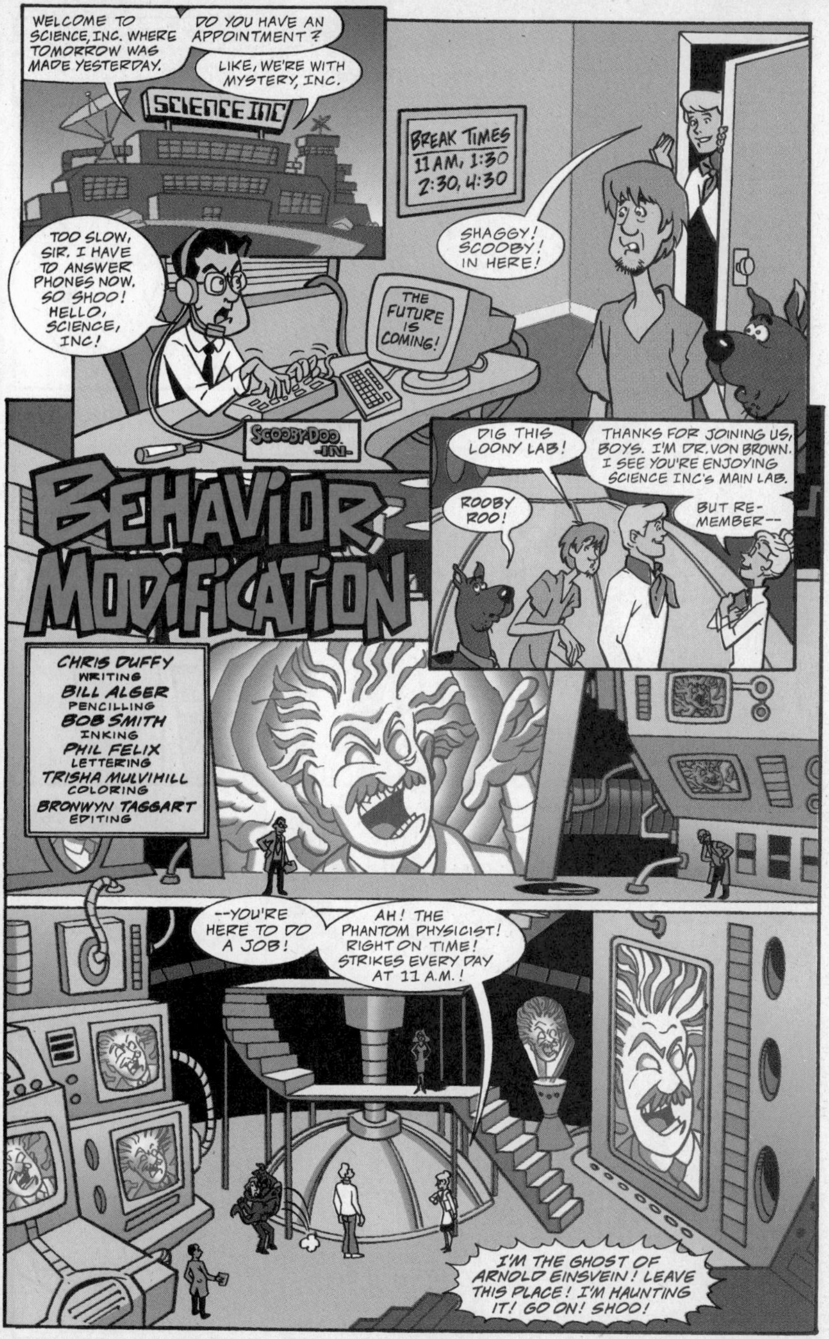
WELCOME TO SCIENCE, INC. WHERE TOMORROW WAS MADE YESTERDAY.
DO YOU HAVE AN APPOINTMENT?
LIKE, WE'RE WITH MYSTERY, INC.
SCIENCE INC
BREAK TIMES 11 AM, 1:30 2:30, 4:30
TOO SLOW, SIR. I HAVE TO ANSWER PHONES NOW. SO SHOO! HELLO, SCIENCE, INC!
THE FUTURE IS COMING!
SHAGGY! SCOOBY! IN HERE!
SCOOBY-DOO -IN-
BEHAVIOR MODIFICATION
CHRIS DUFFY WRITING
BILL ALGER PENCILLING
BOB SMITH INKING
PHIL FELIX LETTERING
TRISHA MULVIHILL COLORING
BRONWYN TAGGART EDITING
DIG THIS LOONY LAB!
ROOBY ROO!
THANKS FOR JOINING US, BOYS. I'M DR. VON BROWN. I SEE YOU'RE ENJOYING SCIENCE INC'S MAIN LAB.
BUT RE-MEMBER--
--YOU'RE HERE TO DO A JOB!
AH! THE PHANTOM PHYSICIST! RIGHT ON TIME! STRIKES EVERY DAY AT 11 A.M.!
I'M THE GHOST OF ARNOLD EINSVEIN! LEAVE THIS PLACE! I'M HAUNTING IT! GO ON! SHOO!

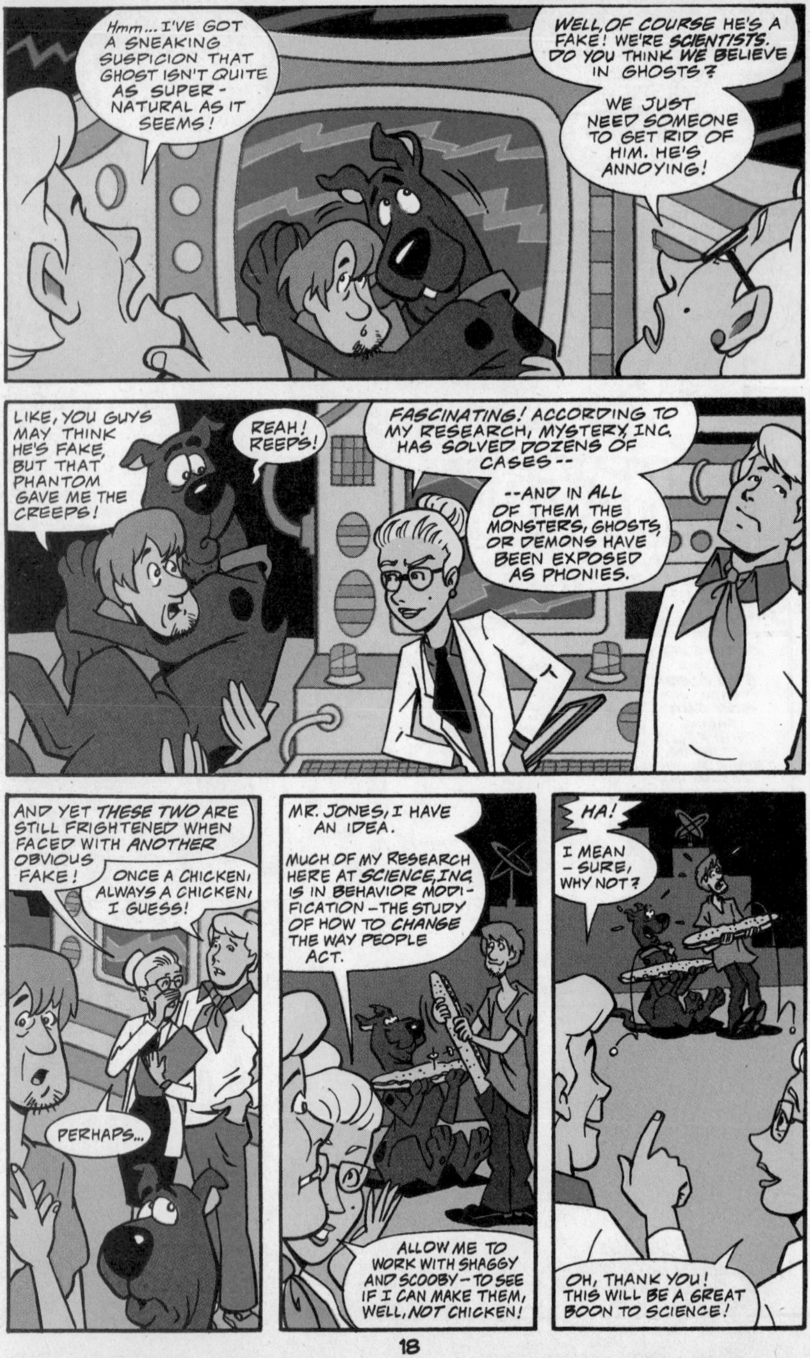
Hmm... I'VE GOT A SNEAKING SUSPICION THAT GHOST ISN'T QUITE AS SUPER-NATURAL AS IT SEEMS!
WELL, OF COURSE HE'S A FAKE! WE'RE SCIENTISTS. DO YOU THINK WE BELIEVE IN GHOSTS?
WE JUST NEED SOMEONE TO GET RID OF HIM. HE'S ANNOYING!
LIKE, YOU GUYS MAY THINK HE'S FAKE, BUT THAT PHANTOM GAVE ME THE CREEPS!
REAH! REEPS!
FASCINATING! ACCORDING TO MY RESEARCH, MYSTERY, INC. HAS SOLVED DOZENS OF CASES --
--AND IN ALL OF THEM THE MONSTERS, GHOSTS, OR DEMONS HAVE BEEN EXPOSED AS PHONIES.
AND YET THESE TWO ARE STILL FRIGHTENED WHEN FACED WITH ANOTHER OBVIOUS FAKE!
ONCE A CHICKEN, ALWAYS A CHICKEN, I GUESS!
PERHAPS...
MR. JONES, I HAVE AN IDEA.
MUCH OF MY RESEARCH HERE AT SCIENCE, INC. IS IN BEHAVIOR MODI-FICATION — THE STUDY OF HOW TO CHANGE THE WAY PEOPLE ACT.
ALLOW ME TO WORK WITH SHAGGY AND SCOOBY — TO SEE IF I CAN MAKE THEM, WELL, NOT CHICKEN!
HA!
I MEAN — SURE, WHY NOT?
OH, THANK YOU! THIS WILL BE A GREAT BOON TO SCIENCE!

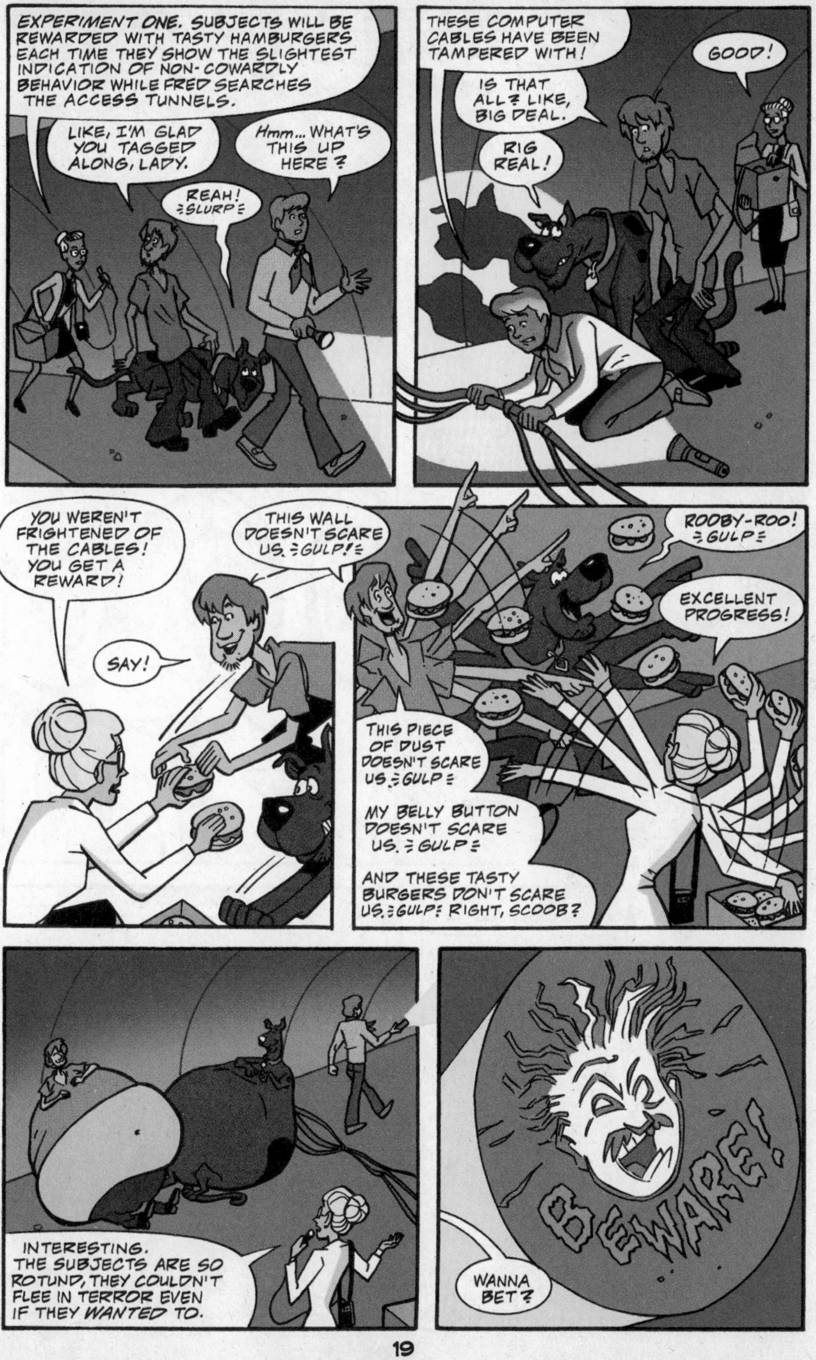
EXPERIMENT ONE. SUBJECTS WILL BE REWARDED WITH TASTY HAMBURGERS EACH TIME THEY SHOW THE SLIGHTEST INDICATION OF NON-COWARDLY BEHAVIOR WHILE FRED SEARCHES THE ACCESS TUNNELS.
LIKE, I'M GLAD YOU TAGGED ALONG, LADY.
Hmm... WHAT'S THIS UP HERE?
REAH! ≡SLURP≡
THESE COMPUTER CABLES HAVE BEEN TAMPERED WITH!
GOOD!
IS THAT ALL? LIKE, BIG DEAL.
RIG REAL!
YOU WEREN'T FRIGHTENED OF THE CABLES! YOU GET A REWARD!
THIS WALL DOESN'T SCARE US. ≡GULP!≡
SAY!
ROOBY-ROO! ≡GULP≡
EXCELLENT PROGRESS!
THIS PIECE OF DUST DOESN'T SCARE US. ≡GULP≡
MY BELLY BUTTON DOESN'T SCARE US. ≡GULP≡
AND THESE TASTY BURGERS DON'T SCARE US. ≡GULP≡ RIGHT, SCOOB?
INTERESTING. THE SUBJECTS ARE SO ROTUND, THEY COULDN'T FLEE IN TERROR EVEN IF THEY *WANTED* TO.
BEWARE!
WANNA BET?

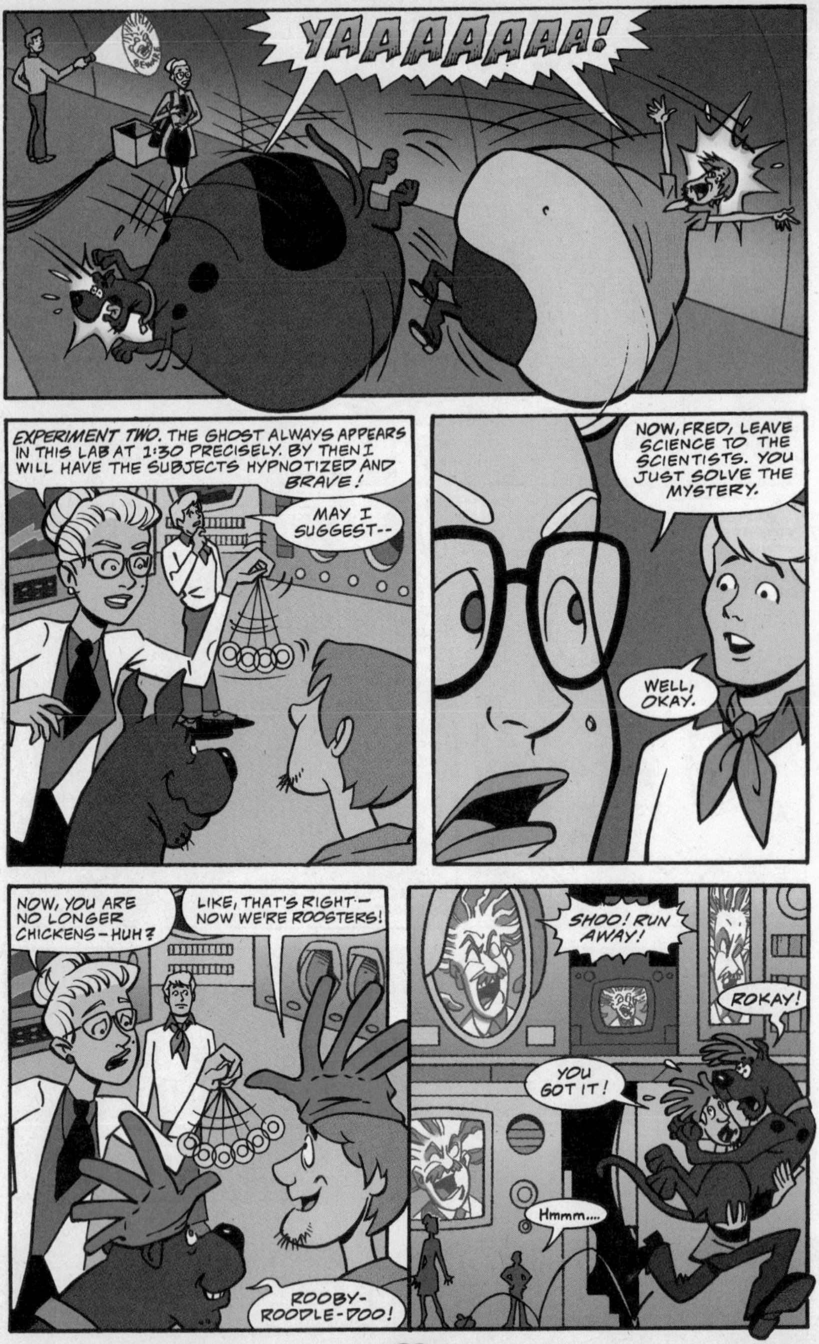
YAAAAAAA!
BEWARE
EXPERIMENT TWO. THE GHOST ALWAYS APPEARS IN THIS LAB AT 1:30 PRECISELY. BY THEN I WILL HAVE THE SUBJECTS HYPNOTIZED AND BRAVE!
MAY I SUGGEST--
NOW, FRED, LEAVE SCIENCE TO THE SCIENTISTS. YOU JUST SOLVE THE MYSTERY.
WELL, OKAY.
NOW, YOU ARE NO LONGER CHICKENS—HUH?
LIKE, THAT'S RIGHT— NOW WE'RE ROOSTERS!
ROOBY-ROODLE-DOO!
SHOO! RUN AWAY!
ROKAY!
YOU GOT IT!
Hmmm....

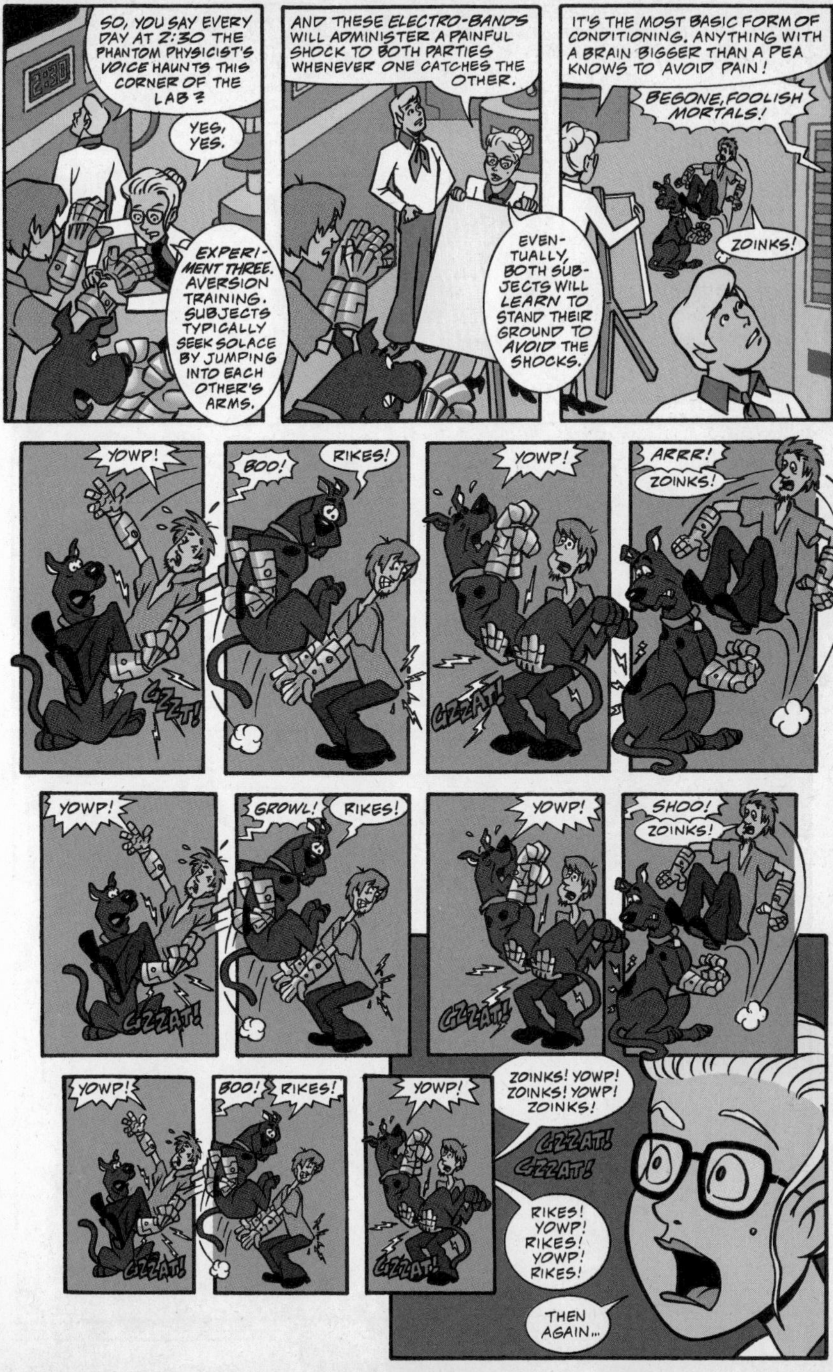
SO, YOU SAY EVERY DAY AT 2:30 THE PHANTOM PHYSICIST'S VOICE HAUNTS THIS CORNER OF THE LAB?
YES, YES.
EXPERIMENT THREE. AVERSION TRAINING. SUBJECTS TYPICALLY SEEK SOLACE BY JUMPING INTO EACH OTHER'S ARMS.
AND THESE ELECTRO-BANDS WILL ADMINISTER A PAINFUL SHOCK TO BOTH PARTIES WHENEVER ONE CATCHES THE OTHER.
EVENTUALLY, BOTH SUBJECTS WILL LEARN TO STAND THEIR GROUND TO AVOID THE SHOCKS.
IT'S THE MOST BASIC FORM OF CONDITIONING. ANYTHING WITH A BRAIN BIGGER THAN A PEA KNOWS TO AVOID PAIN!
BEGONE, FOOLISH MORTALS!
ZOINKS!
YOWP!
GZZT!
BOO!
RIKES!
YOWP!
GZZAT!
ARRR!
ZOINKS!
YOWP!
GZZAT!
GROWL!
RIKES!
YOWP!
GZZAT!
SHOO!
ZOINKS!
YOWP!
GZZAT!
BOO!
RIKES!
YOWP!
GZZAT!
ZOINKS! YOWP! ZOINKS! YOWP! ZOINKS!
GZZAT!
GZZAT!
RIKES! YOWP! RIKES! YOWP! RIKES!
THEN AGAIN...

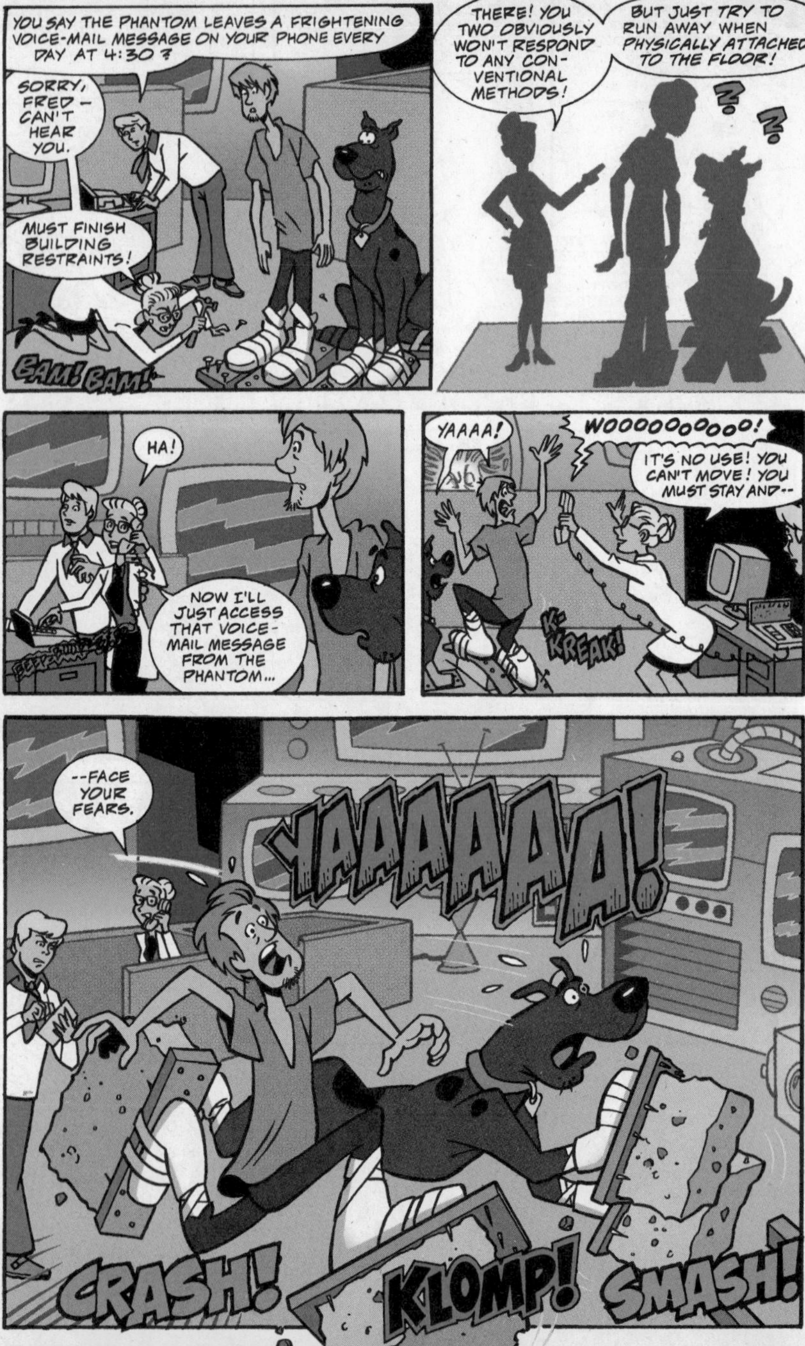
YOU SAY THE PHANTOM LEAVES A FRIGHTENING VOICE-MAIL MESSAGE ON YOUR PHONE EVERY DAY AT 4:30 ?
SORRY, FRED -- CAN'T HEAR YOU.
MUST FINISH BUILDING RESTRAINTS!
BAM! BAM!
THERE! YOU TWO OBVIOUSLY WON'T RESPOND TO ANY CON-VENTIONAL METHODS!
BUT JUST TRY TO RUN AWAY WHEN PHYSICALLY ATTACHED TO THE FLOOR!
? ?
HA!
NOW I'LL JUST ACCESS THAT VOICE-MAIL MESSAGE FROM THE PHANTOM...
YAAAA!
WOOOOOOOOOO!
IT'S NO USE! YOU CAN'T MOVE! YOU MUST STAY AND--
K-KREAK!
--FACE YOUR FEARS.
YAAAAAA!
CRASH!
KLOMP!
SMASH!

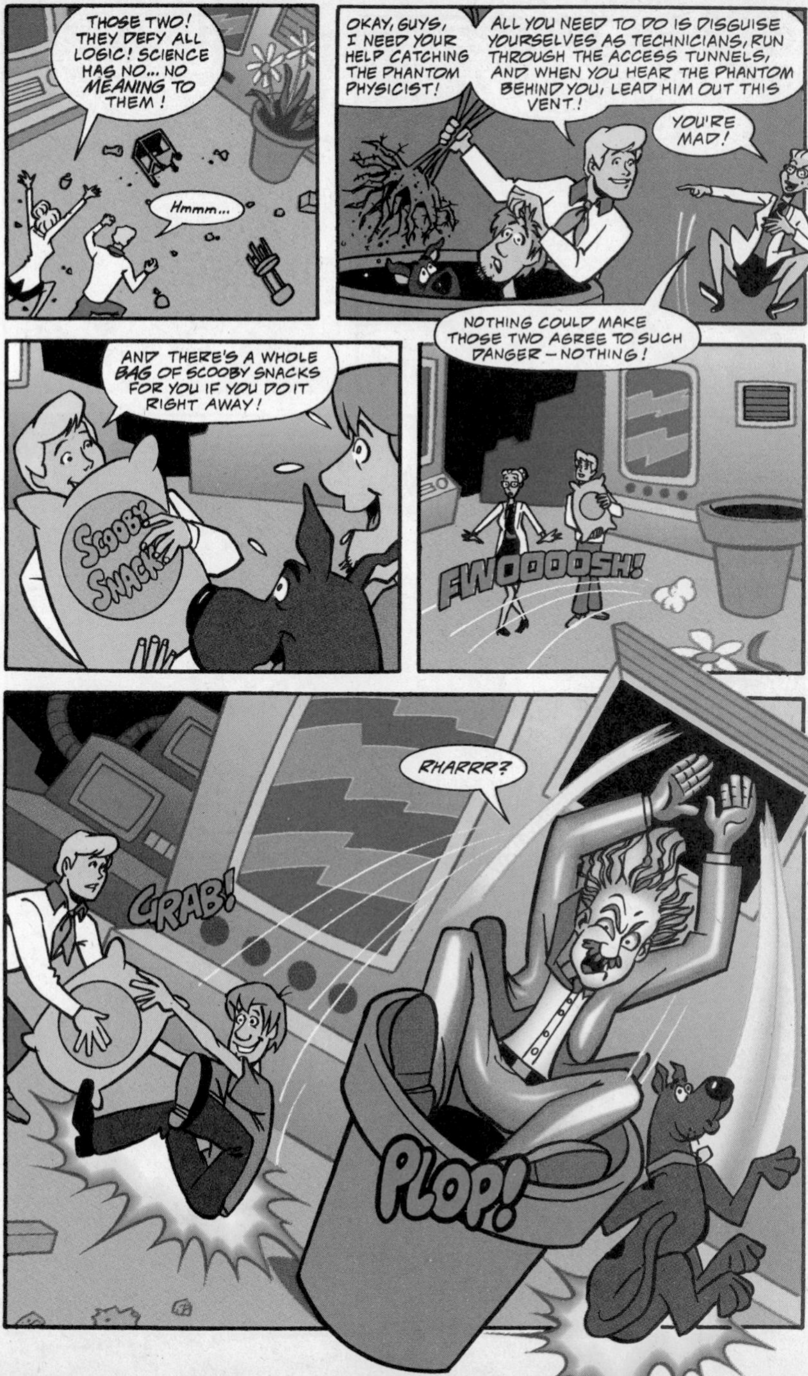
THOSE TWO! THEY DEFY ALL LOGIC! SCIENCE HAS NO... NO MEANING TO THEM!
Hmmm...
OKAY, GUYS, I NEED YOUR HELP CATCHING THE PHANTOM PHYSICIST!
ALL YOU NEED TO DO IS DISGUISE YOURSELVES AS TECHNICIANS, RUN THROUGH THE ACCESS TUNNELS, AND WHEN YOU HEAR THE PHANTOM BEHIND YOU, LEAD HIM OUT THIS VENT!
YOU'RE MAD!
NOTHING COULD MAKE THOSE TWO AGREE TO SUCH DANGER—NOTHING!
AND THERE'S A WHOLE BAG OF SCOOBY SNACKS FOR YOU IF YOU DO IT RIGHT AWAY!
SCOOBY SNACKS
FWOOOOSH!
RHARRR?
GRAB!
PLOP!

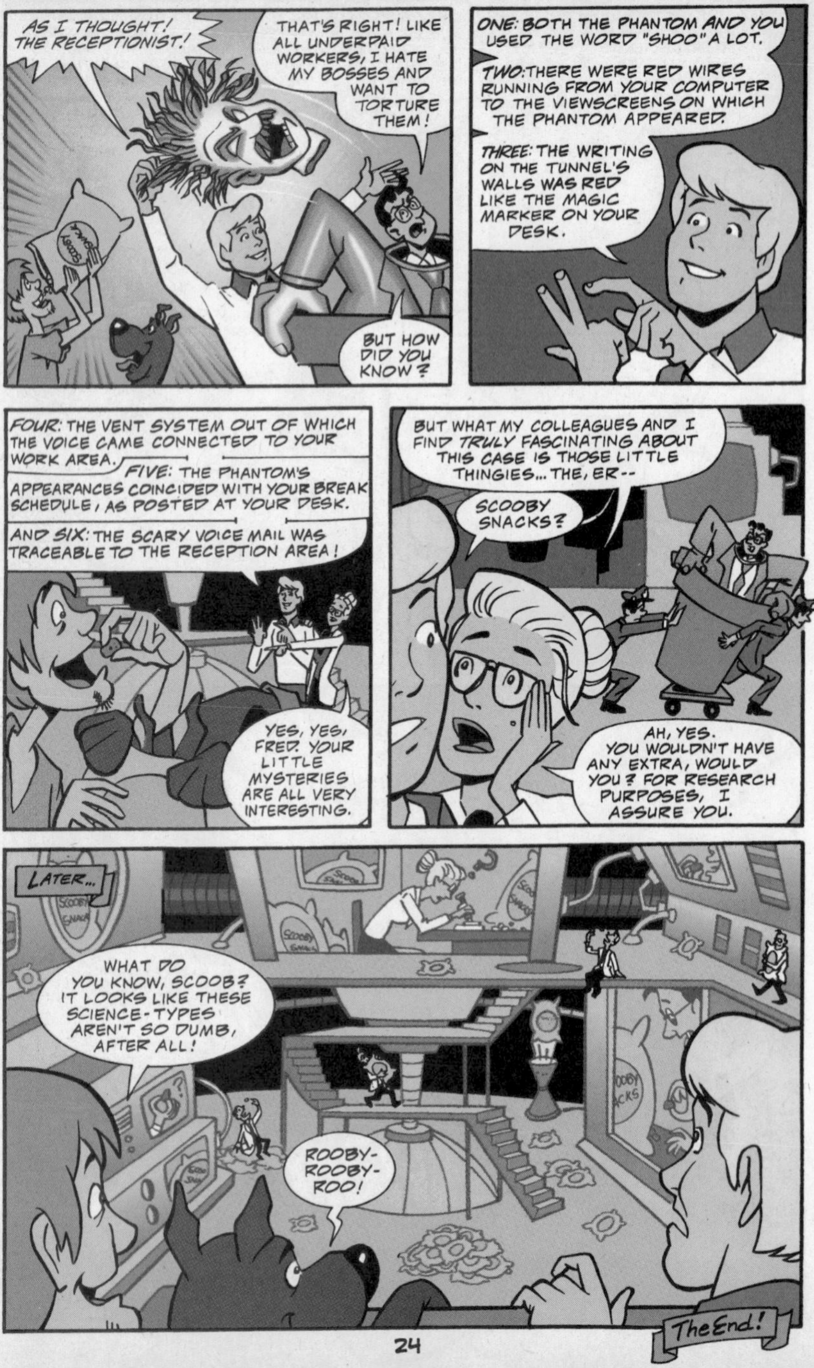
AS I THOUGHT! THE RECEPTIONIST!
THAT'S RIGHT! LIKE ALL UNDERPAID WORKERS, I HATE MY BOSSES AND WANT TO TORTURE THEM!
BUT HOW DID YOU KNOW?
ONE: BOTH THE PHANTOM AND YOU USED THE WORD "SHOO" A LOT.
TWO: THERE WERE RED WIRES RUNNING FROM YOUR COMPUTER TO THE VIEWSCREENS ON WHICH THE PHANTOM APPEARED.
THREE: THE WRITING ON THE TUNNEL'S WALLS WAS RED LIKE THE MAGIC MARKER ON YOUR DESK.
FOUR: THE VENT SYSTEM OUT OF WHICH THE VOICE CAME CONNECTED TO YOUR WORK AREA.
FIVE: THE PHANTOM'S APPEARANCES COINCIDED WITH YOUR BREAK SCHEDULE, AS POSTED AT YOUR DESK.
AND SIX: THE SCARY VOICE MAIL WAS TRACEABLE TO THE RECEPTION AREA!
YES, YES, FRED. YOUR LITTLE MYSTERIES ARE ALL VERY INTERESTING.
BUT WHAT MY COLLEAGUES AND I FIND TRULY FASCINATING ABOUT THIS CASE IS THOSE LITTLE THINGIES... THE, ER--
SCOOBY SNACKS?
AH, YES. YOU WOULDN'T HAVE ANY EXTRA, WOULD YOU? FOR RESEARCH PURPOSES, I ASSURE YOU.
LATER...
WHAT DO YOU KNOW, SCOOB? IT LOOKS LIKE THESE SCIENCE-TYPES AREN'T SO DUMB, AFTER ALL!
ROOBY-ROOBY-ROO!
The End!

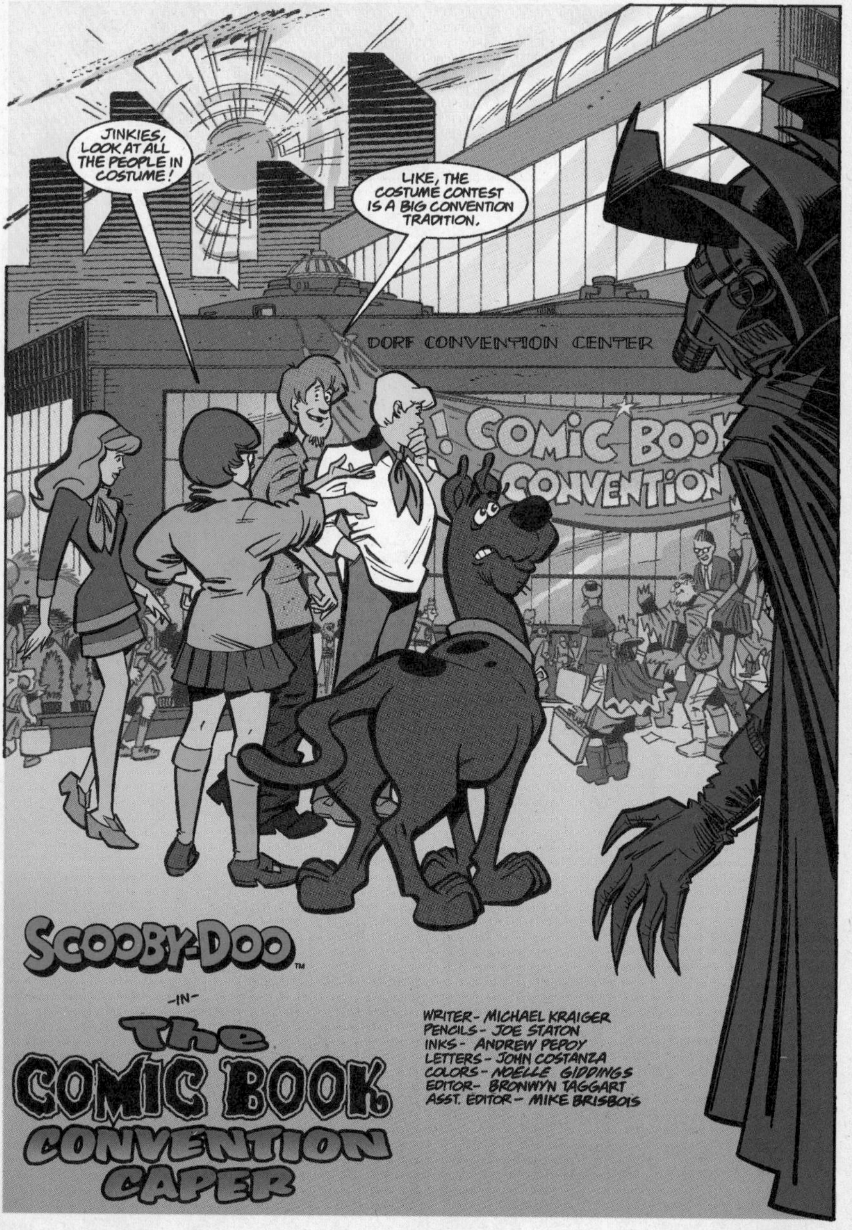
JINKIES, LOOK AT ALL THE PEOPLE IN COSTUME!
LIKE, THE COSTUME CONTEST IS A BIG CONVENTION TRADITION.
DORF CONVENTION CENTER
COMIC BOOK CONVENTION
SCOOBY-DOO™
-IN-
The COMIC BOOK CONVENTION CAPER
WRITER- MICHAEL KRAIGER
PENCILS- JOE STATON
INKS- ANDREW PEPOY
LETTERS- JOHN COSTANZA
COLORS- NOELLE GIDDINGS
EDITOR- BRONWYN TAGGART
ASST. EDITOR- MIKE BRISBOIS

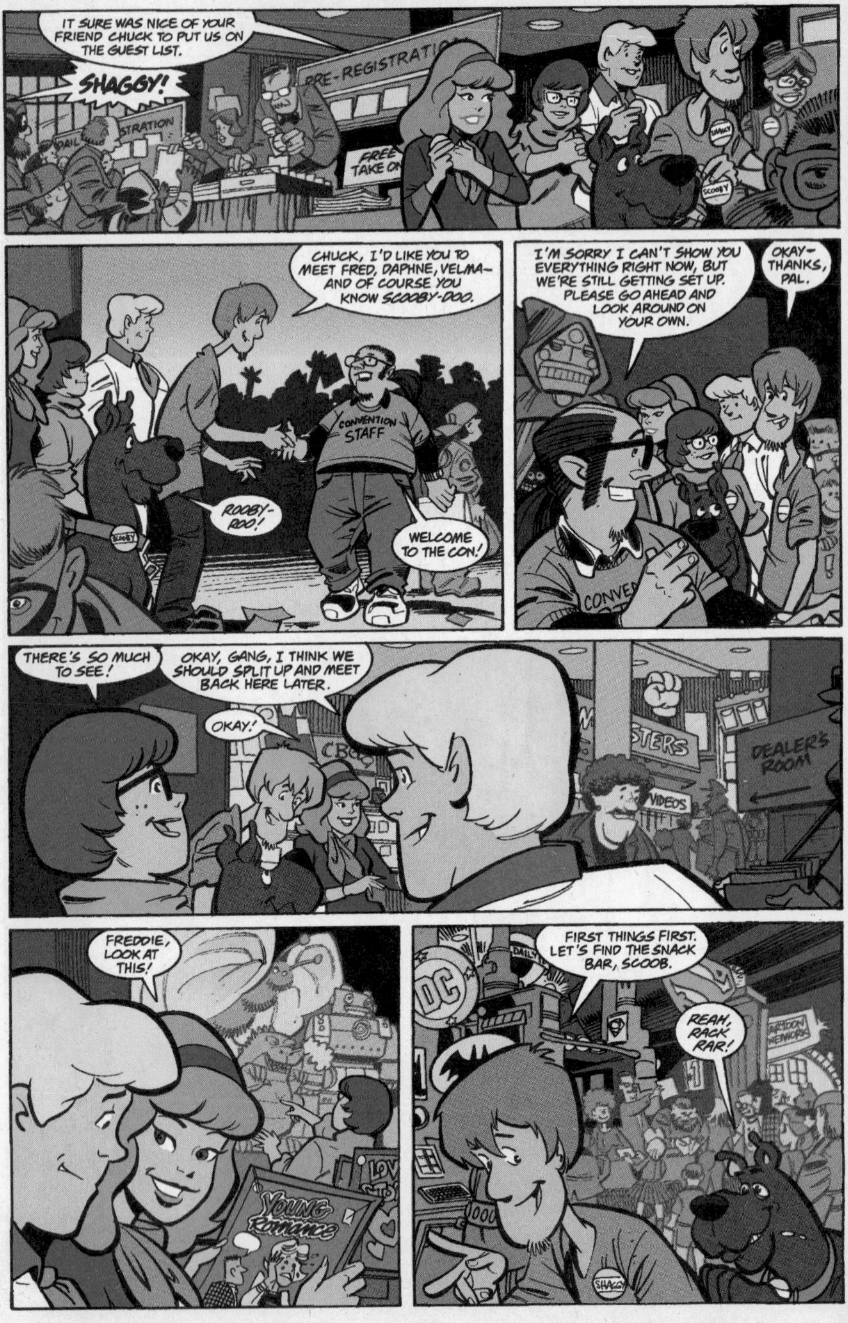
IT SURE WAS NICE OF YOUR FRIEND CHUCK TO PUT US ON THE GUEST LIST.
SHAGGY!
PRE-REGISTRATI
STRATION
FREE TAKE ON
SHAGGY
SCOOBY
CHUCK, I'D LIKE YOU TO MEET FRED, DAPHNE, VELMA-- AND OF COURSE YOU KNOW SCOOBY-DOO.
CONVENTION STAFF
ROOBY-ROO!
SCOOBY
WELCOME TO THE CON!
I'M SORRY I CAN'T SHOW YOU EVERYTHING RIGHT NOW, BUT WE'RE STILL GETTING SET UP. PLEASE GO AHEAD AND LOOK AROUND ON YOUR OWN.
OKAY-- THANKS, PAL.
THERE'S SO MUCH TO SEE!
OKAY, GANG, I THINK WE SHOULD SPLIT UP AND MEET BACK HERE LATER.
OKAY!
DEALER'S ROOM
VIDEOS
FREDDIE, LOOK AT THIS!
YOUNG ROMANCE
FIRST THINGS FIRST. LET'S FIND THE SNACK BAR, SCOOB.
REAH, RACK RAR!
DC
SHAGGY

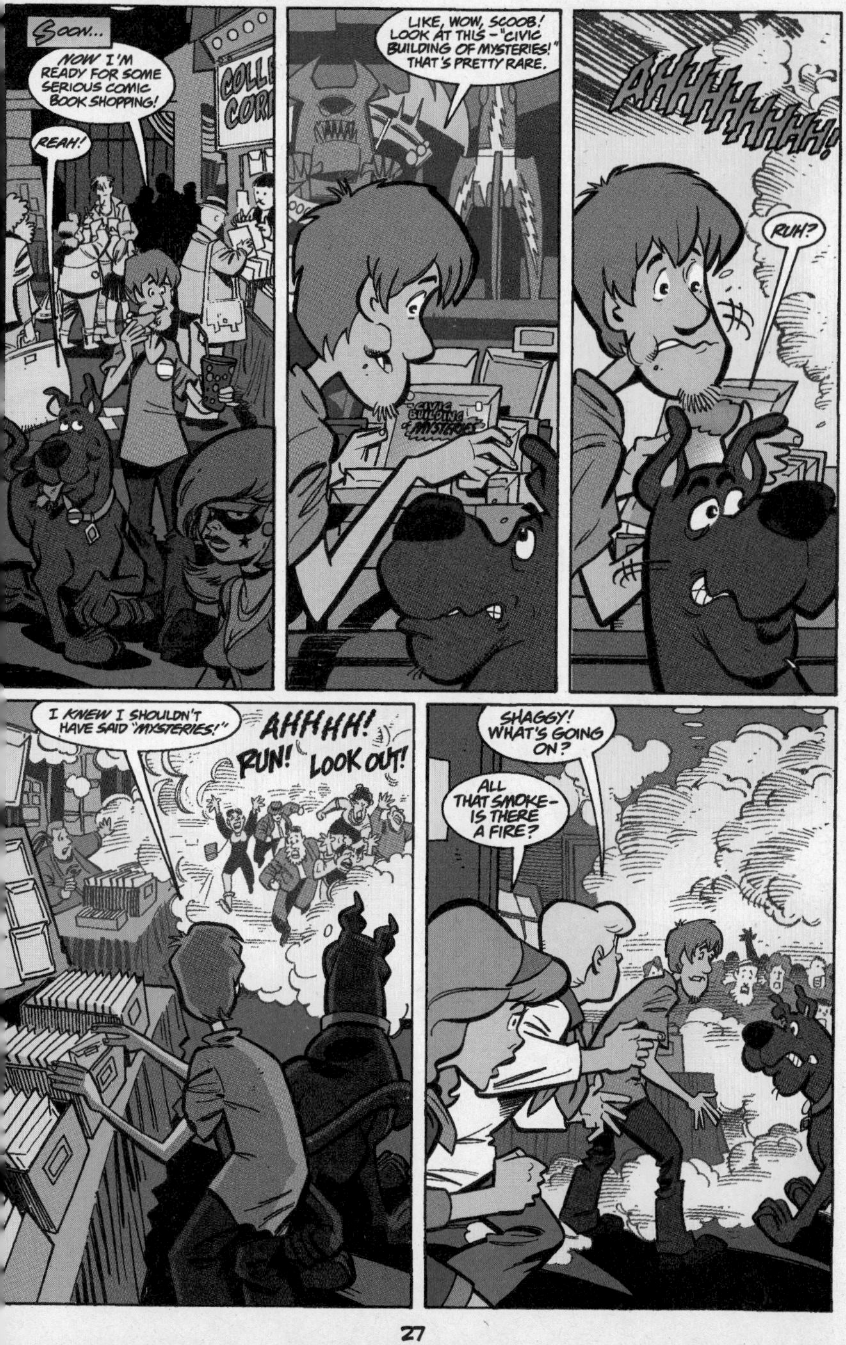
SOON...
NOW I'M READY FOR SOME SERIOUS COMIC BOOK SHOPPING!
REAH!
LIKE, WOW, SCOOB! LOOK AT THIS – "CIVIC BUILDING OF MYSTERIES!" THAT'S PRETTY RARE.
CIVIC BUILDING OF MYSTERIES
AHHHHHHHH!
RUH?
I KNEW I SHOULDN'T HAVE SAID "MYSTERIES!"
AHHHH!
RUN!
LOOK OUT!
SHAGGY! WHAT'S GOING ON?
ALL THAT SMOKE– IS THERE A FIRE?

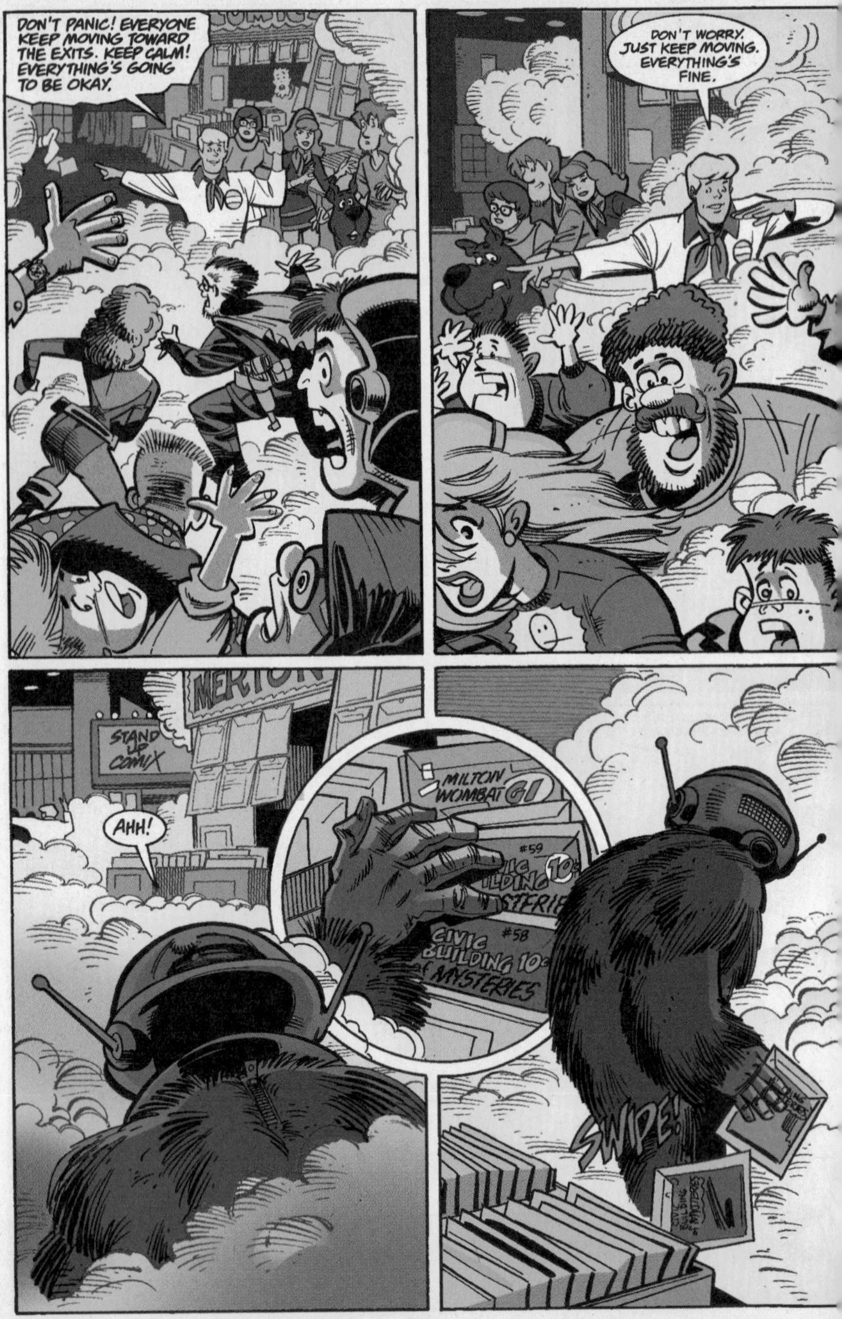
DON'T PANIC! EVERYONE KEEP MOVING TOWARD THE EXITS. KEEP CALM! EVERYTHING'S GOING TO BE OKAY.
DON'T WORRY. JUST KEEP MOVING. EVERYTHING'S FINE.
MERTON
STAND UP COMIX
AHH!
MILTON WOMBAT GI
#59
10¢
#58
CIVIC BUILDING 10¢ of MYSTERIES
SWIPE!

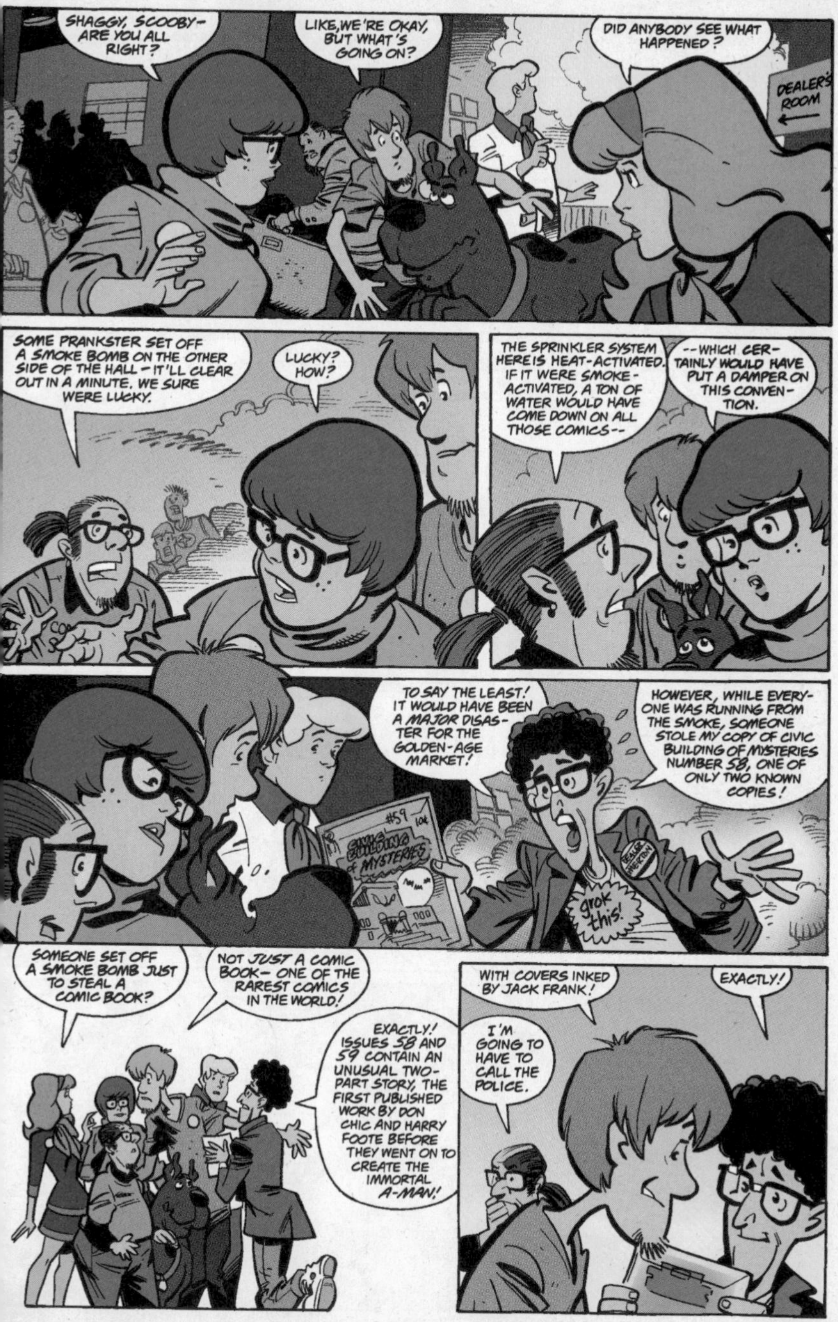
SHAGGY, SCOOBY-- ARE YOU ALL RIGHT?
LIKE, WE'RE OKAY, BUT WHAT'S GOING ON?
DID ANYBODY SEE WHAT HAPPENED?
DEALER'S ROOM
SOME PRANKSTER SET OFF A SMOKE BOMB ON THE OTHER SIDE OF THE HALL -- IT'LL CLEAR OUT IN A MINUTE. WE SURE WERE LUCKY.
LUCKY? HOW?
THE SPRINKLER SYSTEM HERE IS HEAT-ACTIVATED. IF IT WERE SMOKE-ACTIVATED, A TON OF WATER WOULD HAVE COME DOWN ON ALL THOSE COMICS--
--WHICH CERTAINLY WOULD HAVE PUT A DAMPER ON THIS CONVENTION.
TO SAY THE LEAST! IT WOULD HAVE BEEN A MAJOR DISASTER FOR THE GOLDEN-AGE MARKET!
HOWEVER, WHILE EVERYONE WAS RUNNING FROM THE SMOKE, SOMEONE STOLE MY COPY OF CIVIC BUILDING OF MYSTERIES NUMBER 58, ONE OF ONLY TWO KNOWN COPIES!
#59
10¢
CIVIC BUILDING OF MYSTERIES
grok this!
SOMEONE SET OFF A SMOKE BOMB JUST TO STEAL A COMIC BOOK?
NOT JUST A COMIC BOOK-- ONE OF THE RAREST COMICS IN THE WORLD!
EXACTLY! ISSUES 58 AND 59 CONTAIN AN UNUSUAL TWO-PART STORY, THE FIRST PUBLISHED WORK BY DON CHIC AND HARRY FOOTE BEFORE THEY WENT ON TO CREATE THE IMMORTAL A-MAN!
WITH COVERS INKED BY JACK FRANK!
EXACTLY!
I'M GOING TO HAVE TO CALL THE POLICE.

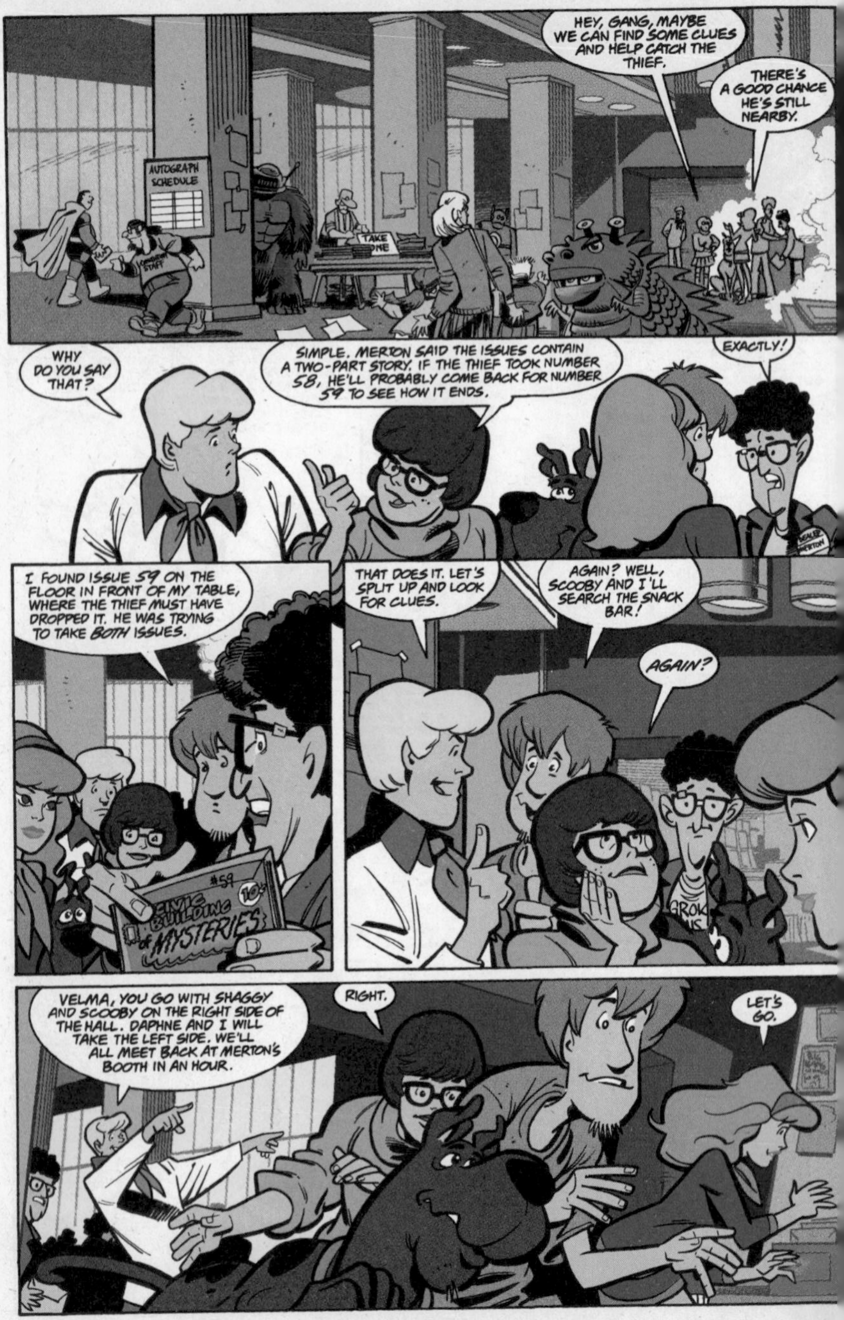
AUTOGRAPH SCHEDULE
TAKE ONE
HEY, GANG, MAYBE WE CAN FIND SOME CLUES AND HELP CATCH THE THIEF.
THERE'S A GOOD CHANCE HE'S STILL NEARBY.
WHY DO YOU SAY THAT?
SIMPLE. MERTON SAID THE ISSUES CONTAIN A TWO-PART STORY. IF THE THIEF TOOK NUMBER 58, HE'LL PROBABLY COME BACK FOR NUMBER 59 TO SEE HOW IT ENDS.
EXACTLY!
I FOUND ISSUE 59 ON THE FLOOR IN FRONT OF MY TABLE, WHERE THE THIEF MUST HAVE DROPPED IT. HE WAS TRYING TO TAKE BOTH ISSUES.
#59 10¢ CIVIC BUILDING of MYSTERIES
THAT DOES IT. LET'S SPLIT UP AND LOOK FOR CLUES.
AGAIN? WELL, SCOOBY AND I'LL SEARCH THE SNACK BAR!
AGAIN?
VELMA, YOU GO WITH SHAGGY AND SCOOBY ON THE RIGHT SIDE OF THE HALL. DAPHNE AND I WILL TAKE THE LEFT SIDE. WE'LL ALL MEET BACK AT MERTON'S BOOTH IN AN HOUR.
RIGHT.
LET'S GO.

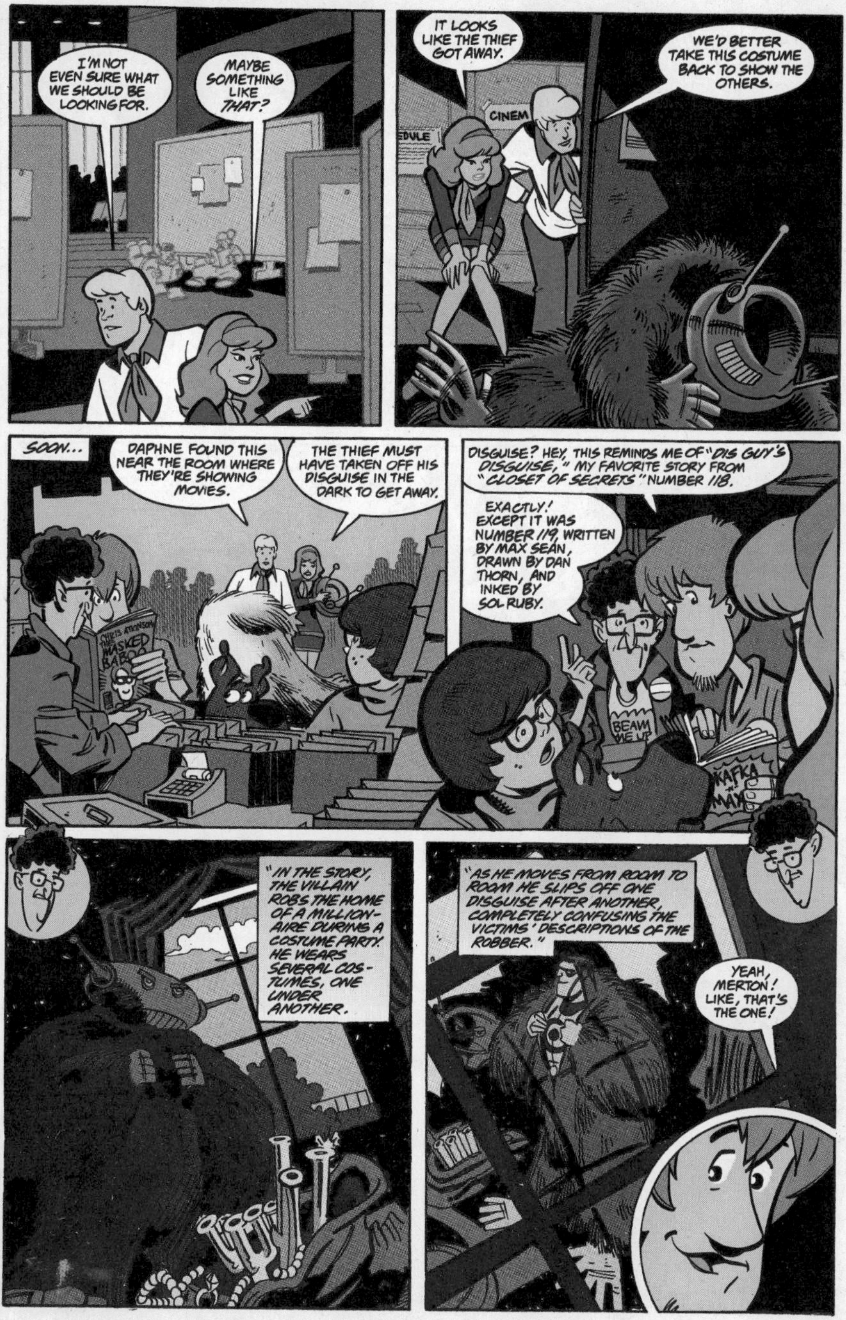
I'M NOT EVEN SURE WHAT WE SHOULD BE LOOKING FOR.
MAYBE SOMETHING LIKE THAT?
IT LOOKS LIKE THE THIEF GOT AWAY.
WE'D BETTER TAKE THIS COSTUME BACK TO SHOW THE OTHERS.
CINEM
EDULE
SOON...
DAPHNE FOUND THIS NEAR THE ROOM WHERE THEY'RE SHOWING MOVIES.
THE THIEF MUST HAVE TAKEN OFF HIS DISGUISE IN THE DARK TO GET AWAY.
CHRIS ATKINSON THE MASKED BABOO
DISGUISE? HEY, THIS REMINDS ME OF "DIS GUY'S DISGUISE," MY FAVORITE STORY FROM "CLOSET OF SECRETS" NUMBER 118.
EXACTLY! EXCEPT IT WAS NUMBER 119, WRITTEN BY MAX SEAN, DRAWN BY DAN THORN, AND INKED BY SOL RUBY.
BEAM ME UP
KAFKA MAX
"IN THE STORY, THE VILLAIN ROBS THE HOME OF A MILLION-AIRE DURING A COSTUME PARTY. HE WEARS SEVERAL COS-TUMES, ONE UNDER ANOTHER.
"AS HE MOVES FROM ROOM TO ROOM HE SLIPS OFF ONE DISGUISE AFTER ANOTHER, COMPLETELY CONFUSING THE VICTIMS' DESCRIPTIONS OF THE ROBBER."
YEAH, MERTON! LIKE, THAT'S THE ONE!

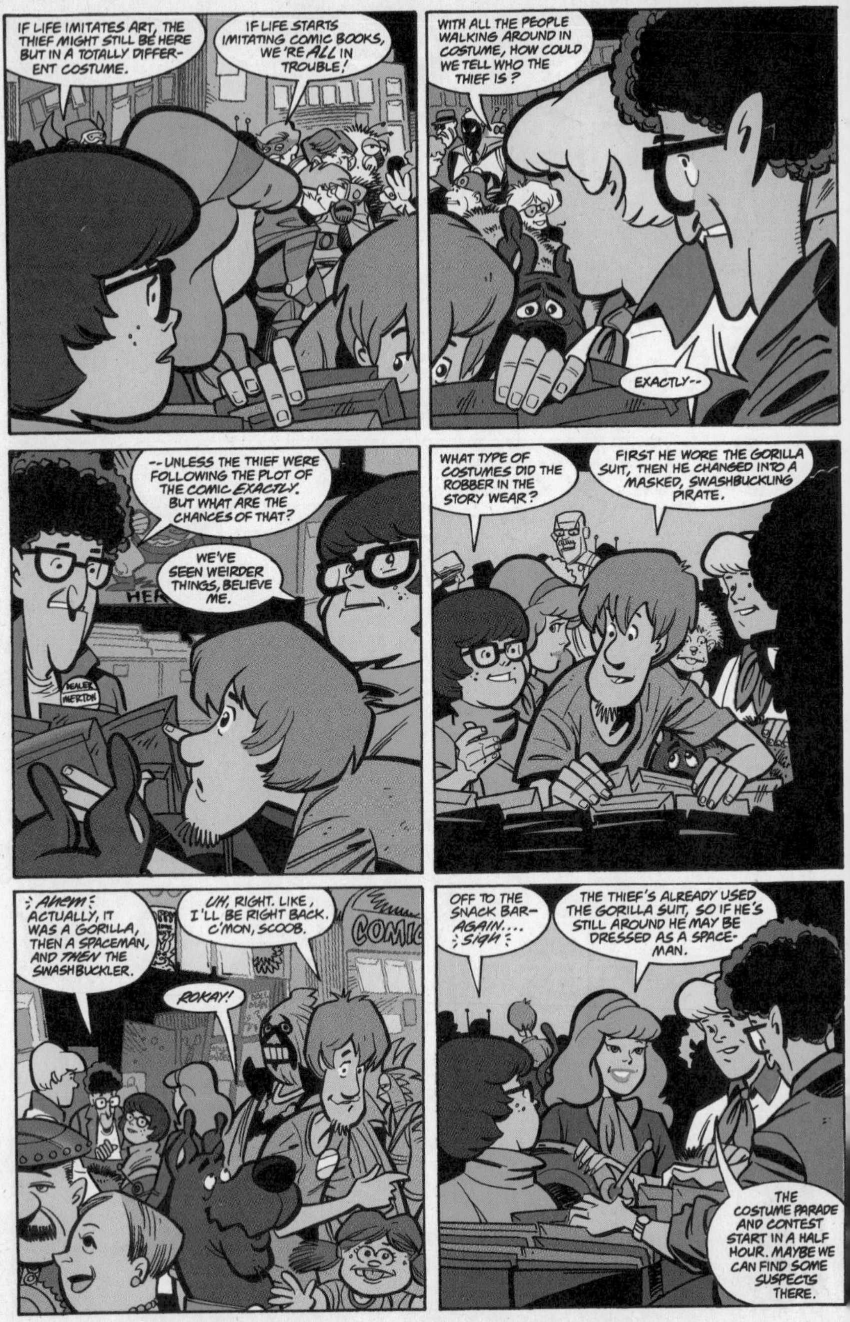
IF LIFE IMITATES ART, THE THIEF MIGHT STILL BE HERE BUT IN A TOTALLY DIFFERENT COSTUME.
IF LIFE STARTS IMITATING COMIC BOOKS, WE'RE ALL IN TROUBLE!
WITH ALL THE PEOPLE WALKING AROUND IN COSTUME, HOW COULD WE TELL WHO THE THIEF IS?
EXACTLY--
--UNLESS THE THIEF WERE FOLLOWING THE PLOT OF THE COMIC EXACTLY. BUT WHAT ARE THE CHANCES OF THAT?
WE'VE SEEN WEIRDER THINGS, BELIEVE ME.
DEALER MERTON
WHAT TYPE OF COSTUMES DID THE ROBBER IN THE STORY WEAR?
FIRST HE WORE THE GORILLA SUIT, THEN HE CHANGED INTO A MASKED, SWASHBUCKLING PIRATE.
AHEM ACTUALLY, IT WAS A GORILLA, THEN A SPACEMAN, AND THEN THE SWASHBUCKLER.
UH, RIGHT. LIKE, I'LL BE RIGHT BACK. C'MON, SCOOB.
ROKAY!
COMIC
OFF TO THE SNACK BAR-- AGAIN.... SIGH
THE THIEF'S ALREADY USED THE GORILLA SUIT, SO IF HE'S STILL AROUND HE MAY BE DRESSED AS A SPACEMAN.
THE COSTUME PARADE AND CONTEST START IN A HALF HOUR. MAYBE WE CAN FIND SOME SUSPECTS THERE.

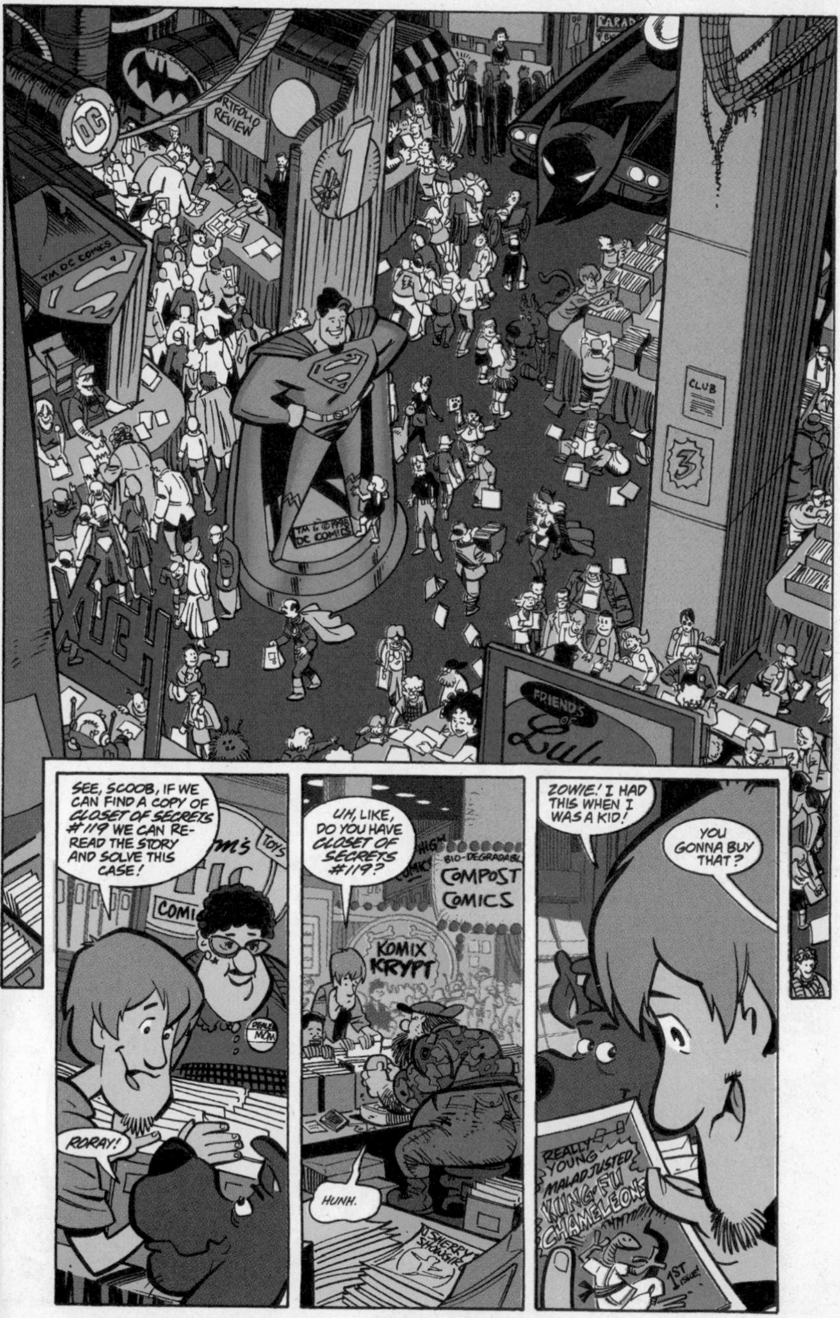
PORTFOLIO REVIEW
CLUB
FRIENDS OF
SEE, SCOOB, IF WE CAN FIND A COPY OF CLOSET OF SECRETS #119 WE CAN RE-READ THE STORY AND SOLVE THIS CASE!
TOYS
RORAY!
UH, LIKE, DO YOU HAVE CLOSET OF SECRETS #119?
BIO-DEGRADABLE
COMPOST COMICS
KOMIX KRYPT
HUNH.
ZOWIE! I HAD THIS WHEN I WAS A KID!
YOU GONNA BUY THAT?
REALLY YOUNG MALADJUSTED KUNG-FU CHAMELEONS
1ST ISSUE!

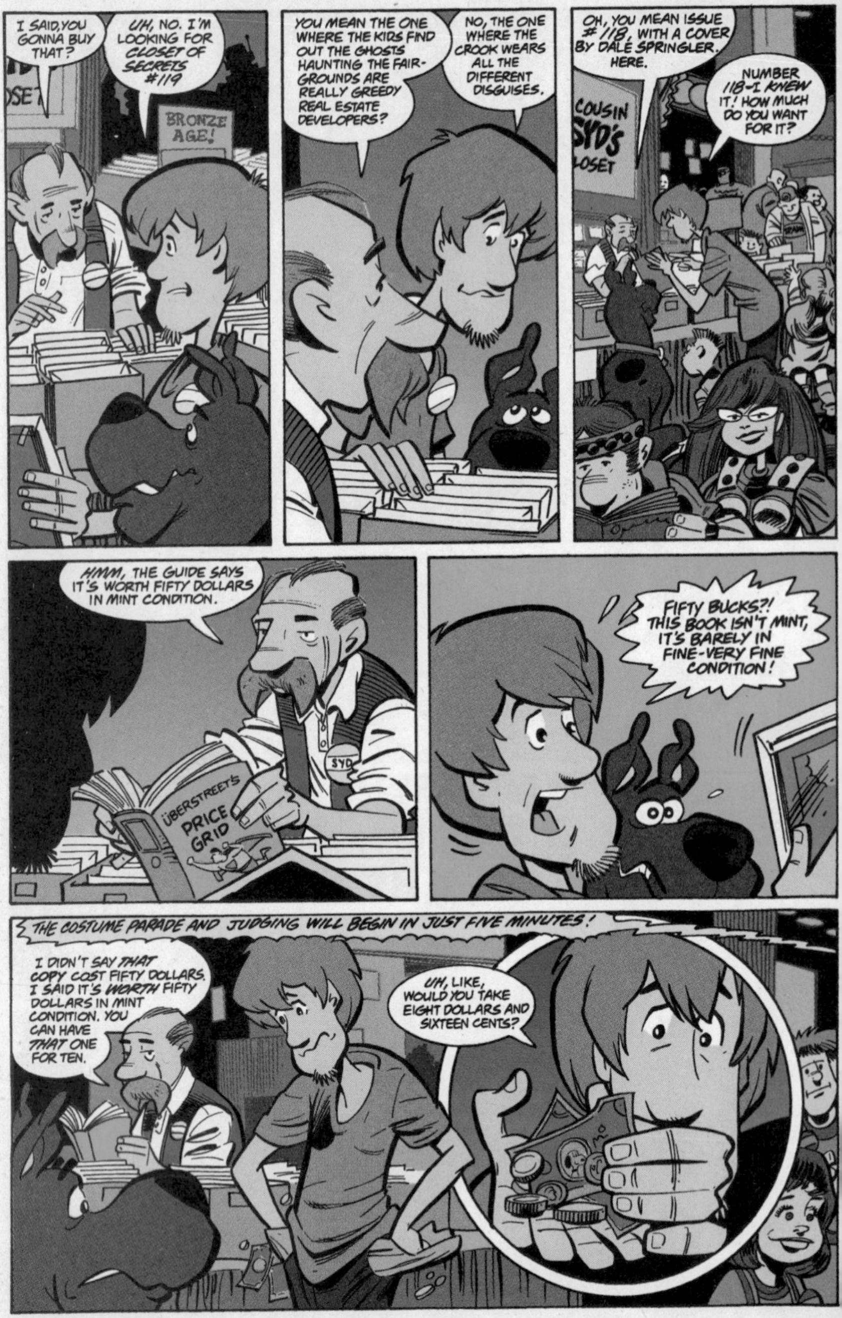
I SAID, YOU GONNA BUY THAT?
UH, NO. I'M LOOKING FOR CLOSET OF SECRETS #119
BRONZE AGE!
YOU MEAN THE ONE WHERE THE KIDS FIND OUT THE GHOSTS HAUNTING THE FAIR-GROUNDS ARE REALLY GREEDY REAL ESTATE DEVELOPERS?
NO, THE ONE WHERE THE CROOK WEARS ALL THE DIFFERENT DISGUISES.
OH, YOU MEAN ISSUE #118, WITH A COVER BY DALE SPRINGLER. HERE.
COUSIN SYD'S CLOSET
NUMBER 118-I KNEW IT! HOW MUCH DO YOU WANT FOR IT?
HMM, THE GUIDE SAYS IT'S WORTH FIFTY DOLLARS IN MINT CONDITION.
SYD
ÜBERSTREET'S PRICE GRID
FIFTY BUCKS?! THIS BOOK ISN'T MINT, IT'S BARELY IN FINE-VERY FINE CONDITION!
THE COSTUME PARADE AND JUDGING WILL BEGIN IN JUST FIVE MINUTES!
I DIDN'T SAY THAT COPY COST FIFTY DOLLARS. I SAID IT'S WORTH FIFTY DOLLARS IN MINT CONDITION. YOU CAN HAVE THAT ONE FOR TEN.
UH, LIKE, WOULD YOU TAKE EIGHT DOLLARS AND SIXTEEN CENTS?

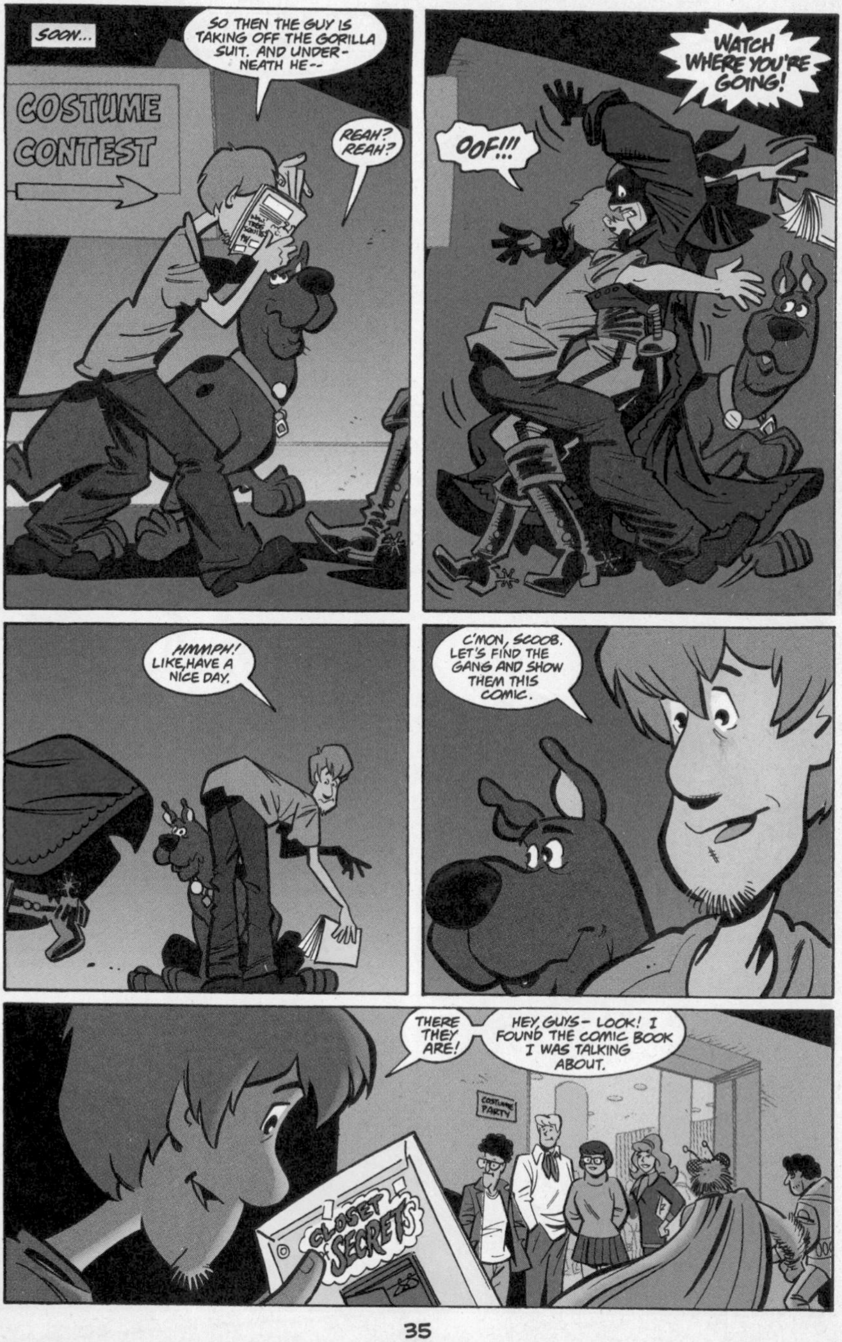
SOON...
SO THEN THE GUY IS TAKING OFF THE GORILLA SUIT. AND UNDER-NEATH HE--
COSTUME CONTEST
REAH? REAH?
WATCH WHERE YOU'RE GOING!
OOF!!!
HMMPH! LIKE, HAVE A NICE DAY.
C'MON, SCOOB. LET'S FIND THE GANG AND SHOW THEM THIS COMIC.
THERE THEY ARE!
HEY, GUYS-- LOOK! I FOUND THE COMIC BOOK I WAS TALKING ABOUT.
COSTUME PARTY
CLOSET SECRETS

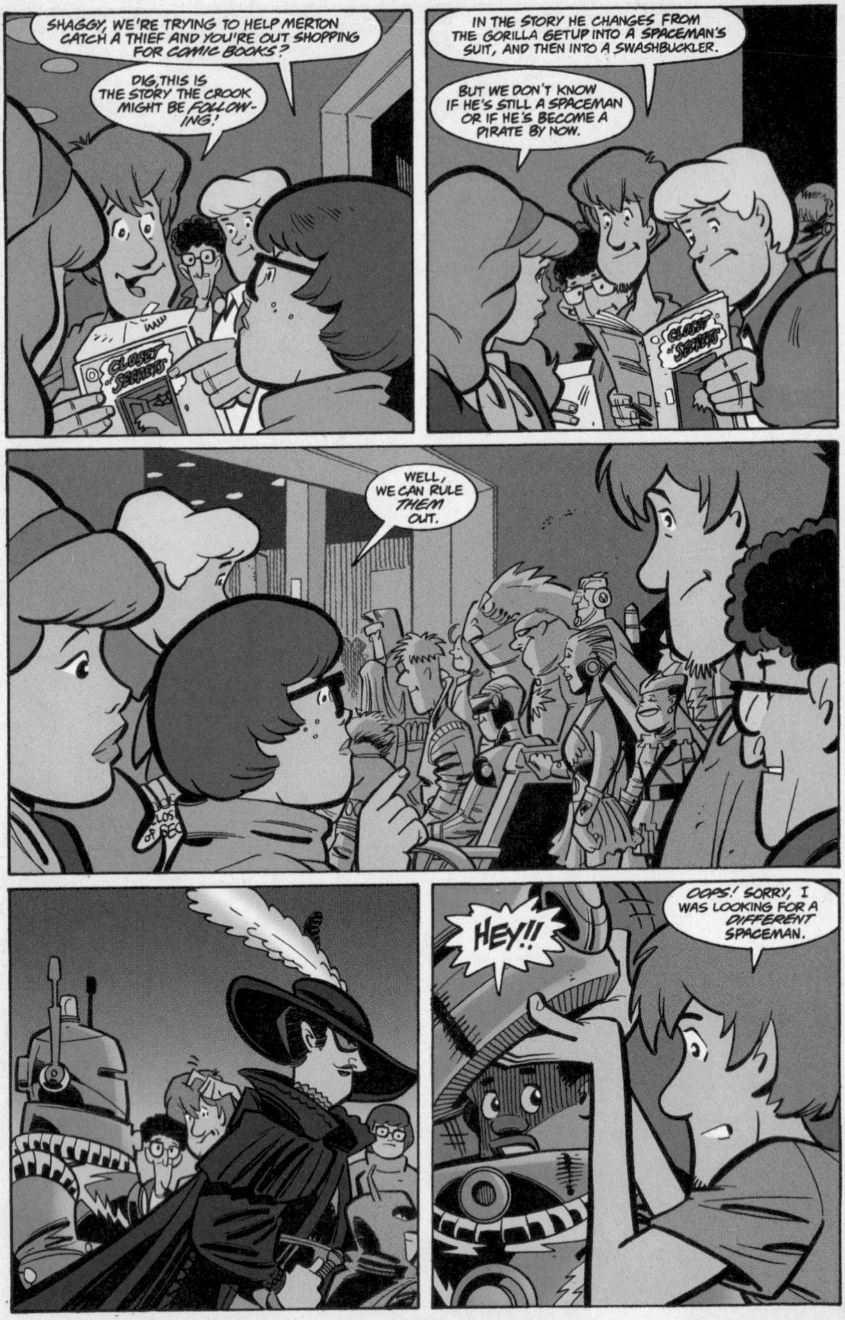
SHAGGY, WE'RE TRYING TO HELP MERTON CATCH A THIEF AND YOU'RE OUT SHOPPING FOR COMIC BOOKS?
DIG, THIS IS THE STORY THE CROOK MIGHT BE FOLLOWING!
CLOSET OF SECRETS
IN THE STORY HE CHANGES FROM THE GORILLA GETUP INTO A SPACEMAN'S SUIT, AND THEN INTO A SWASHBUCKLER.
BUT WE DON'T KNOW IF HE'S STILL A SPACEMAN OR IF HE'S BECOME A PIRATE BY NOW.
CLOSET OF SECRETS
WELL, WE CAN RULE THEM OUT.
HEY!!
OOPS! SORRY, I WAS LOOKING FOR A DIFFERENT SPACEMAN.

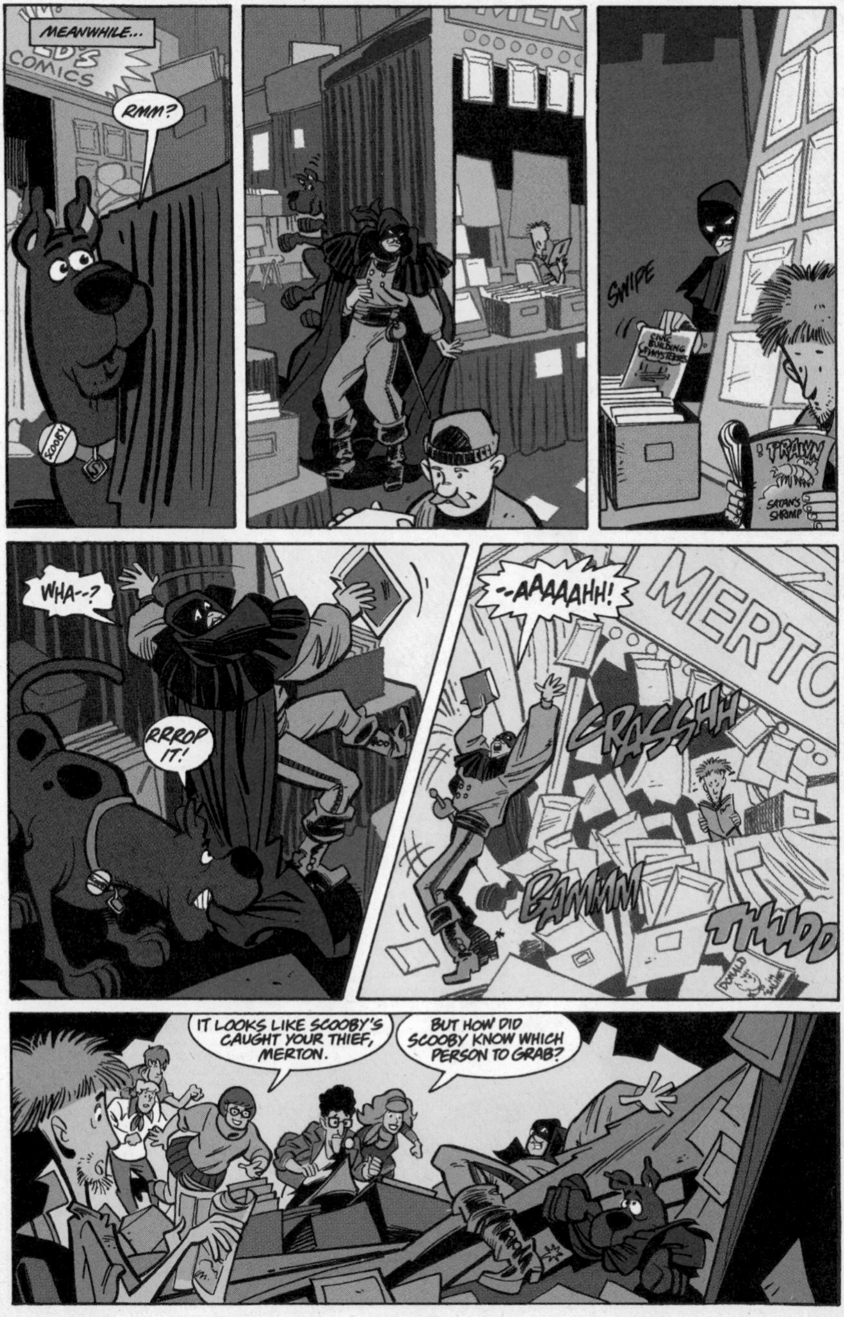
MEANWHILE...
COMICS
RMM?
SCOOBY
SWIPE
T'RAWN
SATAN'S SHRIMP
WHA--?
RRROP IT!
--AAAAAHH!
MERTO
CRASSHH
BAMMM
THUDD
IT LOOKS LIKE SCOOBY'S CAUGHT YOUR THIEF, MERTON.
BUT HOW DID SCOOBY KNOW WHICH PERSON TO GRAB?

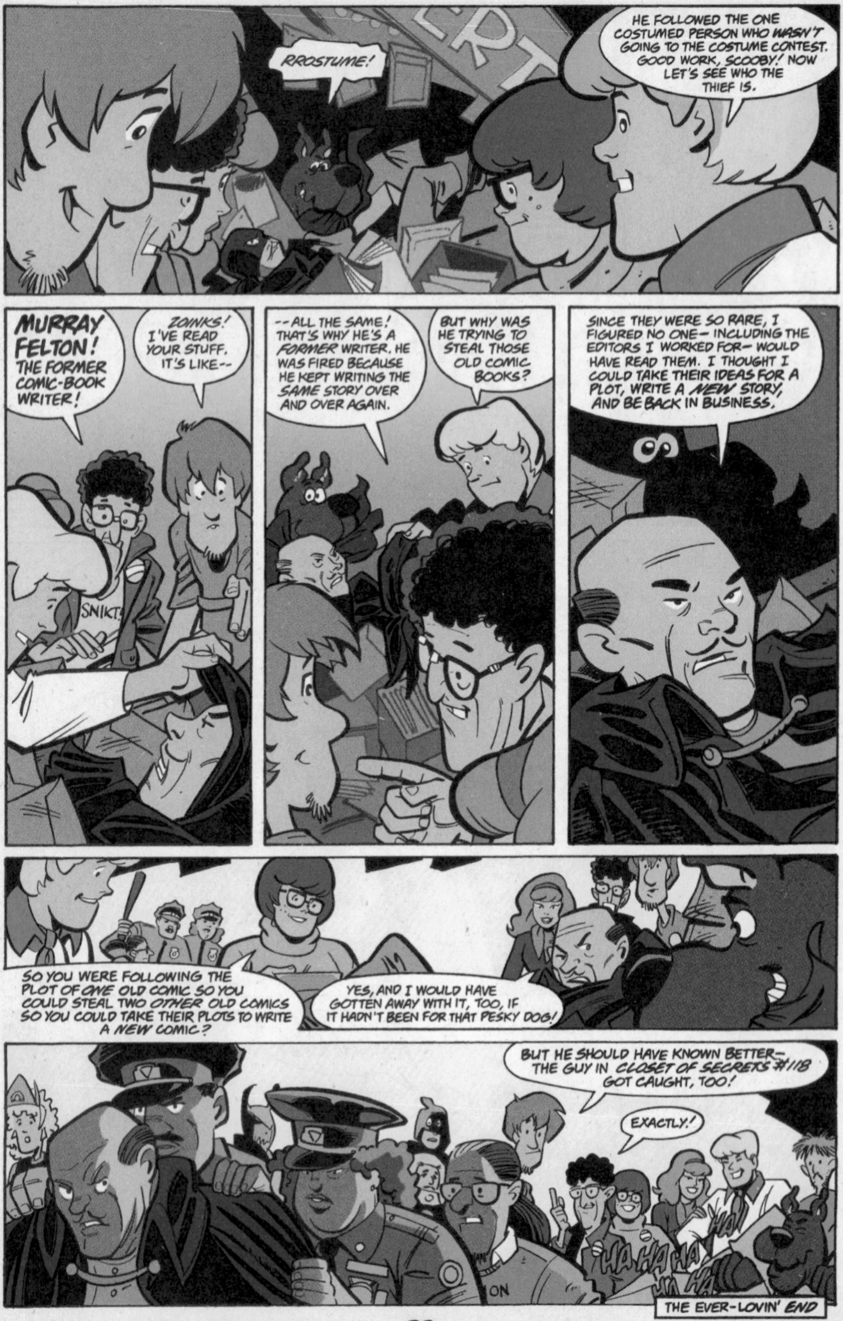
RROSTUME!
HE FOLLOWED THE ONE COSTUMED PERSON WHO WASN'T GOING TO THE COSTUME CONTEST. GOOD WORK, SCOOBY! NOW LET'S SEE WHO THE THIEF IS.
MURRAY FELTON! THE FORMER COMIC-BOOK WRITER!
ZOINKS! I'VE READ YOUR STUFF. IT'S LIKE--
SNIKT!
--ALL THE SAME! THAT'S WHY HE'S A FORMER WRITER. HE WAS FIRED BECAUSE HE KEPT WRITING THE SAME STORY OVER AND OVER AGAIN.
BUT WHY WAS HE TRYING TO STEAL THOSE OLD COMIC BOOKS?
SINCE THEY WERE SO RARE, I FIGURED NO ONE— INCLUDING THE EDITORS I WORKED FOR— WOULD HAVE READ THEM. I THOUGHT I COULD TAKE THEIR IDEAS FOR A PLOT, WRITE A NEW STORY, AND BE BACK IN BUSINESS.
SO YOU WERE FOLLOWING THE PLOT OF ONE OLD COMIC SO YOU COULD STEAL TWO OTHER OLD COMICS SO YOU COULD TAKE THEIR PLOTS TO WRITE A NEW COMIC?
YES, AND I WOULD HAVE GOTTEN AWAY WITH IT, TOO, IF IT HADN'T BEEN FOR THAT PESKY DOG!
BUT HE SHOULD HAVE KNOWN BETTER— THE GUY IN CLOSET OF SECRETS #118 GOT CAUGHT, TOO!
EXACTLY!
HA HA HA HA
THE EVER-LOVIN' END

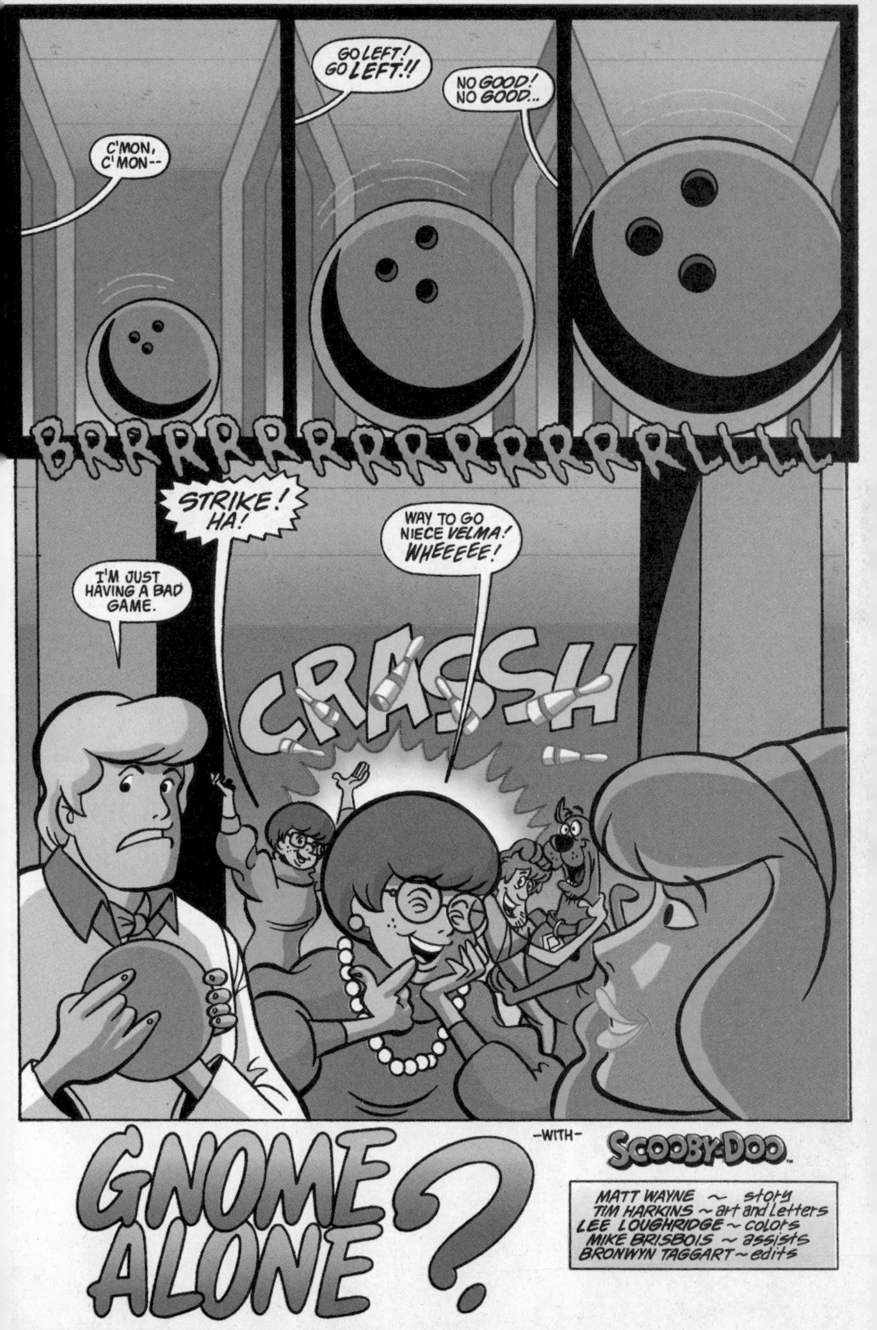
C'MON, C'MON--
GO LEFT! GO LEFT!!
NO GOOD! NO GOOD...
BRRRRRRRRRRRRRLLLL
STRIKE! HA!
I'M JUST HAVING A BAD GAME.
WAY TO GO NIECE VELMA! WHEEEEE!
CRASSH

GNOME ALONE?

-WITH- SCOOBY-DOO™

MATT WAYNE ~ story
TIM HARKINS ~ art and letters
LEE LOUGHRIDGE ~ colors
MIKE BRISBOIS ~ assists
BRONWYN TAGGART ~ edits

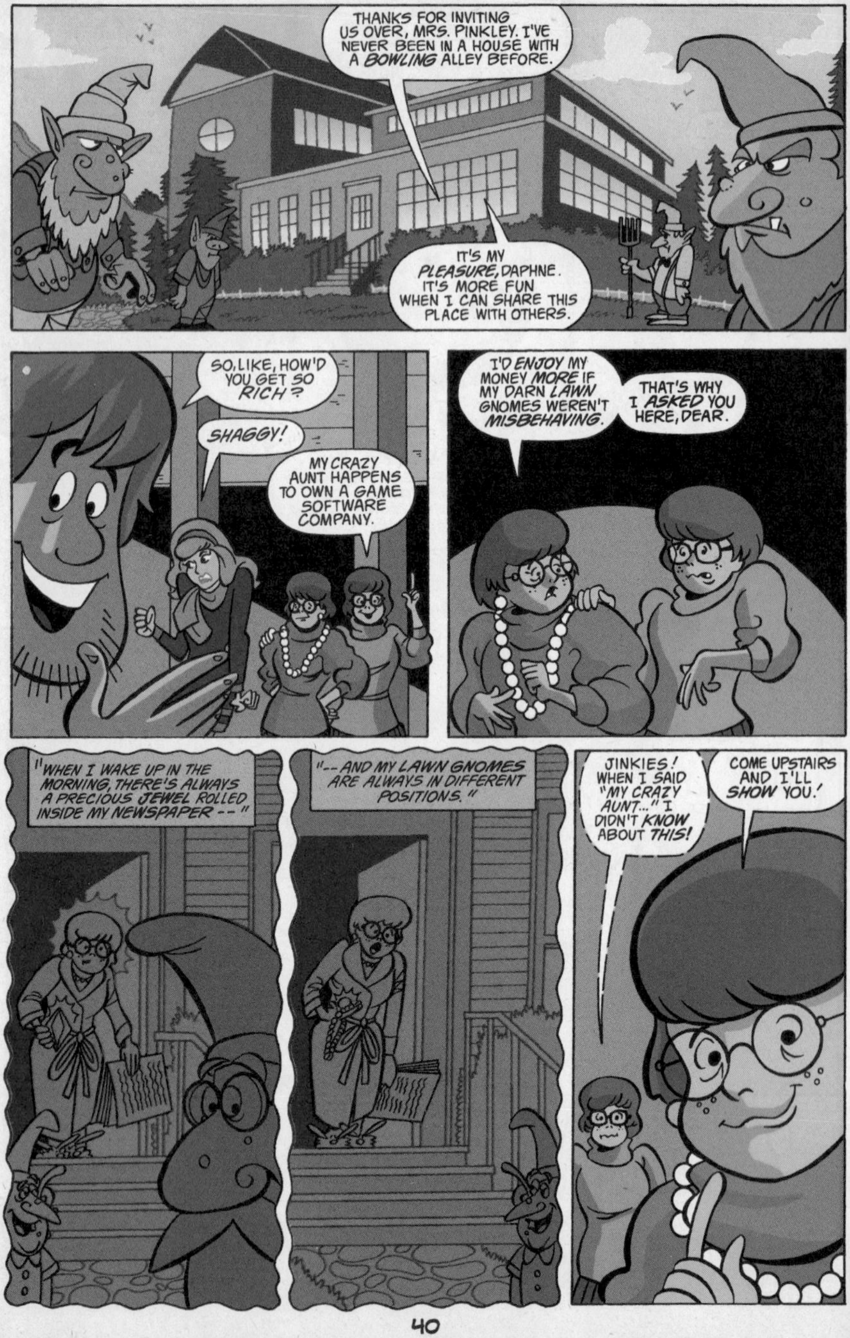
THANKS FOR INVITING US OVER, MRS. PINKLEY. I'VE NEVER BEEN IN A HOUSE WITH A BOWLING ALLEY BEFORE.
IT'S MY PLEASURE, DAPHNE. IT'S MORE FUN WHEN I CAN SHARE THIS PLACE WITH OTHERS.
SO, LIKE, HOW'D YOU GET SO RICH?
SHAGGY!
MY CRAZY AUNT HAPPENS TO OWN A GAME SOFTWARE COMPANY.
I'D ENJOY MY MONEY MORE IF MY DARN LAWN GNOMES WEREN'T MISBEHAVING.
THAT'S WHY I ASKED YOU HERE, DEAR.
"WHEN I WAKE UP IN THE MORNING, THERE'S ALWAYS A PRECIOUS JEWEL ROLLED INSIDE MY NEWSPAPER --"
"-- AND MY LAWN GNOMES ARE ALWAYS IN DIFFERENT POSITIONS."
JINKIES! WHEN I SAID "MY CRAZY AUNT..." I DIDN'T KNOW ABOUT THIS!
COME UPSTAIRS AND I'LL SHOW YOU!

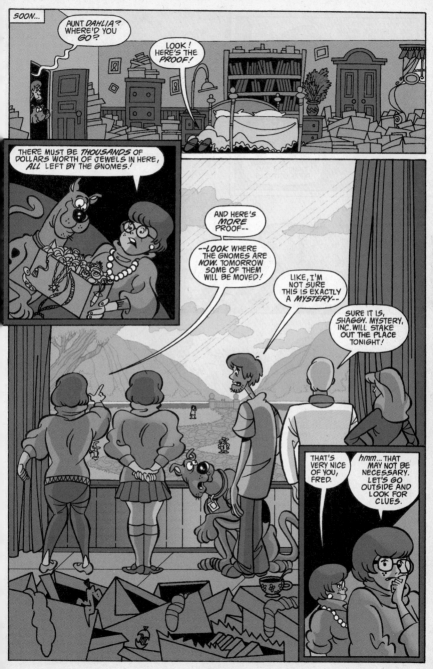

SOON...

AUNT *DAHLIA?* WHERE'D YOU GO?

LOOK! HERE'S THE *PROOF!*

THERE MUST BE *THOUSANDS* OF DOLLARS WORTH OF JEWELS IN HERE, *ALL* LEFT BY THE GNOMES!

AND HERE'S *MORE* PROOF--

--LOOK WHERE THE GNOMES ARE *NOW.* TOMORROW SOME OF THEM WILL BE MOVED!

LIKE, I'M NOT SURE THIS IS EXACTLY A *MYSTERY--*

SURE IT IS, SHAGGY. MYSTERY, INC. WILL STAKE OUT THE PLACE TONIGHT!

THAT'S VERY NICE OF YOU, FRED.

hmm... THAT MAY NOT BE NECESSARY. LET'S GO OUTSIDE AND LOOK FOR CLUES.

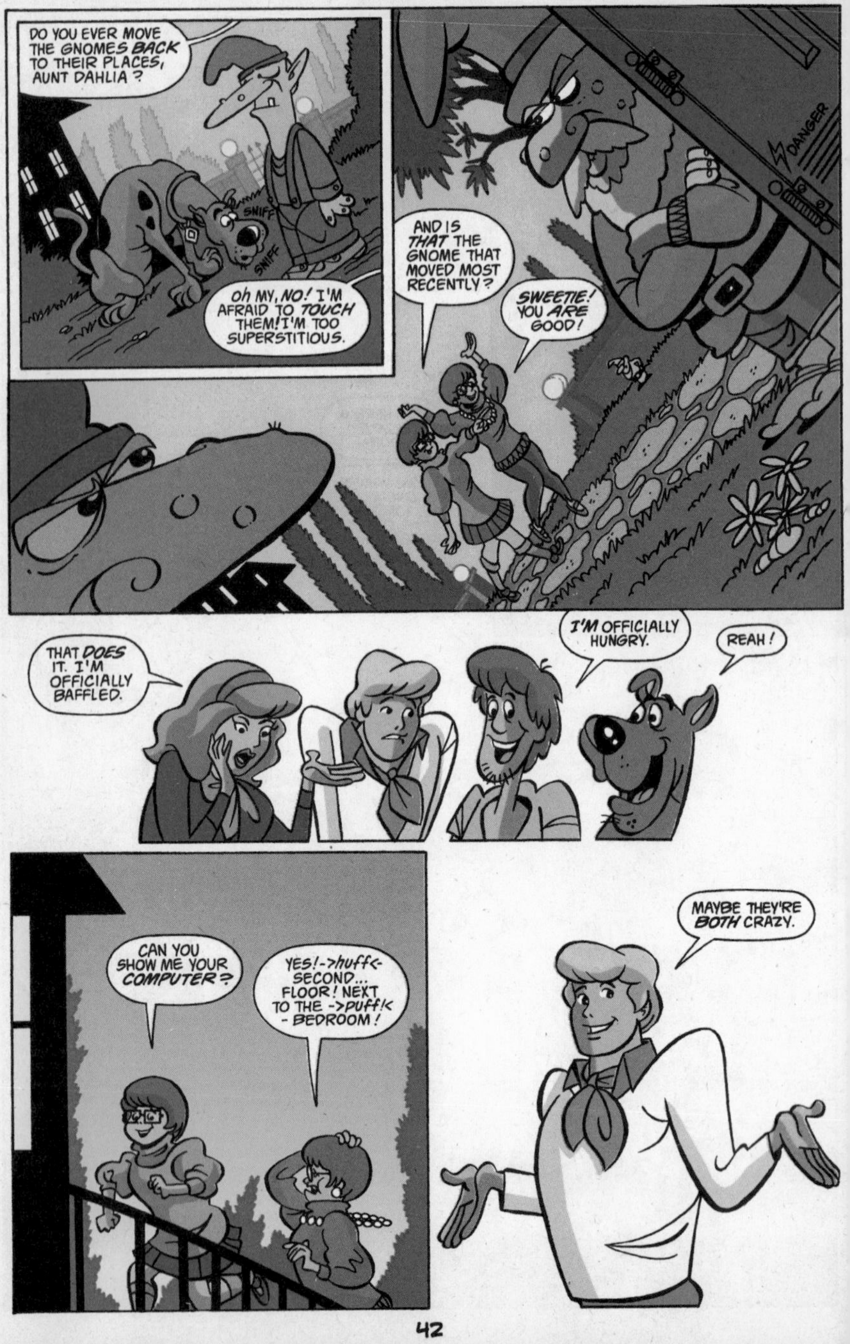
DO YOU EVER MOVE THE GNOMES BACK TO THEIR PLACES, AUNT DAHLIA?
SNIFF
SNIFF
Oh MY, NO! I'M AFRAID TO TOUCH THEM! I'M TOO SUPERSTITIOUS.
AND IS THAT THE GNOME THAT MOVED MOST RECENTLY?
SWEETIE! YOU ARE GOOD!
DANGER
THAT DOES IT. I'M OFFICIALLY BAFFLED.
I'M OFFICIALLY HUNGRY.
REAH!
CAN YOU SHOW ME YOUR COMPUTER?
YES! ->huff<- SECOND... FLOOR! NEXT TO THE ->puff!< - BEDROOM!
MAYBE THEY'RE BOTH CRAZY.

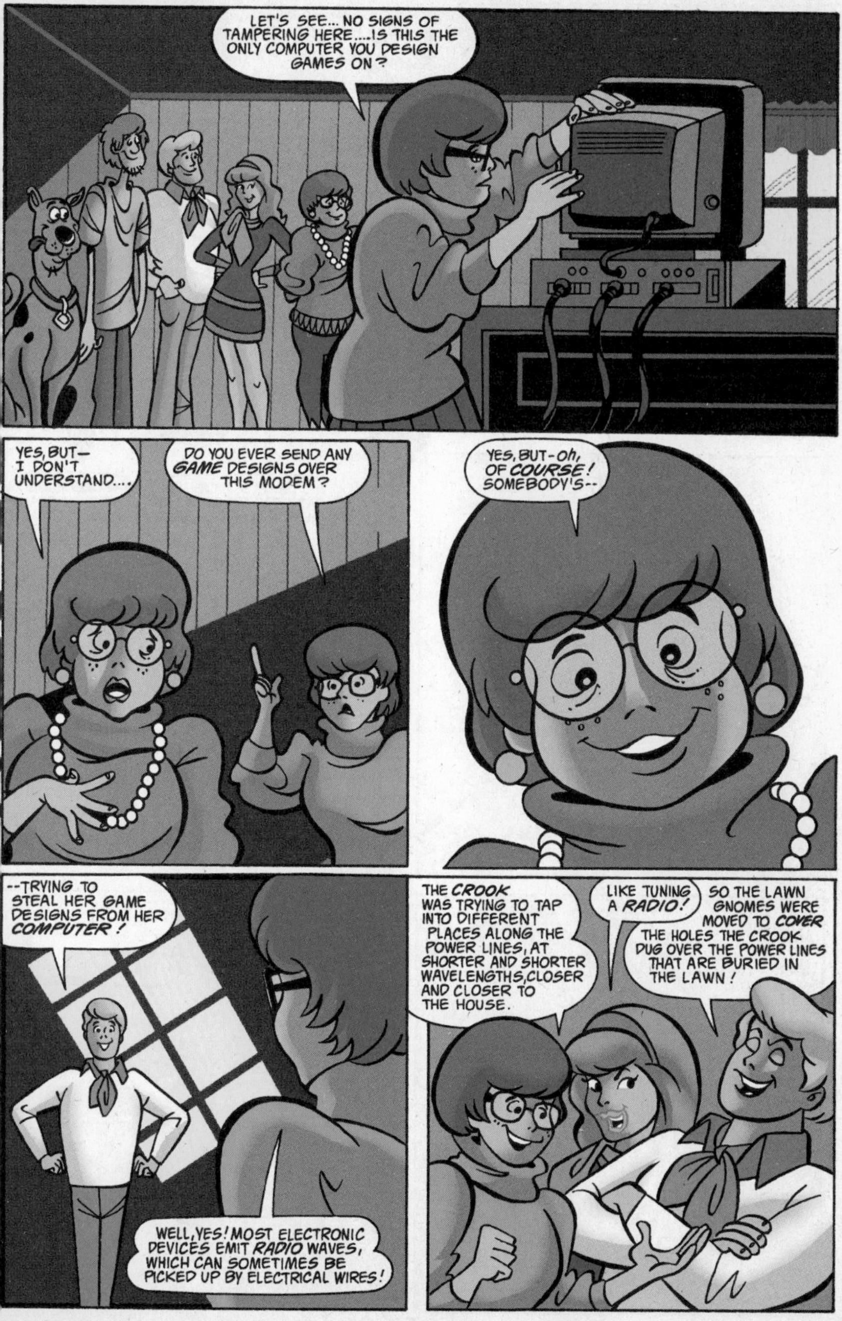
LET'S SEE... NO SIGNS OF TAMPERING HERE....IS THIS THE ONLY COMPUTER YOU DESIGN GAMES ON?
YES, BUT— I DON'T UNDERSTAND....
DO YOU EVER SEND ANY *GAME* DESIGNS OVER THIS MODEM?
YES, BUT-*oh*, OF *COURSE!* SOMEBODY'S--
--TRYING TO STEAL HER GAME DESIGNS FROM HER *COMPUTER!*
WELL, YES! MOST ELECTRONIC DEVICES EMIT *RADIO* WAVES, WHICH CAN SOMETIMES BE PICKED UP BY ELECTRICAL WIRES!
THE *CROOK* WAS TRYING TO TAP INTO DIFFERENT PLACES ALONG THE POWER LINES, AT SHORTER AND SHORTER WAVELENGTHS, CLOSER AND CLOSER TO THE HOUSE.
LIKE TUNING A *RADIO!*
SO THE LAWN GNOMES WERE MOVED TO *COVER* THE HOLES THE *CROOK* DUG OVER THE POWER LINES THAT ARE BURIED IN THE LAWN!

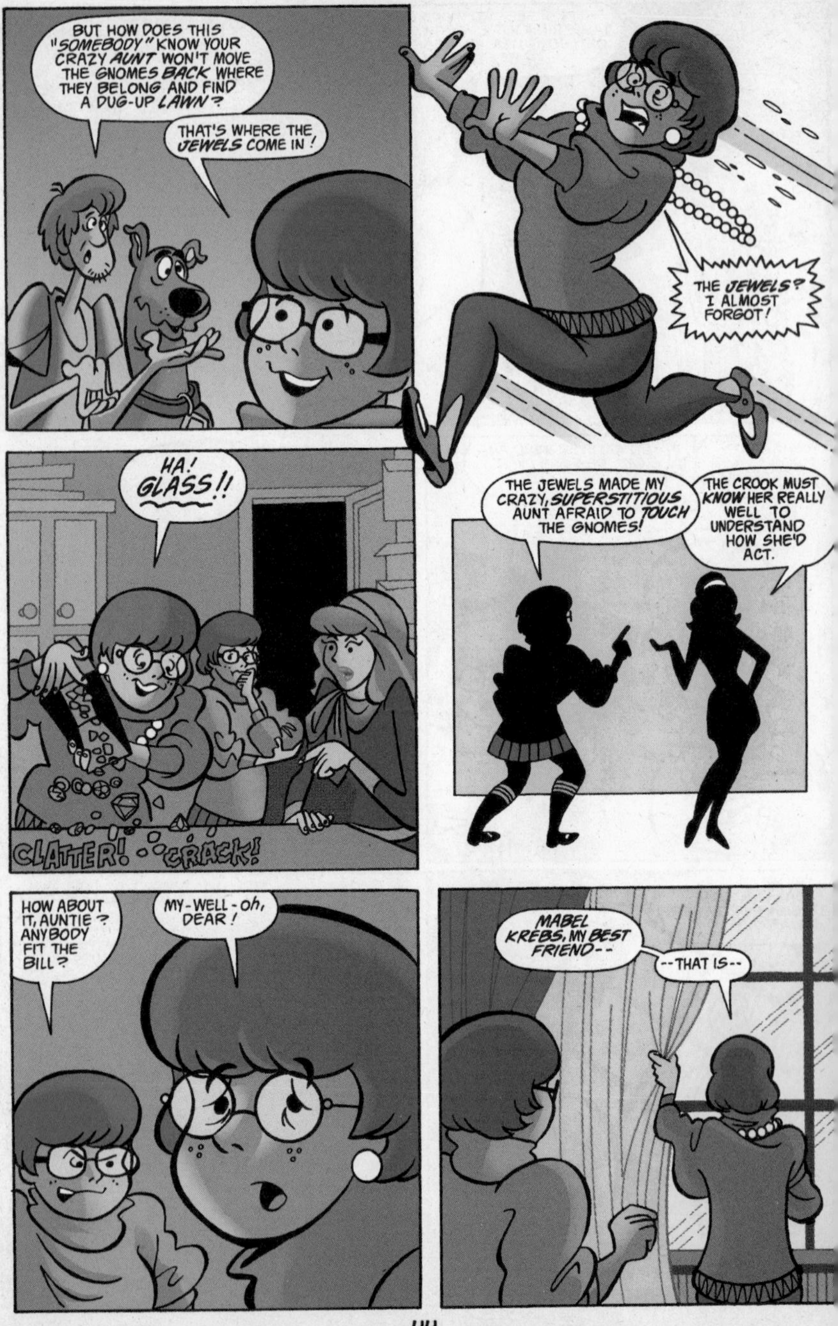
BUT HOW DOES THIS "SOMEBODY" KNOW YOUR CRAZY AUNT WON'T MOVE THE GNOMES BACK WHERE THEY BELONG AND FIND A DUG-UP LAWN?
THAT'S WHERE THE JEWELS COME IN!
THE JEWELS? I ALMOST FORGOT!
HA! GLASS!!
CLATTER! CRACK!
THE JEWELS MADE MY CRAZY, SUPERSTITIOUS AUNT AFRAID TO TOUCH THE GNOMES!
THE CROOK MUST KNOW HER REALLY WELL TO UNDERSTAND HOW SHE'D ACT.
HOW ABOUT IT, AUNTIE? ANYBODY FIT THE BILL?
MY-WELL-oh, DEAR!
MABEL KREBS, MY BEST FRIEND--
--THAT IS--

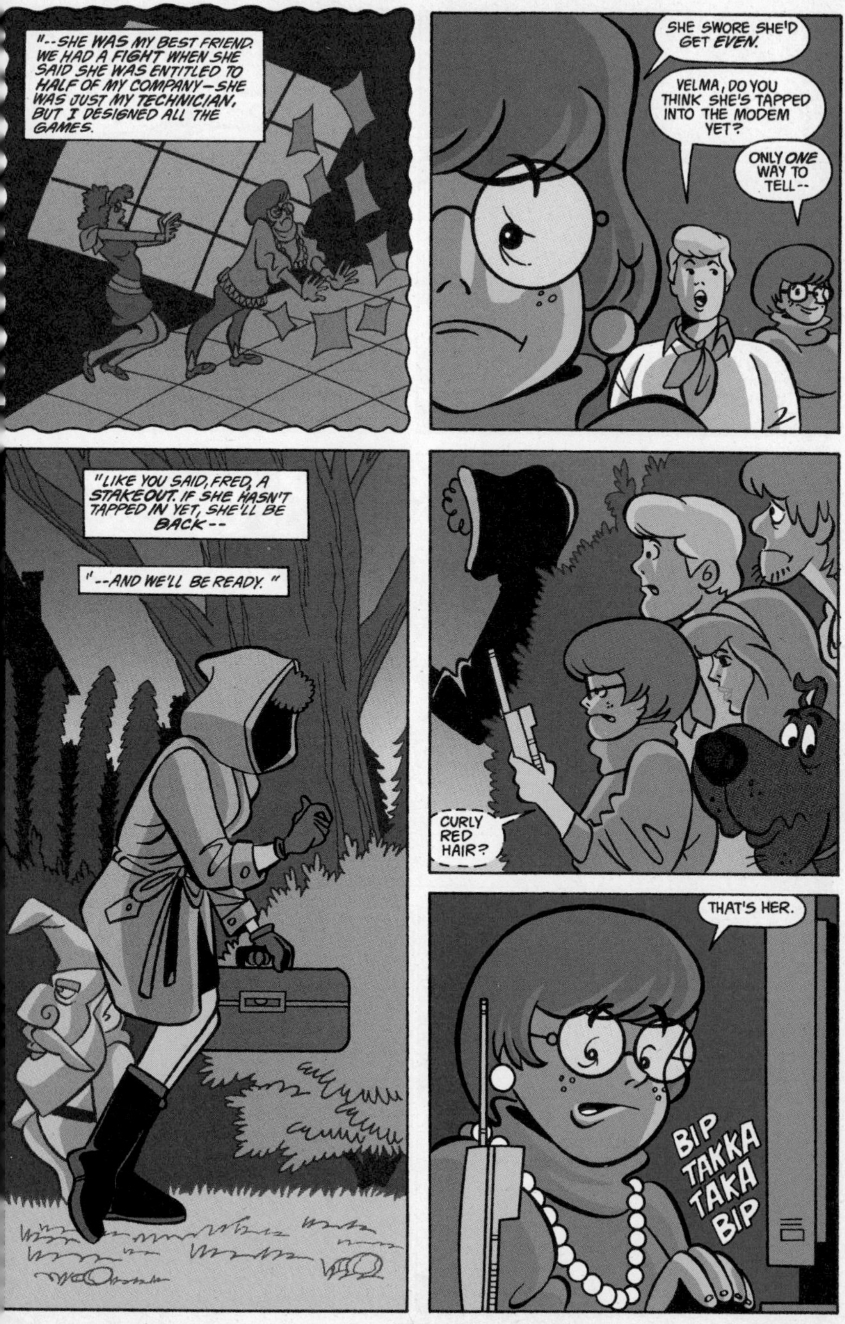
"--SHE WAS MY BEST FRIEND. WE HAD A FIGHT WHEN SHE SAID SHE WAS ENTITLED TO HALF OF MY COMPANY--SHE WAS JUST MY TECHNICIAN, BUT I DESIGNED ALL THE GAMES.
SHE SWORE SHE'D GET EVEN.
VELMA, DO YOU THINK SHE'S TAPPED INTO THE MODEM YET?
ONLY ONE WAY TO TELL--
"LIKE YOU SAID, FRED, A STAKEOUT. IF SHE HASN'T TAPPED IN YET, SHE'LL BE BACK--
"--AND WE'LL BE READY."
CURLY RED HAIR?
THAT'S HER.
BIP TAKKA TAKA BIP

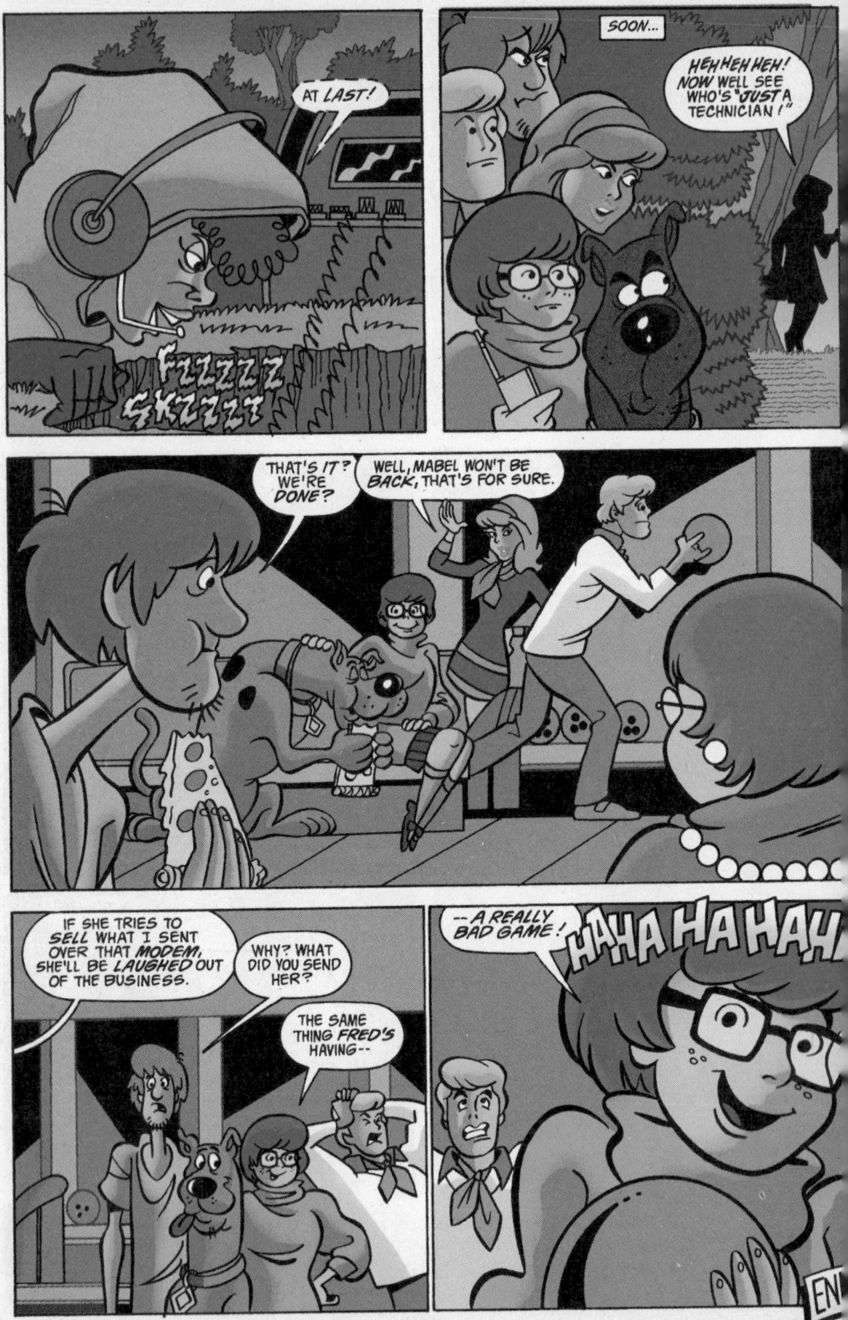
AT LAST!
FZZZZZ
SKZZZZT
SOON...
HEH HEH HEH! NOW WE'LL SEE WHO'S "JUST A TECHNICIAN!"
THAT'S IT? WE'RE DONE?
WELL, MABEL WON'T BE BACK, THAT'S FOR SURE.
IF SHE TRIES TO SELL WHAT I SENT OVER THAT MODEM, SHE'LL BE LAUGHED OUT OF THE BUSINESS.
WHY? WHAT DID YOU SEND HER?
THE SAME THING FRED'S HAVING--
--A REALLY BAD GAME!
HAHA HA HAHA

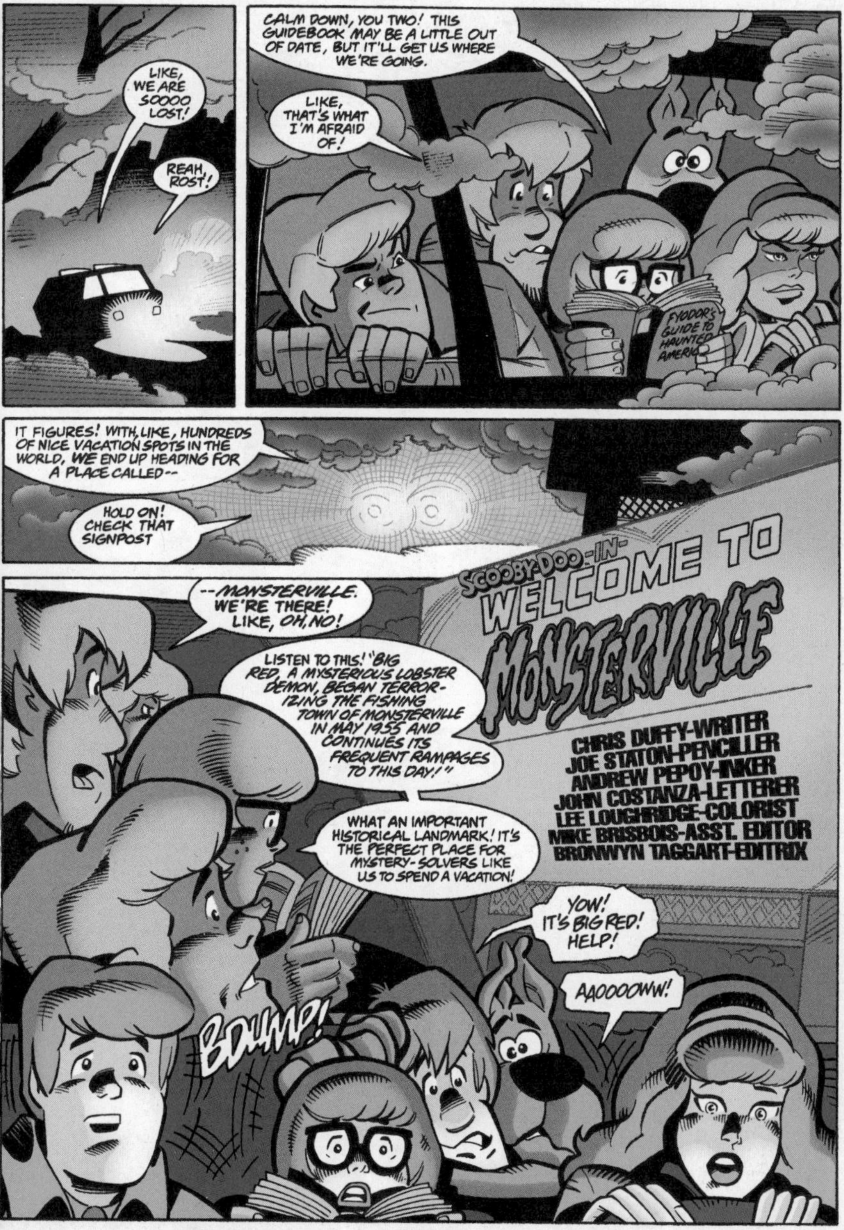
LIKE, WE ARE SOOOO LOST!
REAH, ROST!
CALM DOWN, YOU TWO! THIS GUIDEBOOK MAY BE A LITTLE OUT OF DATE, BUT IT'LL GET US WHERE WE'RE GOING.
LIKE, THAT'S WHAT I'M AFRAID OF!
FYODOR'S GUIDE TO HAUNTED AMERICA
IT FIGURES! WITH, LIKE, HUNDREDS OF NICE VACATION SPOTS IN THE WORLD, WE END UP HEADING FOR A PLACE CALLED--
HOLD ON! CHECK THAT SIGNPOST
--MONSTERVILLE. WE'RE THERE! LIKE, OH, NO!
SCOOBY-DOO-IN- WELCOME TO MONSTERVILLE
CHRIS DUFFY-WRITER
JOE STATON-PENCILLER
ANDREW PEPOY-INKER
JOHN COSTANZA-LETTERER
LEE LOUGHRIDGE-COLORIST
MIKE BRISBOIS-ASST. EDITOR
BRONWYN TAGGART-EDITRIX
LISTEN TO THIS! "BIG RED, A MYSTERIOUS LOBSTER DEMON, BEGAN TERRORIZING THE FISHING TOWN OF MONSTERVILLE IN MAY 1955 AND CONTINUES ITS FREQUENT RAMPAGES TO THIS DAY!"
WHAT AN IMPORTANT HISTORICAL LANDMARK! IT'S THE PERFECT PLACE FOR MYSTERY-SOLVERS LIKE US TO SPEND A VACATION!
YOW! IT'S BIG RED! HELP!
AAOOOOWW!
BDUMP!

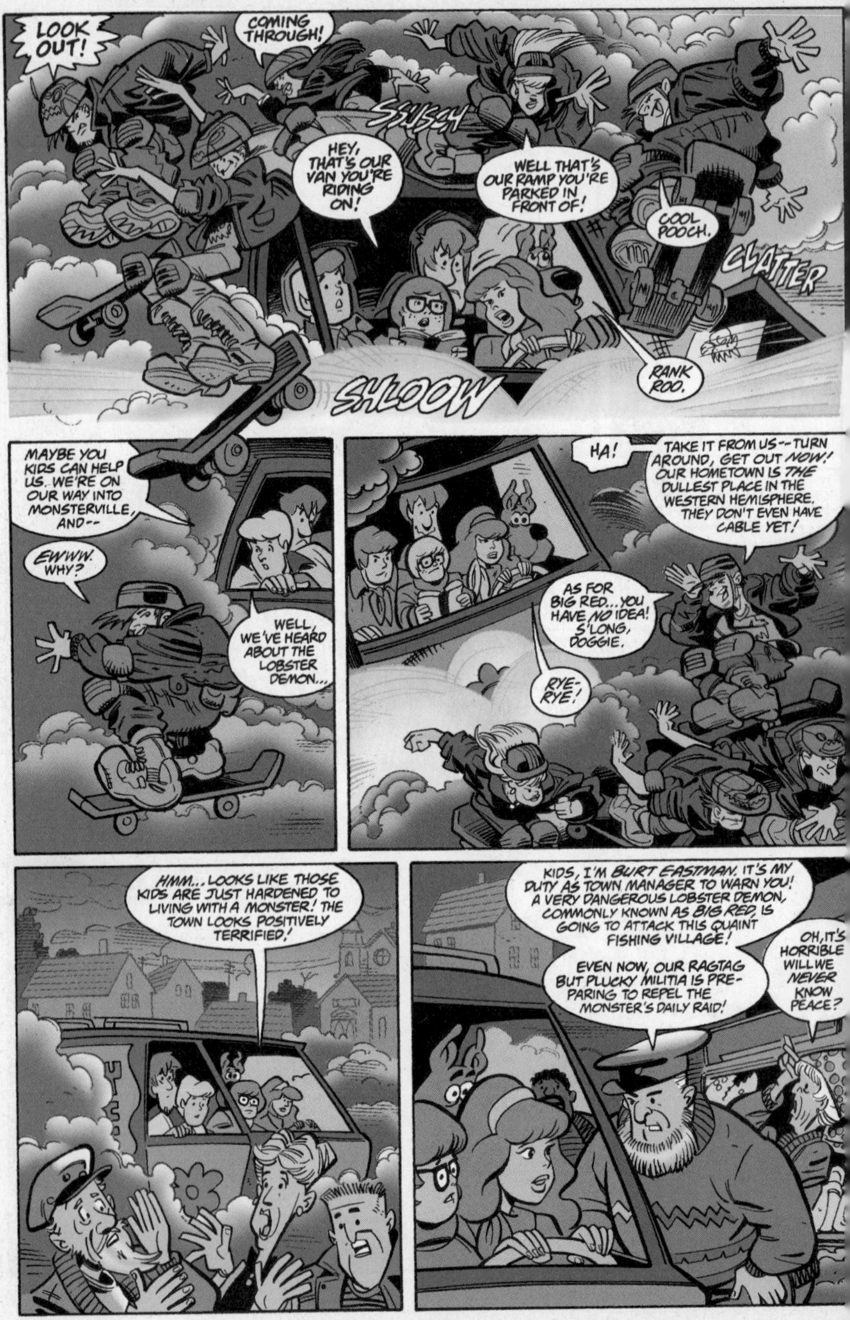
LOOK OUT!
COMING THROUGH!
SSUSSH
HEY, THAT'S OUR VAN YOU'RE RIDING ON!
WELL THAT'S OUR RAMP YOU'RE PARKED IN FRONT OF!
COOL POOCH.
CLATTER
RANK ROO.
SHLOOW
MAYBE YOU KIDS CAN HELP US.. WE'RE ON OUR WAY INTO MONSTERVILLE, AND--
EWWW. WHY?
WELL, WE'VE HEARD ABOUT THE LOBSTER DEMON...
HA!
TAKE IT FROM US--TURN AROUND, GET OUT NOW! OUR HOMETOWN IS THE DULLEST PLACE IN THE WESTERN HEMISPHERE. THEY DON'T EVEN HAVE CABLE YET!
AS FOR BIG RED... YOU HAVE NO IDEA! S'LONG, DOGGIE.
RYE-RYE!
HMM... LOOKS LIKE THOSE KIDS ARE JUST HARDENED TO LIVING WITH A MONSTER! THE TOWN LOOKS POSITIVELY TERRIFIED!
KIDS, I'M BURT EASTMAN. IT'S MY DUTY AS TOWN MANAGER TO WARN YOU! A VERY DANGEROUS LOBSTER DEMON, COMMONLY KNOWN AS BIG RED, IS GOING TO ATTACK THIS QUAINT FISHING VILLAGE!
EVEN NOW, OUR RAGTAG BUT PLUCKY MILITIA IS PREPARING TO REPEL THE MONSTER'S DAILY RAID!
OH, IT'S HORRIBLE WILL WE NEVER KNOW PEACE?

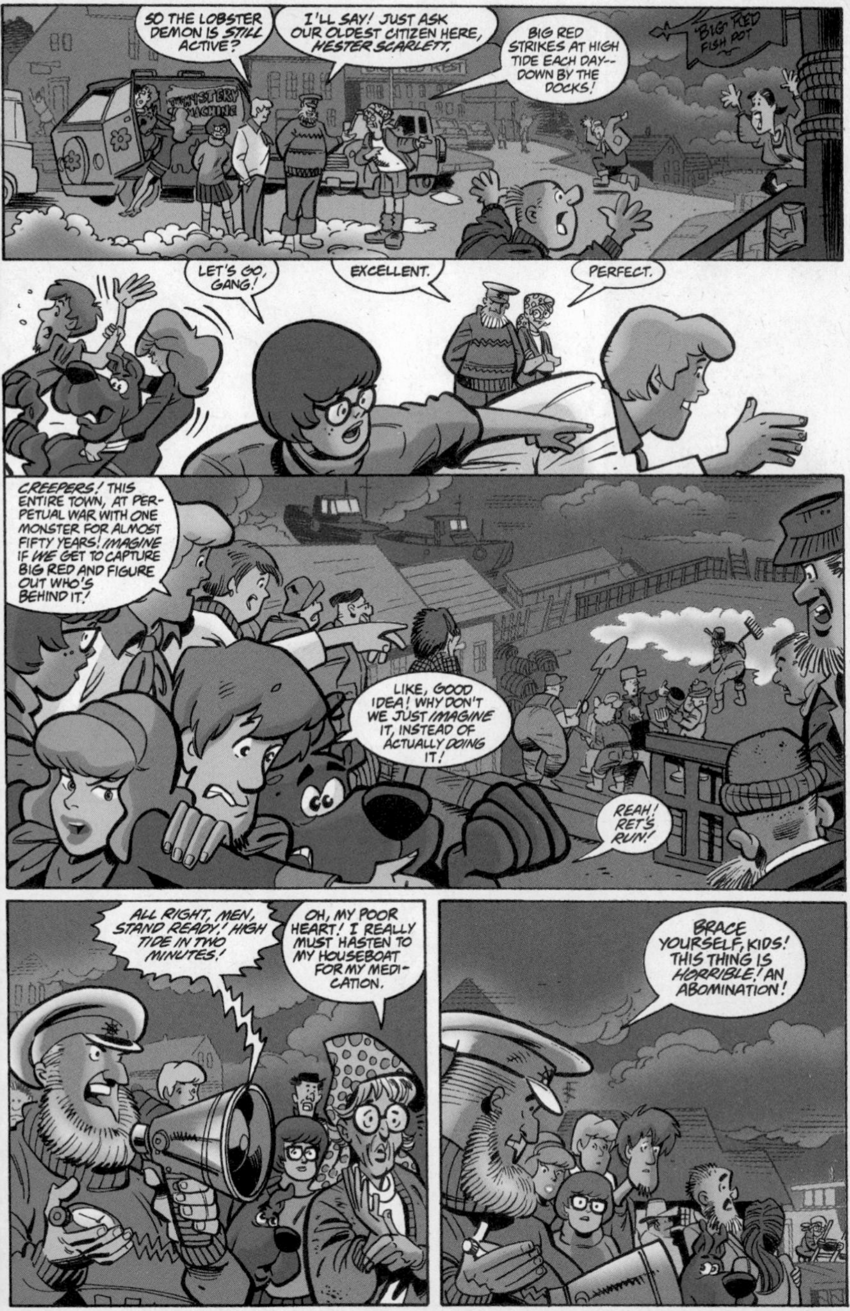
SO THE LOBSTER DEMON IS STILL ACTIVE?
I'LL SAY! JUST ASK OUR OLDEST CITIZEN HERE, HESTER SCARLETT.
BIG RED STRIKES AT HIGH TIDE EACH DAY-- DOWN BY THE DOCKS!
BIG RED FISH POT
THE MYSTERY MACHINE
LET'S GO, GANG!
EXCELLENT.
PERFECT.
CREEPERS! THIS ENTIRE TOWN, AT PERPETUAL WAR WITH ONE MONSTER FOR ALMOST FIFTY YEARS! IMAGINE IF WE GET TO CAPTURE BIG RED AND FIGURE OUT WHO'S BEHIND IT!
LIKE, GOOD IDEA! WHY DON'T WE JUST IMAGINE IT, INSTEAD OF ACTUALLY DOING IT!
REAH! RET'S RUN!
ALL RIGHT, MEN, STAND READY! HIGH TIDE IN TWO MINUTES!
OH, MY POOR HEART! I REALLY MUST HASTEN TO MY HOUSEBOAT FOR MY MEDICATION.
BRACE YOURSELF, KIDS! THIS THING IS HORRIBLE! AN ABOMINATION!

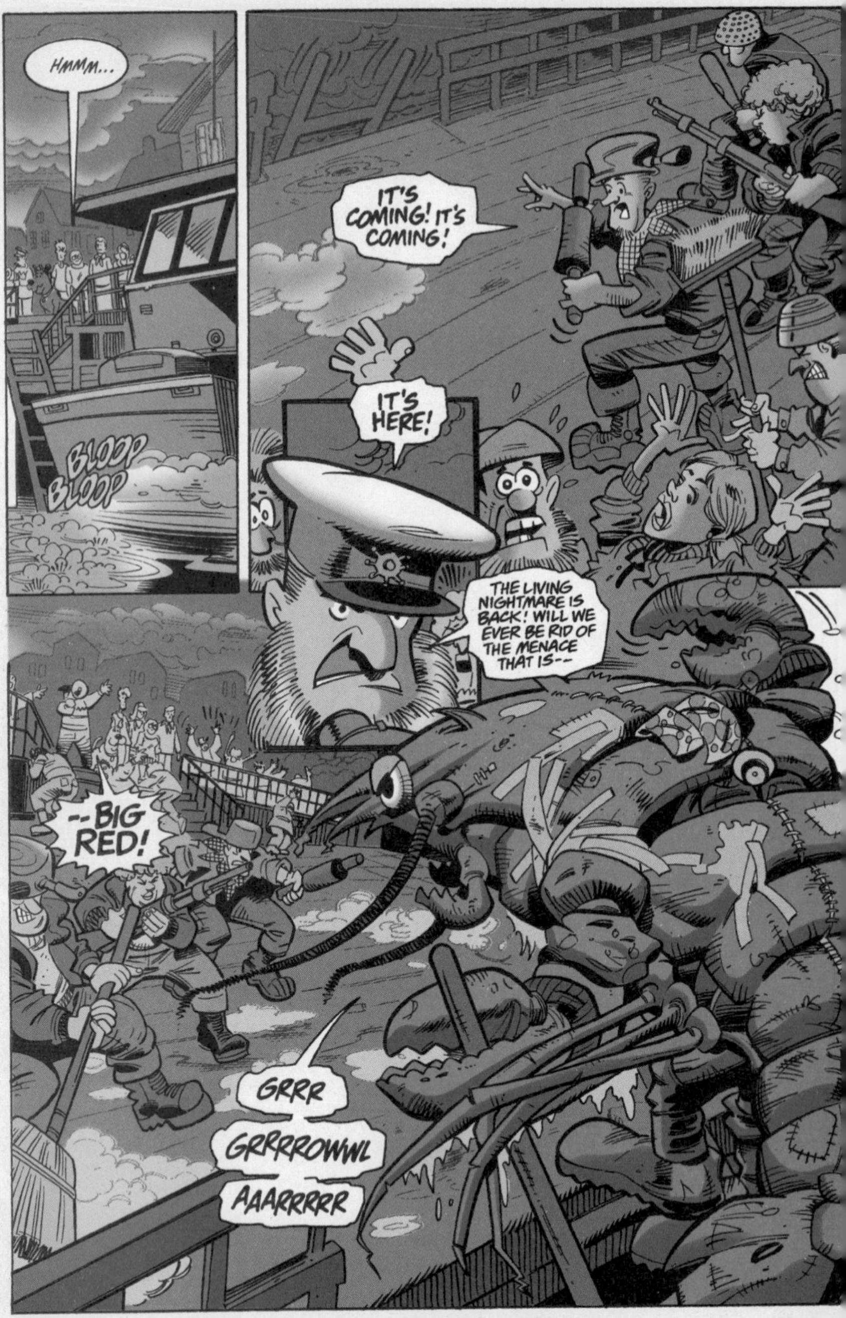
HMMM...
BLOOP BLOOP
IT'S COMING! IT'S COMING!
IT'S HERE!
THE LIVING NIGHTMARE IS BACK! WILL WE EVER BE RID OF THE MENACE THAT IS--
--BIG RED!
GRRR
GRRRROWWL
AAARRRRR

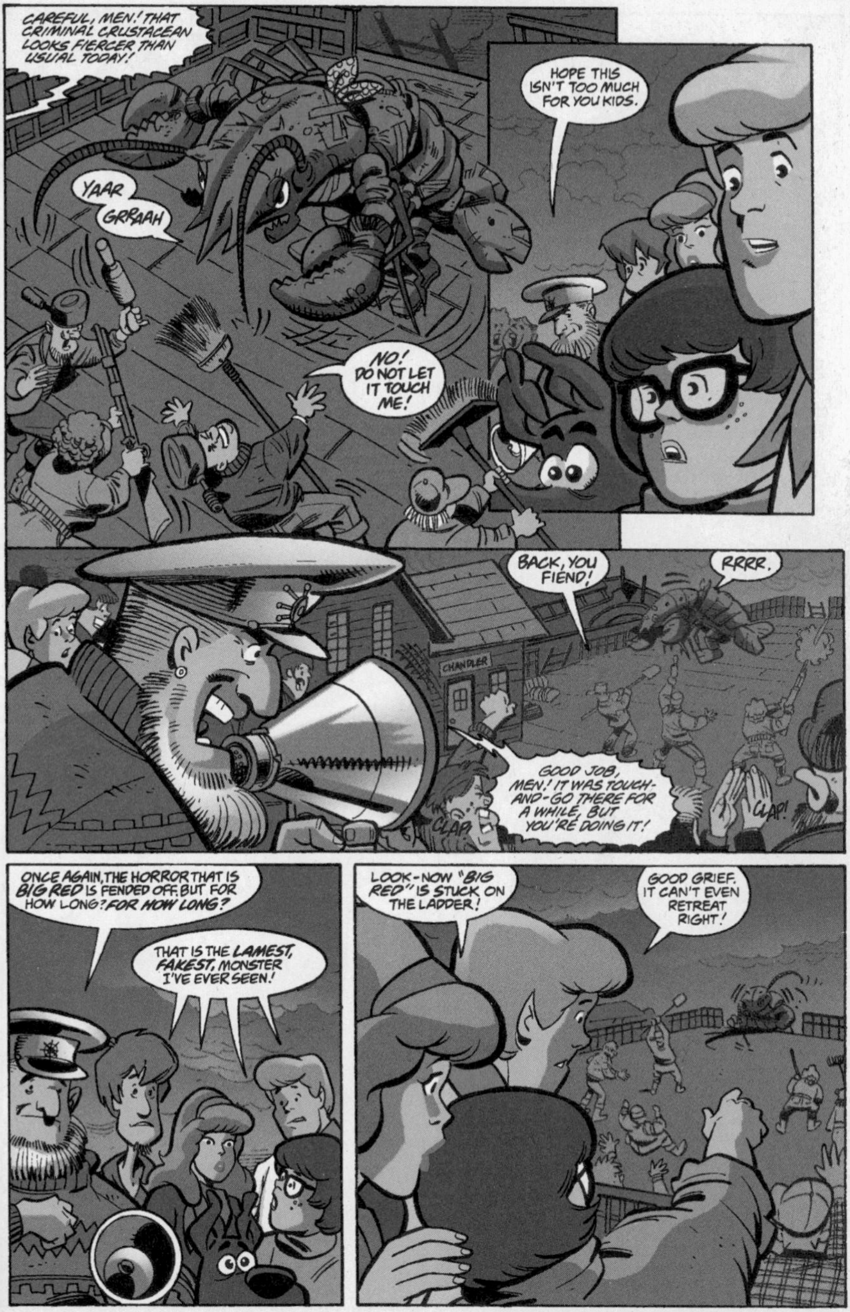
CAREFUL, MEN! THAT CRIMINAL CRUSTACEAN LOOKS FIERCER THAN USUAL TODAY!
HOPE THIS ISN'T TOO MUCH FOR YOU KIDS.
YAAR GRRAAH
NO! DO NOT LET IT TOUCH ME!
BACK, YOU FIEND!
RRRR.
CHANDLER
GOOD JOB, MEN! IT WAS TOUCH-AND-GO THERE FOR A WHILE, BUT YOU'RE DOING IT!
CLAP!
CLAP!
ONCE AGAIN, THE HORROR THAT IS BIG RED IS FENDED OFF. BUT FOR HOW LONG? FOR HOW LONG?
THAT IS THE LAMEST, FAKEST, MONSTER I'VE EVER SEEN!
LOOK-NOW "BIG RED" IS STUCK ON THE LADDER!
GOOD GRIEF. IT CAN'T EVEN RETREAT RIGHT!

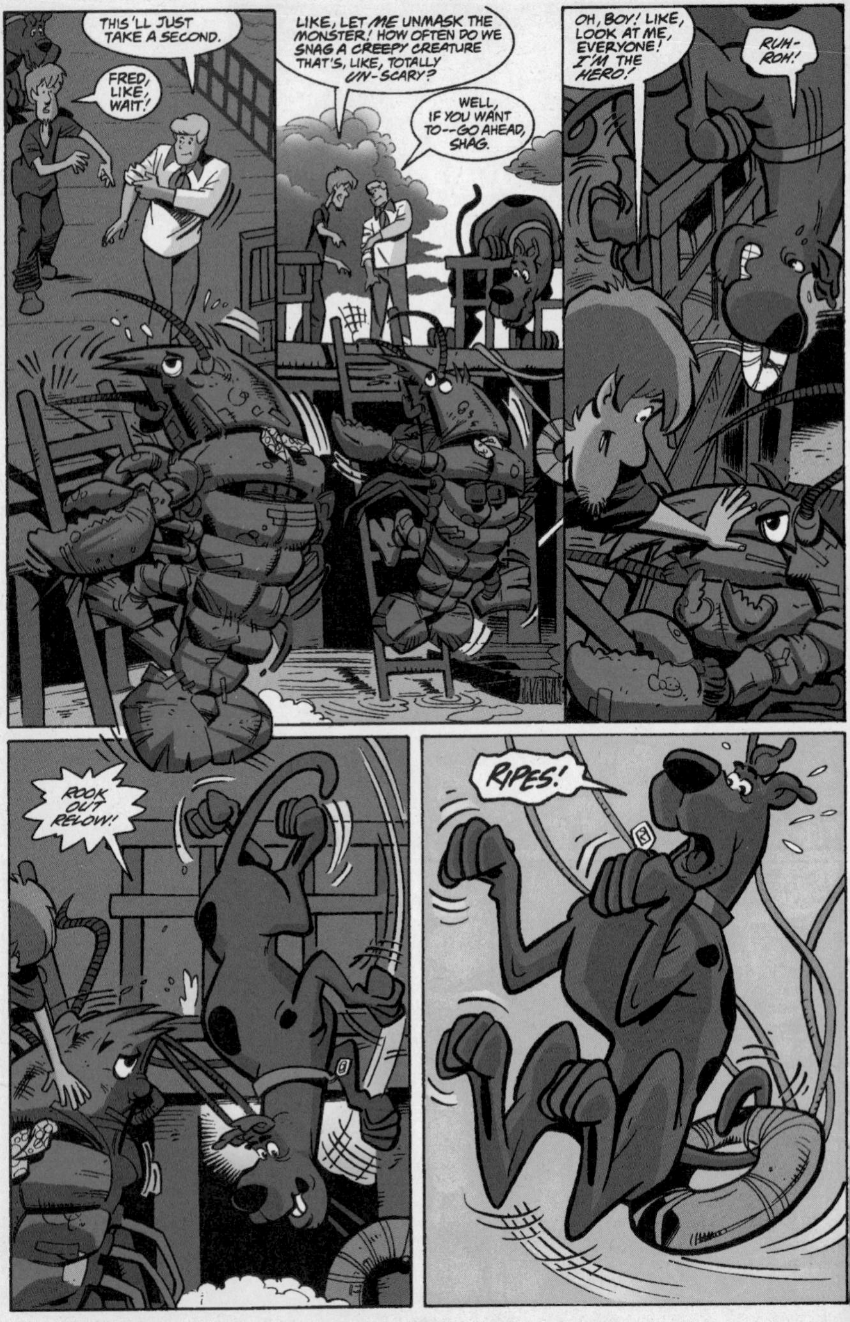
FRED, LIKE, WAIT!
THIS'LL JUST TAKE A SECOND.
LIKE, LET ME UNMASK THE MONSTER! HOW OFTEN DO WE SNAG A CREEPY CREATURE THAT'S, LIKE, TOTALLY UN-SCARY?
WELL, IF YOU WANT TO--GO AHEAD, SHAG.
OH, BOY! LIKE, LOOK AT ME, EVERYONE! I'M THE HERO!
RUH-ROH!
ROOK OUT RELOW!
RIPES!

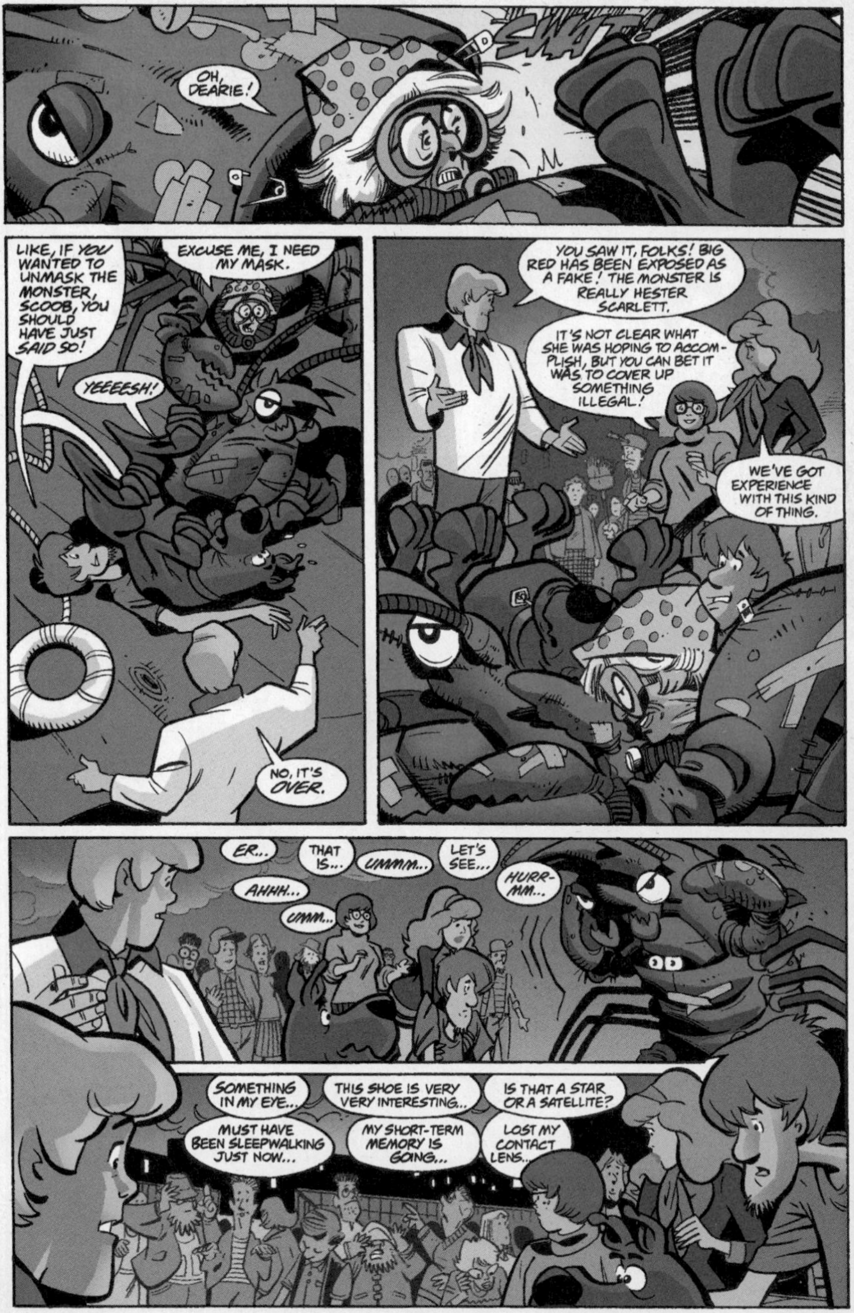
SWAT!
OH, DEARIE!
LIKE, IF YOU WANTED TO UNMASK THE MONSTER, SCOOB, YOU SHOULD HAVE JUST SAID SO!
EXCUSE ME, I NEED MY MASK.
YEEEESH!
NO, IT'S OVER.
YOU SAW IT, FOLKS! BIG RED HAS BEEN EXPOSED AS A FAKE! THE MONSTER IS REALLY HESTER SCARLETT.
IT'S NOT CLEAR WHAT SHE WAS HOPING TO ACCOMPLISH, BUT YOU CAN BET IT WAS TO COVER UP SOMETHING ILLEGAL!
WE'VE GOT EXPERIENCE WITH THIS KIND OF THING.
ER...
THAT IS...
UMMM...
LET'S SEE...
HURR-MM...
AHHH...
UMM...
SOMETHING IN MY EYE...
THIS SHOE IS VERY VERY INTERESTING...
IS THAT A STAR OR A SATELLITE?
MUST HAVE BEEN SLEEPWALKING JUST NOW...
MY SHORT-TERM MEMORY IS GOING...
LOST MY CONTACT LENS...

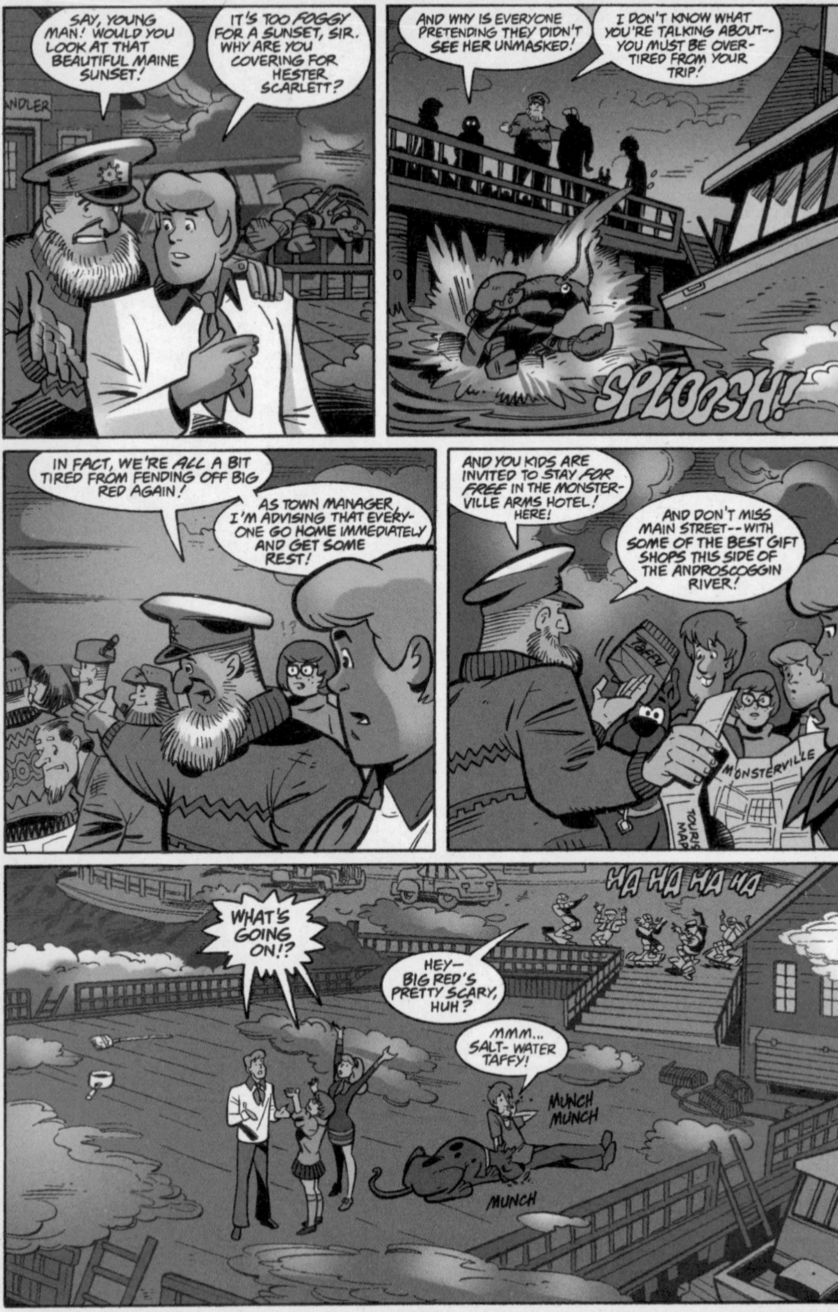
SAY, YOUNG MAN! WOULD YOU LOOK AT THAT BEAUTIFUL MAINE SUNSET!
IT'S TOO FOGGY FOR A SUNSET, SIR. WHY ARE YOU COVERING FOR HESTER SCARLETT?
ANDLER
AND WHY IS EVERYONE PRETENDING THEY DIDN'T SEE HER UNMASKED!
I DON'T KNOW WHAT YOU'RE TALKING ABOUT-- YOU MUST BE OVER-TIRED FROM YOUR TRIP!
SPLOOSH!
IN FACT, WE'RE ALL A BIT TIRED FROM FENDING OFF BIG RED AGAIN!
AS TOWN MANAGER, I'M ADVISING THAT EVERY-ONE GO HOME IMMEDIATELY AND GET SOME REST!
!?
AND YOU KIDS ARE INVITED TO STAY FOR FREE IN THE MONSTER-VILLE ARMS HOTEL! HERE!
AND DON'T MISS MAIN STREET--WITH SOME OF THE BEST GIFT SHOPS THIS SIDE OF THE ANDROSCOGGIN RIVER!
TAFFY
MONSTERVILLE
HA HA HA HA
WHAT'S GOING ON!?
HEY— BIG RED'S PRETTY SCARY, HUH?
MMM... SALT- WATER TAFFY!
MUNCH MUNCH
MUNCH

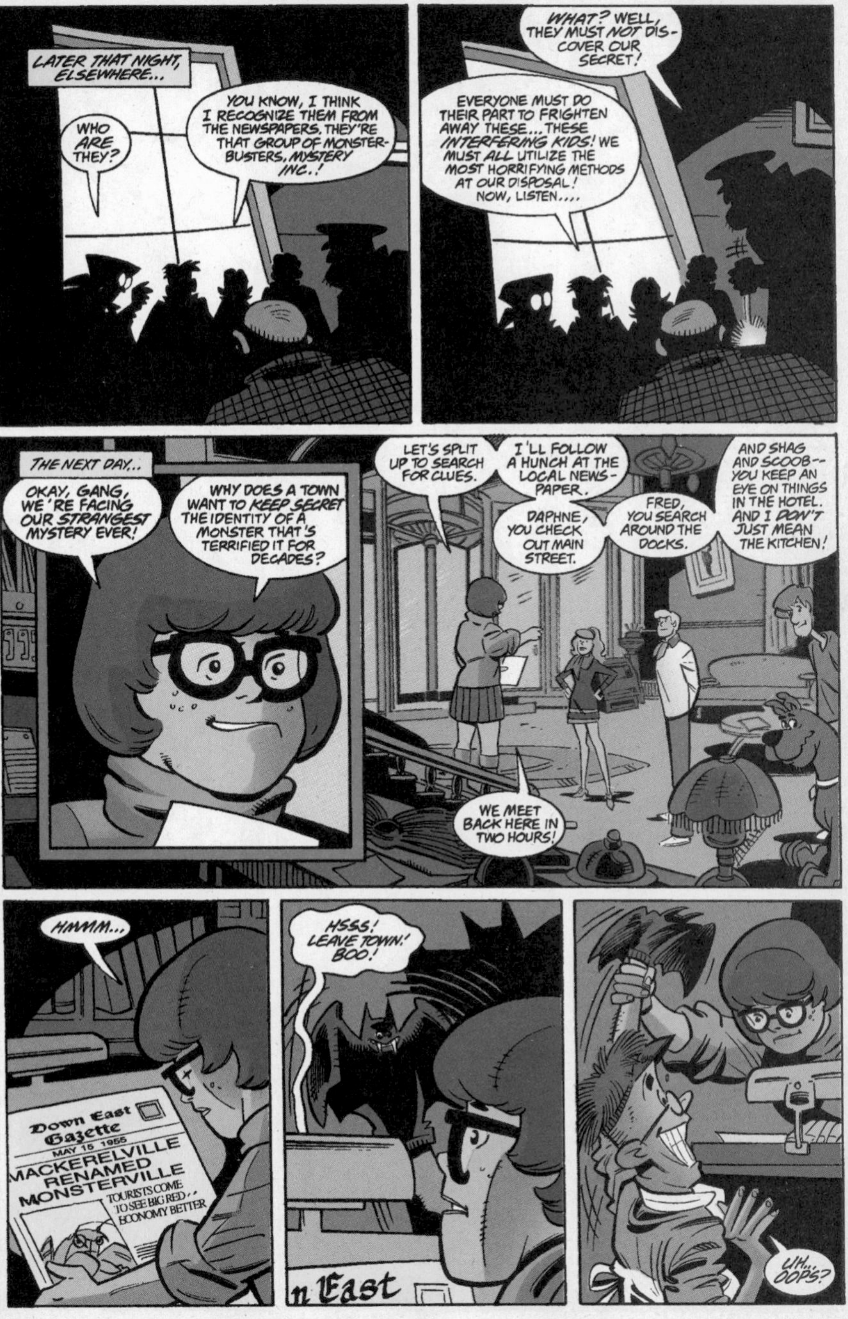
LATER THAT NIGHT, ELSEWHERE...
WHO ARE THEY?
YOU KNOW, I THINK I RECOGNIZE THEM FROM THE NEWSPAPERS. THEY'RE THAT GROUP OF MONSTER-BUSTERS, MYSTERY INC.!
WHAT? WELL, THEY MUST NOT DIS-COVER OUR SECRET!
EVERYONE MUST DO THEIR PART TO FRIGHTEN AWAY THESE... THESE INTERFERING KIDS! WE MUST ALL UTILIZE THE MOST HORRIFYING METHODS AT OUR DISPOSAL! NOW, LISTEN....
THE NEXT DAY...
OKAY, GANG, WE'RE FACING OUR STRANGEST MYSTERY EVER!
WHY DOES A TOWN WANT TO KEEP SECRET THE IDENTITY OF A MONSTER THAT'S TERRIFIED IT FOR DECADES?
LET'S SPLIT UP TO SEARCH FOR CLUES.
I'LL FOLLOW A HUNCH AT THE LOCAL NEWS-PAPER.
DAPHNE, YOU CHECK OUT MAIN STREET.
FRED, YOU SEARCH AROUND THE DOCKS.
AND SHAG AND SCOOB-- YOU KEEP AN EYE ON THINGS IN THE HOTEL. AND I DON'T JUST MEAN THE KITCHEN!
WE MEET BACK HERE IN TWO HOURS!
HMMM...
Down East Gazette
MAY 15 1955
MACKERELVILLE RENAMED MONSTERVILLE
TOURISTS COME TO SEE BIG RED,, ECONOMY BETTER
HSSS! LEAVE TOWN! BOO!
n East
UH... OOPS?

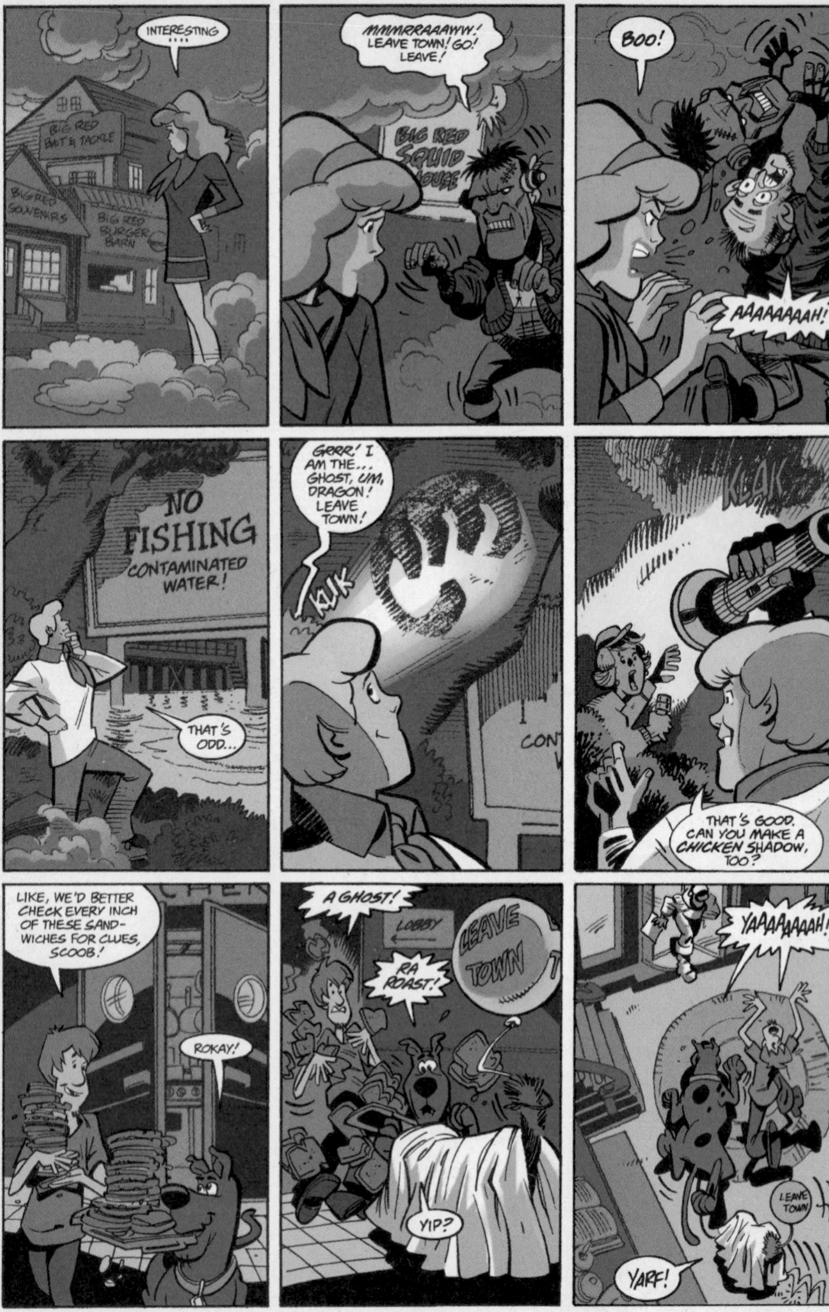
INTERESTING ....
BIG RED BAIT & TACKLE
BIG RED SOUVENIRS
BIG RED BURGER BARN
MMMRRAAAWW! LEAVE TOWN! GO! LEAVE!
BIG RED SQUID HOUSE
BOO!
AAAAAAAAH!
NO FISHING CONTAMINATED WATER!
THAT'S ODD...
GRRR! I AM THE... GHOST, UM, DRAGON! LEAVE TOWN!
KLIK
KLAK
THAT'S GOOD. CAN YOU MAKE A CHICKEN SHADOW, TOO?
LIKE, WE'D BETTER CHECK EVERY INCH OF THESE SAND-WICHES FOR CLUES, SCOOB!
ROKAY!
A GHOST!
LOBBY
RA ROAST!
LEAVE TOWN
YIP?
YAAAAAAAAH!
LEAVE TOWN
YARF!

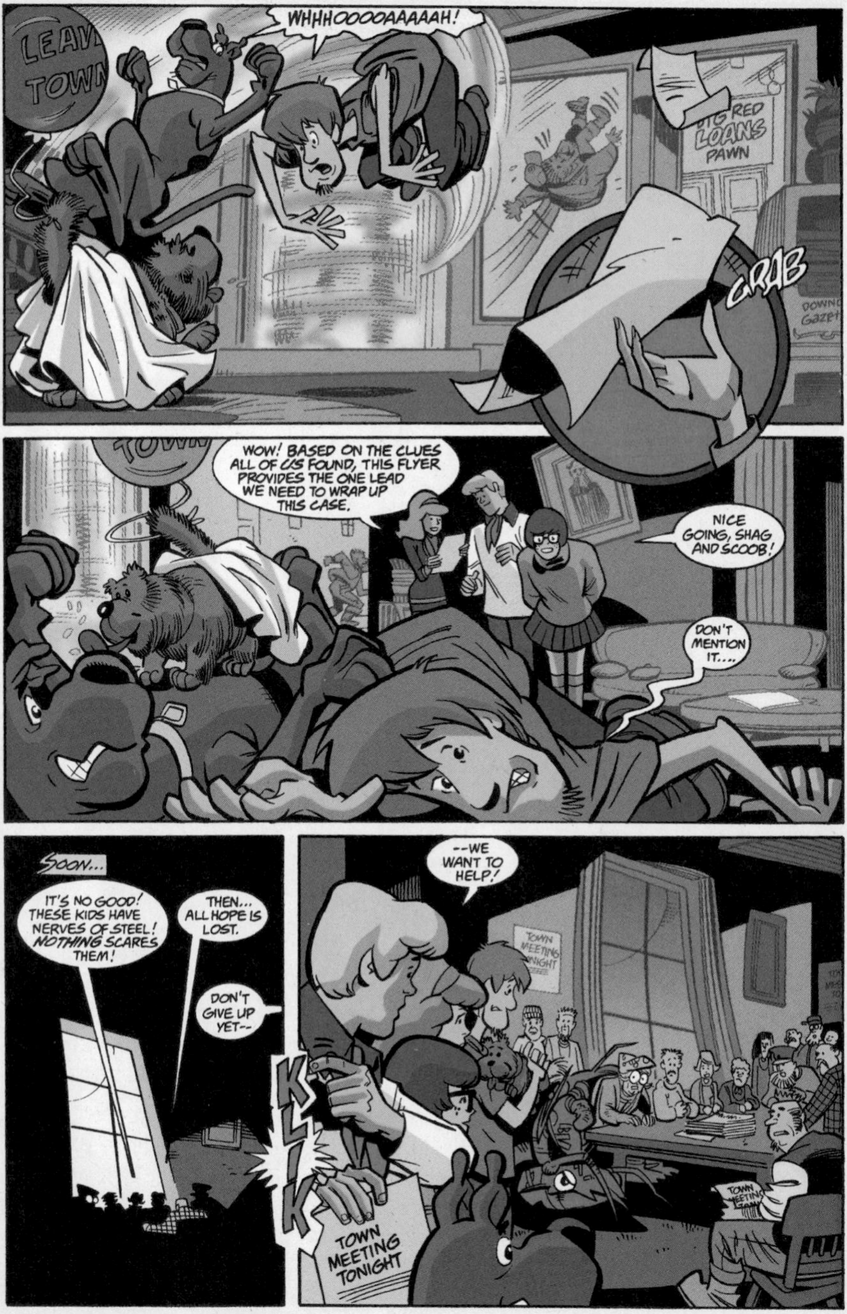
WHHHOOOOAAAAAH!
LEAVE TOWN
BIG RED LOANS PAWN
GRAB
WOW! BASED ON THE CLUES ALL OF US FOUND, THIS FLYER PROVIDES THE ONE LEAD WE NEED TO WRAP UP THIS CASE.
NICE GOING, SHAG AND SCOOB!
DON'T MENTION IT....
SOON...
IT'S NO GOOD! THESE KIDS HAVE NERVES OF STEEL! NOTHING SCARES THEM!
THEN... ALL HOPE IS LOST.
DON'T GIVE UP YET--
KLIK
--WE WANT TO HELP!
TOWN MEETING TONIGHT
TOWN MEETING TONIGHT

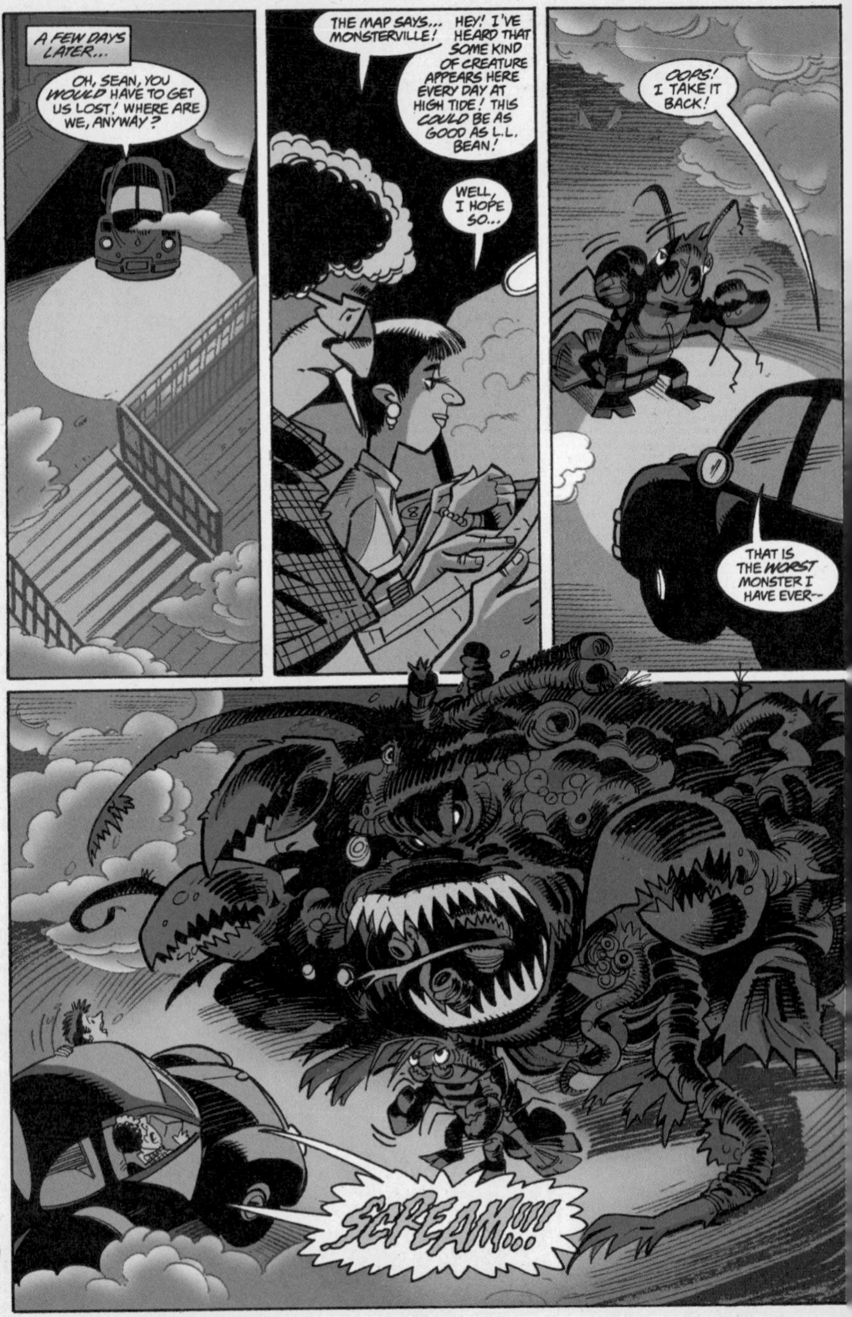
A FEW DAYS LATER...
OH, SEAN, YOU WOULD HAVE TO GET US LOST! WHERE ARE WE, ANYWAY?
THE MAP SAYS... MONSTERVILLE!
HEY! I'VE HEARD THAT SOME KIND OF CREATURE APPEARS HERE EVERY DAY AT HIGH TIDE! THIS COULD BE AS GOOD AS L.L. BEAN!
WELL, I HOPE SO...
OOPS! I TAKE IT BACK!
THAT IS THE WORST MONSTER I HAVE EVER--
SCREAM!!!

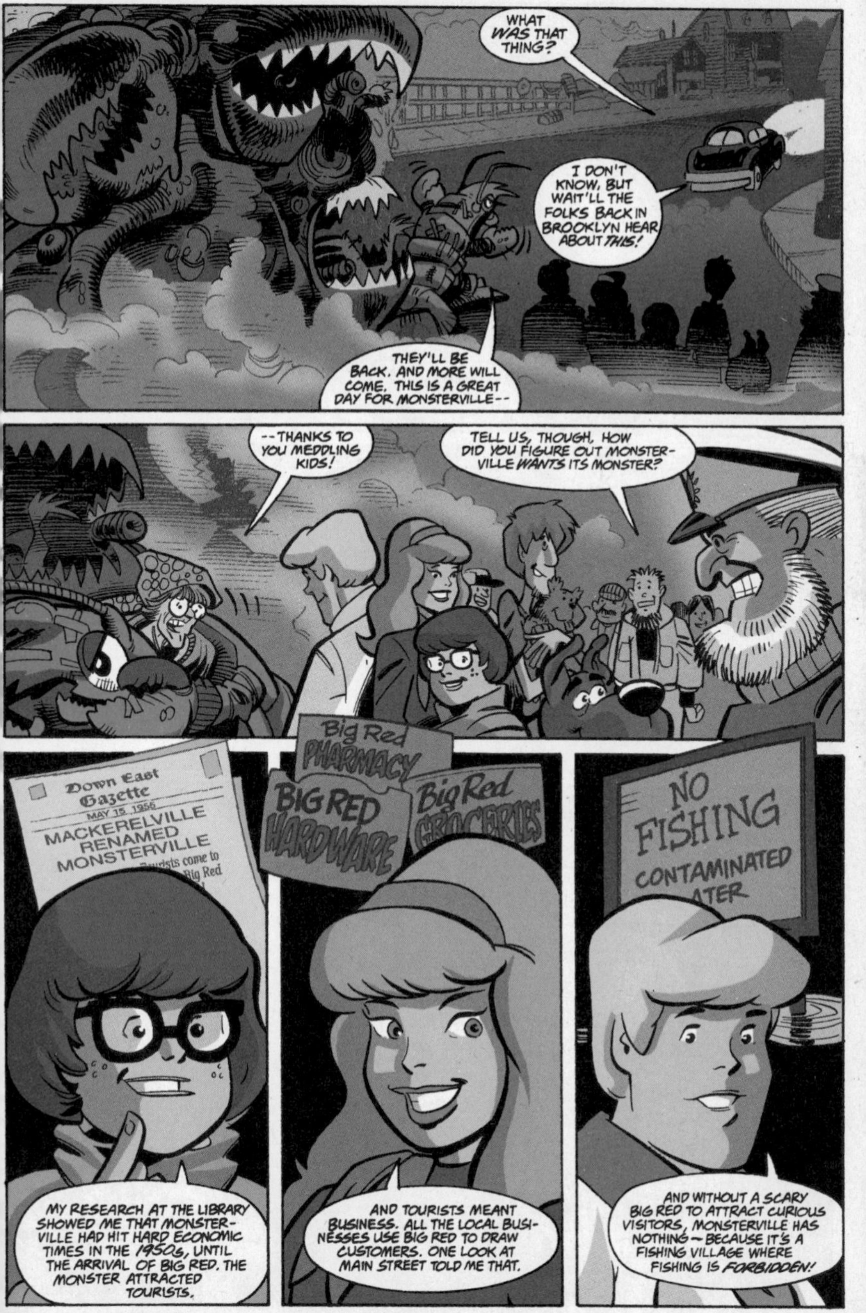
WHAT WAS THAT THING?
I DON'T KNOW, BUT WAIT'LL THE FOLKS BACK IN BROOKLYN HEAR ABOUT THIS!
THEY'LL BE BACK. AND MORE WILL COME. THIS IS A GREAT DAY FOR MONSTERVILLE--
--THANKS TO YOU MEDDLING KIDS!
TELL US, THOUGH, HOW DID YOU FIGURE OUT MONSTERVILLE WANTS ITS MONSTER?
Down East Gazette
MAY 15, 1956
MACKERELVILLE RENAMED MONSTERVILLE
MY RESEARCH AT THE LIBRARY SHOWED ME THAT MONSTERVILLE HAD HIT HARD ECONOMIC TIMES IN THE 1950s, UNTIL THE ARRIVAL OF BIG RED. THE MONSTER ATTRACTED TOURISTS.
Big Red PHARMACY
BIG RED HARDWARE
Big Red GROCERIES
AND TOURISTS MEANT BUSINESS. ALL THE LOCAL BUSINESSES USE BIG RED TO DRAW CUSTOMERS. ONE LOOK AT MAIN STREET TOLD ME THAT.
NO FISHING
CONTAMINATED
AND WITHOUT A SCARY BIG RED TO ATTRACT CURIOUS VISITORS, MONSTERVILLE HAS NOTHING — BECAUSE IT'S A FISHING VILLAGE WHERE FISHING IS FORBIDDEN!

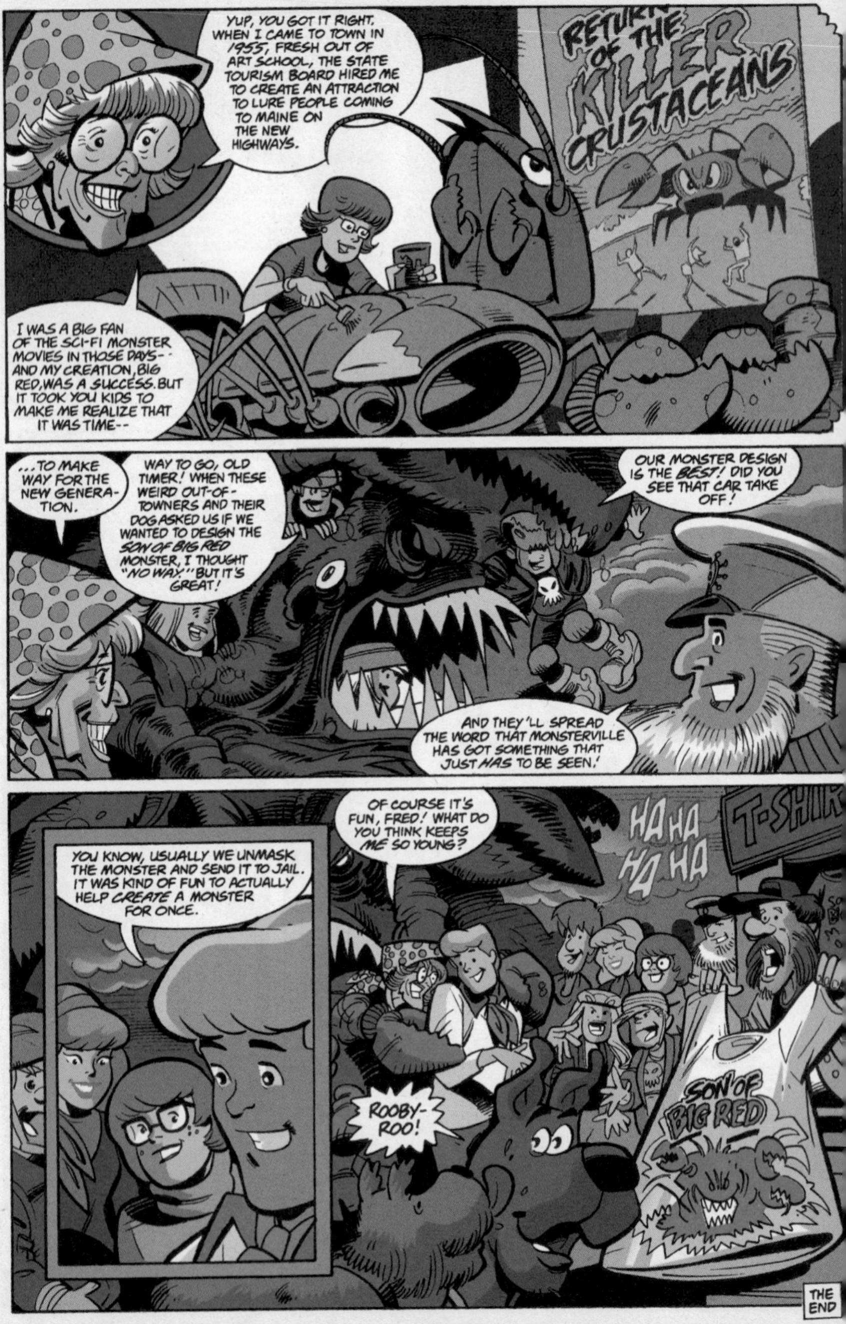
YUP, YOU GOT IT RIGHT. WHEN I CAME TO TOWN IN 1955, FRESH OUT OF ART SCHOOL, THE STATE TOURISM BOARD HIRED ME TO CREATE AN ATTRACTION TO LURE PEOPLE COMING TO MAINE ON THE NEW HIGHWAYS.
RETURN OF THE KILLER CRUSTACEANS
I WAS A BIG FAN OF THE SCI-FI MONSTER MOVIES IN THOSE DAYS-- AND MY CREATION, BIG RED, WAS A SUCCESS. BUT IT TOOK YOU KIDS TO MAKE ME REALIZE THAT IT WAS TIME--
...TO MAKE WAY FOR THE NEW GENERATION.
WAY TO GO, OLD TIMER! WHEN THESE WEIRD OUT-OF-TOWNERS AND THEIR DOG ASKED US IF WE WANTED TO DESIGN THE SON OF BIG RED MONSTER, I THOUGHT "NO WAY." BUT IT'S GREAT!
OUR MONSTER DESIGN IS THE BEST! DID YOU SEE THAT CAR TAKE OFF!
AND THEY'LL SPREAD THE WORD THAT MONSTERVILLE HAS GOT SOMETHING THAT JUST HAS TO BE SEEN!
YOU KNOW, USUALLY WE UNMASK THE MONSTER AND SEND IT TO JAIL. IT WAS KIND OF FUN TO ACTUALLY HELP CREATE A MONSTER FOR ONCE.
OF COURSE IT'S FUN, FRED! WHAT DO YOU THINK KEEPS ME SO YOUNG?
HA HA HA HA
ROOBY-ROO!
SON OF BIG RED
THE END

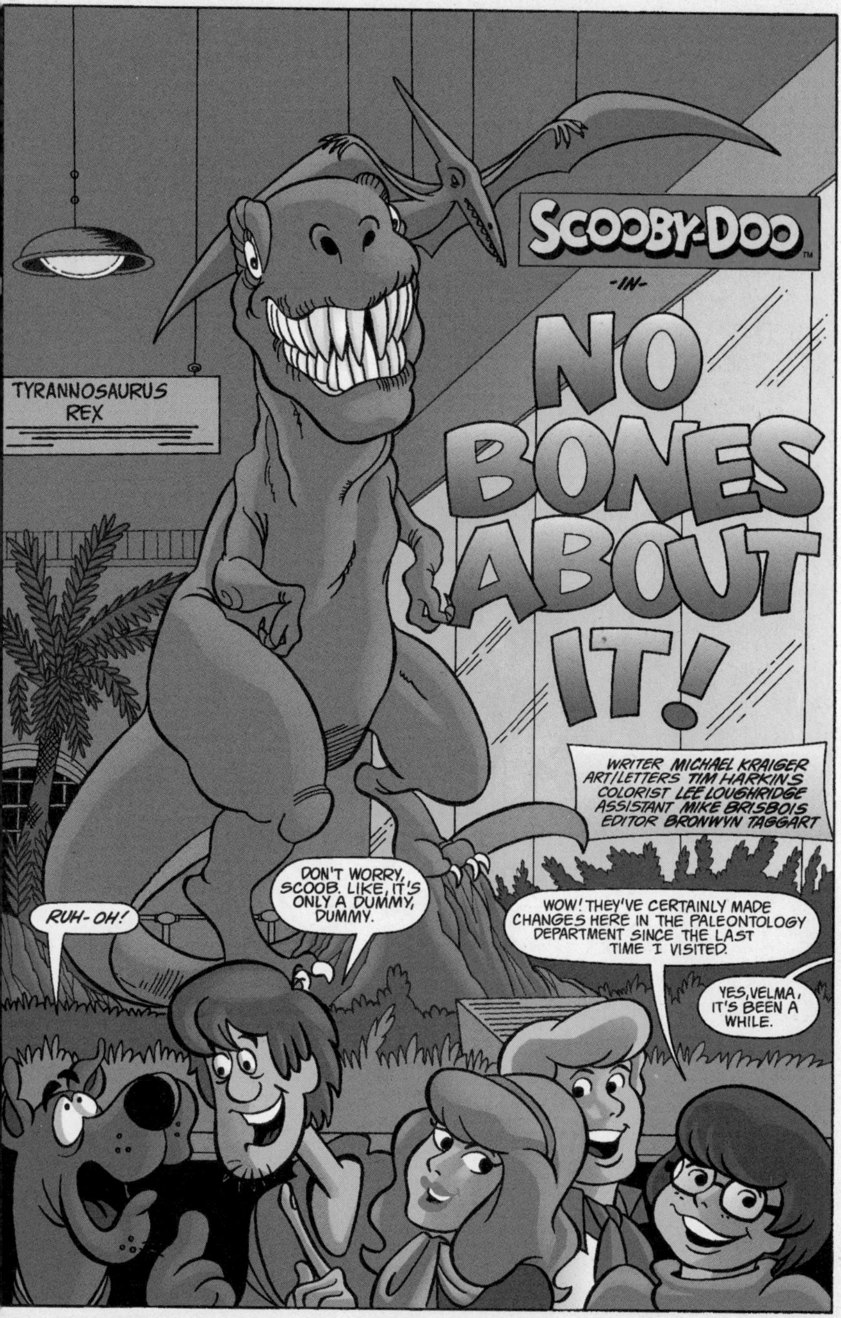
TYRANNOSAURUS REX
SCOOBY-DOO™
-IN-
NO BONES ABOUT IT!
WRITER MICHAEL KRAIGER
ART/LETTERS TIM HARKINS
COLORIST LEE LOUGHRIDGE
ASSISTANT MIKE BRISBOIS
EDITOR BRONWYN TAGGART
RUH-OH!
DON'T WORRY, SCOOB. LIKE, IT'S ONLY A DUMMY, DUMMY.
WOW! THEY'VE CERTAINLY MADE CHANGES HERE IN THE PALEONTOLOGY DEPARTMENT SINCE THE LAST TIME I VISITED.
YES, VELMA, IT'S BEEN A WHILE.

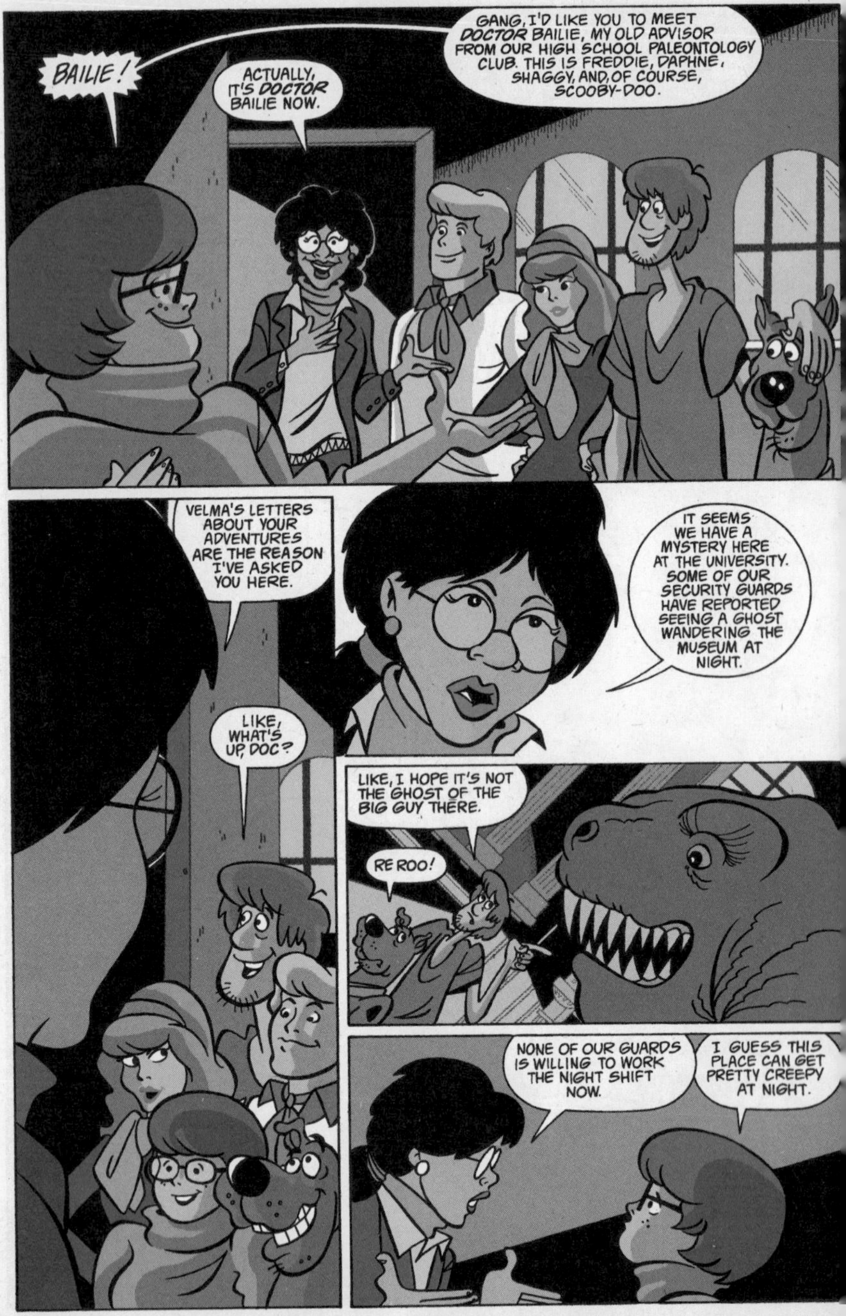
BAILIE!
GANG, I'D LIKE YOU TO MEET DOCTOR BAILIE, MY OLD ADVISOR FROM OUR HIGH SCHOOL PALEONTOLOGY CLUB. THIS IS FREDDIE, DAPHNE, SHAGGY, AND, OF COURSE, SCOOBY-DOO.
ACTUALLY, IT'S DOCTOR BAILIE NOW.
VELMA'S LETTERS ABOUT YOUR ADVENTURES ARE THE REASON I'VE ASKED YOU HERE.
IT SEEMS WE HAVE A MYSTERY HERE AT THE UNIVERSITY. SOME OF OUR SECURITY GUARDS HAVE REPORTED SEEING A GHOST WANDERING THE MUSEUM AT NIGHT.
LIKE, WHAT'S UP, DOC?
LIKE, I HOPE IT'S NOT THE GHOST OF THE BIG GUY THERE.
RE ROO!
NONE OF OUR GUARDS IS WILLING TO WORK THE NIGHT SHIFT NOW.
I GUESS THIS PLACE CAN GET PRETTY CREEPY AT NIGHT.

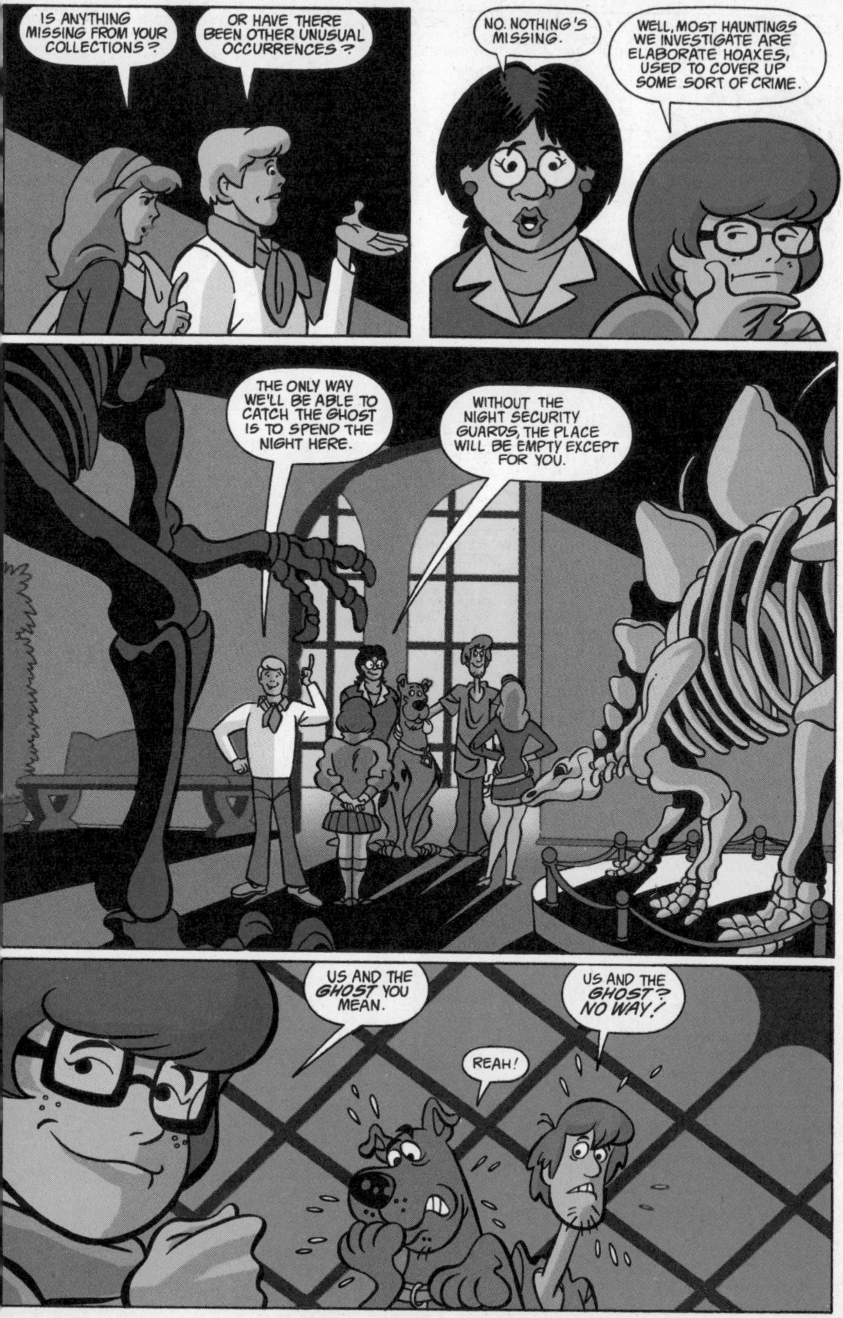
IS ANYTHING MISSING FROM YOUR COLLECTIONS?
OR HAVE THERE BEEN OTHER UNUSUAL OCCURRENCES?
NO. NOTHING'S MISSING.
WELL, MOST HAUNTINGS WE INVESTIGATE ARE ELABORATE HOAXES, USED TO COVER UP SOME SORT OF CRIME.
THE ONLY WAY WE'LL BE ABLE TO CATCH THE GHOST IS TO SPEND THE NIGHT HERE.
WITHOUT THE NIGHT SECURITY GUARDS, THE PLACE WILL BE EMPTY EXCEPT FOR YOU.
US AND THE *GHOST* YOU MEAN.
US AND THE *GHOST*? *NO WAY!*
REAH!

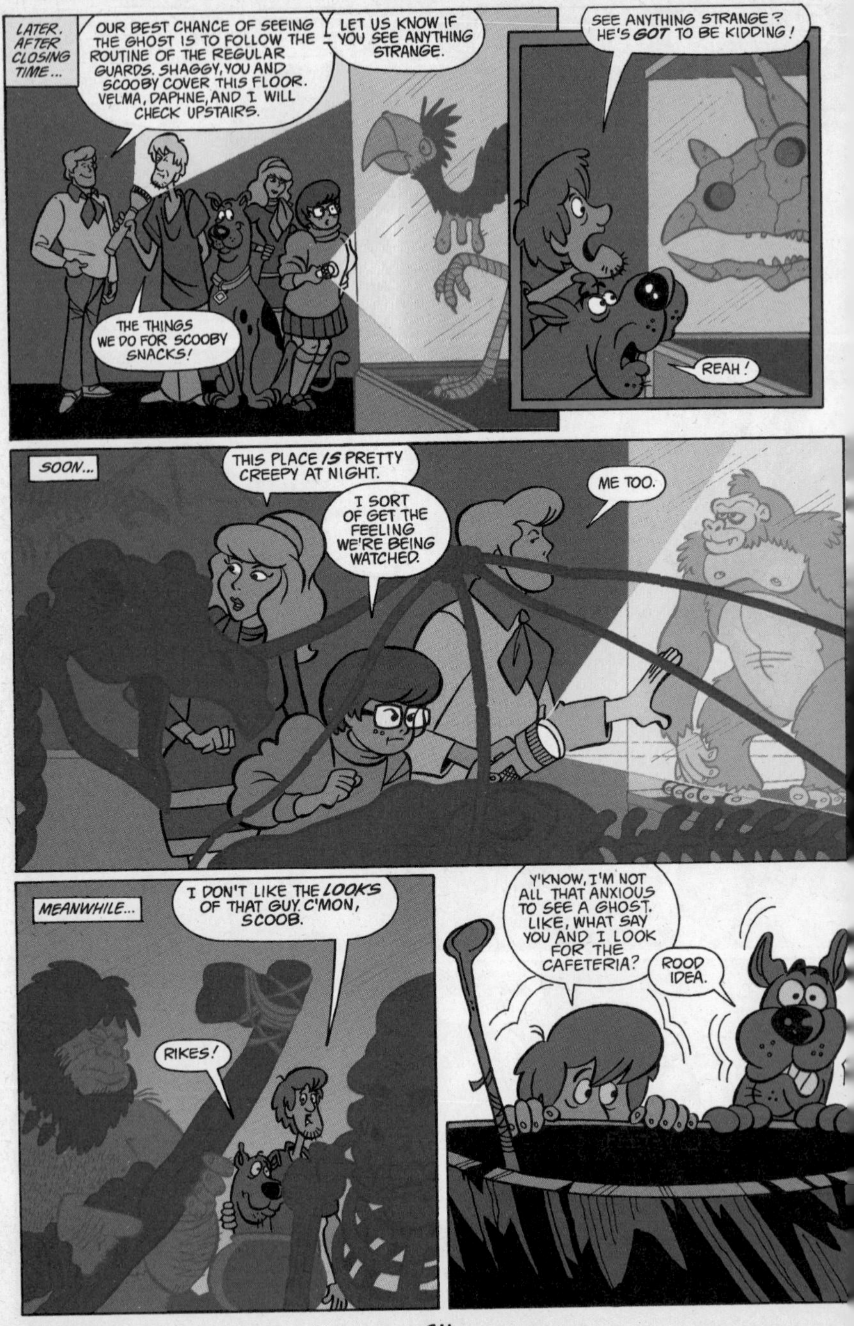
LATER. AFTER CLOSING TIME...
OUR BEST CHANCE OF SEEING THE GHOST IS TO FOLLOW THE ROUTINE OF THE REGULAR GUARDS. SHAGGY, YOU AND SCOOBY COVER THIS FLOOR. VELMA, DAPHNE, AND I WILL CHECK UPSTAIRS.
LET US KNOW IF YOU SEE ANYTHING STRANGE.
THE THINGS WE DO FOR SCOOBY SNACKS!
SEE ANYTHING STRANGE? HE'S GOT TO BE KIDDING!
REAH!
SOON...
THIS PLACE IS PRETTY CREEPY AT NIGHT.
I SORT OF GET THE FEELING WE'RE BEING WATCHED.
ME TOO.
MEANWHILE...
I DON'T LIKE THE LOOKS OF THAT GUY. C'MON, SCOOB.
RIKES!
Y'KNOW, I'M NOT ALL THAT ANXIOUS TO SEE A GHOST. LIKE, WHAT SAY YOU AND I LOOK FOR THE CAFETERIA?
ROOD IDEA.

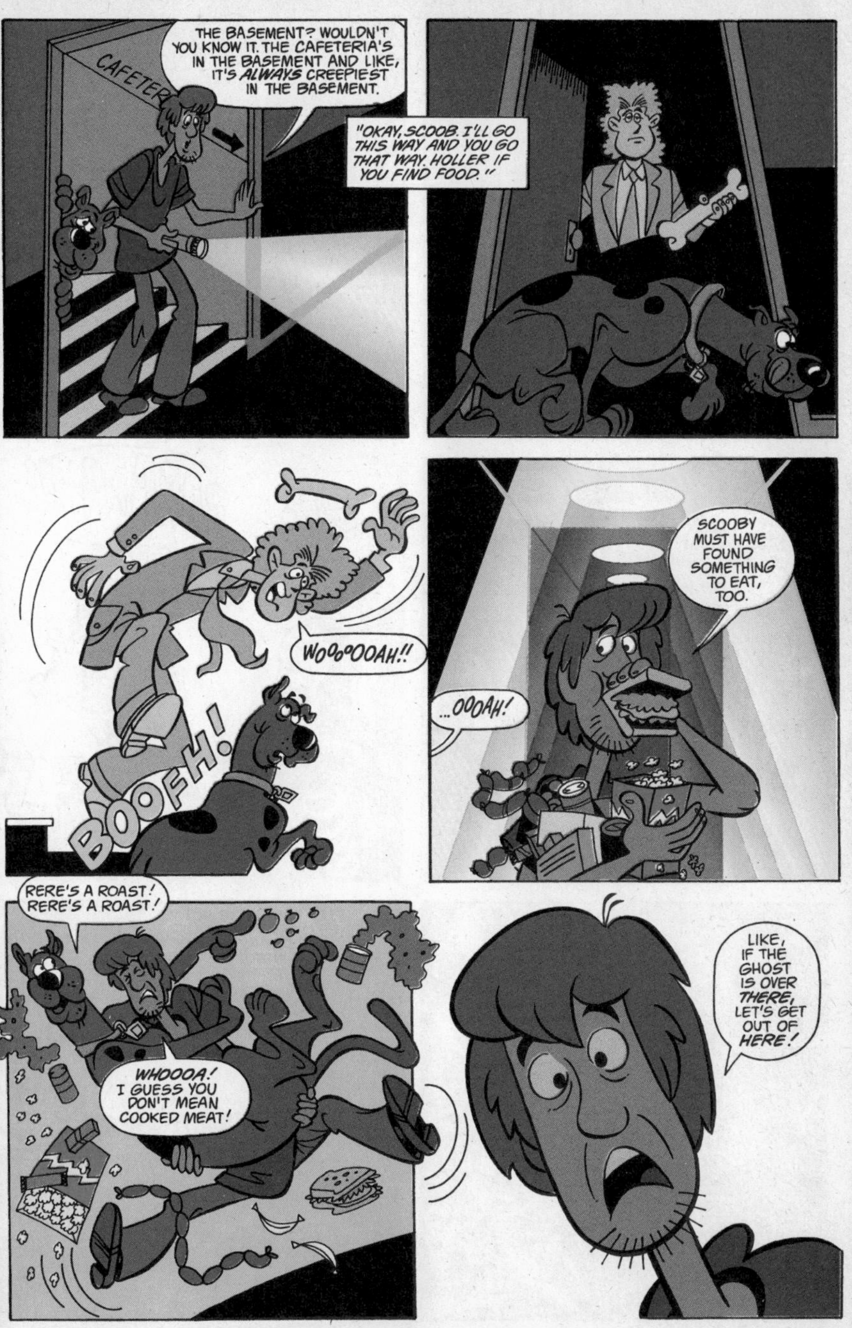
THE BASEMENT? WOULDN'T YOU KNOW IT. THE CAFETERIA'S IN THE BASEMENT AND LIKE, IT'S ALWAYS CREEPIEST IN THE BASEMENT.
CAFETER
"OKAY, SCOOB. I'LL GO THIS WAY AND YOU GO THAT WAY. HOLLER IF YOU FIND FOOD."
WOoooOOAH!!
BOOFH!
SCOOBY MUST HAVE FOUND SOMETHING TO EAT, TOO.
...OOOAH!
RERE'S A ROAST! RERE'S A ROAST!
WHOOOA! I GUESS YOU DON'T MEAN COOKED MEAT!
LIKE, IF THE GHOST IS OVER THERE, LET'S GET OUT OF HERE!

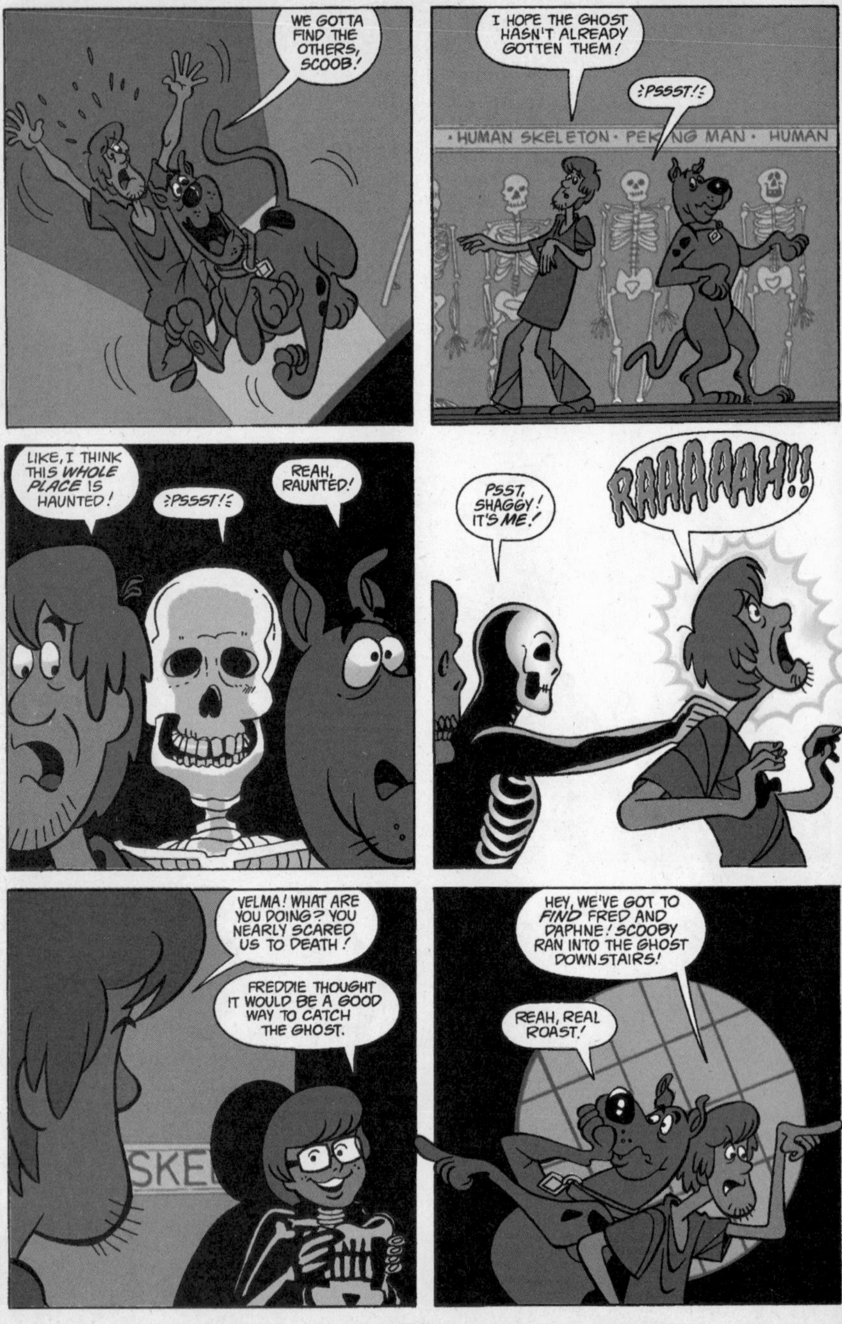
WE GOTTA FIND THE OTHERS, SCOOB!
I HOPE THE GHOST HASN'T ALREADY GOTTEN THEM!
PSSST!
HUMAN SKELETON · PEKING MAN · HUMAN
LIKE, I THINK THIS WHOLE PLACE IS HAUNTED!
PSSST!
REAH, RAUNTED!
PSST, SHAGGY! IT'S ME!
RAAAAAH!!
VELMA! WHAT ARE YOU DOING? YOU NEARLY SCARED US TO DEATH!
FREDDIE THOUGHT IT WOULD BE A GOOD WAY TO CATCH THE GHOST.
SKEL
HEY, WE'VE GOT TO FIND FRED AND DAPHNE! SCOOBY RAN INTO THE GHOST DOWNSTAIRS!
REAH, REAL ROAST!

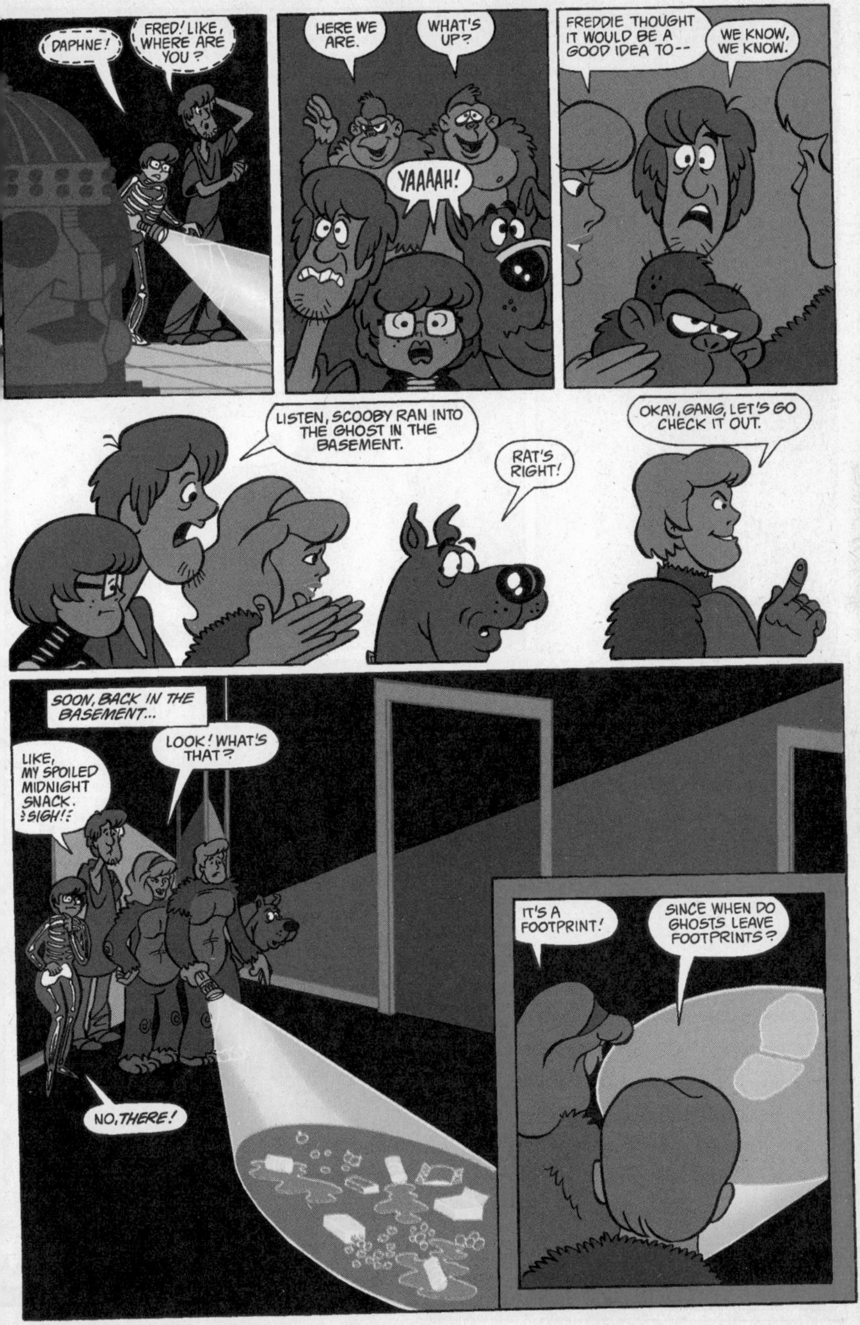
DAPHNE!
FRED! LIKE, WHERE ARE YOU?
HERE WE ARE.
WHAT'S UP?
YAAAAH!
FREDDIE THOUGHT IT WOULD BE A GOOD IDEA TO--
WE KNOW, WE KNOW.
LISTEN, SCOOBY RAN INTO THE GHOST IN THE BASEMENT.
RAT'S RIGHT!
OKAY, GANG, LET'S GO CHECK IT OUT.
SOON, BACK IN THE BASEMENT...
LOOK! WHAT'S THAT?
LIKE, MY SPOILED MIDNIGHT SNACK. SIGH!
NO, THERE!
IT'S A FOOTPRINT!
SINCE WHEN DO GHOSTS LEAVE FOOTPRINTS?

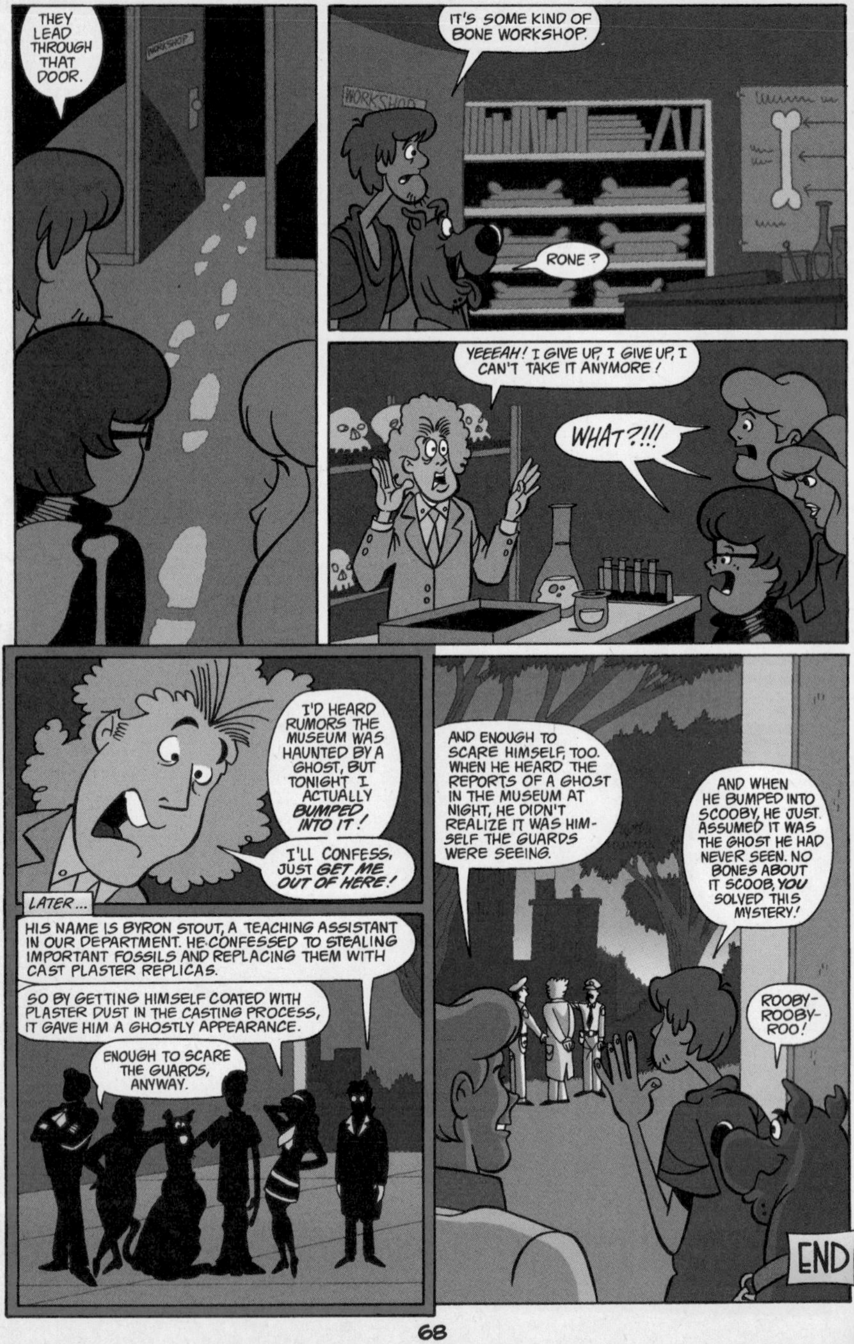
THEY LEAD THROUGH THAT DOOR.
WORKSHOP
IT'S SOME KIND OF BONE WORKSHOP.
WORKSHOP
RONE?
YEEEAH! I GIVE UP, I GIVE UP, I CAN'T TAKE IT ANYMORE!
WHAT?!!!
I'D HEARD RUMORS THE MUSEUM WAS HAUNTED BY A GHOST, BUT TONIGHT I ACTUALLY BUMPED INTO IT!
I'LL CONFESS, JUST GET ME OUT OF HERE!
LATER...
HIS NAME IS BYRON STOUT, A TEACHING ASSISTANT IN OUR DEPARTMENT. HE CONFESSED TO STEALING IMPORTANT FOSSILS AND REPLACING THEM WITH CAST PLASTER REPLICAS.
SO BY GETTING HIMSELF COATED WITH PLASTER DUST IN THE CASTING PROCESS, IT GAVE HIM A GHOSTLY APPEARANCE.
ENOUGH TO SCARE THE GUARDS, ANYWAY.
AND ENOUGH TO SCARE HIMSELF, TOO. WHEN HE HEARD THE REPORTS OF A GHOST IN THE MUSEUM AT NIGHT, HE DIDN'T REALIZE IT WAS HIMSELF THE GUARDS WERE SEEING.
AND WHEN HE BUMPED INTO SCOOBY, HE JUST ASSUMED IT WAS THE GHOST HE HAD NEVER SEEN. NO BONES ABOUT IT SCOOB, YOU SOLVED THIS MYSTERY!
ROOBY-ROOBY-ROO!
END

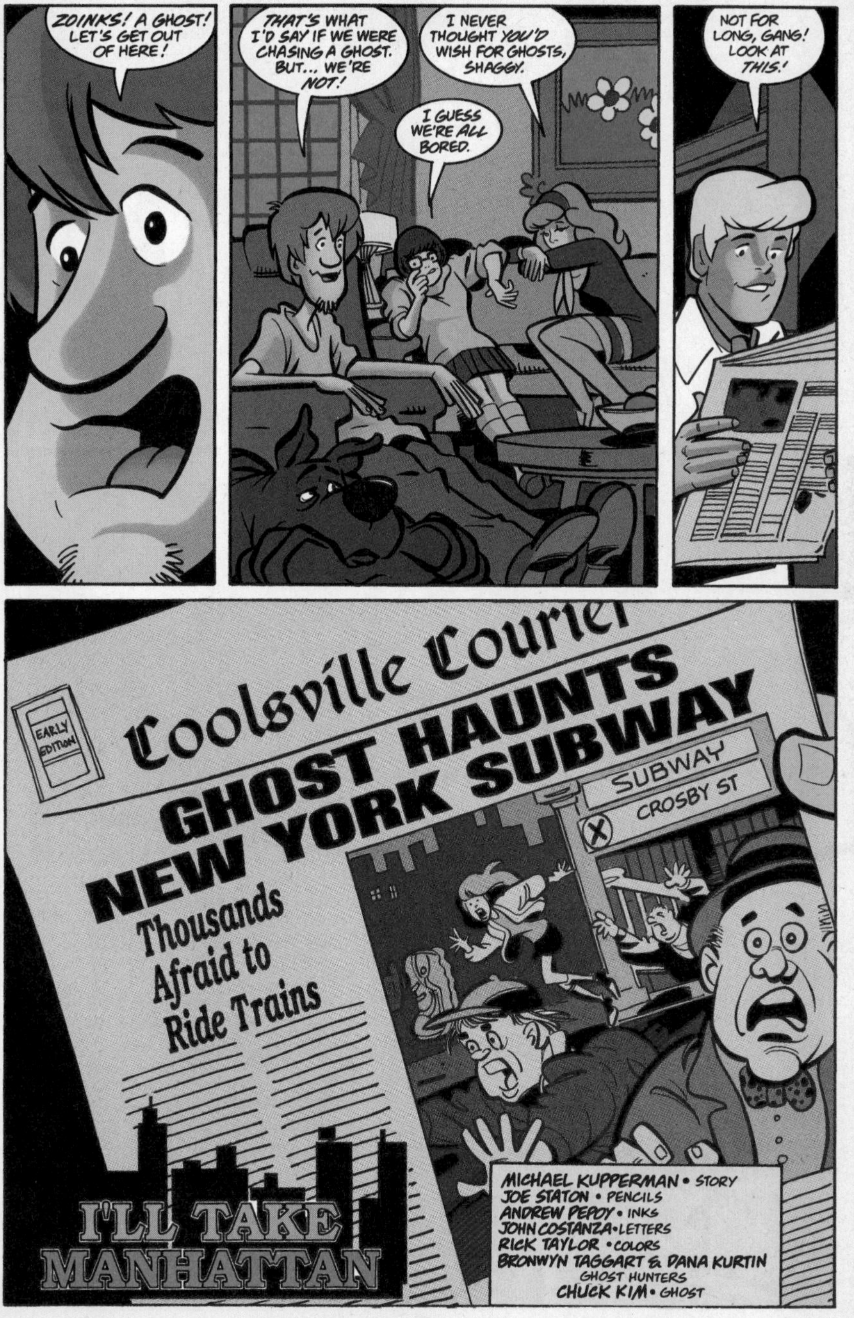

ZOINKS! A GHOST! LET'S GET OUT OF HERE!
THAT'S WHAT I'D SAY IF WE WERE CHASING A GHOST. BUT... WE'RE NOT!
I NEVER THOUGHT YOU'D WISH FOR GHOSTS, SHAGGY.
I GUESS WE'RE ALL BORED.
NOT FOR LONG, GANG! LOOK AT THIS!
EARLY EDITION
Coolsville Courier
GHOST HAUNTS NEW YORK SUBWAY
Thousands Afraid to Ride Trains
SUBWAY
CROSBY ST
I'LL TAKE MANHATTAN
MICHAEL KUPPERMAN • STORY
JOE STATON • PENCILS
ANDREW PEPOY • INKS
JOHN COSTANZA • LETTERS
RICK TAYLOR • COLORS
BRONWYN TAGGART & DANA KURTIN GHOST HUNTERS
CHUCK KIM • GHOST

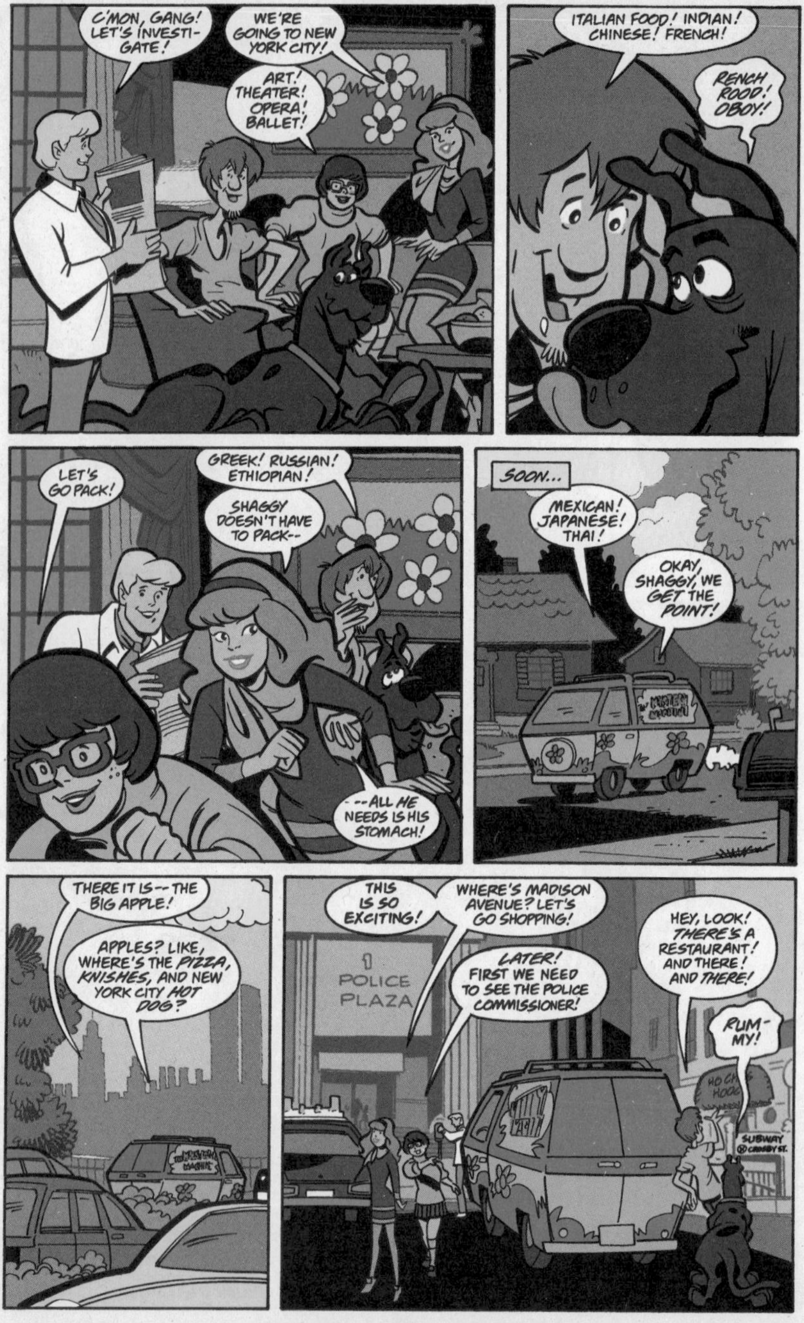
C'MON, GANG! LET'S INVESTIGATE!
WE'RE GOING TO NEW YORK CITY!
ART! THEATER! OPERA! BALLET!
ITALIAN FOOD! INDIAN! CHINESE! FRENCH!
RENCH ROOD! OBOY!
LET'S GO PACK!
GREEK! RUSSIAN! ETHIOPIAN!
SHAGGY DOESN'T HAVE TO PACK--
--ALL HE NEEDS IS HIS STOMACH!
SOON...
MEXICAN! JAPANESE! THAI!
OKAY, SHAGGY, WE GET THE POINT!
THERE IT IS--THE BIG APPLE!
APPLES? LIKE, WHERE'S THE PIZZA, KNISHES, AND NEW YORK CITY HOT DOG?
THIS IS SO EXCITING!
WHERE'S MADISON AVENUE? LET'S GO SHOPPING!
1 POLICE PLAZA
LATER! FIRST WE NEED TO SEE THE POLICE COMMISSIONER!
HEY, LOOK! THERE'S A RESTAURANT! AND THERE! AND THERE!
RUM-MY!
SUBWAY
CROSBY ST.

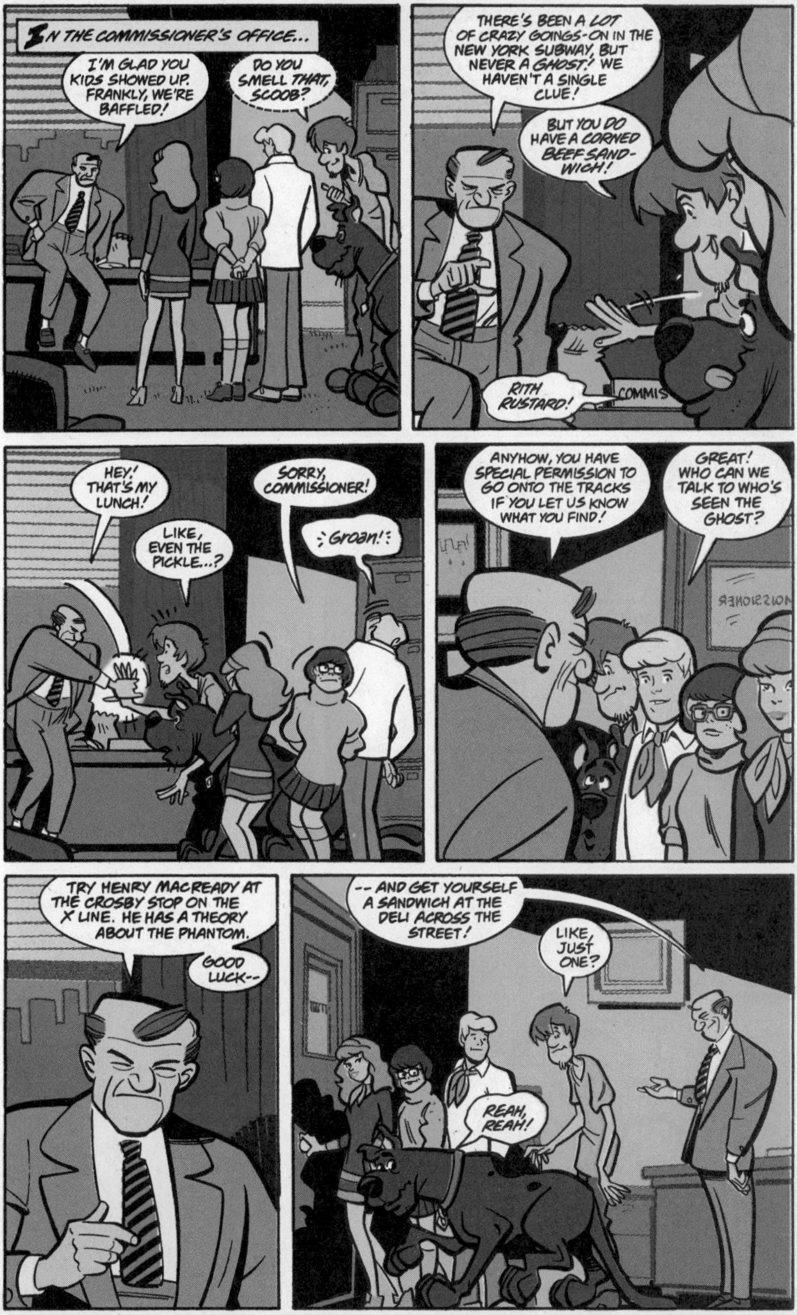
IN THE COMMISSIONER'S OFFICE...
I'M GLAD YOU KIDS SHOWED UP. FRANKLY, WE'RE BAFFLED!
DO YOU SMELL THAT, SCOOB?
THERE'S BEEN A LOT OF CRAZY GOINGS-ON IN THE NEW YORK SUBWAY, BUT NEVER A GHOST! WE HAVEN'T A SINGLE CLUE!
BUT YOU DO HAVE A CORNED BEEF SAND-WICH!
RITH RUSTARD!
COMMIS
HEY! THAT'S MY LUNCH!
LIKE, EVEN THE PICKLE...?
SORRY, COMMISSIONER!
Groan!
ANYHOW, YOU HAVE SPECIAL PERMISSION TO GO ONTO THE TRACKS IF YOU LET US KNOW WHAT YOU FIND!
GREAT! WHO CAN WE TALK TO WHO'S SEEN THE GHOST?
TRY HENRY MACREADY AT THE CROSBY STOP ON THE X LINE. HE HAS A THEORY ABOUT THE PHANTOM.
GOOD LUCK--
-- AND GET YOURSELF A SANDWICH AT THE DELI ACROSS THE STREET!
LIKE, JUST ONE?
REAH, REAH!

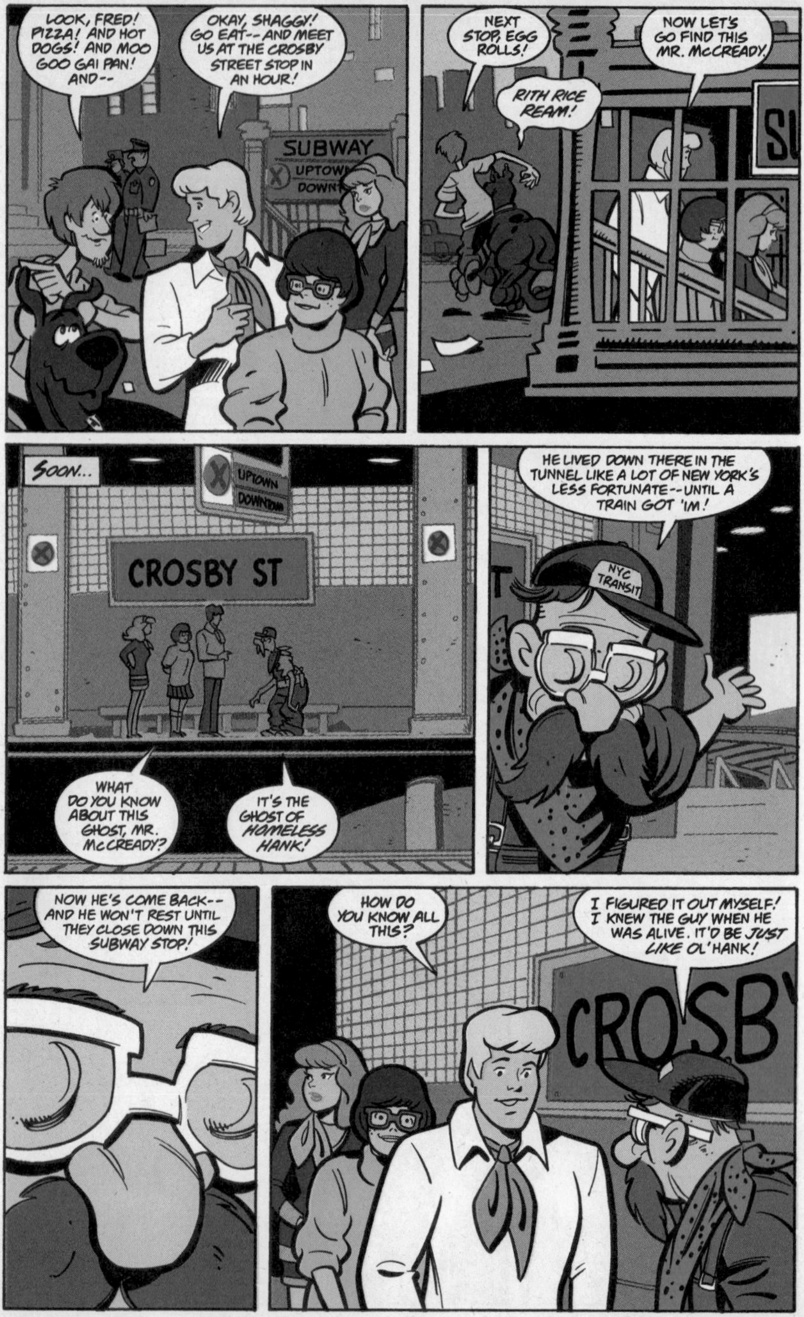
LOOK, FRED! PIZZA! AND HOT DOGS! AND MOO GOO GAI PAN! AND--
OKAY, SHAGGY! GO EAT--AND MEET US AT THE CROSBY STREET STOP IN AN HOUR!
SUBWAY
UPTOWN
DOWNT
NEXT STOP, EGG ROLLS!
RITH RICE REAM!
NOW LET'S GO FIND THIS MR. McCREADY.
SOON...
UPTOWN
DOWNTOWN
CROSBY ST
WHAT DO YOU KNOW ABOUT THIS GHOST, MR. McCREADY?
IT'S THE GHOST OF *HOMELESS HANK!*
HE LIVED DOWN THERE IN THE TUNNEL LIKE A LOT OF NEW YORK'S LESS FORTUNATE--UNTIL A TRAIN GOT 'IM!
NYC TRANSIT
NOW HE'S COME BACK--AND HE WON'T REST UNTIL THEY CLOSE DOWN THIS SUBWAY STOP!
HOW DO YOU KNOW ALL THIS?
I FIGURED IT OUT MYSELF! I KNEW THE GUY WHEN HE WAS ALIVE. IT'D BE *JUST LIKE* OL' HANK!
CROSBY

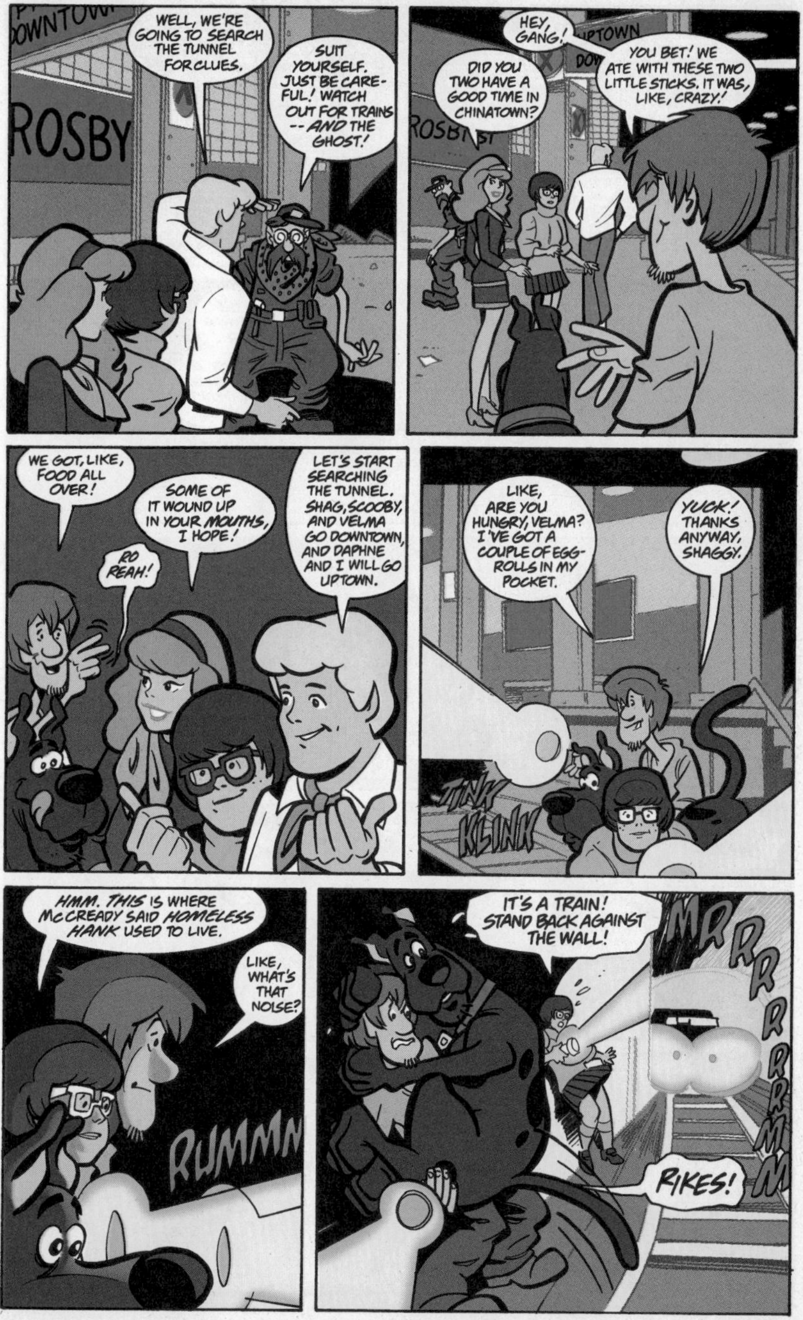
DOWNTOWN
ROSBY
WELL, WE'RE GOING TO SEARCH THE TUNNEL FOR CLUES.
SUIT YOURSELF. JUST BE CAREFUL! WATCH OUT FOR TRAINS -- AND THE GHOST!
HEY, GANG!
UPTOWN
DID YOU TWO HAVE A GOOD TIME IN CHINATOWN?
YOU BET! WE ATE WITH THESE TWO LITTLE STICKS. IT WAS, LIKE, CRAZY!
WE GOT, LIKE, FOOD ALL OVER!
SOME OF IT WOUND UP IN YOUR MOUTHS, I HOPE!
RO REAH!
LET'S START SEARCHING THE TUNNEL. SHAG, SCOOBY, AND VELMA GO DOWNTOWN, AND DAPHNE AND I WILL GO UPTOWN.
LIKE, ARE YOU HUNGRY, VELMA? I'VE GOT A COUPLE OF EGG-ROLLS IN MY POCKET.
YUCK! THANKS ANYWAY, SHAGGY.
TINK
KLINK
HMM. THIS IS WHERE McCREADY SAID HOMELESS HANK USED TO LIVE.
LIKE, WHAT'S THAT NOISE?
RUMMM
IT'S A TRAIN! STAND BACK AGAINST THE WALL!
MRRRRRRRMM
RIKES!

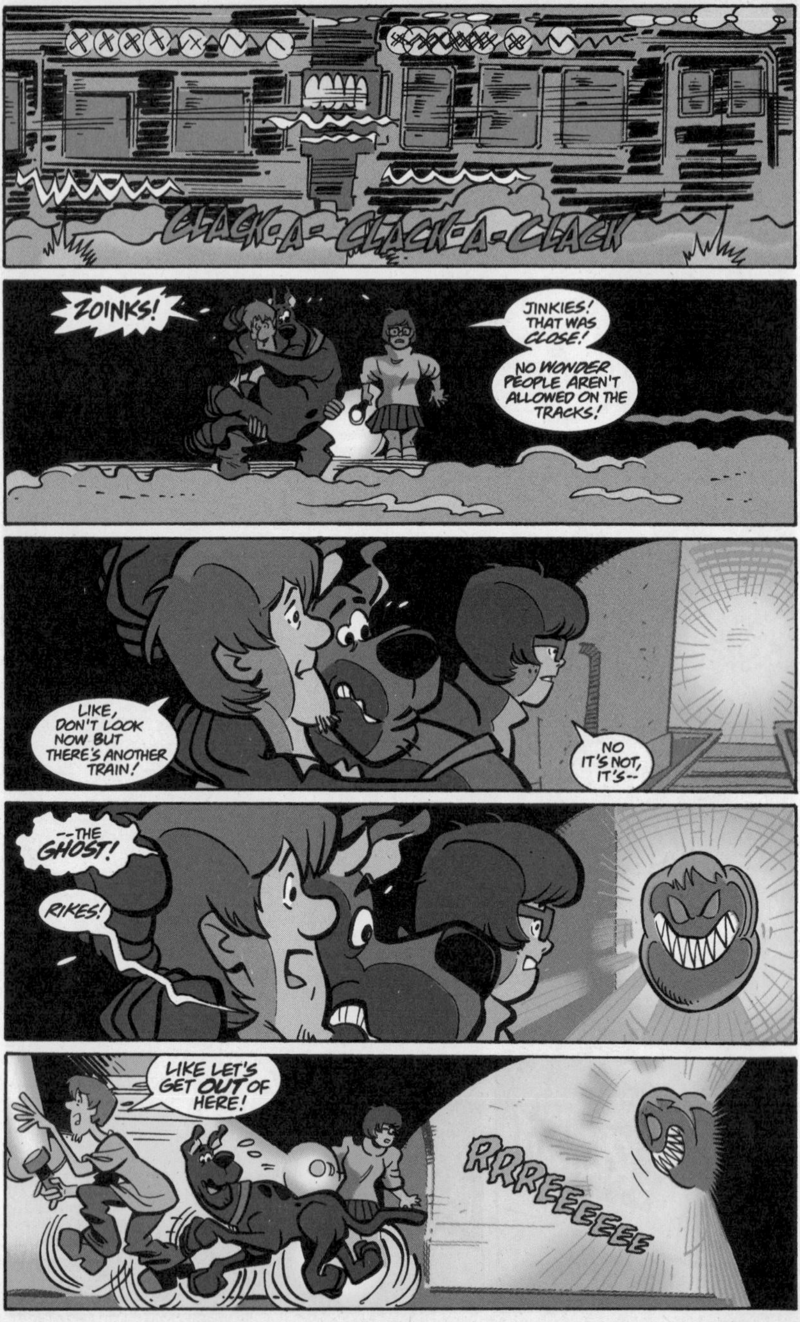
CLACK-A-CLACK-A-CLACK
ZOINKS!
JINKIES! THAT WAS CLOSE!
NO WONDER PEOPLE AREN'T ALLOWED ON THE TRACKS!
LIKE, DON'T LOOK NOW BUT THERE'S ANOTHER TRAIN!
NO IT'S NOT, IT'S--
--THE GHOST!
RIKES!
LIKE LET'S GET OUT OF HERE!
RRREEEEEEE

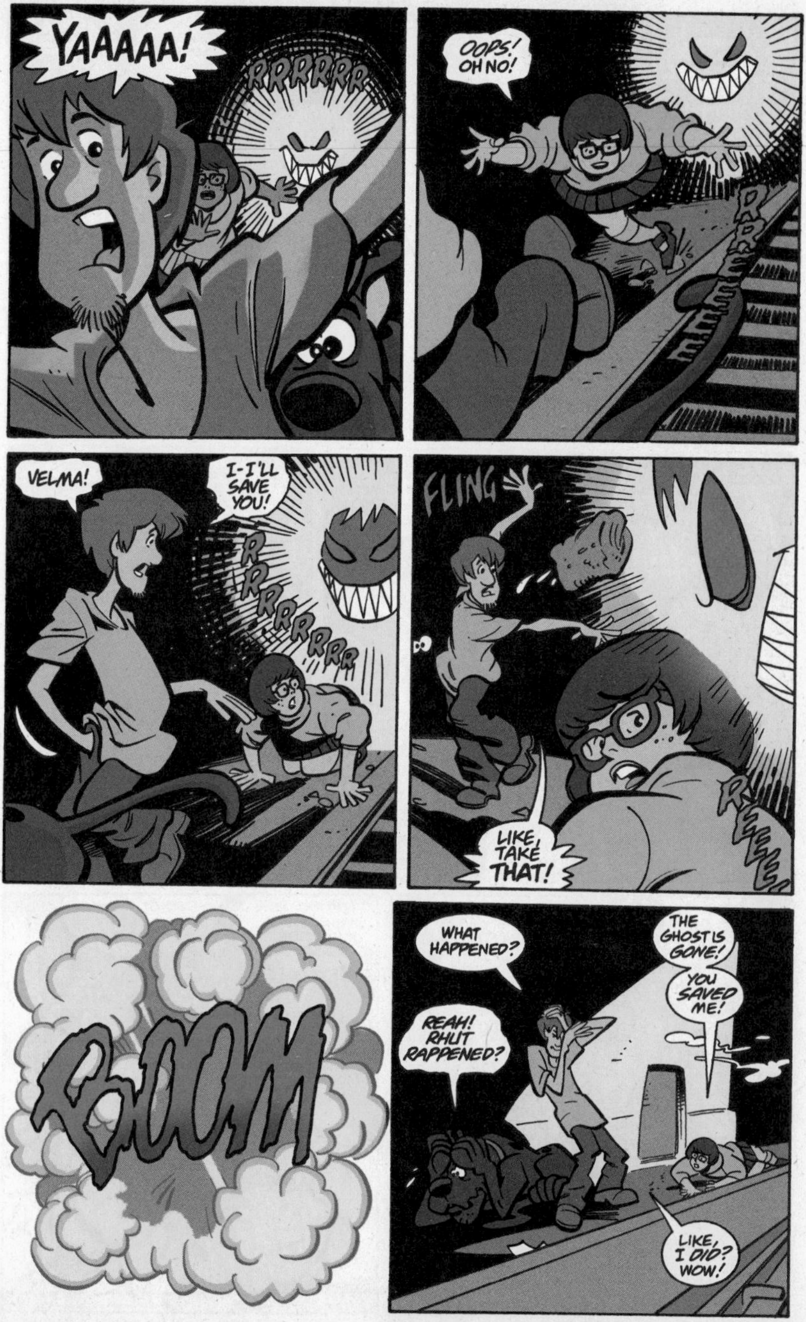
YAAAAA!
RRRRRR
OOPS! OH NO!
RRRR
VELMA!
I-I'LL SAVE YOU!
RRRRRRRRR
FLING
LIKE, TAKE THAT!
BOOM
WHAT HAPPENED?
REAH! RHUT RAPPENED?
THE GHOST IS GONE!
YOU SAVED ME!
LIKE, I DID? WOW!

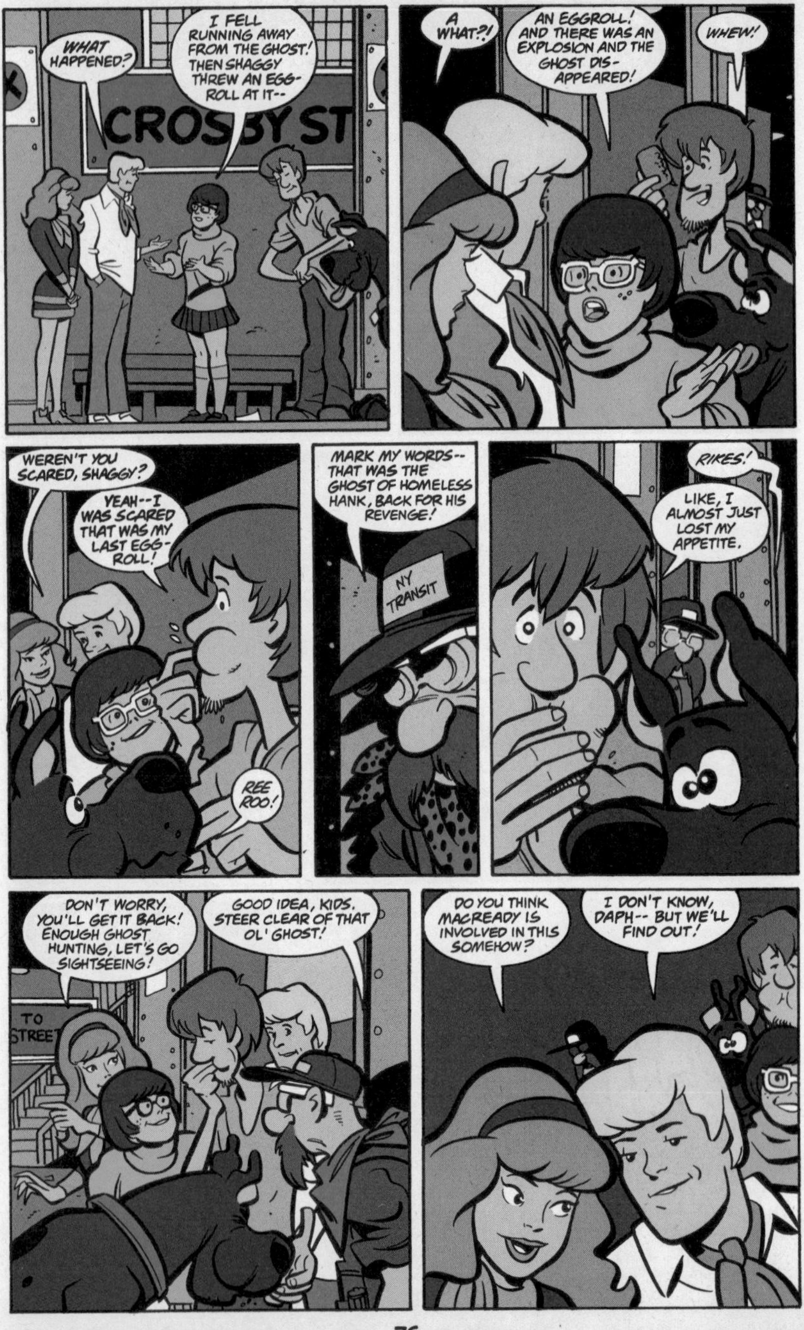

WHAT HAPPENED?
I FELL RUNNING AWAY FROM THE GHOST! THEN SHAGGY THREW AN EGG-ROLL AT IT--
CROSBY ST
A WHAT?!
AN EGGROLL! AND THERE WAS AN EXPLOSION AND THE GHOST DIS-APPEARED!
WHEW!
WEREN'T YOU SCARED, SHAGGY?
YEAH--I WAS SCARED THAT WAS MY LAST EGG-ROLL!
REE ROO!
MARK MY WORDS--THAT WAS THE GHOST OF HOMELESS HANK, BACK FOR HIS REVENGE!
NY TRANSIT
RIKES!
LIKE, I ALMOST JUST LOST MY APPETITE.
DON'T WORRY, YOU'LL GET IT BACK! ENOUGH GHOST HUNTING, LET'S GO SIGHTSEEING!
GOOD IDEA, KIDS. STEER CLEAR OF THAT OL' GHOST!
TO STREET
DO YOU THINK MACREADY IS INVOLVED IN THIS SOMEHOW?
I DON'T KNOW, DAPH-- BUT WE'LL FIND OUT!

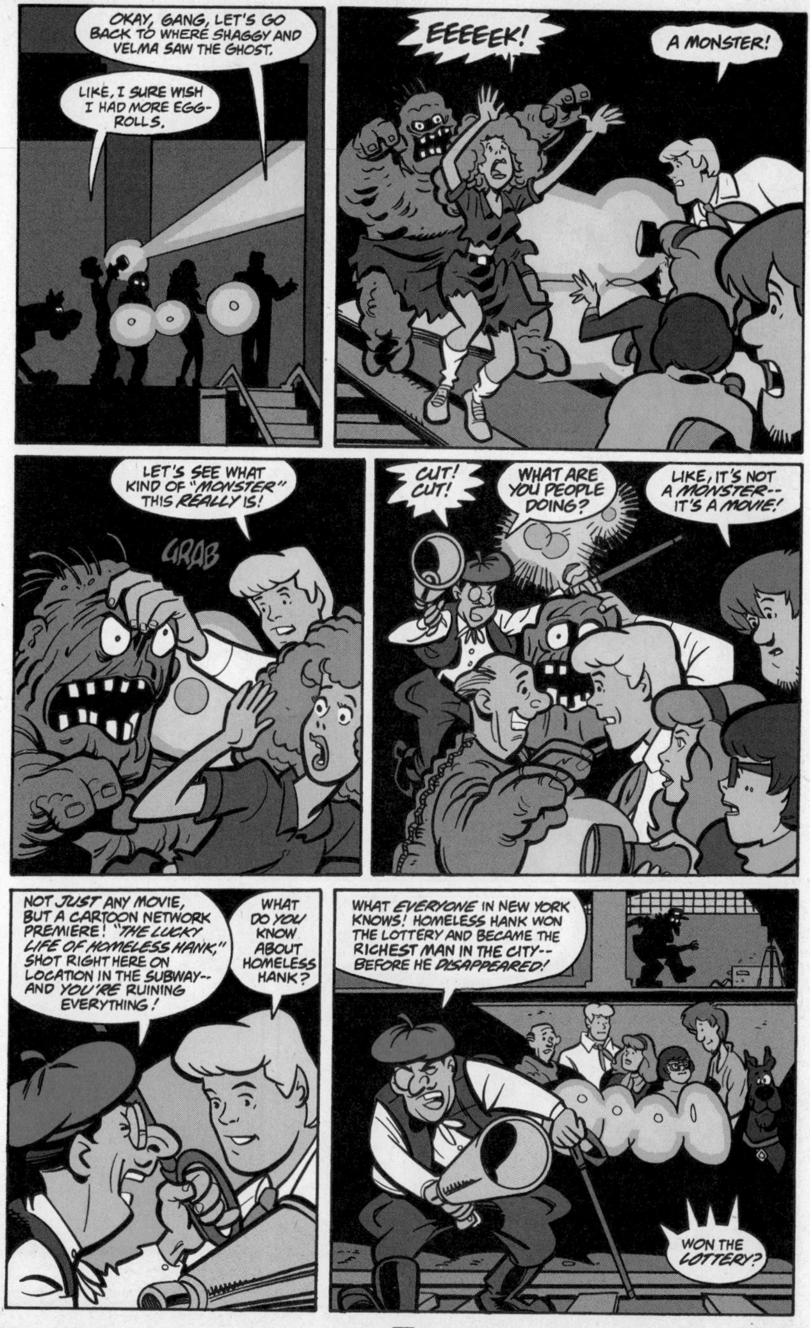
OKAY, GANG, LET'S GO BACK TO WHERE SHAGGY AND VELMA SAW THE GHOST.
LIKE, I SURE WISH I HAD MORE EGG-ROLLS.
EEEEEK!
A MONSTER!
LET'S SEE WHAT KIND OF "MONSTER" THIS REALLY IS!
GRAB
CUT! CUT!
WHAT ARE YOU PEOPLE DOING?
LIKE, IT'S NOT A MONSTER-- IT'S A MOVIE!
NOT JUST ANY MOVIE, BUT A CARTOON NETWORK PREMIERE! "THE LUCKY LIFE OF HOMELESS HANK," SHOT RIGHT HERE ON LOCATION IN THE SUBWAY-- AND YOU'RE RUINING EVERYTHING!
WHAT DO YOU KNOW ABOUT HOMELESS HANK?
WHAT EVERYONE IN NEW YORK KNOWS! HOMELESS HANK WON THE LOTTERY AND BECAME THE RICHEST MAN IN THE CITY-- BEFORE HE DISAPPEARED!
WON THE LOTTERY?

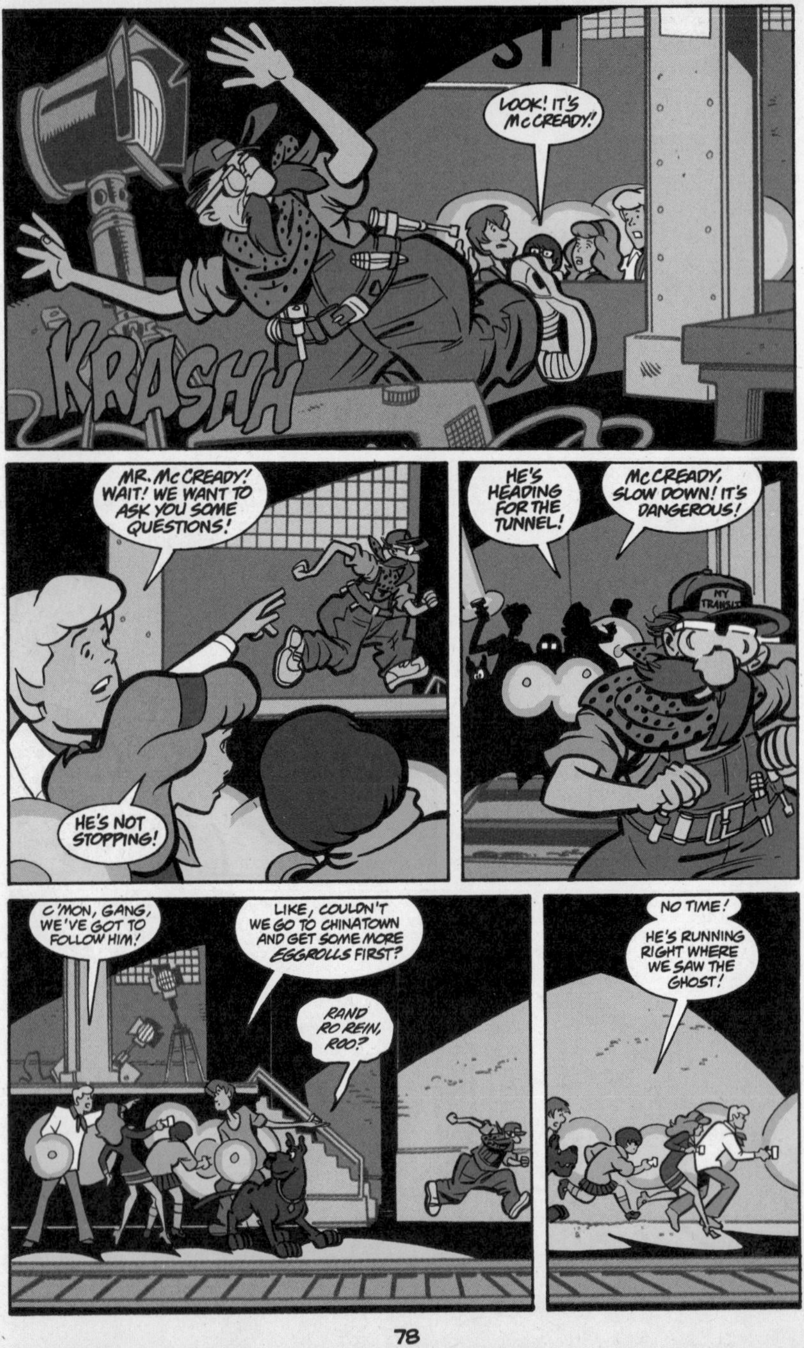
LOOK! IT'S McCREADY!
KRASHH
MR. McCREADY! WAIT! WE WANT TO ASK YOU SOME QUESTIONS!
HE'S NOT STOPPING!
HE'S HEADING FOR THE TUNNEL!
McCREADY, SLOW DOWN! IT'S DANGEROUS!
NY TRANSIT
C'MON, GANG, WE'VE GOT TO FOLLOW HIM!
LIKE, COULDN'T WE GO TO CHINATOWN AND GET SOME MORE EGGROLLS FIRST?
RAND RO REIN, ROO?
NO TIME!
HE'S RUNNING RIGHT WHERE WE SAW THE GHOST!

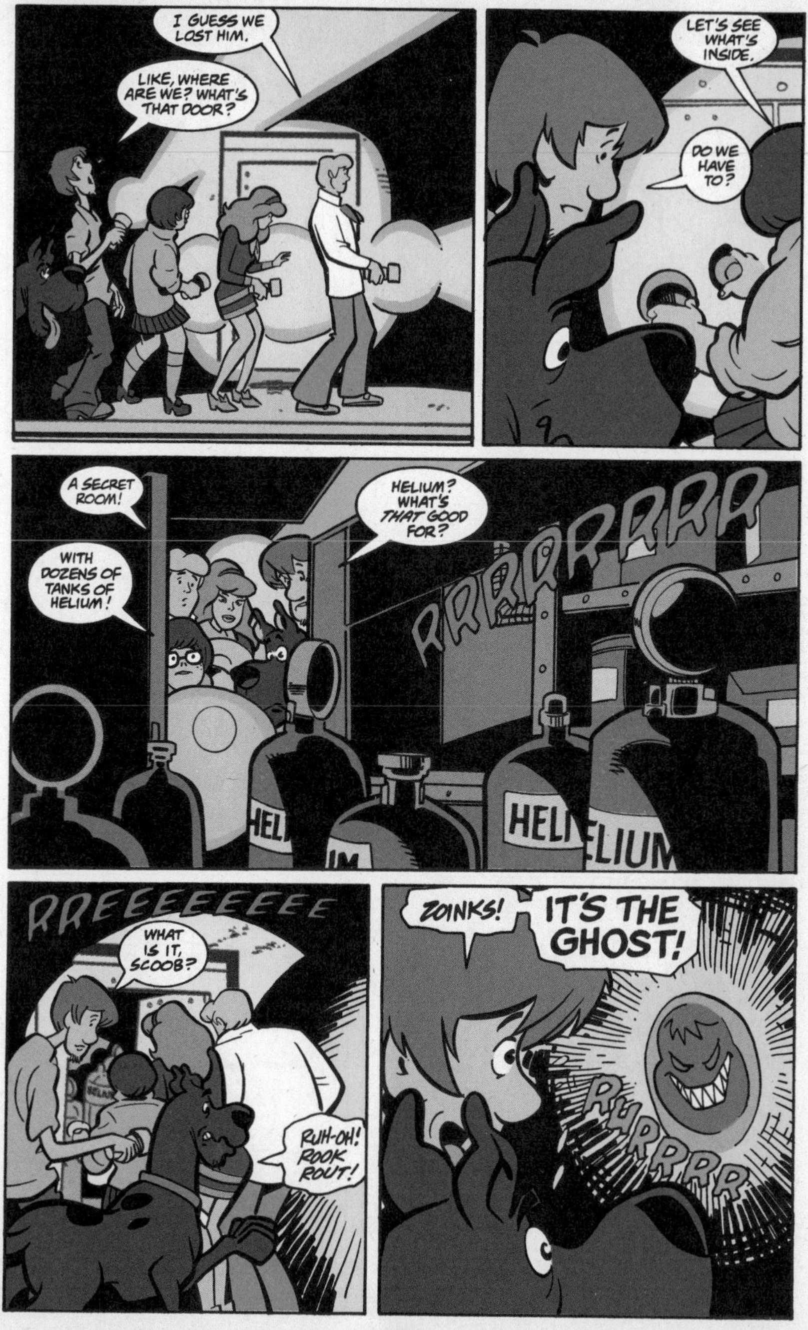
I GUESS WE LOST HIM.
LIKE, WHERE ARE WE? WHAT'S THAT DOOR?
LET'S SEE WHAT'S INSIDE.
DO WE HAVE TO?
A SECRET ROOM!
WITH DOZENS OF TANKS OF HELIUM!
HELIUM? WHAT'S THAT GOOD FOR?
RRRRRRRRRRRR
HELI
HELI
ELIUM
RREEEEEEEEEE
WHAT IS IT, SCOOB?
RUH-OH! ROOK ROUT!
ZOINKS!
IT'S THE GHOST!
RURRRRR

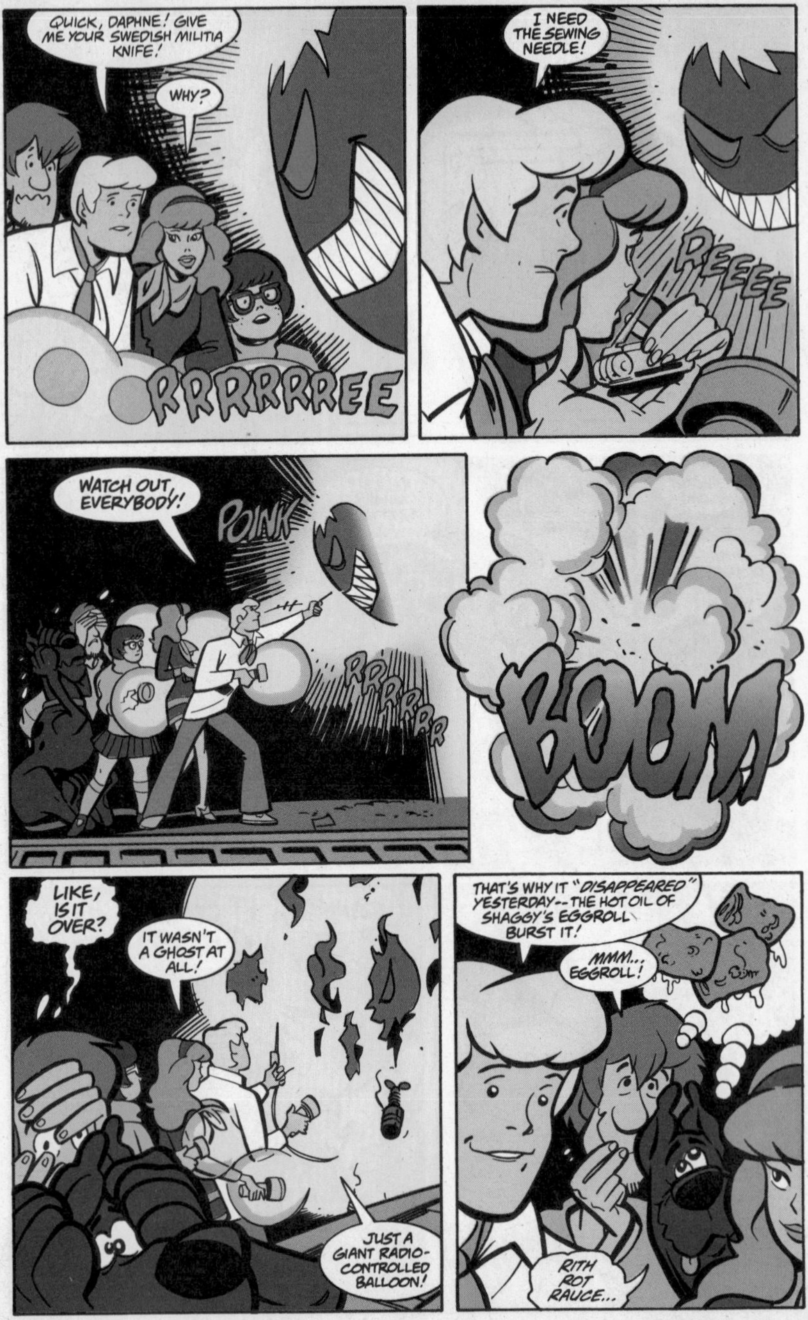
QUICK, DAPHNE! GIVE ME YOUR SWEDISH MILITIA KNIFE!
WHY?
RRRRRRREE
I NEED THE SEWING NEEDLE!
REEEEE
WATCH OUT, EVERYBODY!
POINK
RRRRRRR
BOOM
LIKE, IS IT OVER?
IT WASN'T A GHOST AT ALL!
JUST A GIANT RADIO-CONTROLLED BALLOON!
THAT'S WHY IT "DISAPPEARED" YESTERDAY-- THE HOT OIL OF SHAGGY'S EGGROLL BURST IT!
MMM... EGGROLL!
RITH ROT RAUCE...

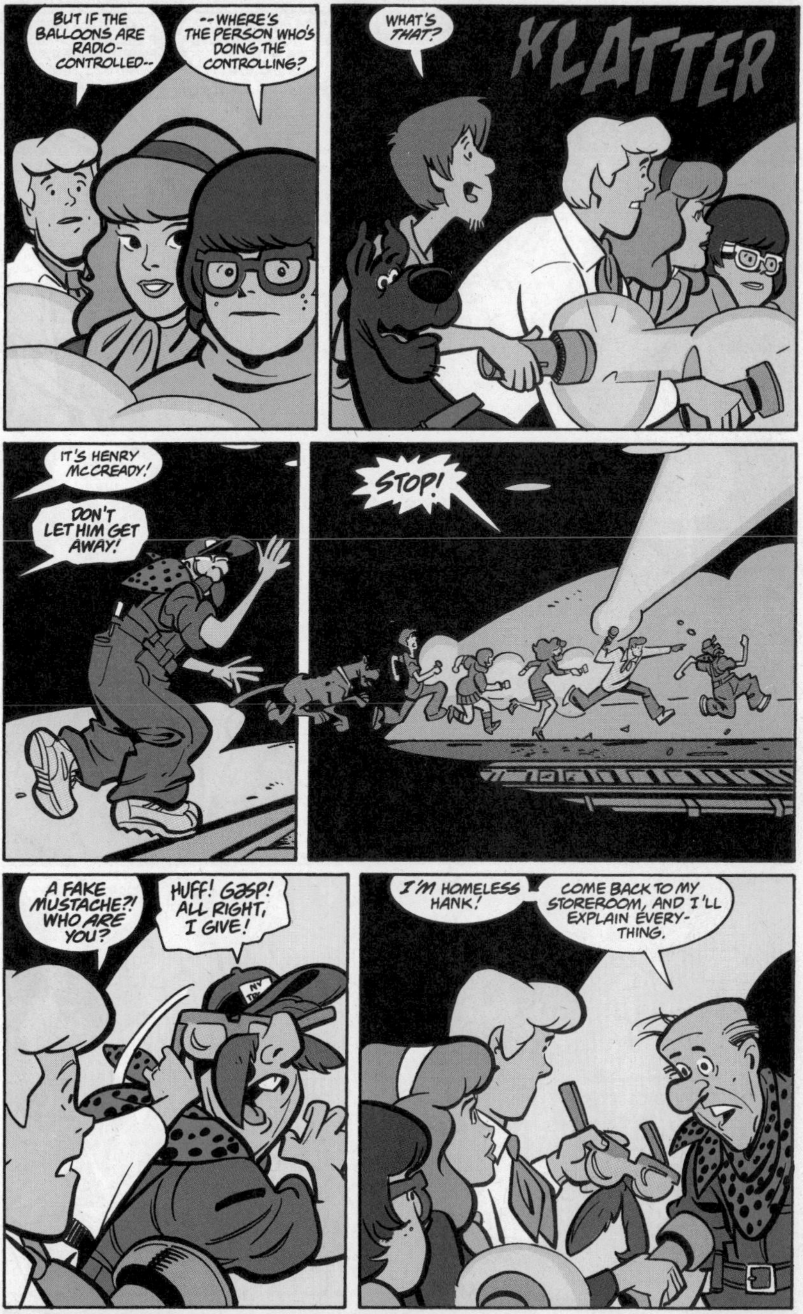
BUT IF THE BALLOONS ARE RADIO-CONTROLLED--
--WHERE'S THE PERSON WHO'S DOING THE CONTROLLING?
WHAT'S *THAT*?
KLATTER
IT'S HENRY McCREADY!
DON'T LET HIM GET AWAY!
STOP!
A FAKE MUSTACHE?! WHO *ARE* YOU?
HUFF! GASP! ALL RIGHT, I GIVE!
NY
I'M HOMELESS HANK!
COME BACK TO MY STOREROOM, AND I'LL EXPLAIN EVERY-THING.

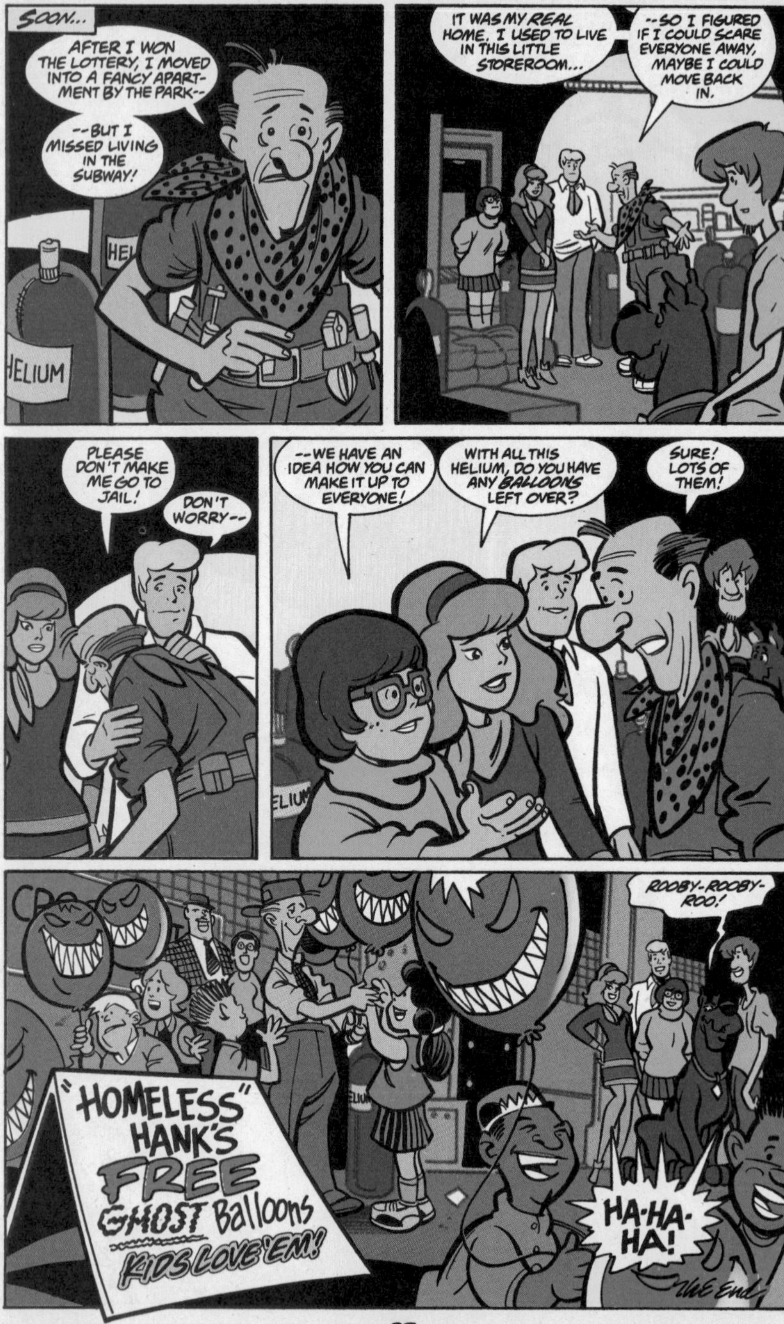
SOON...
AFTER I WON THE LOTTERY, I MOVED INTO A FANCY APARTMENT BY THE PARK--
--BUT I MISSED LIVING IN THE SUBWAY!
HELIUM
IT WAS MY REAL HOME. I USED TO LIVE IN THIS LITTLE STOREROOM...
--SO I FIGURED IF I COULD SCARE EVERYONE AWAY, MAYBE I COULD MOVE BACK IN.
PLEASE DON'T MAKE ME GO TO JAIL!
DON'T WORRY--
--WE HAVE AN IDEA HOW YOU CAN MAKE IT UP TO EVERYONE!
WITH ALL THIS HELIUM, DO YOU HAVE ANY BALLOONS LEFT OVER?
SURE! LOTS OF THEM!
ROOBY-ROOBY-ROO!
"HOMELESS" HANK'S FREE GHOST Balloons
KIDS LOVE 'EM!
HA-HA-HA!
The End

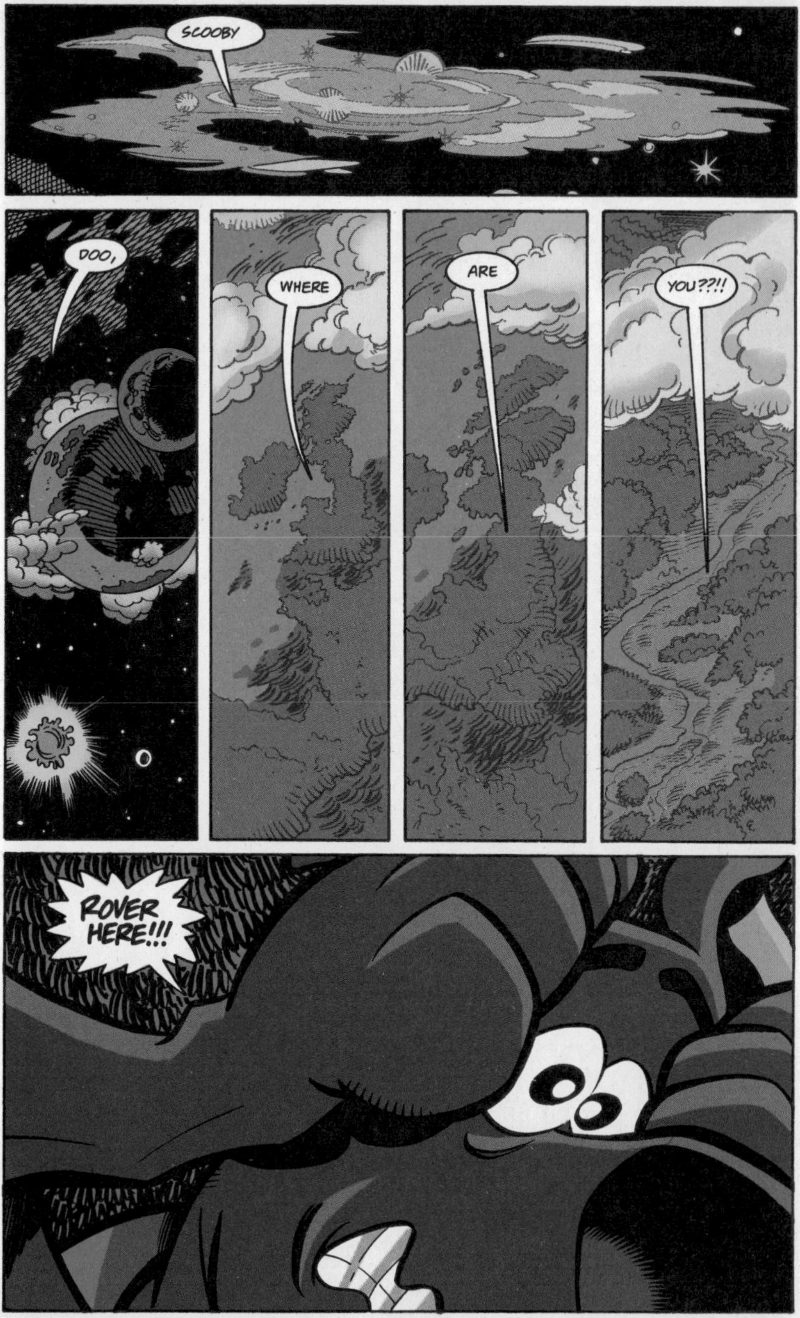
SCOOBY
DOO,
WHERE
ARE
YOU??!!
ROVER HERE!!!

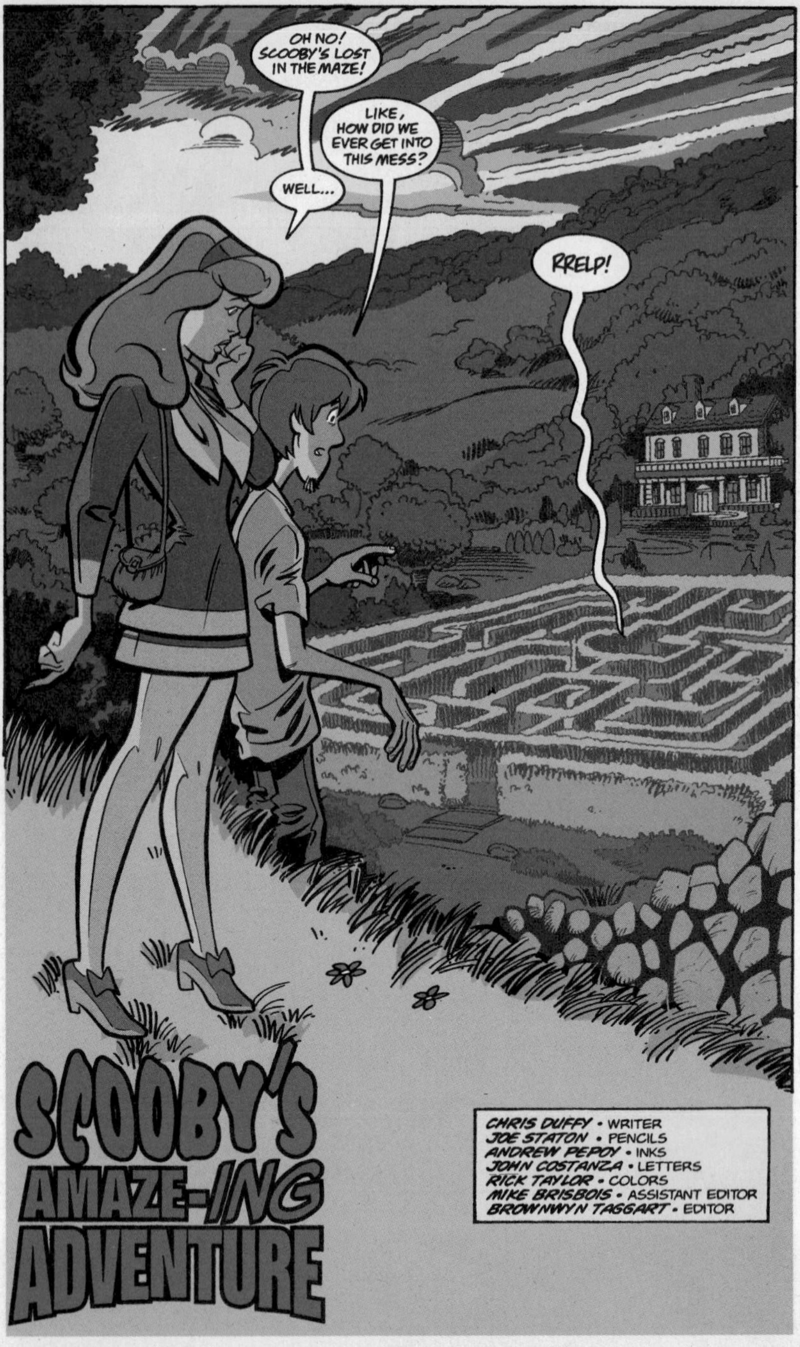
OH NO! SCOOBY'S LOST IN THE MAZE!
LIKE, HOW DID WE EVER GET INTO THIS MESS?
WELL...
RRELP!
SCOOBY'S AMAZE-ING ADVENTURE
CHRIS DUFFY • WRITER
JOE STATON • PENCILS
ANDREW PEPOY • INKS
JOHN COSTANZA • LETTERS
RICK TAYLOR • COLORS
MIKE BRISBOIS • ASSISTANT EDITOR
BROWNWYN TAGGART • EDITOR

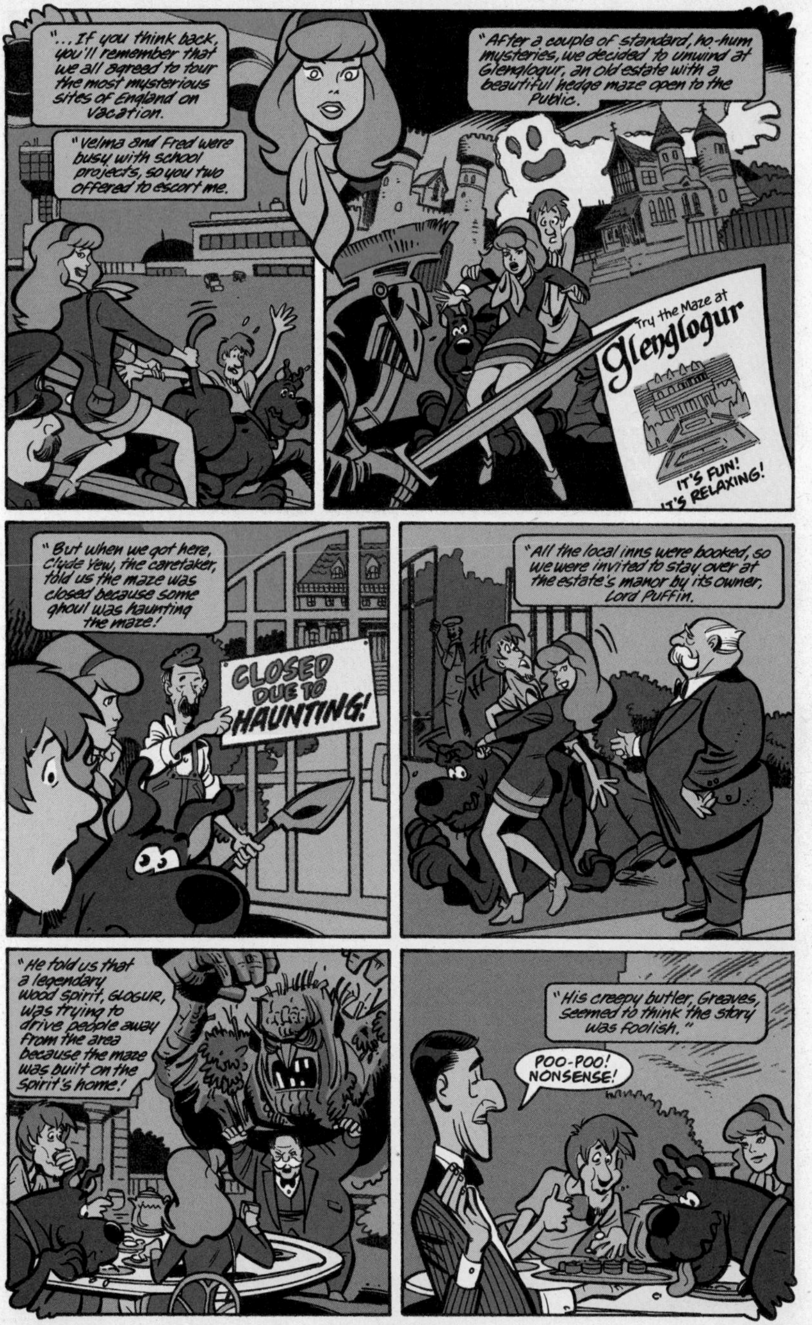
"...If you think back, you'll remember that we all agreed to tour the most mysterious sites of England on vacation.
"Velma and Fred were busy with school projects, so you two offered to escort me.
"After a couple of standard, ho-hum mysteries, we decided to unwind at Glenglogur, an old estate with a beautiful hedge maze open to the public.
Try the Maze at Glenglogur
IT'S FUN! IT'S RELAXING!
"But when we got here, Clyde Yew, the caretaker, told us the maze was closed because some ghoul was haunting the maze!
CLOSED DUE TO HAUNTING!
"All the local inns were booked, so we were invited to stay over at the estate's manor by its owner, Lord Puffin.
"He told us that a legendary wood spirit, GLOGUR, was trying to drive people away from the area because the maze was built on the spirit's home!
"His creepy butler, Greaves, seemed to think the story was foolish."
POO-POO! NONSENSE!

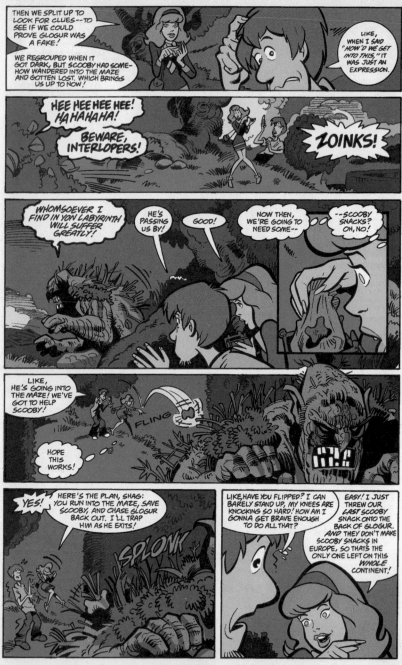

THEN WE SPLIT UP TO LOOK FOR CLUES--TO SEE IF WE COULD PROVE GLOGUR WAS A FAKE!

WE REGROUPED WHEN IT GOT DARK, BUT SCOOBY HAD SOMEHOW WANDERED INTO THE MAZE AND GOTTEN LOST. WHICH BRINGS US UP TO NOW!

LIKE, WHEN I SAID "HOW'D WE GET INTO THIS," IT WAS JUST AN EXPRESSION.

HEE HEE HEE HEE! HA HA HA HA!

BEWARE, INTERLOPERS!

ZOINKS!

WHOMSOEVER I FIND IN YON LABYRINTH WILL SUFFER GREATLY!

HE'S PASSING US BY!

GOOD!

NOW THEN, WE'RE GOING TO NEED SOME--

--SCOOBY SNACKS? OH, NO!

LIKE, HE'S GOING INTO THE MAZE! WE'VE GOT TO HELP SCOOBY!

FLING

HOPE THIS WORKS!

YES!

HERE'S THE PLAN, SHAG: YOU RUN INTO THE MAZE, SAVE SCOOBY, AND CHASE GLOGUR BACK OUT. I'LL TRAP HIM AS HE EXITS!

SPLONK

LIKE, HAVE YOU FLIPPED? I CAN BARELY STAND UP, MY KNEES ARE KNOCKING SO HARD! HOW AM I GONNA GET BRAVE ENOUGH TO DO ALL THAT?

EASY! I JUST THREW OUR LAST SCOOBY SNACK ONTO THE BACK OF GLOGUR, AND THEY DON'T MAKE SCOOBY SNACKS IN EUROPE, SO THAT'S THE ONLY ONE LEFT ON THIS WHOLE CONTINENT!

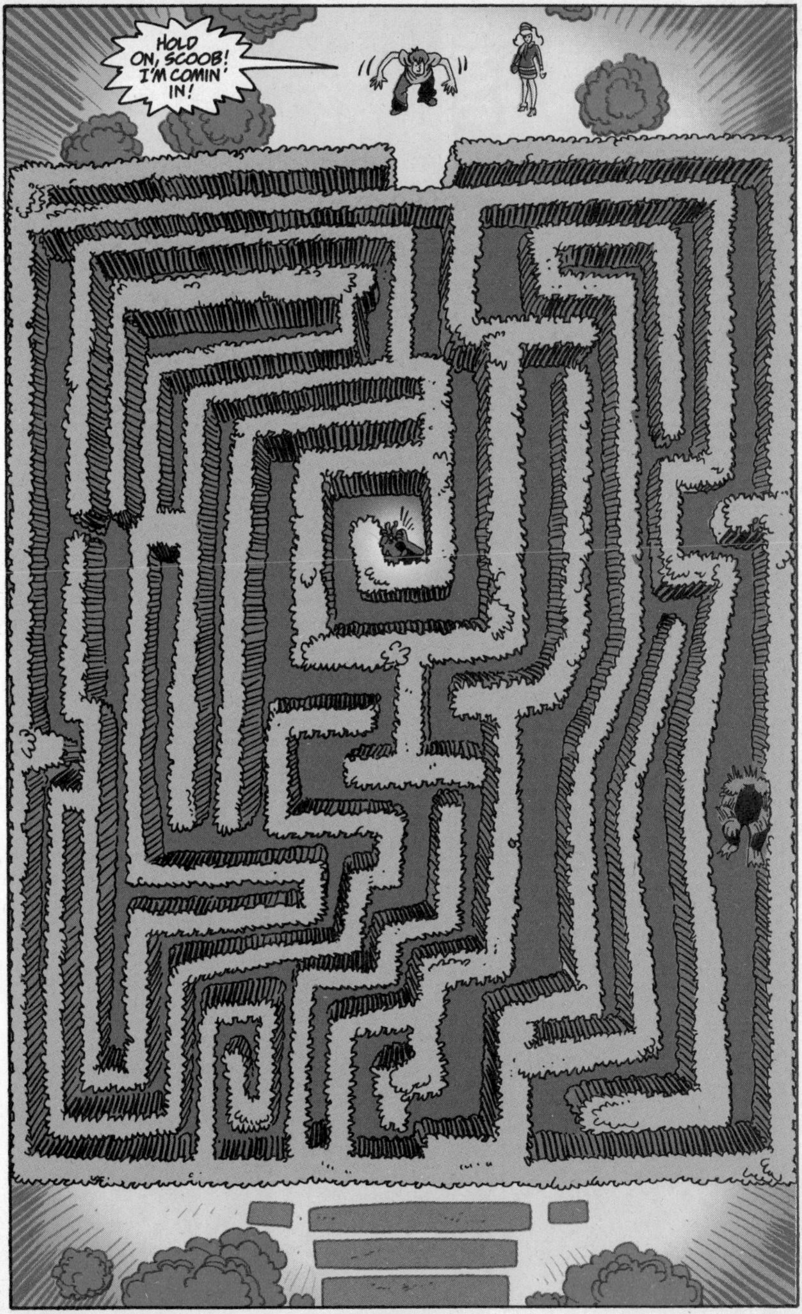
HOLD ON, SCOOB! I'M COMIN' IN!

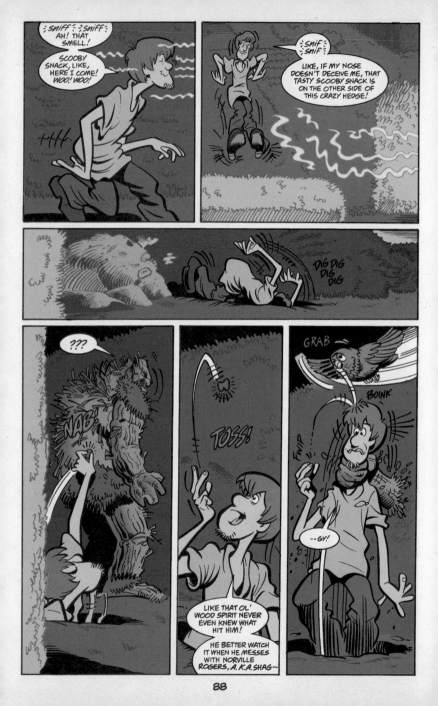

SNIFF! SNIFF! AH! THAT SMELL!

SCOOBY SNACK, LIKE, HERE I COME! WOO! WOO!

SNIF! SNIF!

LIKE, IF MY NOSE DOESN'T DECEIVE ME, THAT TASTY SCOOBY SNACK IS ON THE OTHER SIDE OF THIS CRAZY HEDGE!

DIG DIG DIG DIG

???

NAB!

TOSS!

LIKE THAT OL' WOOD SPIRIT NEVER EVEN KNEW WHAT HIT HIM!

HE BETTER WATCH IT WHEN HE MESSES WITH NORVILLE ROGERS, A.K.A. SHAG--

GRAB

BOINK

FWIP!

--GY!

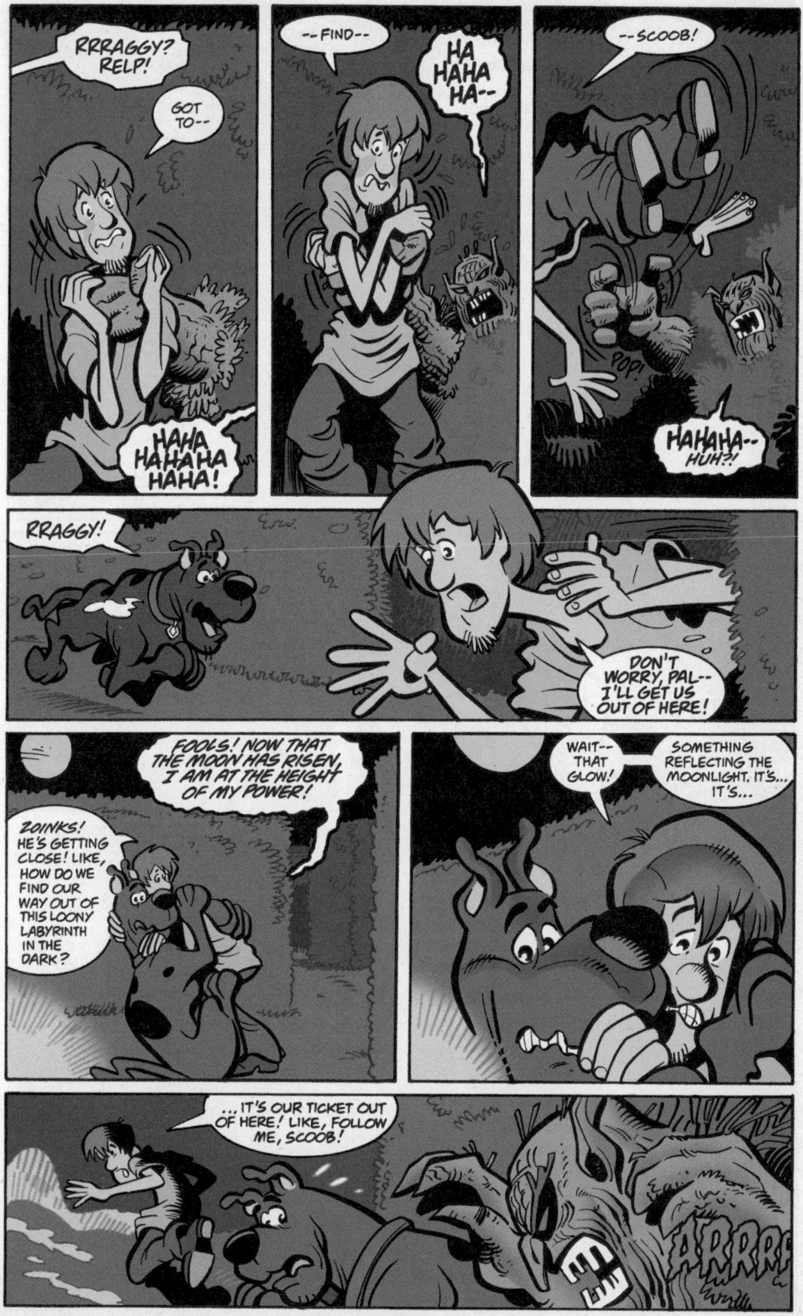
RRRAGGY? RELP!
GOT TO--
HAHA HAHAHA HAHA!
--FIND--
HA HAHAHA HA--
--SCOOB!
POP!
HAHAHA-- HUH?!
RRAGGY!
DON'T WORRY, PAL-- I'LL GET US OUT OF HERE!
FOOLS! NOW THAT THE MOON HAS RISEN, I AM AT THE HEIGHT OF MY POWER!
ZOINKS! HE'S GETTING CLOSE! LIKE, HOW DO WE FIND OUR WAY OUT OF THIS LOONY LABYRINTH IN THE DARK?
WAIT-- THAT GLOW!
SOMETHING REFLECTING THE MOONLIGHT. IT'S... IT'S...
...IT'S OUR TICKET OUT OF HERE! LIKE, FOLLOW ME, SCOOB!
ARRR

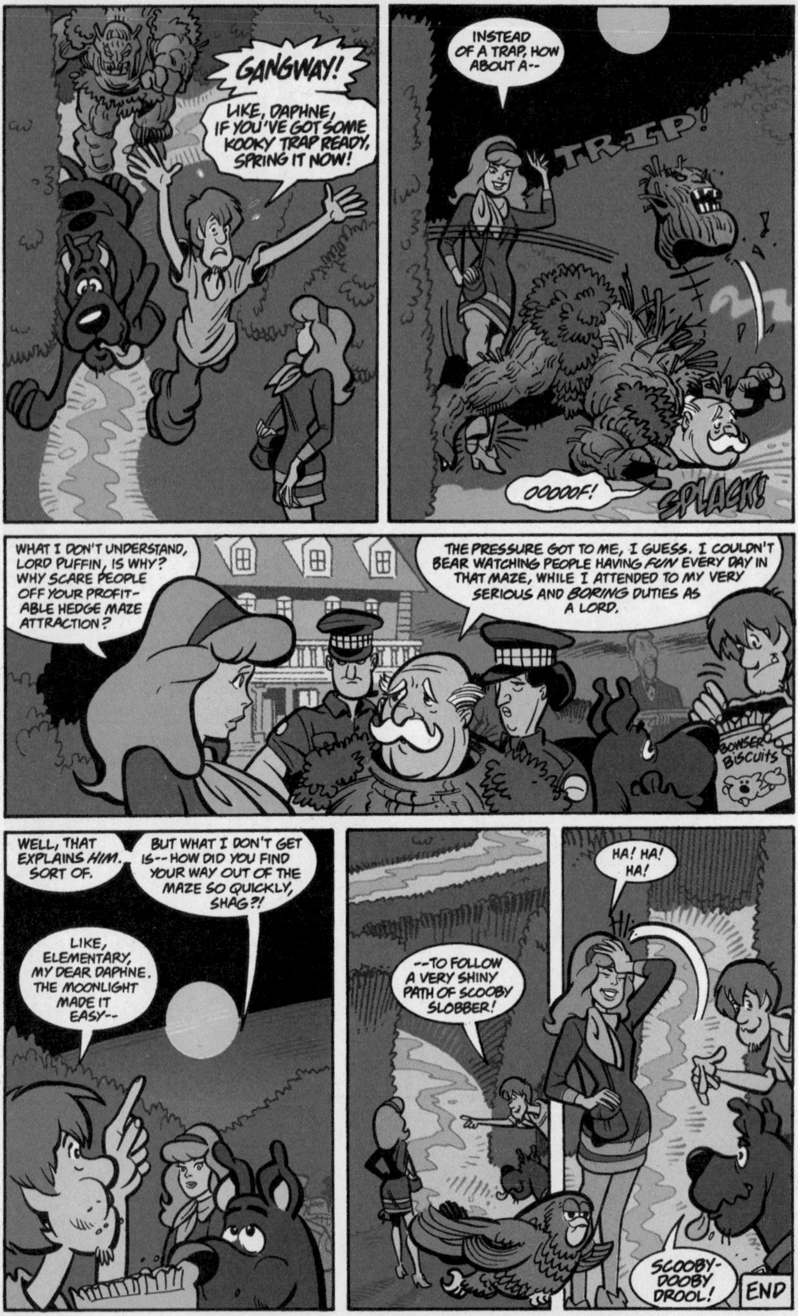
GANGWAY!
LIKE, DAPHNE, IF YOU'VE GOT SOME KOOKY TRAP READY, SPRING IT NOW!
INSTEAD OF A TRAP, HOW ABOUT A--
TRIP!
OOOOOF!
SPLACK!
WHAT I DON'T UNDERSTAND, LORD PUFFIN, IS WHY? WHY SCARE PEOPLE OFF YOUR PROFIT-ABLE HEDGE MAZE ATTRACTION?
THE PRESSURE GOT TO ME, I GUESS. I COULDN'T BEAR WATCHING PEOPLE HAVING FUN EVERY DAY IN THAT MAZE, WHILE I ATTENDED TO MY VERY SERIOUS AND BORING DUTIES AS A LORD.
BOWSER BISCUITS
WELL, THAT EXPLAINS HIM. SORT OF.
BUT WHAT I DON'T GET IS-- HOW DID YOU FIND YOUR WAY OUT OF THE MAZE SO QUICKLY, SHAG?!
LIKE, ELEMENTARY, MY DEAR DAPHNE. THE MOONLIGHT MADE IT EASY--
--TO FOLLOW A VERY SHINY PATH OF SCOOBY SLOBBER!
HA! HA! HA!
SCOOBY-DOOBY DROOL!
END

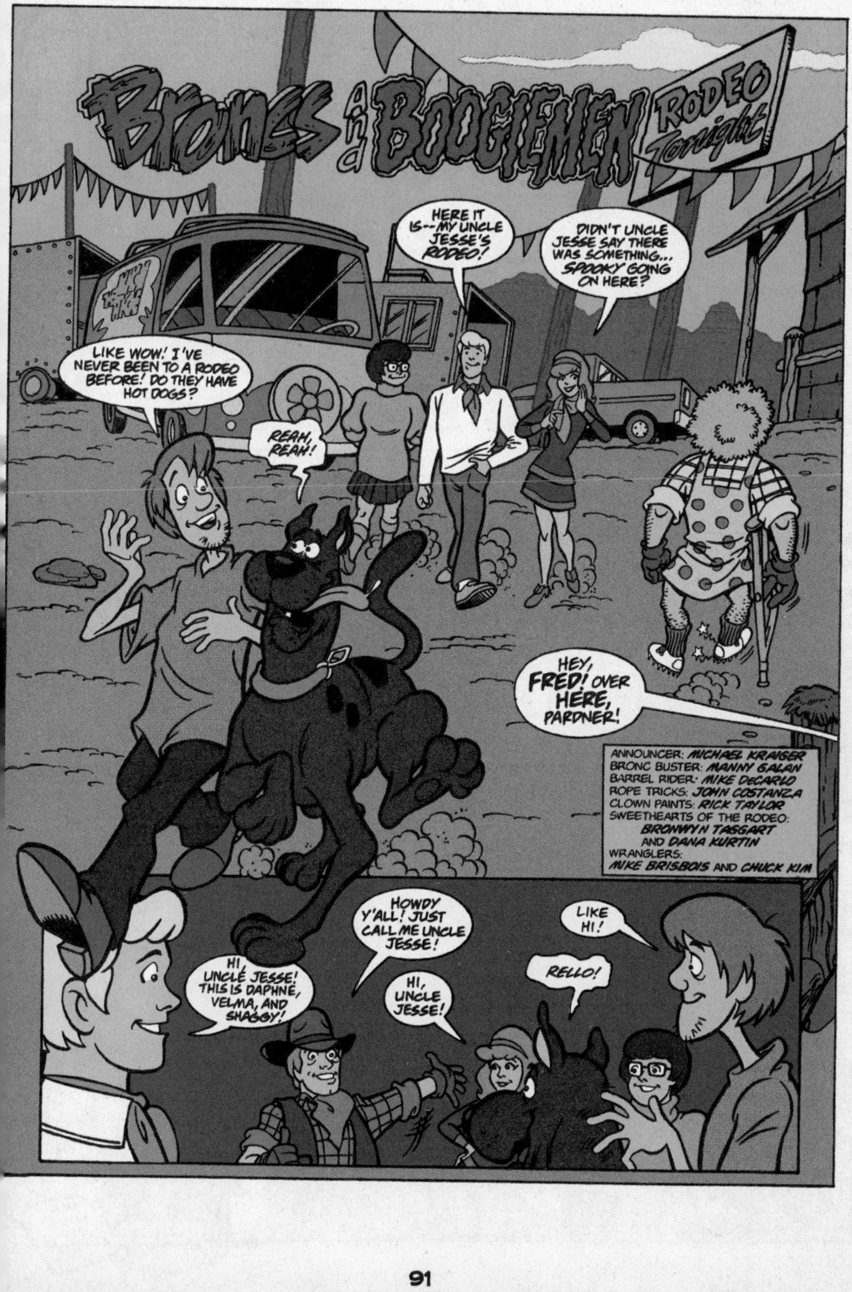
Broncs and Boogiemen
RODEO Tonight
HERE IT IS--MY UNCLE JESSE'S RODEO!
DIDN'T UNCLE JESSE SAY THERE WAS SOMETHING... SPOOKY GOING ON HERE?
LIKE WOW! I'VE NEVER BEEN TO A RODEO BEFORE! DO THEY HAVE HOT DOGS?
REAH, REAH!
HEY, FRED! OVER HERE, PARDNER!
ANNOUNCER: MICHAEL KRAIGER
BRONC BUSTER: MANNY GALAN
BARREL RIDER: MIKE DeCARLO
ROPE TRICKS: JOHN COSTANZA
CLOWN PAINTS: RICK TAYLOR
SWEETHEARTS OF THE RODEO: BRONWYN TAGGART AND DANA KURTIN
WRANGLERS: MIKE BRISBOIS AND CHUCK KIM
HOWDY Y'ALL! JUST CALL ME UNCLE JESSE!
HI, UNCLE JESSE! THIS IS DAPHNE, VELMA, AND SHAGGY!
HI, UNCLE JESSE!
LIKE HI!
RELLO!

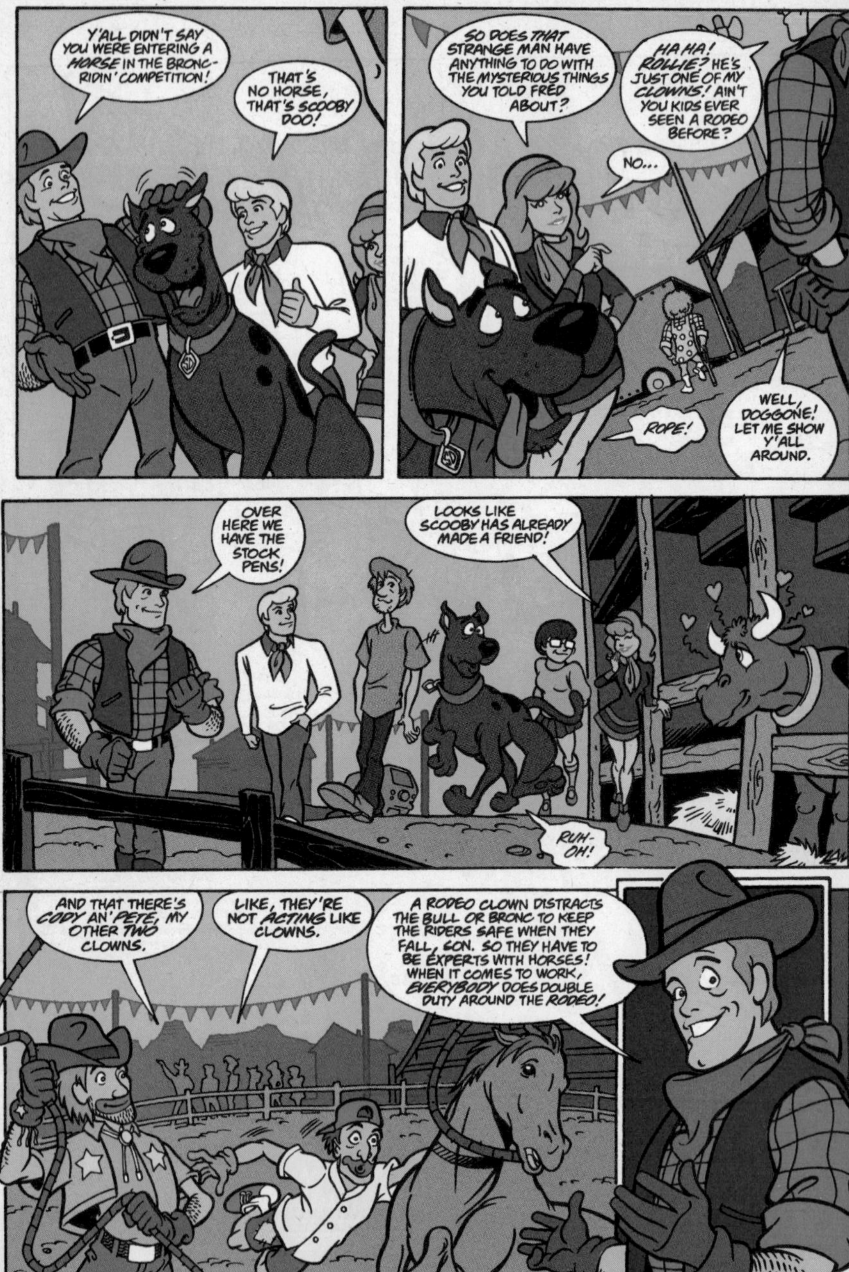

Y'ALL DIDN'T SAY YOU WERE ENTERING A HORSE IN THE BRONC-RIDIN' COMPETITION!
THAT'S NO HORSE, THAT'S SCOOBY DOO!
SO DOES THAT STRANGE MAN HAVE ANYTHING TO DO WITH THE MYSTERIOUS THINGS YOU TOLD FRED ABOUT?
HA HA! ROLLIE? HE'S JUST ONE OF MY CLOWNS! AIN'T YOU KIDS EVER SEEN A RODEO BEFORE?
NO...
ROPE!
WELL, DOGGONE! LET ME SHOW Y'ALL AROUND.
OVER HERE WE HAVE THE STOCK PENS!
LOOKS LIKE SCOOBY HAS ALREADY MADE A FRIEND!
RUH-OH!
AND THAT THERE'S CODY AN' PETE, MY OTHER TWO CLOWNS.
LIKE, THEY'RE NOT ACTING LIKE CLOWNS.
A RODEO CLOWN DISTRACTS THE BULL OR BRONC TO KEEP THE RIDERS SAFE WHEN THEY FALL, SON. SO THEY HAVE TO BE EXPERTS WITH HORSES! WHEN IT COMES TO WORK, EVERYBODY DOES DOUBLE DUTY AROUND THE RODEO!

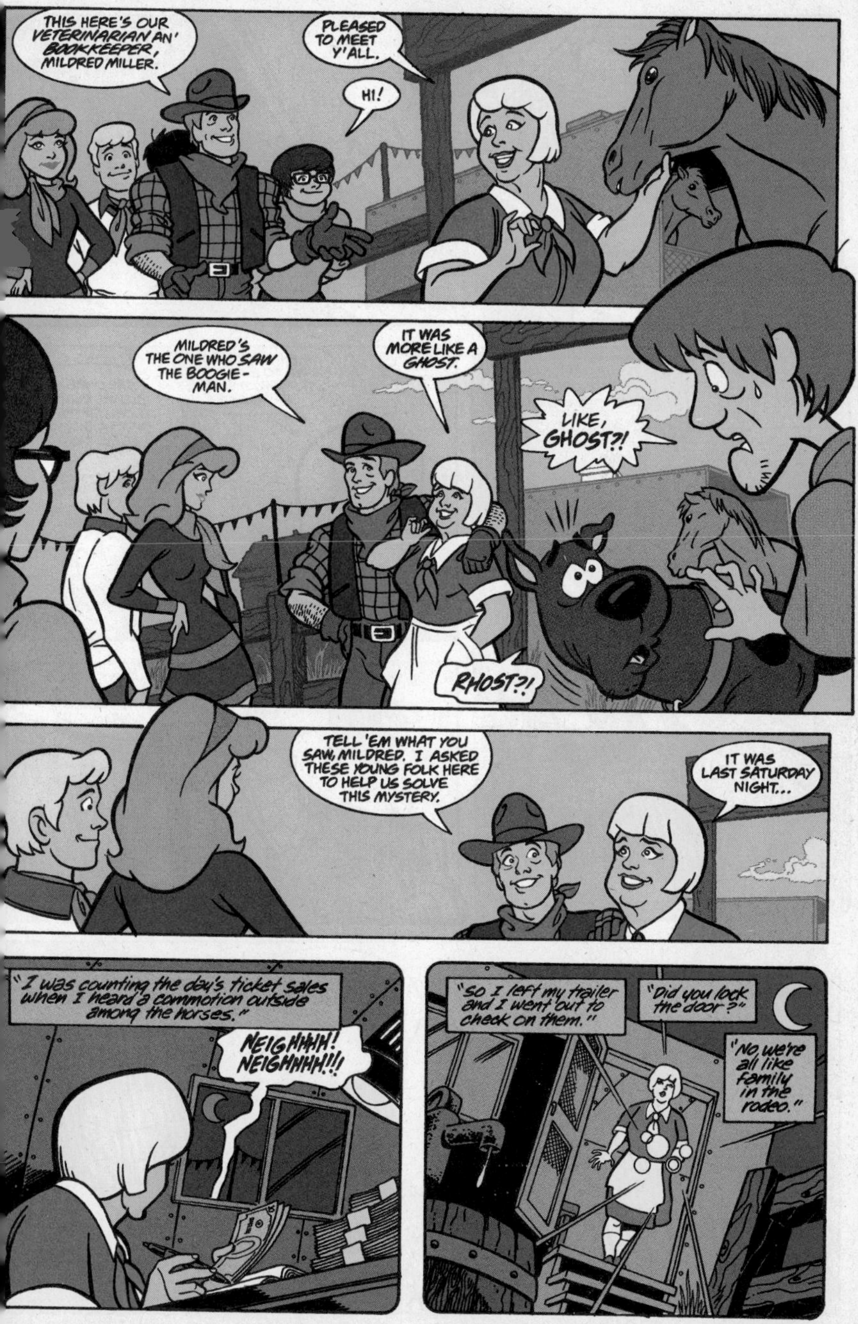
THIS HERE'S OUR VETERINARIAN AN' BOOKKEEPER, MILDRED MILLER.
PLEASED TO MEET Y'ALL.
HI!
MILDRED'S THE ONE WHO SAW THE BOOGIE-MAN.
IT WAS MORE LIKE A GHOST.
LIKE, GHOST?!
RHOST?!
TELL 'EM WHAT YOU SAW, MILDRED. I ASKED THESE YOUNG FOLK HERE TO HELP US SOLVE THIS MYSTERY.
IT WAS LAST SATURDAY NIGHT...
"I was counting the day's ticket sales when I heard a commotion outside among the horses."
NEIGHHHH! NEIGHHHH!!!
"So I left my trailer and I went out to check on them."
"Did you lock the door?"
"No, we're all like family in the rodeo."

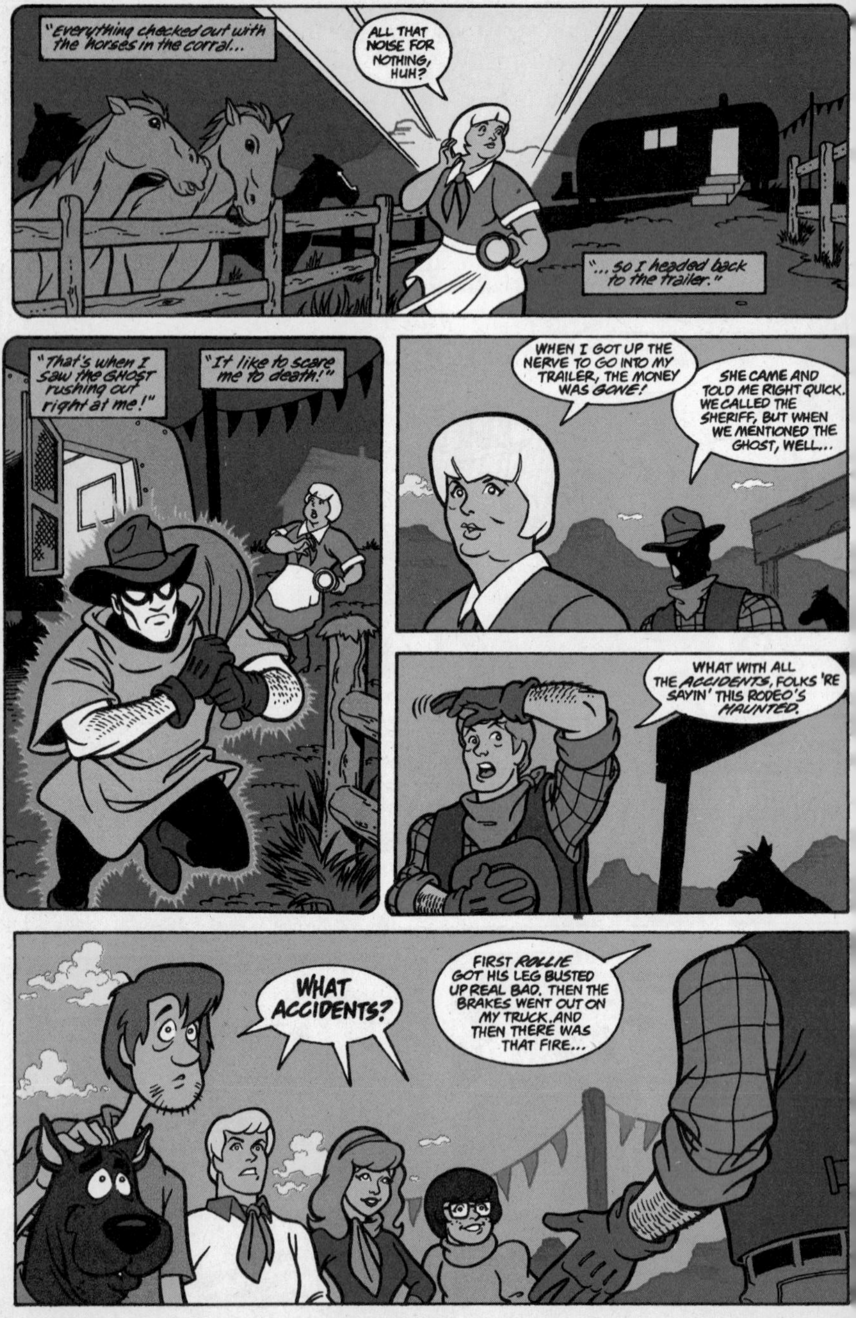
"Everything checked out with the horses in the corral...
ALL THAT NOISE FOR NOTHING, HUH?
"...so I headed back to the trailer."
"That's when I saw the GHOST rushing out right at me!"
"It like to scare me to death!"
WHEN I GOT UP THE NERVE TO GO INTO MY TRAILER, THE MONEY WAS GONE!
SHE CAME AND TOLD ME RIGHT QUICK. WE CALLED THE SHERIFF, BUT WHEN WE MENTIONED THE GHOST, WELL...
WHAT WITH ALL THE ACCIDENTS, FOLKS 'RE SAYIN' THIS RODEO'S HAUNTED.
WHAT ACCIDENTS?
FIRST ROLLIE GOT HIS LEG BUSTED UP REAL BAD. THEN THE BRAKES WENT OUT ON MY TRUCK. AND THEN THERE WAS THAT FIRE...

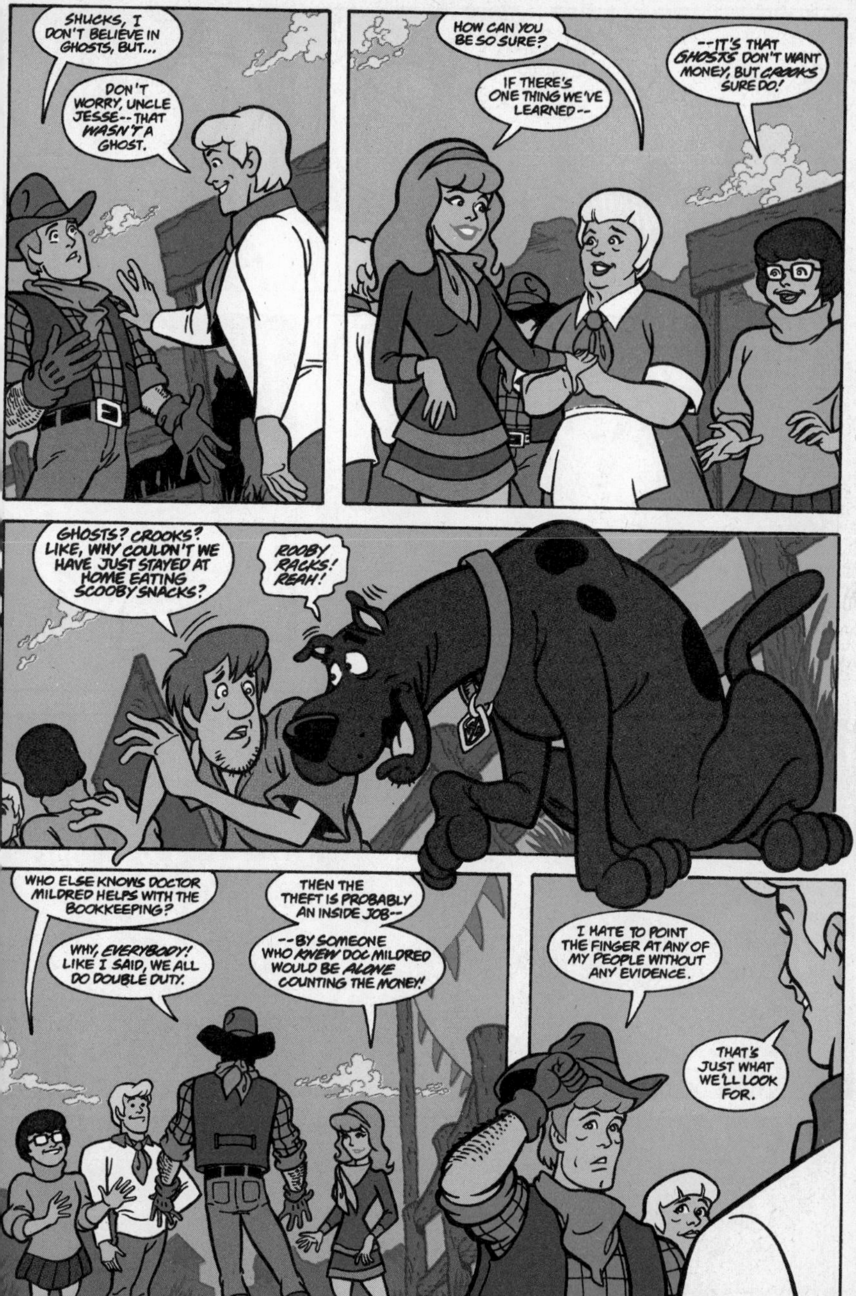
SHUCKS, I DON'T BELIEVE IN GHOSTS, BUT...
DON'T WORRY, UNCLE JESSE--THAT WASN'T A GHOST.
HOW CAN YOU BE SO SURE?
IF THERE'S ONE THING WE'VE LEARNED--
--IT'S THAT GHOSTS DON'T WANT MONEY, BUT CROOKS SURE DO!
GHOSTS? CROOKS? LIKE, WHY COULDN'T WE HAVE JUST STAYED AT HOME EATING SCOOBY SNACKS?
ROOBY RACKS! REAH!
WHO ELSE KNOWS DOCTOR MILDRED HELPS WITH THE BOOKKEEPING?
WHY, EVERYBODY! LIKE I SAID, WE ALL DO DOUBLE DUTY.
THEN THE THEFT IS PROBABLY AN INSIDE JOB--
--BY SOMEONE WHO KNEW DOC MILDRED WOULD BE ALONE COUNTING THE MONEY!
I HATE TO POINT THE FINGER AT ANY OF MY PEOPLE WITHOUT ANY EVIDENCE.
THAT'S JUST WHAT WE'LL LOOK FOR.

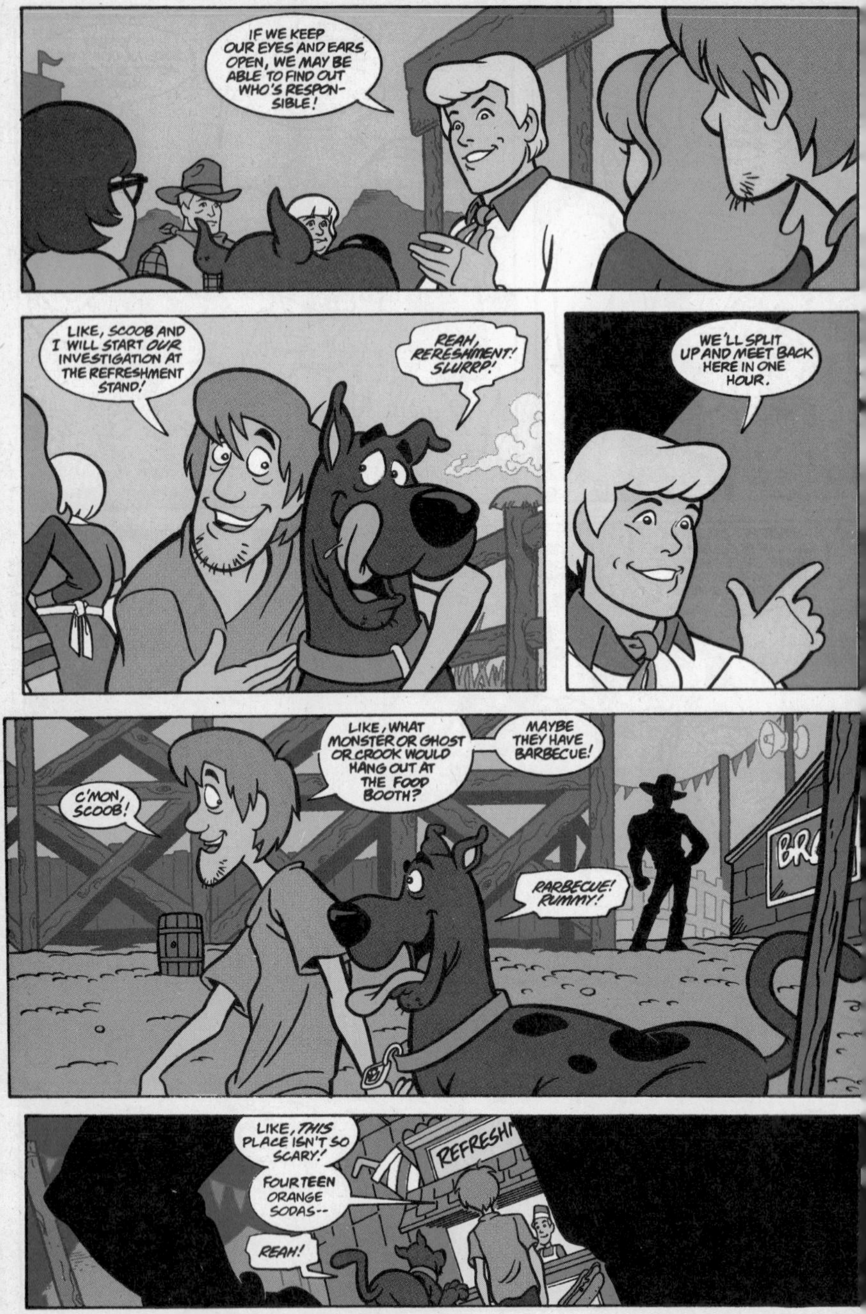
IF WE KEEP OUR EYES AND EARS OPEN, WE MAY BE ABLE TO FIND OUT WHO'S RESPONSIBLE!
LIKE, SCOOB AND I WILL START OUR INVESTIGATION AT THE REFRESHMENT STAND!
REAH, RERESHMENT! SLURRP!
WE'LL SPLIT UP AND MEET BACK HERE IN ONE HOUR.
C'MON, SCOOB!
LIKE, WHAT MONSTER OR GHOST OR CROOK WOULD HANG OUT AT THE FOOD BOOTH?
MAYBE THEY HAVE BARBECUE!
RARBECUE! RUMMY!
BR
LIKE, THIS PLACE ISN'T SO SCARY!
FOURTEEN ORANGE SODAS--
REAH!
REFRESH

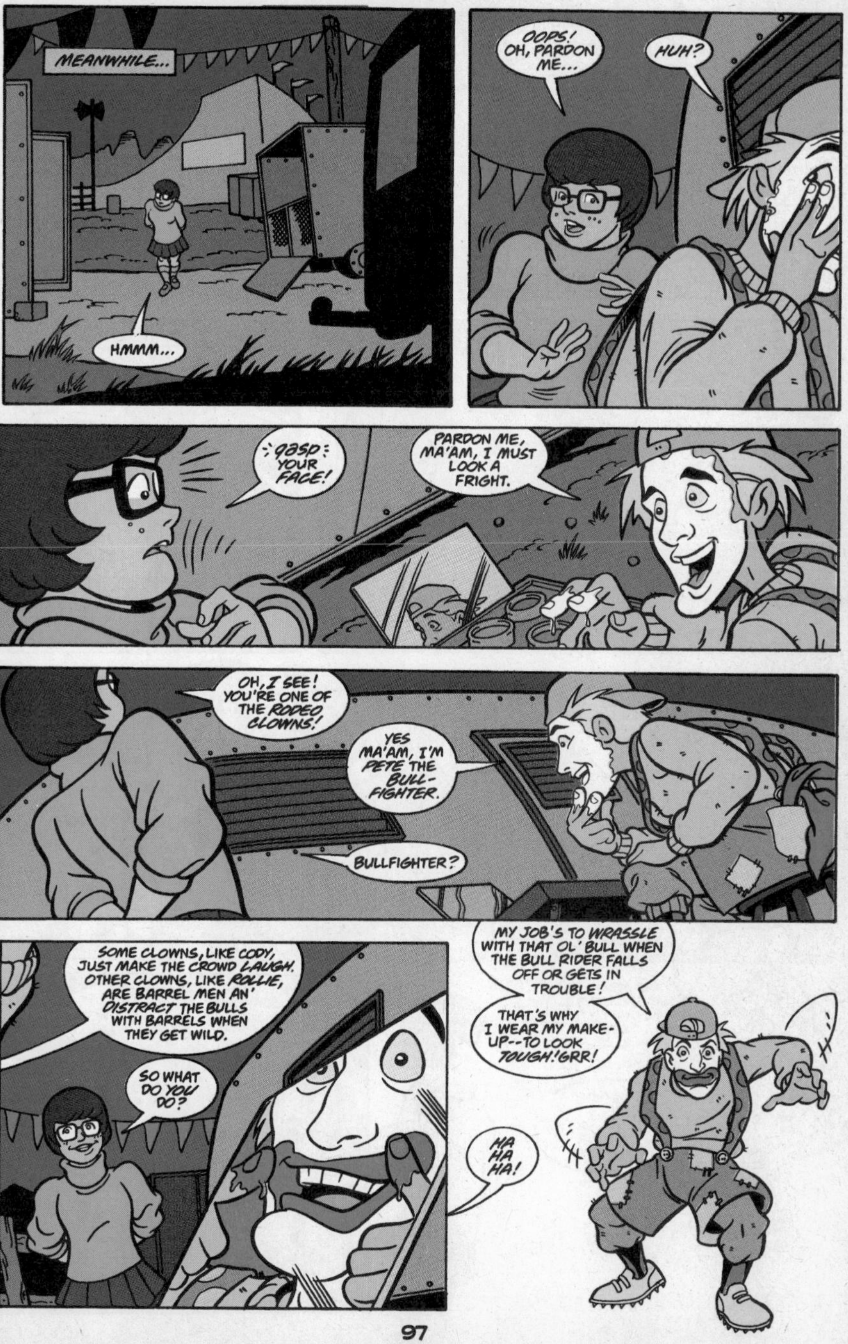
MEANWHILE...
HMMM...
OOPS! OH, PARDON ME...
HUH?
gasp YOUR FACE!
PARDON ME, MA'AM, I MUST LOOK A FRIGHT.
OH, I SEE! YOU'RE ONE OF THE RODEO CLOWNS!
YES MA'AM, I'M PETE THE BULL-FIGHTER.
BULLFIGHTER?
SOME CLOWNS, LIKE CODY, JUST MAKE THE CROWD LAUGH. OTHER CLOWNS, LIKE ROLLIE, ARE BARREL MEN AN' DISTRACT THE BULLS WITH BARRELS WHEN THEY GET WILD.
SO WHAT DO YOU DO?
MY JOB'S TO WRASSLE WITH THAT OL' BULL WHEN THE BULL RIDER FALLS OFF OR GETS IN TROUBLE!
THAT'S WHY I WEAR MY MAKE-UP--TO LOOK TOUGH! GRR!
HA HA HA!

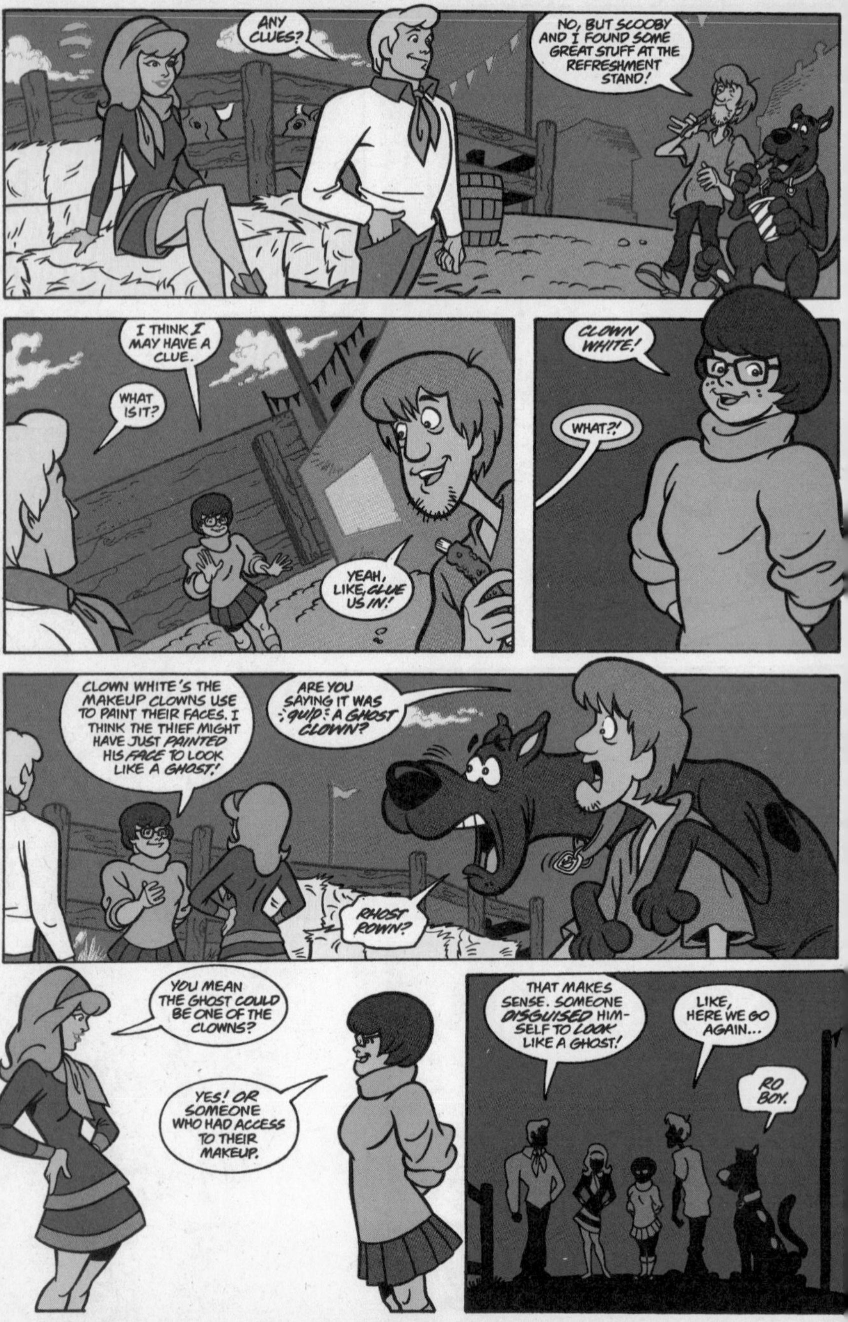
ANY CLUES?
NO, BUT SCOOBY AND I FOUND SOME GREAT STUFF AT THE REFRESHMENT STAND!
I THINK I MAY HAVE A CLUE.
WHAT IS IT?
YEAH, LIKE, CLUE US IN!
CLOWN WHITE!
WHAT?!
CLOWN WHITE'S THE MAKEUP CLOWNS USE TO PAINT THEIR FACES. I THINK THE THIEF MIGHT HAVE JUST PAINTED HIS FACE TO LOOK LIKE A GHOST!
ARE YOU SAYING IT WAS :GULP: A GHOST CLOWN?
RHOST ROWN?
YOU MEAN THE GHOST COULD BE ONE OF THE CLOWNS?
YES! OR SOMEONE WHO HAD ACCESS TO THEIR MAKEUP.
THAT MAKES SENSE. SOMEONE DISGUISED HIM-SELF TO LOOK LIKE A GHOST!
LIKE, HERE WE GO AGAIN...
RO BOY.

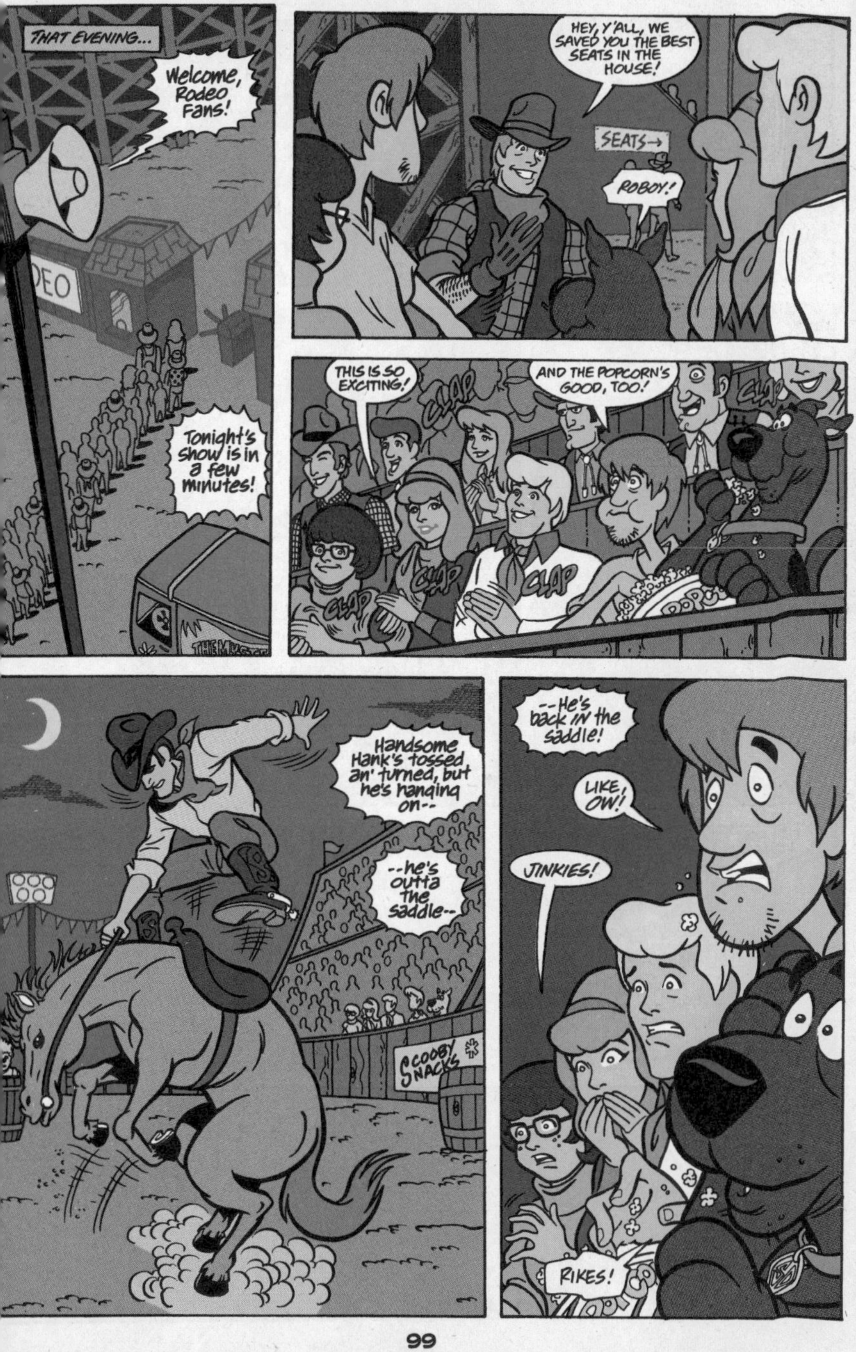
THAT EVENING...
Welcome, Rodeo Fans!
Tonight's show is in a few minutes!
RODEO
HEY, Y'ALL, WE SAVED YOU THE BEST SEATS IN THE HOUSE!
SEATS→
ROBOY!
THIS IS SO EXCITING!
AND THE POPCORN'S GOOD, TOO!
CLAP
CLAP
CLAP
CLAP
CLAP
Handsome Hank's tossed an' turned, but he's hanging on--
--he's outta the saddle--
SCOOBY SNACKS
--He's back in the saddle!
LIKE, OW!
JINKIES!
RIKES!

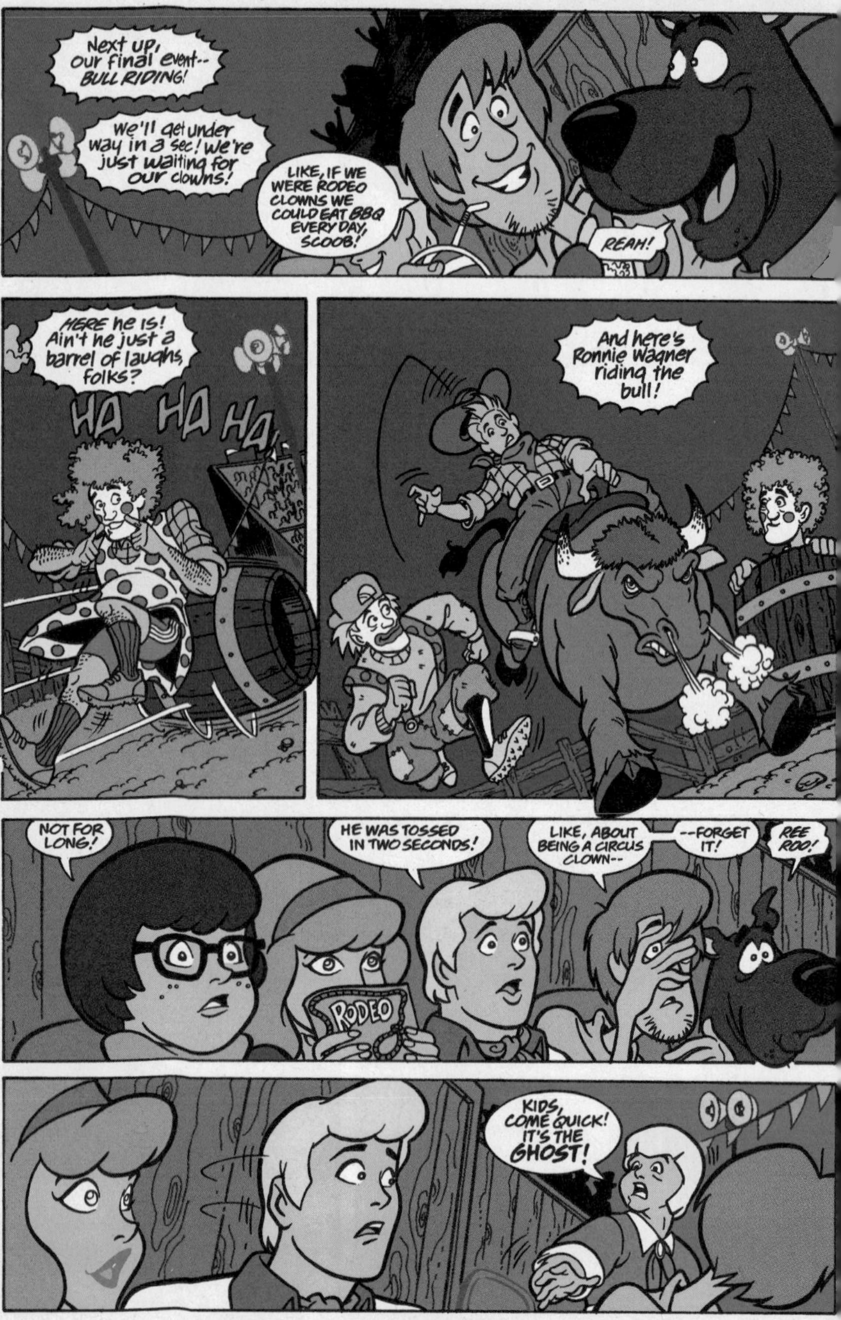
Next up, our final event-- BULL RIDING!
We'll get under way in a sec! We're just waiting for our clowns!
LIKE, IF WE WERE RODEO CLOWNS WE COULD EAT BBQ EVERY DAY, SCOOB!
REAH!
HERE he is! Ain't he just a barrel of laughs, folks?
HA HA HA
And here's Ronnie Wagner riding the bull!
NOT FOR LONG!
HE WAS TOSSED IN TWO SECONDS!
LIKE, ABOUT BEING A CIRCUS CLOWN--
--FORGET IT!
REE ROO!
RODEO
KIDS, COME QUICK! IT'S THE GHOST!

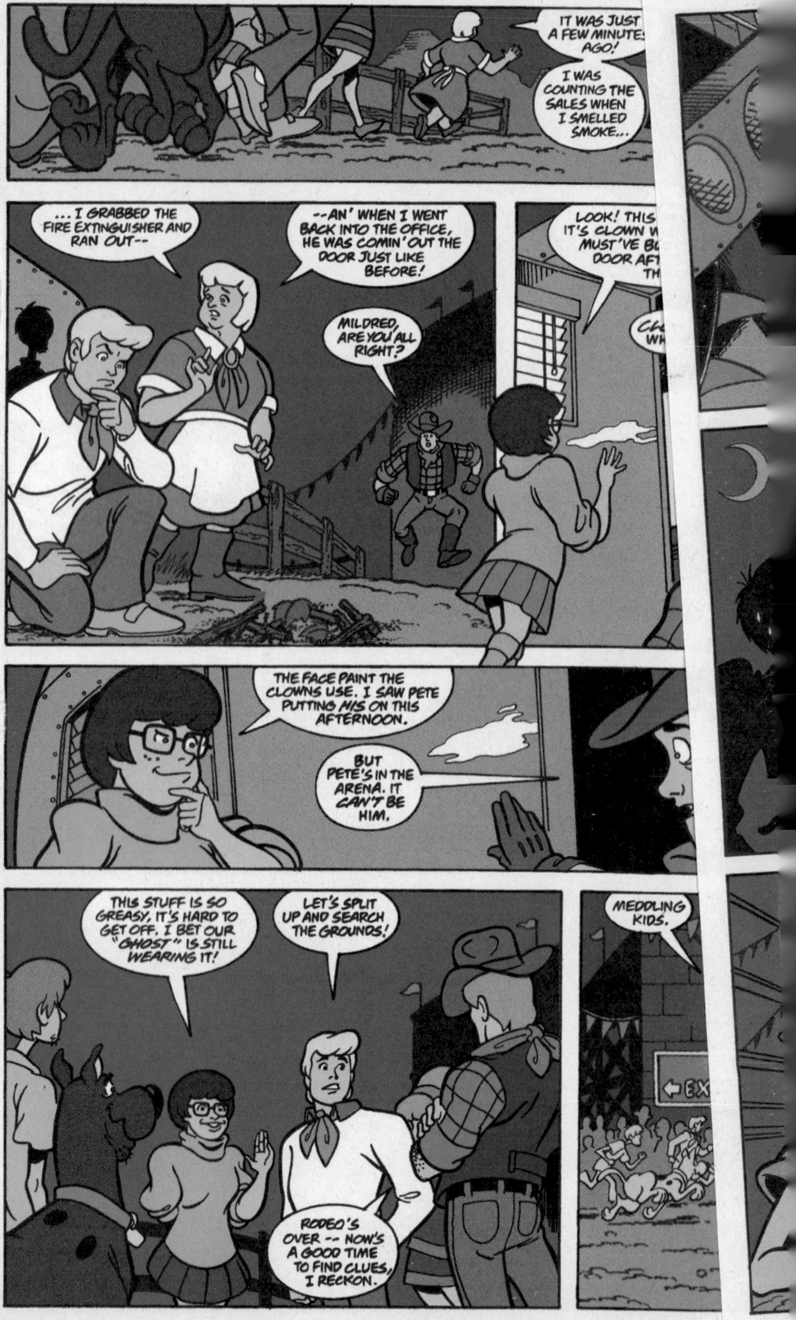
IT WAS JUST A FEW MINUTES AGO!
I WAS COUNTING THE SALES WHEN I SMELLED SMOKE...
... I GRABBED THE FIRE EXTINGUISHER AND RAN OUT--
--AN' WHEN I WENT BACK INTO THE OFFICE, HE WAS COMIN' OUT THE DOOR JUST LIKE BEFORE!
MILDRED, ARE YOU ALL RIGHT?
LOOK! THIS
IT'S CLOWN
MUST'VE
DOOR
THE FACE PAINT THE CLOWNS USE. I SAW PETE PUTTING HIS ON THIS AFTERNOON.
BUT PETE'S IN THE ARENA. IT CAN'T BE HIM.
THIS STUFF IS SO GREASY, IT'S HARD TO GET OFF. I BET OUR "GHOST" IS STILL WEARING IT!
LET'S SPLIT UP AND SEARCH THE GROUNDS!
RODEO'S OVER -- NOW'S A GOOD TIME TO FIND CLUES, I RECKON.
MEDDLING KIDS.

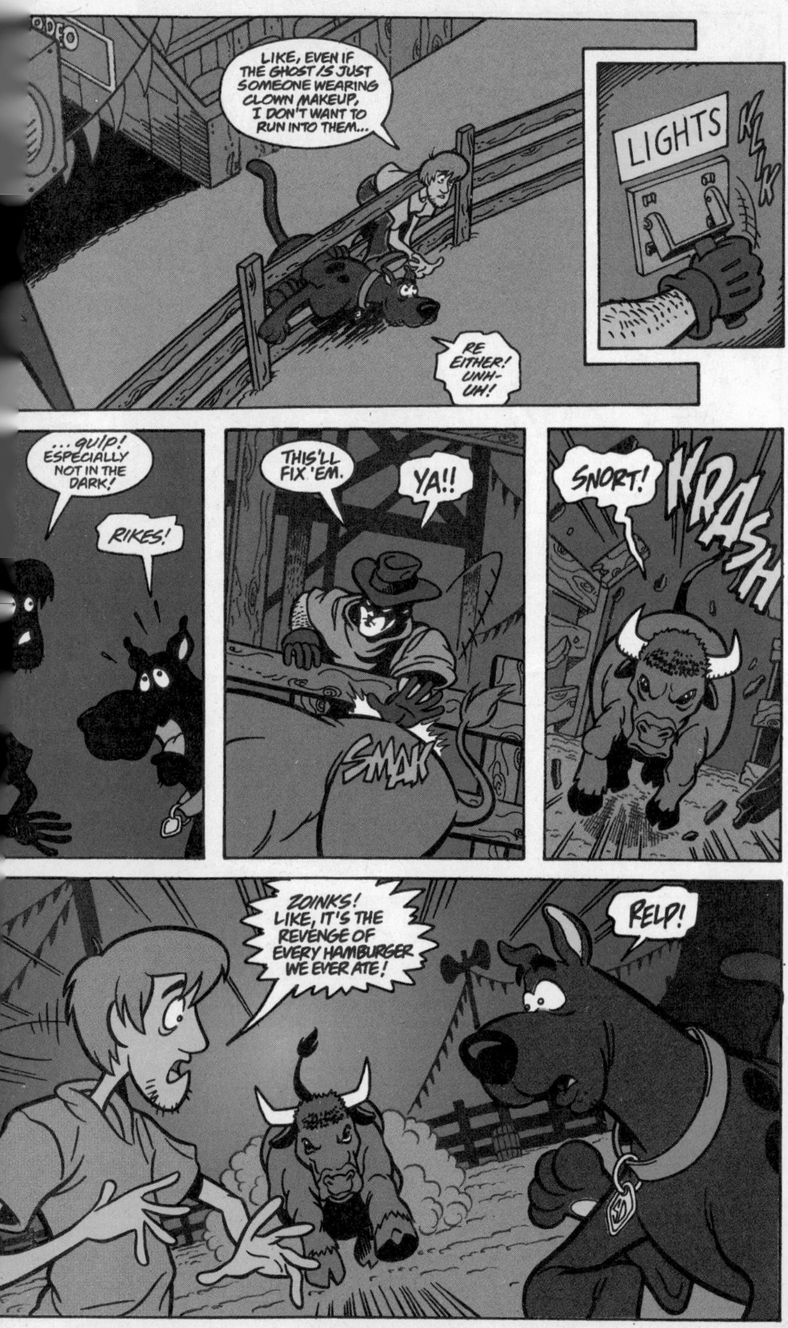
RODEO
LIKE, EVEN IF THE GHOST IS JUST SOMEONE WEARING CLOWN MAKEUP, I DON'T WANT TO RUN INTO THEM...
RE EITHER! UNH-UH!
LIGHTS
KLIK
...gulp! ESPECIALLY NOT IN THE DARK!
RIKES!
THIS'LL FIX 'EM.
YA!!
SMAK
SNORT!
KRASH
ZOINKS! LIKE, IT'S THE REVENGE OF EVERY HAMBURGER WE EVER ATE!
RELP!

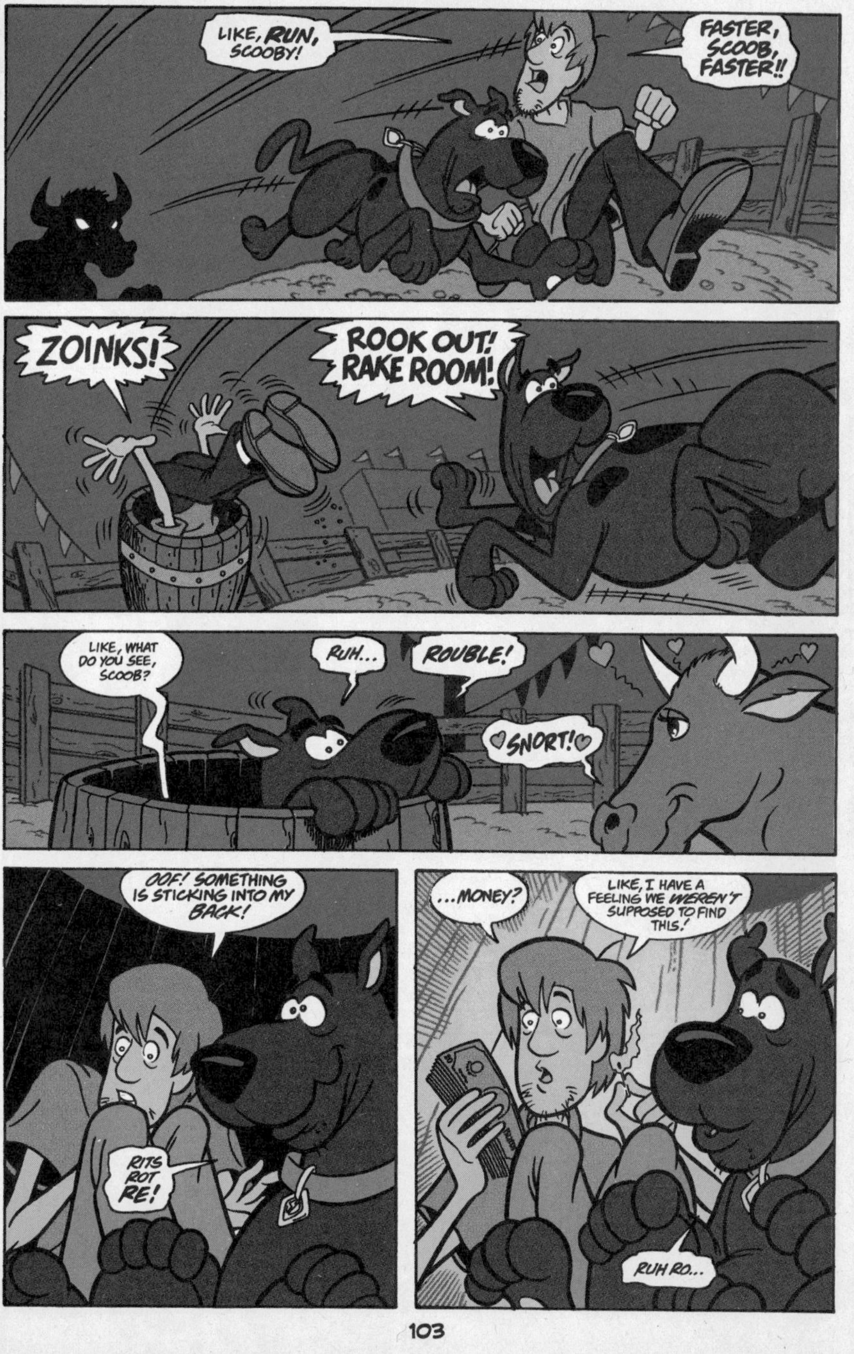
LIKE, RUN, SCOOBY!
FASTER, SCOOB, FASTER!!
ZOINKS!
ROOK OUT! RAKE ROOM!
LIKE, WHAT DO YOU SEE, SCOOB?
RUH...
ROUBLE!
SNORT!
OOF! SOMETHING IS STICKING INTO MY BACK!
RITS ROT RE!
...MONEY?
LIKE, I HAVE A FEELING WE WEREN'T SUPPOSED TO FIND THIS!
RUH RO...

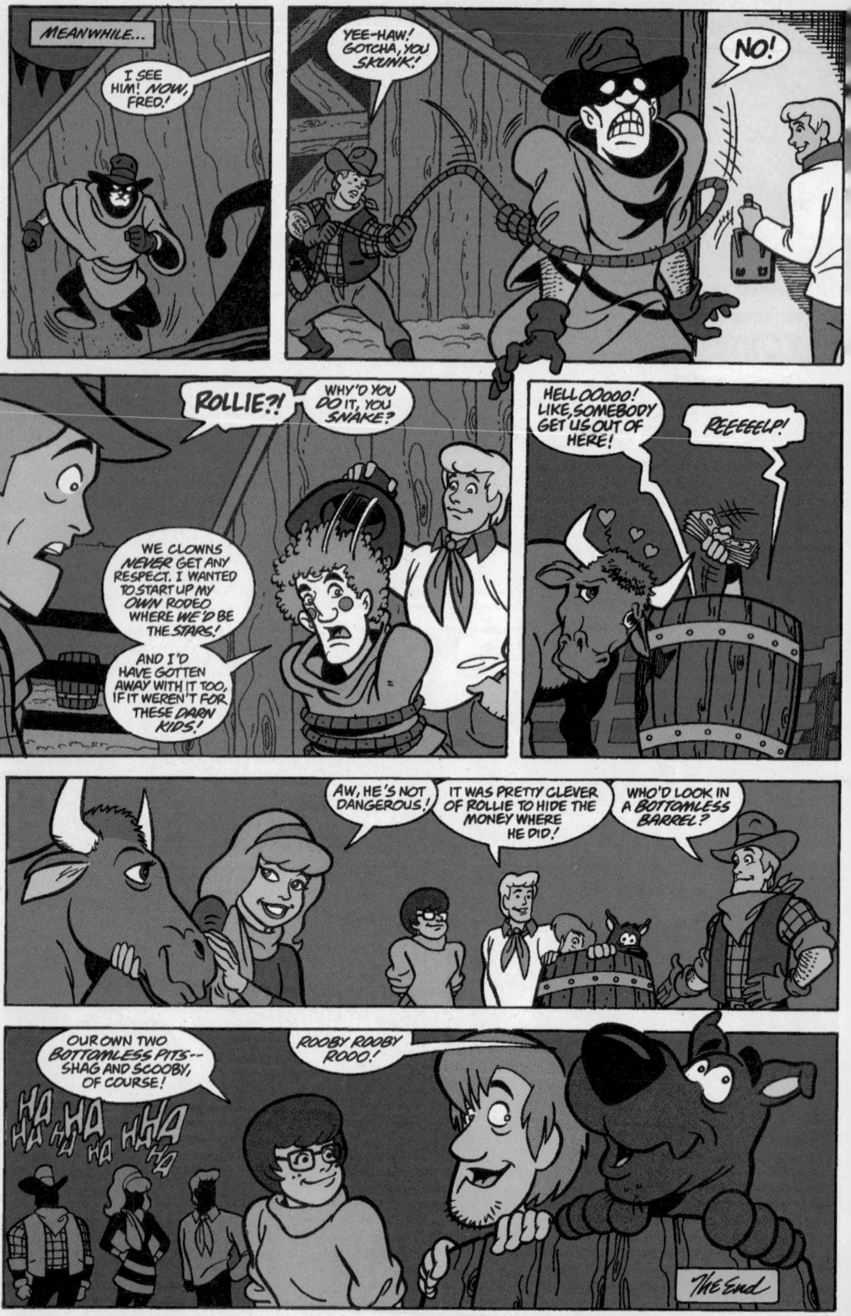
MEANWHILE...
I SEE HIM! NOW, FRED!
YEE-HAW! GOTCHA, YOU SKUNK!
NO!
ROLLIE?!
WHY'D YOU DO IT, YOU SNAKE?
WE CLOWNS NEVER GET ANY RESPECT. I WANTED TO START UP MY OWN RODEO WHERE WE'D BE THE STARS!
AND I'D HAVE GOTTEN AWAY WITH IT TOO, IF IT WEREN'T FOR THESE DARN KIDS!
HELLOOOOO! LIKE, SOMEBODY GET US OUT OF HERE!
REEEEELP!
AW, HE'S NOT DANGEROUS!
IT WAS PRETTY CLEVER OF ROLLIE TO HIDE THE MONEY WHERE HE DID!
WHO'D LOOK IN A BOTTOMLESS BARREL?
OUR OWN TWO BOTTOMLESS PITS-- SHAG AND SCOOBY, OF COURSE!
ROOBY ROOBY ROOO!
HA HA HA HA HA HA HA HA HA HA
THE End

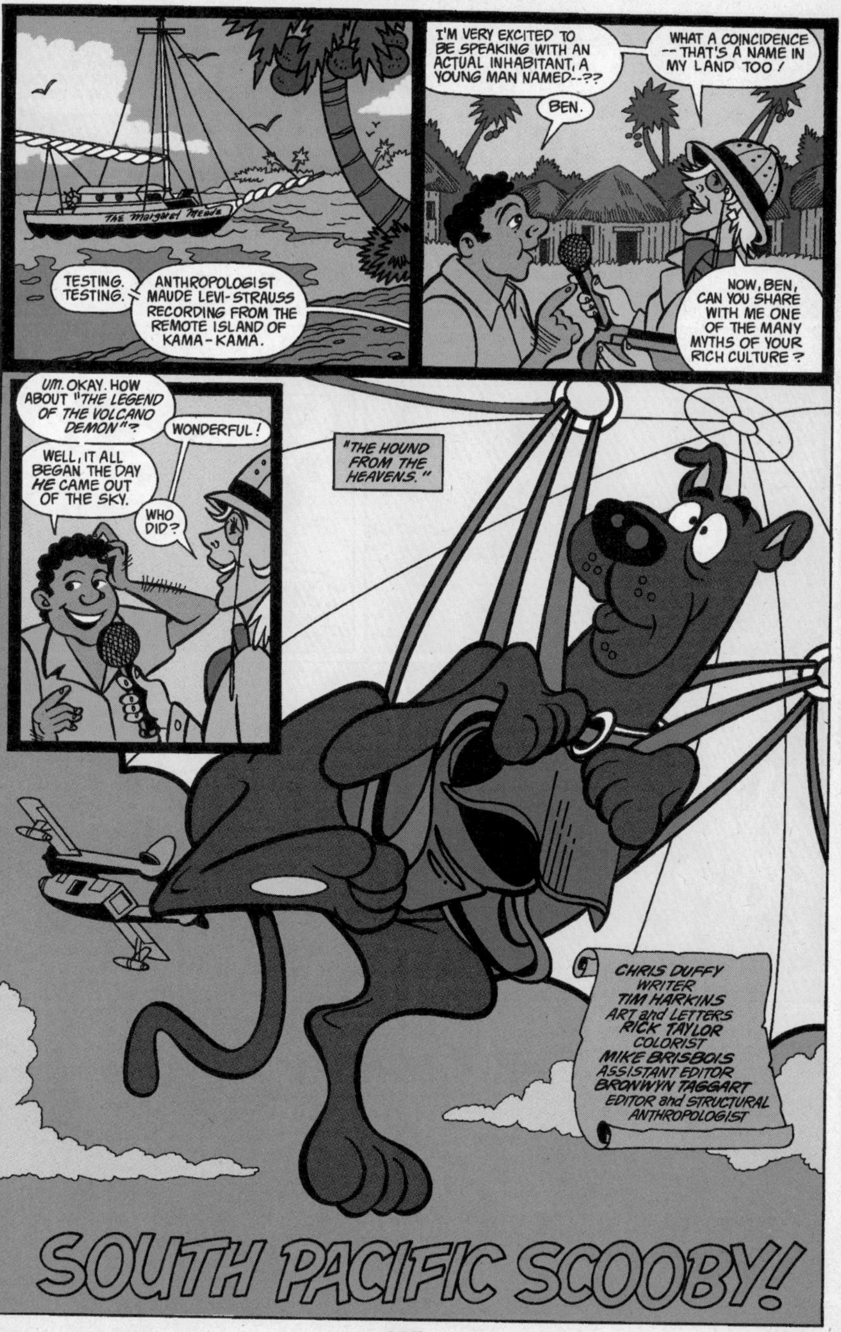
THE Margaret Meade
TESTING. TESTING.
ANTHROPOLOGIST MAUDE LEVI-STRAUSS RECORDING FROM THE REMOTE ISLAND OF KAMA-KAMA.
I'M VERY EXCITED TO BE SPEAKING WITH AN ACTUAL INHABITANT, A YOUNG MAN NAMED--??
BEN.
WHAT A COINCIDENCE -- THAT'S A NAME IN MY LAND TOO!
NOW, BEN, CAN YOU SHARE WITH ME ONE OF THE MANY MYTHS OF YOUR RICH CULTURE?
UM. OKAY. HOW ABOUT "THE LEGEND OF THE VOLCANO DEMON"?
WONDERFUL!
WELL, IT ALL BEGAN THE DAY HE CAME OUT OF THE SKY.
WHO DID?
"THE HOUND FROM THE HEAVENS."
CHRIS DUFFY WRITER
TIM HARKINS ART and LETTERS
RICK TAYLOR COLORIST
MIKE BRISBOIS ASSISTANT EDITOR
BRONWYN TAGGART EDITOR and STRUCTURAL ANTHROPOLOGIST
SOUTH PACIFIC SCOOBY!

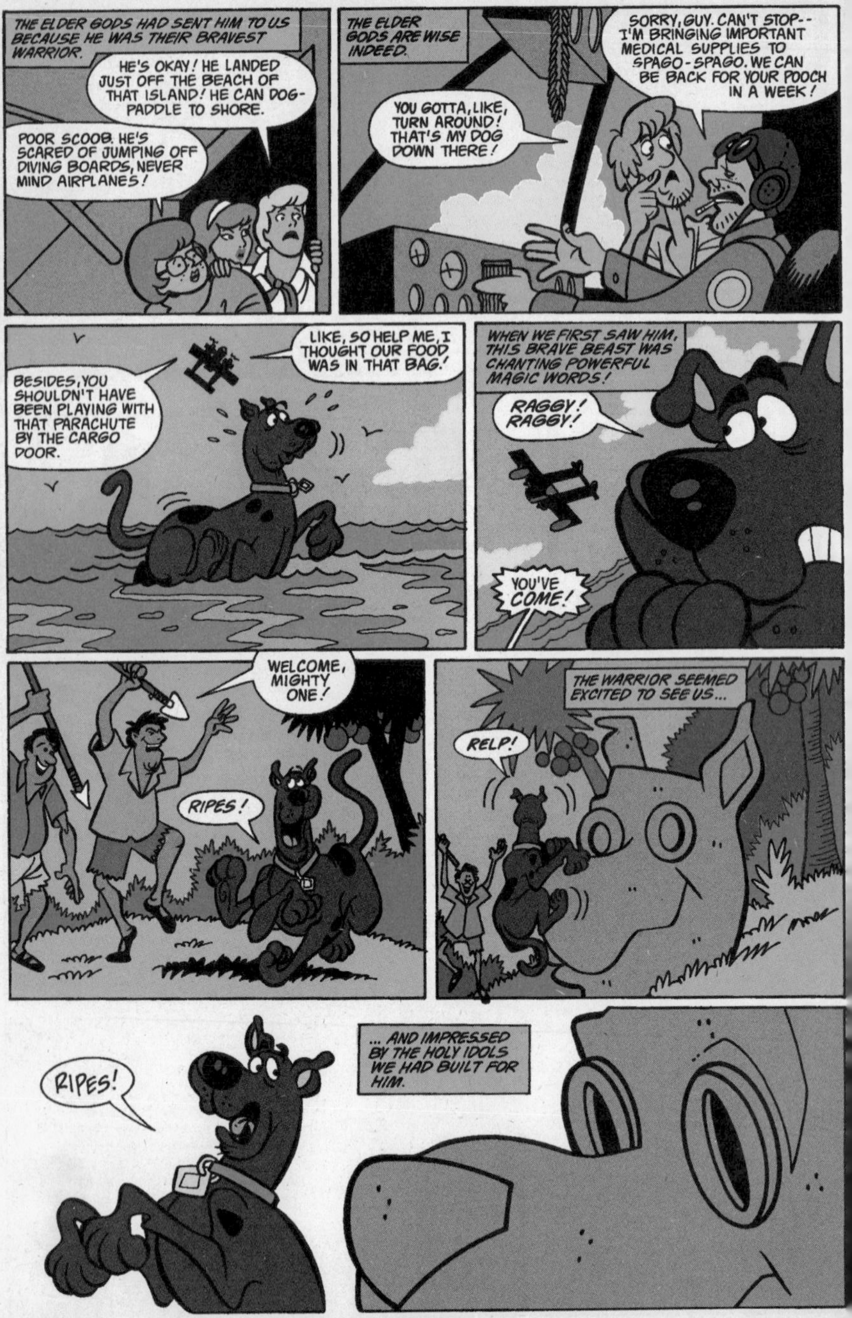
THE ELDER GODS HAD SENT HIM TO US BECAUSE HE WAS THEIR BRAVEST WARRIOR.
HE'S OKAY! HE LANDED JUST OFF THE BEACH OF THAT ISLAND! HE CAN DOG-PADDLE TO SHORE.
POOR SCOOB. HE'S SCARED OF JUMPING OFF DIVING BOARDS, NEVER MIND AIRPLANES!
THE ELDER GODS ARE WISE INDEED.
SORRY, GUY. CAN'T STOP--I'M BRINGING IMPORTANT MEDICAL SUPPLIES TO SPAGO-SPAGO. WE CAN BE BACK FOR YOUR POOCH IN A WEEK!
YOU GOTTA, LIKE, TURN AROUND! THAT'S MY DOG DOWN THERE!
LIKE, SO HELP ME, I THOUGHT OUR FOOD WAS IN THAT BAG!
BESIDES, YOU SHOULDN'T HAVE BEEN PLAYING WITH THAT PARACHUTE BY THE CARGO DOOR.
WHEN WE FIRST SAW HIM, THIS BRAVE BEAST WAS CHANTING POWERFUL MAGIC WORDS!
RAGGY! RAGGY!
YOU'VE COME!
WELCOME, MIGHTY ONE!
RIPES!
THE WARRIOR SEEMED EXCITED TO SEE US...
RELP!
RIPES!
... AND IMPRESSED BY THE HOLY IDOLS WE HAD BUILT FOR HIM.

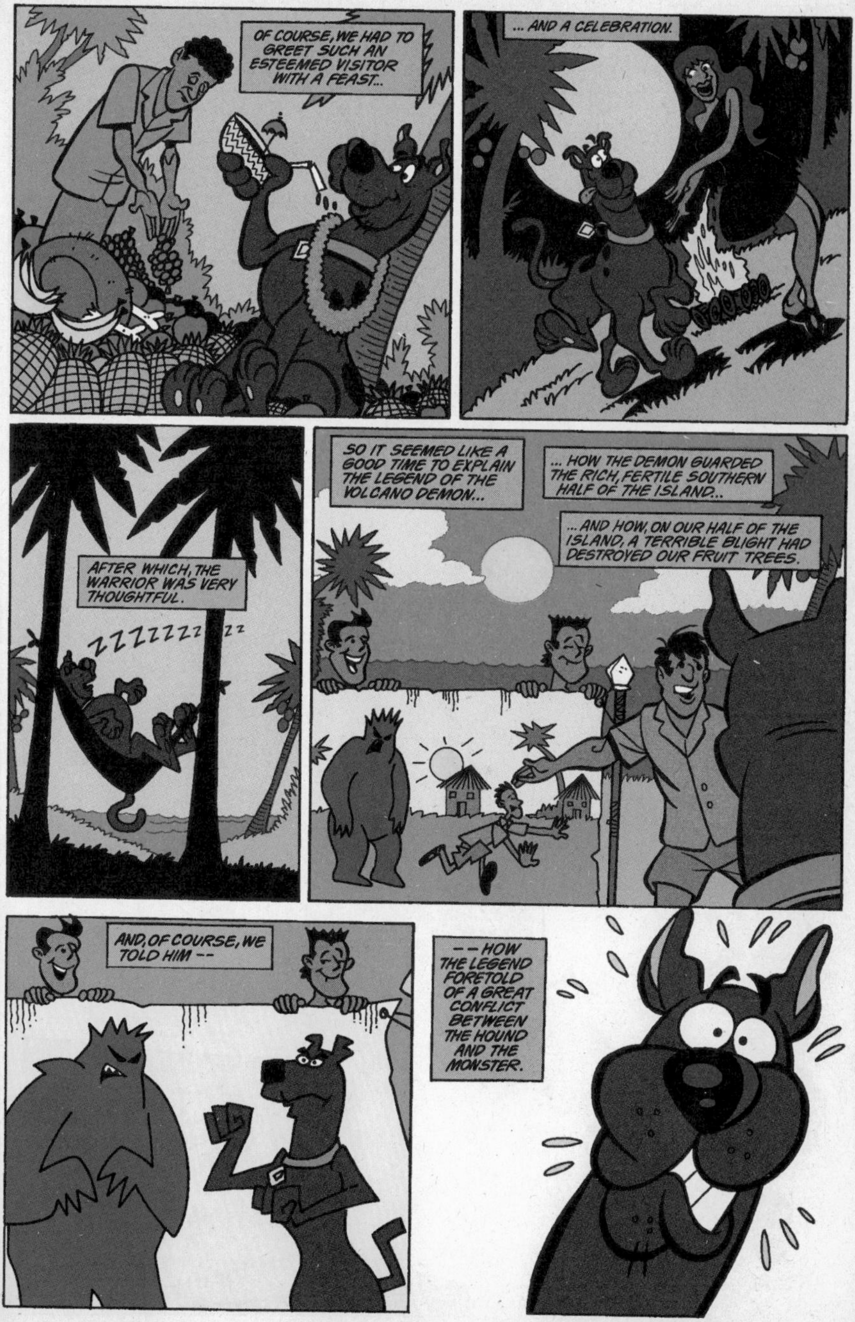
OF COURSE, WE HAD TO GREET SUCH AN ESTEEMED VISITOR WITH A FEAST...
... AND A CELEBRATION.
AFTER WHICH, THE WARRIOR WAS VERY THOUGHTFUL.
ZZZZZZZzzzz
SO IT SEEMED LIKE A GOOD TIME TO EXPLAIN THE LEGEND OF THE VOLCANO DEMON...
... HOW THE DEMON GUARDED THE RICH, FERTILE SOUTHERN HALF OF THE ISLAND...
...AND HOW, ON OUR HALF OF THE ISLAND, A TERRIBLE BLIGHT HAD DESTROYED OUR FRUIT TREES.
AND, OF COURSE, WE TOLD HIM --
-- HOW THE LEGEND FORETOLD OF A GREAT CONFLICT BETWEEN THE HOUND AND THE MONSTER.

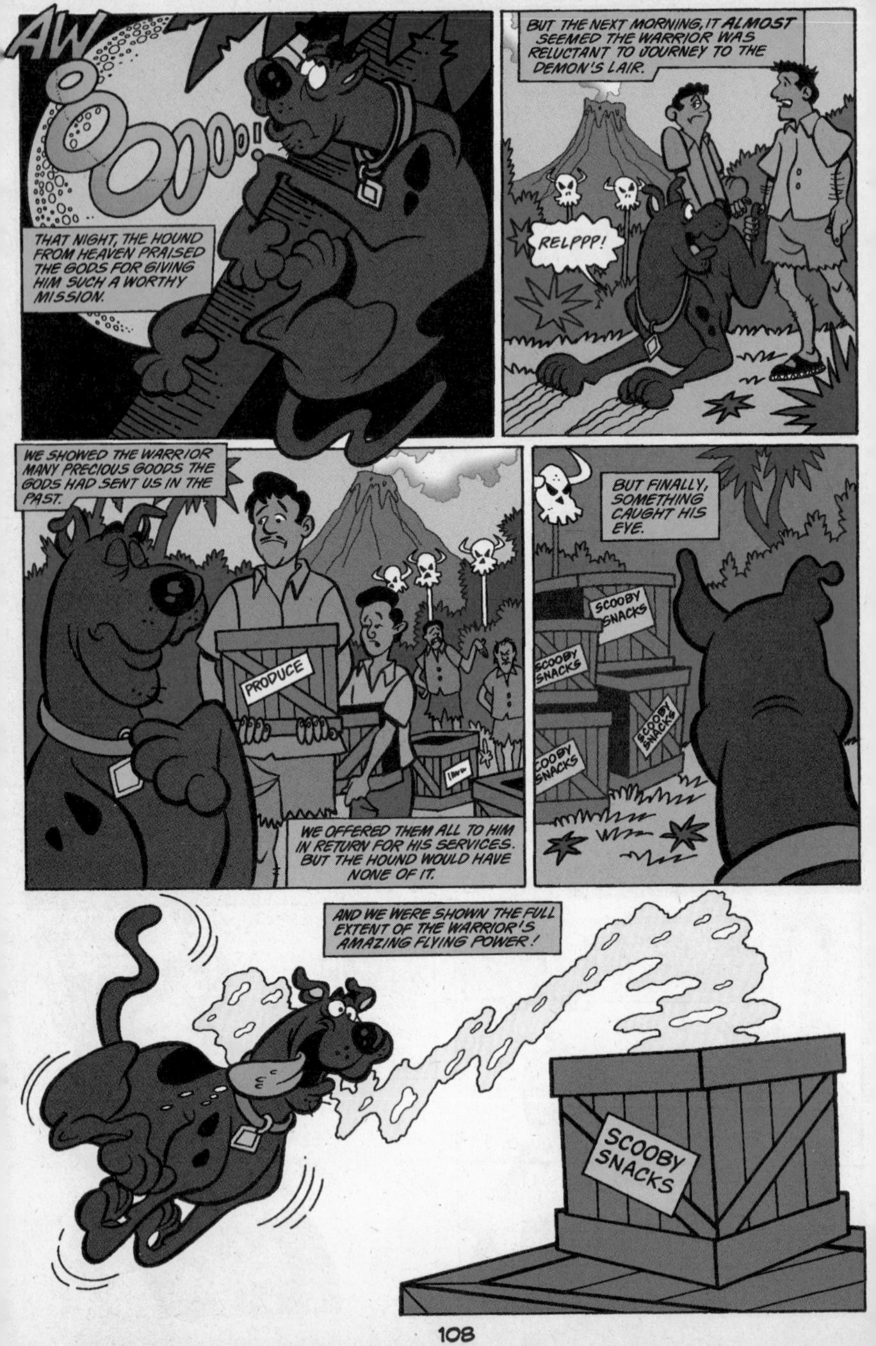
AWOOOOOOO!
THAT NIGHT, THE HOUND FROM HEAVEN PRAISED THE GODS FOR GIVING HIM SUCH A WORTHY MISSION.
BUT THE NEXT MORNING, IT ALMOST SEEMED THE WARRIOR WAS RELUCTANT TO JOURNEY TO THE DEMON'S LAIR.
RELPPP!
WE SHOWED THE WARRIOR MANY PRECIOUS GOODS THE GODS HAD SENT US IN THE PAST.
PRODUCE
WE OFFERED THEM ALL TO HIM IN RETURN FOR HIS SERVICES. BUT THE HOUND WOULD HAVE NONE OF IT.
BUT FINALLY, SOMETHING CAUGHT HIS EYE.
SCOOBY SNACKS
SCOOBY SNACKS
SCOOBY SNACKS
SCOOBY SNACKS
AND WE WERE SHOWN THE FULL EXTENT OF THE WARRIOR'S AMAZING FLYING POWER!
SCOOBY SNACKS

WE WERE NOT FAMILIAR WITH THE MORSELS HE FEASTED ON...

SCOOBY SNACKS

SCOOBY

SCOOBY SNACKS

SCOOBY

BUT CLEARLY THEY WERE THE BISCUITS OF THE GODS!

RUFF! RUFF! RET'S RO! RET'S RO!

NO ONE WITNESSED THE EPIC BATTLE THAT TRANSPIRED THAT DAY...

RET'S... RUH-ROH...

BUT NO DOUBT, THE FEARLESS HOUND HUNTED DOWN THE VOLCANO DEMON WITH HIS KEEN SENSES.

TWANG

THE DEMON MUST HAVE KNOWN HE'D MET HIS MATCH WHEN FIRST HE GLIMPSED THIS BRAVE, GOD-SENT GUARDIAN.

RIPES!

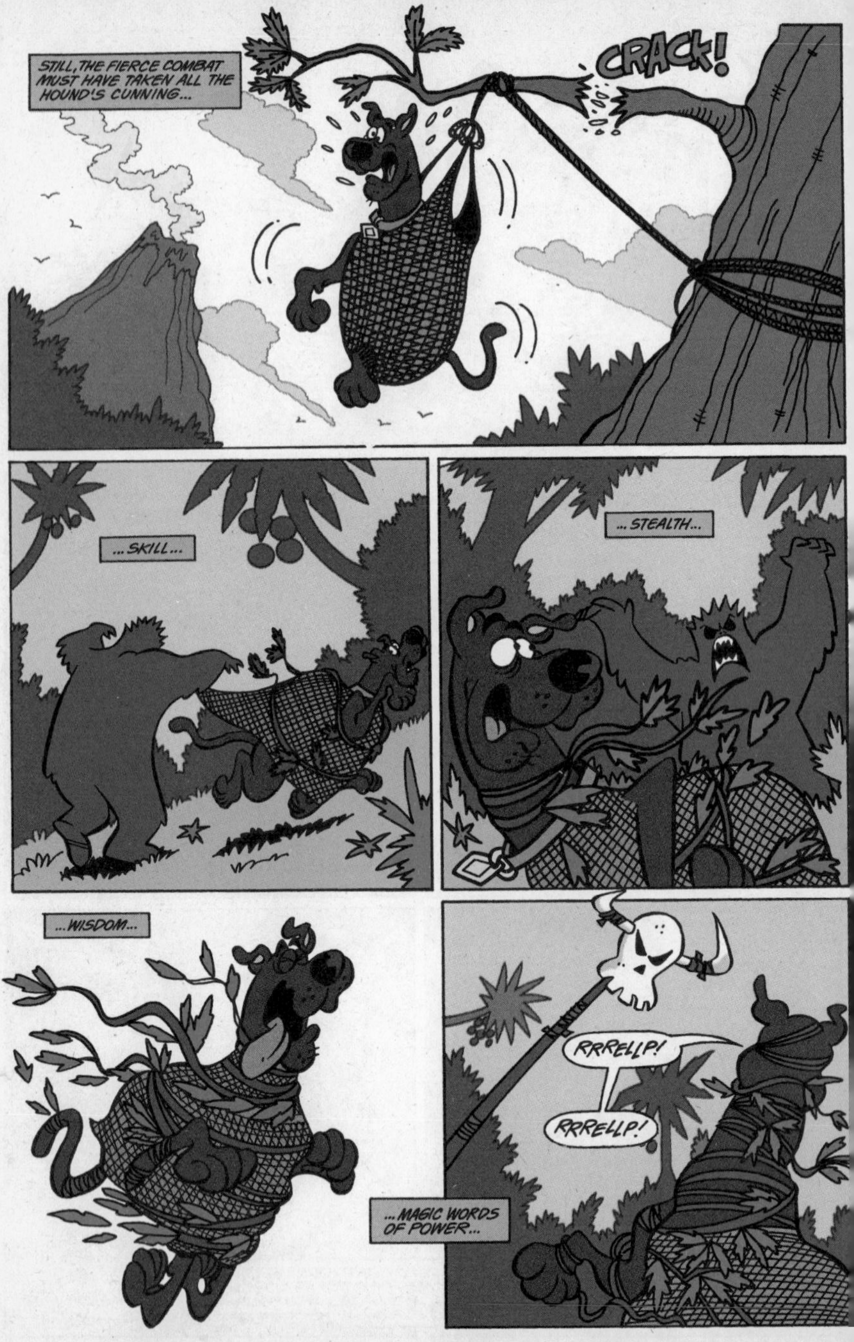
STILL, THE FIERCE COMBAT MUST HAVE TAKEN ALL THE HOUND'S CUNNING...
CRACK!
...SKILL...
...STEALTH...
...WISDOM...
RRRELLP!
RRRELLP!
...MAGIC WORDS OF POWER...

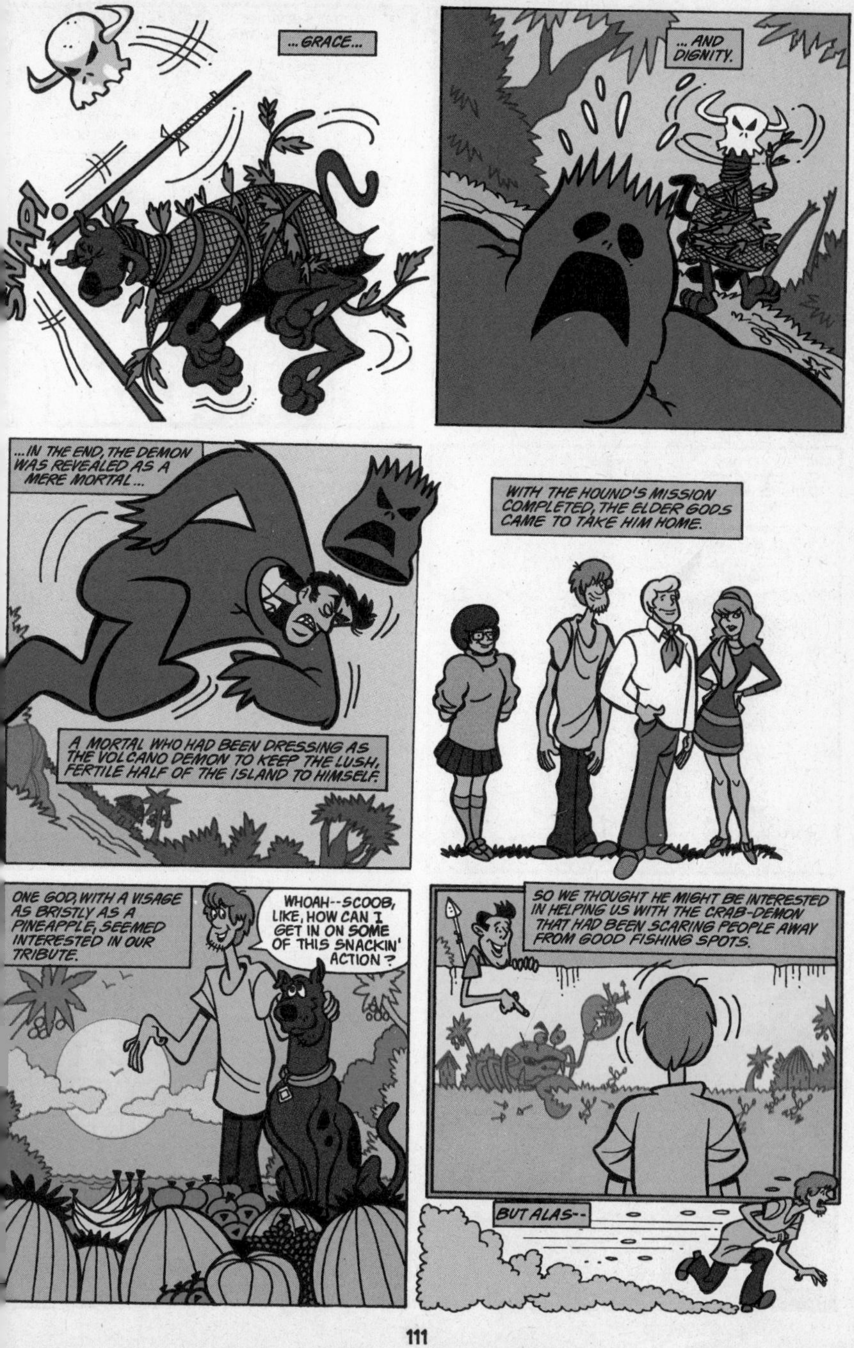
...GRACE...
SNAP!
...AND DIGNITY.
...IN THE END, THE DEMON WAS REVEALED AS A MERE MORTAL...
A MORTAL WHO HAD BEEN DRESSING AS THE VOLCANO DEMON TO KEEP THE LUSH, FERTILE HALF OF THE ISLAND TO HIMSELF.
WITH THE HOUND'S MISSION COMPLETED, THE ELDER GODS CAME TO TAKE HIM HOME.
ONE GOD, WITH A VISAGE AS BRISTLY AS A PINEAPPLE, SEEMED INTERESTED IN OUR TRIBUTE.
WHOAH--SCOOB, LIKE, HOW CAN I GET IN ON SOME OF THIS SNACKIN' ACTION?
SO WE THOUGHT HE MIGHT BE INTERESTED IN HELPING US WITH THE CRAB-DEMON THAT HAD BEEN SCARING PEOPLE AWAY FROM GOOD FISHING SPOTS.
BUT ALAS--

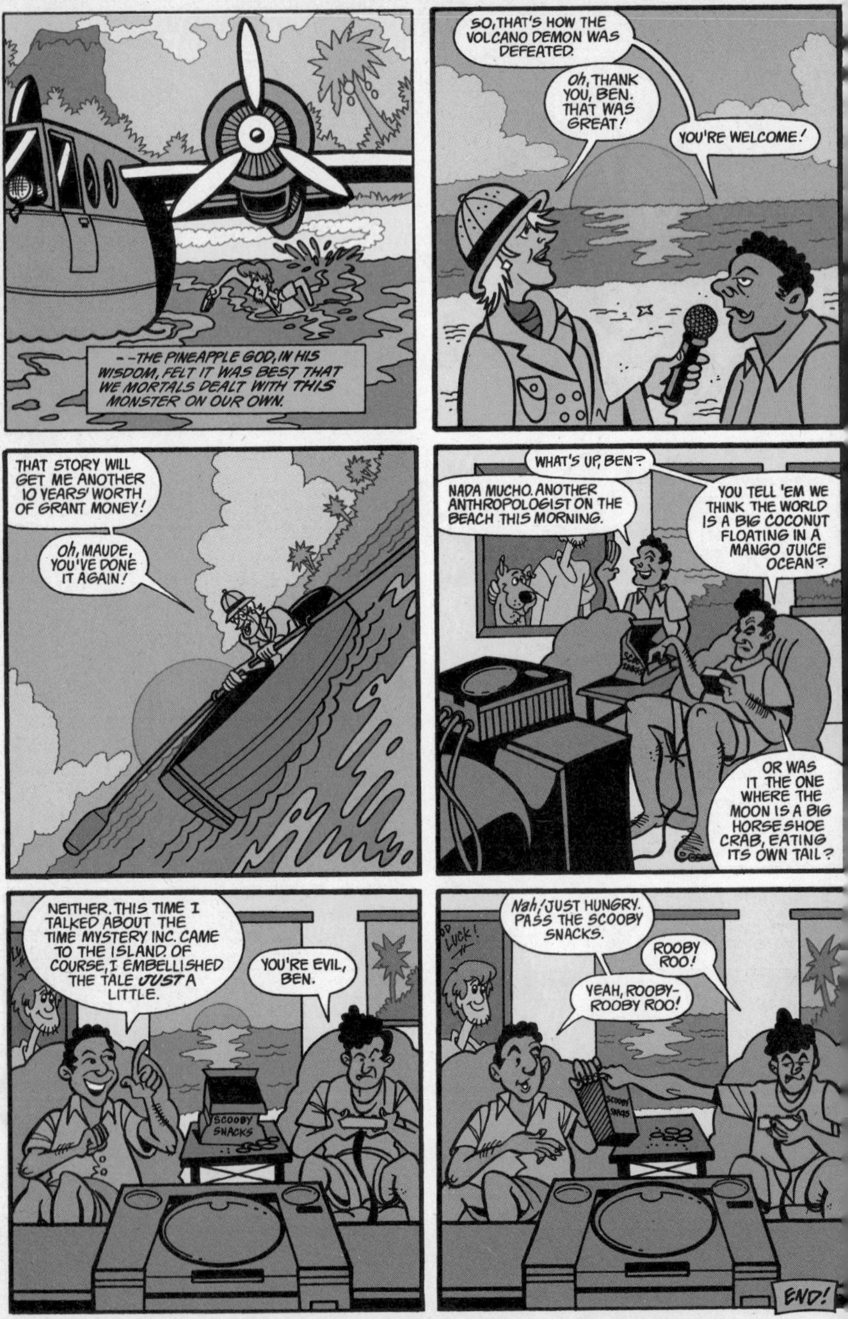
--THE PINEAPPLE GOD, IN HIS WISDOM, FELT IT WAS BEST THAT WE MORTALS DEALT WITH THIS MONSTER ON OUR OWN.
SO, THAT'S HOW THE VOLCANO DEMON WAS DEFEATED.
Oh, THANK YOU, BEN. THAT WAS GREAT!
YOU'RE WELCOME!
THAT STORY WILL GET ME ANOTHER 10 YEARS' WORTH OF GRANT MONEY!
Oh, MAUDE, YOU'VE DONE IT AGAIN!
WHAT'S UP, BEN?
NADA MUCHO. ANOTHER ANTHROPOLOGIST ON THE BEACH THIS MORNING.
YOU TELL 'EM WE THINK THE WORLD IS A BIG COCONUT FLOATING IN A MANGO JUICE OCEAN?
OR WAS IT THE ONE WHERE THE MOON IS A BIG HORSESHOE CRAB, EATING ITS OWN TAIL?
NEITHER. THIS TIME I TALKED ABOUT THE TIME MYSTERY INC. CAME TO THE ISLAND. OF COURSE, I EMBELLISHED THE TALE JUST A LITTLE.
YOU'RE EVIL, BEN.
SCOOBY SNACKS
Nah! JUST HUNGRY. PASS THE SCOOBY SNACKS.
ROOBY ROO!
YEAH, ROOBY-ROOBY ROO!
SCOOBY SNACKS
END!